Jemmabeth Forrester just never learns...

Obviously, she shouldn't have picked a fight
with the meanest judge around.
And maybe it wasn't too smart to have
the town's peeping Tom sit for a portrait.
Jemma knows that—now.

But in spite of a pickup load of advice
from most everybody in Chillaton, she remains stubborn,
wanting to go her own way, like the Texas Panhandle wind.

Someday she'll grow old and wise, like her grandmother,
a strong woman of faith,
but Jemma's got a ways to go yet....

Corner of Blue

❦

Sharon McAnear

CAPSTONE
FICTION

WATERFORD, VIRGINIA

Corner of Blue

Published in the U.S. by:
Capstone Publishing Group LLC
P.O. Box 8
Waterford, VA 20197

Visit Capstone Fiction at
www.capstonefiction.com

Cover design by David LaPlaca/debest design co.
Cover image © 2007, Sharon McAnear

Scripture is taken from *The Holy Bible,* King James Version.

ISBN: 978-1-60290-064-6

For my grandparents,
Rev. Charlie & Addie Williams
DeVerdie & Grace Leathers

Acknowledgments

With thanks to:

My sons, for their uncommon wit.

My uncle, Johnny Leathers, Mary Wilson, and Kelly Mull for their continued encouragement.

Josh, for his kindness and patience.

Maureen Rowlatt, who inspires me from across the Atlantic.

Ramona Tucker, for believing.

My parents and brothers for their fine humor.

Dwight, who showed me Paris.

Carried Away

Golden-eyed Zephyr
Making up time,
Hear it on the wind,
Better clear the line.

Come, silver chariot,
Long overdue,
Carry me away
To that corner of blue.

Dancing on the track
Until the whistle blows,
Runaway heart;
She comes,
She goes.

—Jemmabeth Forrester

CHAPTER ONE

Promises

Rats. She felt it pop at her garter belt tab and zip its way into her shoe. She should've known better than to buy dimestore nylons. Jemma wrangled the giant Dodge into a parking spot, then checked the run. Maybe Granny's eyesight was bad, and she wouldn't notice. She read the ad again:

Floral delivery/Apply in person/Granny's Basket/
Must have a Texas driver's license.

She admired elderly businesswomen, especially spunky old maids because they could've actually outfoxed any number of men over the years. She might become an old maid herself if she didn't watch out. There weren't many guys left for her to outfox.

She checked her lipstick in the mirror and caught a glimpse of a couple kissing in the car behind her. She drummed her fingers on the steering wheel. The time had come for her to crawl back to Spence, confess what a waste this year been, and admit that he really was The One. That plan of action would be next on her agenda. At the moment, she needed this job.

A small bell tolled above her as she pushed open the door, and the air inside dripped with the scent of carnations. One bump and hundreds of trinkets would come crashing to the floor from the glass and metal shelves lining the walls. The knickknacks were probably ready to be dusted, too, but not by her. She was going to deliver floral poetry and get paid to do it.

A ceramic fawn caught her eye, and she touched its spotted coat. A buck had jumped in front of Spencer's Corvette once. He would have hit it, too, if she'd kissed him one second longer. Those were the kisses

1

she wanted again. Those were the first ones she'd ever had, not counting family, and as things were turning out, they were also the best. Now he could be kissing somebody else on a steady basis. Double rats. She should send him some flowers and let them do the talking, like the TV commercials advised. Surely employees got a discount. Maybe Granny would offer her a glass of lemonade as they chatted about roses. She could ask about the discount then.

"Don't handle the merchandise." Norman Bates' mother spat out the order. All she lacked was a big knife and a shower curtain to put them on the set of *Psycho*. Jemma was at least a head taller and could see the woman's scalp through her lavender hair. Mother Bates ran her finger along the counter, then examined it with her bifocals. "I assume you are looking rather than shopping."

Jemma had read about projecting a positive attitude at interviews, so she put out her hand. "My name is Jemmabeth Forrester, and I'm your new delivery girl."

"Handshaking passes germs, and you'll get nowhere with sassiness."

"Yes, ma'am." Granny might want to hear about this attitude. It wasn't exactly spunky; it was more along the lines of spiteful.

"I'm The Proprietor and we don't hire girls for various reasons. We use boys to deliver our orders." She moved to adjust the deer, and her shoes squeaked on the linoleum. They were nurse shoes like those Mrs. Bach, Jemma's fourth-grade teacher, had worn. She could still picture Billy Joe Ferris tying Mrs. Bach's laces together as the woman snored through geography. The Proprietor sniffed. "Are you a local?"

"My dad has been the football coach at Wicklow High School for two years, since '63, and I live at Helene Neblitt's." That should carry some weight in her favor.

"Sports are a waste of energy." The Proprietor eyed her for a moment, then checked her watch. "Mrs. Neblitt, you say? I'll call her even though she never trades with us. Grows her own flowers. At least you're big enough to be a boy."

They retreated to a large workroom being minded by a woman chopping the stem tips off carnations with a vengeance and a butcher knife. Her pale blue hair wobbled with each chop as did her hips. Hmm…maybe these two were Granny's daughters or some black sheep cousins, and what was a *proprietor* anyway, the manager? Perhaps she should forget about the lemonade.

"Don't touch anything," the chopper said. A vision of Papa's best milk cow, its tail swishing, made Jemma bite her lip. She wiped her forehead too, quite discreetly. Those cheap stockings clung to her like damp tissue, and the run had to be as wide as a Band-Aid by now.

The Proprietor hung up the phone, then turned to her associate. "Sister, I need quiet for a minute." She rapped her fingers on a counter laden with floral arrangements. "Show me your driver's license." Jemma forked it over. "I assume you know your way around Wicklow since you live with the former mayor's snobby widow. Remove the tickets but leave the sender's card. There is a spray to be positioned on a loved one's casket at the funeral home. You will follow the bereavement spray placement diagram in the car. Any monetary tips are to be given to me immediately upon your return. You should have no questions if you have been listening. Do you promise to follow my instructions to the letter?"

Jemma nodded, but "loved one's casket" swarmed around in her ears until the chopping resumed. Sister knew when a minute was up.

The Proprietor unbolted numerous locks on a sliding door that opened into the alley, then led the way to a Buick Woody station wagon. The butcher knife remained in Sister's hand.

"Remember," The Proprietor said, "I will be calling the delivery addresses to see if there were problems. This is only a test because we are behind on our deliveries. You are not hired yet." She surrendered the car keys and Jemma's license.

The sisters stood guard while she loaded the wagon. Craning their necks like a couple of Papa's chickens, they loomed in her rearview mirror until she turned out of sight. Jemma unleashed a giggle and turned on the radio. She pulled over and did her hair up in a ponytail, then whipped off the stockings and stuck them in her purse. Prepared for an impressive job audition with resultant employment, she sallied forth.

కింరా

The dreaded casket spray was the only delivery left. The last time she had been in a funeral home was in high school when she and her best friend, Sandy Kay Baker, had to sing a duet for a service at the Boxwright Brothers Funeral Parlor. They were seated behind two heart-shaped floral arrangements that centered exactly on their chests until they stood to sing. Sandy would die laughing when she heard about these sisters.

Cars lined the street and the big semi-circle driveway, but a wide space in front of the funeral home was empty. It was perfect for the station wagon. Jemma studied the pseudo antebellum mansion—a poor man's Tara. On the lawn, matching cherubs sputtered water onto concrete slabs. Miss Scarlett wouldn't twitter down these tacky steps with her hoop skirt flouncing, but then Scarlett would have a sure-fire plan to get Spencer back. If he'd found somebody else, now that she wanted him, it would be the pits.

Right in the middle of a reconciliation scenario, the car died. She pumped the accelerator and turned the key, producing a dismal grinding noise until a hearse pulled up behind her. One of the men got out and came alongside her. He stuck his round head in the window, cigarette dangling. "You need to get out of the way, kitten. Flowers go around to the back."

"It won't start."

"You've flooded it. Scoot over."

The wagon started on his first try. He flipped his ashes out the window and winked. She drove to the delivery door and slipped inside. Distant groans of organ music greeted her. To the left was a small, roped-off room with an occupied coffin. She cradled the casket spray with *Uncle Dear* written in gold letters on the ribbon, ready to follow The Proprietor's directions. At least somebody's dear uncle wouldn't spring up and spit like Thurman Talley said his wife did at midnight while he sat with her coffin at Boxwright's. That was a perennial Halloween story in Chillaton.

Giving the diagram a quick look, Jemma laid the paper, along with the flowers, on the casket. She avoided viewing the old fellow as she eased the spray towards him, then backed up to the door to check the results. His folded hands were lost among the carnations, a palm branch was curved up against his nostrils, and the diagram rested in an unseemly fashion on his forehead. Otherwise, he looked good. Someone coughed behind her and Jemma, studying Uncle Dear's features, shrieked.

"Shh. There's a service in progress, kitten." The roundhead who had started the car rearranged the spray and handed her the instruction sheet. "Anything else I can do to please you, sweet cakes?"

4

"No, thanks," she said. She could take him with The Sleeper hold. That would be a good story to tell Spencer, to break the ice.

He put an arm across the door, releasing an unsavory combination of sweat and Old Spice, and his eyes swarmed over her. "Nice to see a girl for a change, 'specially one who's a real looker, like you. I bet you're on a soap opera or somethin' or you could be a stewardess with them long legs." He took a cigarette out of his pocket and stuck it behind his ear. "The sisters always hire boys to make deliveries, due to the fact that they ain't as likely to be scared of the deceased. How 'bout you, kitten? Don't you think it's a little spooky in here?"

She glanced at Uncle Dear. "Not really, but if you will excuse me."

"I'm a generous tipper with the delivery boys, so here's a little somethin' for your trouble." He held up a coin, and as Jemma swept by him, he clutched her arm. "See you real soon, hon," he said, then tucked the coin in her hand. She shoved it in her skirt pocket and raced to the car.

Not only did the station wagon start, but it left a little rubber on the driveway just like Spencer did the night she broke up with him. She turned on the radio and sang along.

Jemma parked the car precisely where she had found it. She left the placement diagram on the dashboard, and she took the keys and the tickets with her. Perfect. She knocked on the alley door.

"Who is it?" Sister asked.

"It's me, the delivery girl."

The door slid open and there they stood, giving her the eye.

"Is there anything you need to tell me?" The Proprietor asked.

"No, ma'am, I can't think of anything."

The sisters exchanged glances. Maybe laying rubber on the funeral home driveway was frowned upon in the delivery business.

"Don't play coy with me. I just got off the phone with Mr. Tiller." The Proprietor's hands were on her hips, fingers together, just like Jemma had learned at cheerleading camp. "I told you that follow-up calls would be made and questions would be asked. Mr. Tiller reported that he gave you a quarter for a tip, and you promised to turn all tips over to me at once."

"Oh, that." Jemma fumbled in her pocket. "It's right here." The Proprietor pursed her lips in victory as Jemma handed it over, accompanied by a weak smile. "I'm sorry. I forgot all about it." She looked to Sister for comfort.

Sister adjusted her bosom. "Young people don't appreciate money these days."

Mother Bates plunked the coin in a Mason jar above her desk. "We run an honest establishment here, but it appears you don't adhere to those standards."

"Because I forgot about the quarter?" Jemma asked.

"Girls always get silly over things. I warned you, we don't hire girls."

Sister clicked her tongue.

Jemma's mind churned. "Ma'am, this isn't fair. I wasn't being dishonest; I just forgot." Then it came to her. "I want to speak with Granny."

The sisters raised their voices in chorus. "Who?"

"The Granny on the window, on the car, and in the ad, too. It's her shop."

"There is no Granny," Mother said. "That's just our business name. I told you, I am *the proprietor*. Are you daft?"

Jemma's hands flew to her hips, as well. "Well, isn't this great? You got an afternoon's work out of me, accused me of stealing and lying, and now you're admitting there is no Granny. This job isn't what I thought it was going to be. You can pay me for my hours and I'll go."

"I never said I would pay you. This was a trial period, and it hasn't worked out. Obviously, you don't honor promises."

"You don't even know me! I've gone to church all my life, and I have a boxful of perfect Sunday school attendance certificates to prove it."

Mother's mouth twitched. "Religion is nothing more than a crutch for the simple-minded."

Jemma caught her breath. She was in the presence of a heathen. "Look, whoever you are, ma'am, I delivered your flowers and that alone is worth a stinking quarter."

Sister shifted her weight, possibly wishing she had her knife.

Mother fished the coin out of the jar and held it out to Jemma like a departed slug. "Twenty-five cents for services rendered."

Jemma propelled herself towards the front door, ignoring the offer. The bell jingled wildly as she flung it open, and the ceramic deer caught her attention, his soft brown eyes belying its role as a harbinger of trouble. She slammed the door a little harder than she intended, but the sisters had finished listening to her anyway. Their heads were bent over the workroom counters as they resumed their duties.

Guilt nagged at her, but not because she had tried to keep money from them. She had let a couple of elderly ladies haul out her temper. Papa would say that she should have been more respectful, and Jemma couldn't believe she had been fired, before she was hired, for the only job in the *Wicklow Weekly*.

She languished against the hot bricks outside the barbershop and bawled until the barber came out to ask if there was anything he could do to help. It was too late now for help. Maybe she should have prayed about it. A good, solid prayer couldn't have done any harm. That's what her Gram would've done. Jemma wiped her eyes and stepped off the sidewalk to the Dodge. Across the street the sun sparkled on the glass doors of the solitary law office in town. Gold lettering, edged in black, spelled out the lawyers' names:

Lloyd D. Turner—Stevens P. Turner
Attorneys at Law

A hand-printed sign was taped on the door: *Part-time position available. Must be bonded.*

Jemma undid her ponytail, licked her lips, and opened the door to a rush of frosty air-conditioning. There was no time for stockings. Classical music wafted from a radio and a dish of buttermints rested on the receptionist's desk.

A smartly dressed woman looked up from her typewriter and smiled. "May I help you?"

Jemma cleared her throat. "I'm here about the job."

The woman gave her some forms to fill out, she met with one of the lawyers, and she was in. It was that simple.

"Are you bonded?" the secretary asked before she left.

"No," Jemma said, "but I want to be."

❧ ☙

That night she sat on the steps outside her sticky hot garage apartment, listening to the crickets. Spent clouds masked the moon, but the nearby lights of Dallas made the moonlight pointless anyway. The glow messed up her stargazing, too. In high school she and Spencer had watched the stars and talked about life from the hood of his car, but in the eighth grade they had promised to love one another forever, among other things. Maybe she really didn't keep promises since she had given up his love easy enough. Now she wanted it back. No, she wanted *him* back. It was small comfort that he was somewhere under that same moon, maybe even loving her, still. She should call him, but then if he had a girlfriend, she would just die.

The clouds moved off and she searched the heavens for Orion, like they'd always done. It was no use. Jemma returned to the thick heat of her room. Spencer's senior picture smiled from the dresser, and she touched the little scar, barely visible, on his chin. She longed to touch him in person. He stared back at her with his big gray eyes. She sighed out loud, then sat down at the typewriter. She was running low on sleep, vocabulary, and paper. The old portable didn't help much, either. She gathered her damp hair on top of her head, then put in another sheet.

Title: Joy, In Light—Artist's Statement
Medium: oil on canvas

> *Scenes wash across my path in a kaleidoscope refrain and I am compelled to capture them as they reveal themselves in the light. A delicate line, sensuous curve, or subtle shade of color could release even the most fleeting response in another soul, thereby validating some common ground in the human experience.*
>
> *In this piece, the woman's face and the text are illuminated, capturing the effect of the letter on her heart. One hand is held midair as in sudden realization, while the other quells the paper. The tilt of the woman's head and the curl of her mouth suggest the text is one of joy.*
>
> *Signed: Jemmabeth Alexandra Forrester, May 9, 1965*
> *Le Claire College of the Arts, Dallas, Texas*

She yanked it out and typed it again on her last sheet of paper, translating the title into French: *Joie, Dans La Lumière*. She had looked up the right words at school. Maybe, by some miracle, she would win the competition and Spence would call to congratulate her. Slathering the statement with rubber cement, she positioned it on the back of the canvas. She piled her art history research paper beside it on the floor, wound her clock, said her prayers, and collapsed into sleep.

Caruso's scratchy voice floated through her window. She sat on the side of her bed for a groggy minute, then splashed cold water on her face and looked down on Helene's backyard. Her English landlady was cutting the first flush of roses and singing along with the gramophone. Jemma threw on one of her daddy's old white shirts and a pair of her painting jeans. She squeezed into her loafers as she descended the stairs where Helene greeted her at the bottom.

"You are up so early, *Zhemma*." Helene pronounced her name in the continental style, further proof that anything sounded better in French. "I have had a brainstorm, dear, and I think you may be quite interested."

"I'll come by later because today is my family's big move to Arizona." Jemma said but couldn't resist the roses. "My mom would love one of those, if you don't mind."

Helene offered her all of the creamy pink flowers. "Give my regards to your family. Tell them I'll look after you. Now carry on, dear."

Everybody had said that her grandpapa would want her to have his 1957 Dodge, a gas-guzzling, two-toned green monster with fins. Poking at the pushbutton gear selector on the dashboard, Papa had always been full of advice. "You gotta keep up with the times, Jemmabeth, and pushing buttons is the wave of the future," he had said, looking at her out of the corner of his eye. The Dodge was losing charm, but it still got her around.

She needed to get around to calling Spence, but there remained the problem of what she would say. He was too smart and would pick up on any weak excuses, so it would have to be flat-out honesty. This had been her big idea and, looking back, it was truly dumb. She only hoped that his feelings hadn't changed at all in the last year. She was willing to beg, if necessary, and begging could be good if nobody else had entered the picture. It might also help if she apologized for dumping him. There. That was the rough draft. Not exactly spectacular, but heartfelt.

The sun peeked between the stands of old elm and oak trees, scattering patches of blackish-green along the country lanes. Jemma concocted another tender reunion situation with Spence, loaded with prolonged bouts of kissing, and it sucked her into the other lane around a curve. A delivery truck swerved and honked, but she couldn't help resuming the daydream. After all, it had been a whole year since she kissed him good-bye, and she'd kissed many a dud in the meantime.

Her parents' ranch-style house was set on a knoll and shaded by elms. Her daddy and her little brother had built a tree house in the largest one, and she had stayed all night in it with Robby on his seventh birthday just the past week. Now a realtor's sign was nailed to it.

Robby ran out of the house, shouting, "Mom, she's here." He jumped on his sister, spilling a collection of trip entertainment on the steps.

She helped him clean it up and looked into his sky blue eyes. "You need to lick your lips. There are crumbs and syrup shining under them." She handed him a thick tablet of paper and some of her own colored pencils. "You also have to draw the desert for me, and I mean fill each page."

"Maybe," he said. "Since you're not coming, you have to write me a lot of letters."

She rubbed his buzz haircut, like velvet against her hand. "That means you have to answer every single one, big boy."

"Aw, c'mon; that's too much spelling."

"A letter a month, then," she yelled after him as he was off to watch his bicycle being loaded into the U-Haul.

Alexandra Forrester appeared in the doorway, dressed in her new Arizona outfit, complete with a purple bandana tied at her neck. Her mother knew how to turn heads. People commented that Jemma had become the image of her, right down to their pouty lips, as her daddy called them, but Alex's auburn hair was cut in an Italian bob, and Jemma's was below her shoulders in natural waves. Jemma did have those uncanny golden eyes, too, unlike the hazel eyes of her mother, and she had outgrown Alex by a good three inches. Not exactly twins.

Alex held out her arms. "Come here, Sweet Pea. I miss you already. Promise you will call us and you'll take your vitamins."

10

"Sure, Mom." Jemma saluted. "Here's a bouquet to keep you company."

Alex first tucked her daughter's hair behind her ears, then took the roses. "I mean it now."

"Yes, ma'am. It's not like I'm going to prison or something."

"I know a kid whose grandpa is in prison," Robby said, climbing on Jemma's back. "He was our class pen pal."

Alex and Jemma exchanged glances and giggled.

Jim Forrester set an ice chest, which Jemma knew was full of sodas and pimiento cheese sandwiches, in the rental truck and strode over to hug her. Tall and lanky with brown hair, high forehead, deep-set eyes the color of a lion's, a generous nose, and a toothy smile, he looked like Jemma's grandmother, Lizbeth.

"Daddy, you watch the road and don't be looking around for deer or antelope," Jemma said.

"Or buffalo?" Jim laughed as he inspected their new Rambler station wagon that was hitched securely to the back of the truck. He had made this trip once already with an even bigger load. He wiped the back of his neck and pointed a finger at her. "You be smart, young lady. Watch out for those burly cello players, and you be in church every Sunday."

"Yes sir, I know. I've been learning some wrestling moves from TV," she said, assuming a stance and hoping for a laugh. None was forthcoming.

"We'll be in Chillaton tonight, so you can call us at Gram's if you want." He opened his wallet and held out a fifty-dollar bill. "You hide this in your sock drawer because it may come in handy. Now don't be shaking your head at me."

"Thanks, Daddy, but I got that cleaning job yesterday."

He stuffed the money in her pocket, along with a quick hug and kiss. "Love you, baby girl. Let's go, troops."

"Wait." Robby came running with a piece of wood. "It's for your hope chest thing. I messed up on the P, but Daddy says nobody will notice." It was smooth, gray driftwood, over a foot long, with JEMMA'S PLACE carved into it. The P was once backwards, but then sanded out to face the right way—there was a reason he didn't like spelling. "It's that wood we found on the beach last summer," he said.

She held him until he wriggled away.

Jim started the U-Haul. "Give Spence a call. Don't let that boy get away from you. I don't think you know which end is up in that department."

Jemma nodded again, like things were under control in every department. She knew that her mother was crying as they pulled out of the lane. "I love you," she shouted and blew one last kiss.

Sunlight glinted off the chrome luggage rack as the Rambler vanished over the hilltop behind the U-Haul. Jemma left without looking back, but her mother's perfume lingered on her blouse. She turned up the radio full blast and sang "Ticket to Ride" with the Beatles. Her new job would start tomorrow, and she would call Spence by the weekend. Life was good. Helene's old red MG was gone when she got home so she set her alarm for eight o'clock, turned on the fan, and fell asleep.

❧ ❧

The pouting room was just a whatnot of a room, originally intended as a pantry. Lizbeth Forrester propped open the window, then dusted the shelves and the bulky trunk with its tin, leaf-shaped hinges. The floor was too small to fiddle with, but she scrubbed it on her knees anyway. She laid back the lid of the trunk to get the medals. With tiny, even, circles she rubbed the cleanser into the Purple Hearts. She polished them with a corner of her apron until a bird outside the window caught her attention for a moment. The song was somehow familiar, but it vanished before she could get a look at it. She rested, massaging the bridge of her nose, then stared blankly at the hearts. Such trifles to honor her babies. She returned them to their velvet boxes and the lids snapped shut. This was her private ritual. She didn't know if it made her feel better or worse after all these years, but she had kept it up.

Cameron had never brought himself to look at the medals from the time they put them in the trunk, the soldier box, until he died. Instead, he planted flowers and built fancy little birdhouses to deal with the sorrow. He put them all over their place until folks started driving by just to look at the mass of blooms and birdhouses that filled the yard. Now he was gone, too. Lizbeth closed the window and replaced the little hook on the door just as the 6:23 Zephyr blew by on the tracks behind the house.

She poured herself a tall glass of sweet tea and went to the hollyhock patch. Her dress was already clinging to her skin, so she laid her hand on a metal chair with peeling Getaway Green paint to see if it was still cool enough to sit in. Cam had painted his chair Thunder Red on the screened-in porch one winter day and the fumes had lingered for a week.

Lizbeth touched the cold glass to her forehead, then rolled her neck on the back of the chair and gazed into the branches of the pecan tree. It was going to make a heavy crop this year and provide plenty of pecans for her holiday pies. A movement in the foliage caught her eye. It was a cardinal, bright red, the same one she had heard outside the pouting room. She had never seen one in this part of Texas, but knew them well growing up along the banks of the Bosque River. The bird shook itself and let out two long, shrill whistles then a burst of short chirps. It hopped to another spot and was lost in the branches. They saw lots of birds back in Erath County when Cam was courting her, and he could name them all. His birdhouses were trifles, too. She missed the man.

The wind picked up, snapping her laundry on the line and flushing a bevy of birds from the trees. A fly crept around the edge of her glass, leaving a threadlike trail in the condensation. She poured out the last bits of ice and went inside to bake cookies before it got too hot, and especially before her neighbor could bring the mail. The man could eat a dozen before any were offered, but he kept her entertained.

She checked her watch. Her dear ones, Jimmy, Alexandra, and Robby, would be pulling into the driveway in about five hours. Jemmabeth, bless her, was on her own now, but she would make it. Lizbeth had survived, despite all the grief, with the same mettle she had as the only female in her college class. Jenkins girls always did, somehow, and Jemma had just as much Jenkins in her as she did Forrester.

CHAPTER TWO

Snakeskin

The Le Claire College of the Arts was in an older part of Dallas, the area where a squirrel could travel from one tree to another for blocks at a time and never touch the ground. The campus had been a private boys' school at the turn of the century, but it now sheltered minds and hands bent on creativity. The buildings had been refurbished through a generous donation from a patron of the arts now living abroad. Jemma wanted to live abroad someday, too. Maybe Spence would like to live on the French Riviera or in a quaint Italian village. Their children could be multi-lingual, that is, if he took her back.

She read the inscription over the entryway aloud, as always:

> *Criticism is easy, Art is difficult.*
> *—Philippe Nericault 1680-1754*

Art had never been difficult for her, but she liked the quote anyway. He was French.

The smell of paint and brush cleaner saturated the room. Ceiling fans whirred overhead and windows the size of Volkswagens were cranked open, infusing the room with humid Dallas air. The wooden floors, spattered with color flicked in moments of inspiration or frustration, creaked in certain spots. Jemma closed her eyes and inhaled.

Professor Rossi leaned across a counter and tapped on its surface. "Jemmabeth, have you come to bring me your competition piece or are you taking a tour of the school?" His white hair curled around his ears, and his bushy brows sprang up.

She laughed. "I missed you, too. How was y'all's trip to Italy?"

He patted his belly. "Perfect. You should have come with us.

14

Florence would have ignited your senses."

"Maybe next year."

The professor wagged his finger. "Come, give me your painting. The competition will be intense." His eyes widened as she revealed the piece. "Ah, exquisite," he said, kissing his fingers and tossing them in the air. It was his idea for her to enter the contest for the fellowship. He propped the painting on a display ledge that lined the room, then stepped back to scrutinize her work, talking to himself. Jemma smiled and left him to his artistic dissection.

She was late to meet Melanie Glazer, a fellow Le Claireian and concert violinist. Melanie had been invited to play with the Dallas Symphony Orchestra for the summer season, and the two girls had a date to go shopping.

"Over here," Melanie yelled across the fountain plaza.

Jemma waved. "Ready to go?"

"Always willing to spend my hard-earned money."

Jemma pulled out of the school parking lot. "I haven't been shopping since Christmas. I hope I remember how to get to this place."

"Go to SMU, then it's easy. You should know how to get there since you've spent all year checking out the men on that campus."

"Southern Methodist University, where all the good-looking, rich guys are," Jemma said, although she knew better.

"Not always," Melanie said, flashing her engagement ring.

"I assume Michael is doing well."

"He's my accompanist for the recital. Any luck with Robert?" Melanie asked.

"Clammy hands."

"Clayton?"

"He makes this weird clucking noise when he can't think of anything to say, and his lips fold under or something when he kisses. I just get a lot of teeth."

"Yuck. Now that's what I'll think about every time I see him. He is cute, though. Whatever happened to that guy you dated your freshman year? Wasn't he your childhood sweetheart or something?"

"Yeah. We'd never even looked at anybody else in thirteen years. Well, maybe I looked at a few cowboys, but who wouldn't? Anyway, I haven't seen Spencer since last summer when I said that I needed some time to see if I really loved him." She pulled into a parking spot.

They got out and stood before a row of posh shops. "Not exactly middle class."

"Nope. Listen, I found that song you told me about," Melanie said as they surveyed the mannequins.

"Papa's favorite? Isn't it great?"

"It's sweet but melancholy."

"It follows me around."

"Like other things from your past?"

Jemma took a breath. "Let's shop."

∽೨ ⌀∾

She hammered the shiny brass knocker on the door several times in case Helene wasn't wearing her hearing aid. The Tudor style house was unique in the town of Wicklow. It was gabled with tall windows, half-timbers, and four chimneys. Helene had lived alone in the great house for the last several years until she took in Jemma, her first boarder. She opened the door dressed impeccably in a linen suit. She was a spry, petite woman. As always, she was wearing her double strand of pearls and her emerald earrings.

"Jemma, dear," she said, adjusting her hearing aid. "Let's visit in the kitchen, shall we? Come along." Only at the corners of Helene's brown eyes was there a hint of wrinkles and her silver hair was forever pulled back into a bun. Jemma followed her through the house, past loaded bookshelves, rich floral fabrics, photographs of Mr. Neblitt and her in exotic places, and paintings of Helene's stuffy ancestors.

Helene went on the whole time about her fat white cat, Chelsea, while Jemma considered how similar the antique mirror above the fireplace was to one at the Chase's house in Chillaton. This home smelled of wood polish and lavender, and recently, toast. At her landlady's invitation over the past several months, Jemma had studied at Mr. Neblitt's desk in the drawing room as Helene read, reclining on a pillow-strewn window seat. They had charmed one another. Helene always wanted a child and Jemma loved her companionship, style, and spirit. Helene was also a gourmet cook, which didn't hurt anything.

A dazzling collection of china filled every cabinet and shelf in the kitchen. The cookstove was a huge black thing shipped from England, and the breakfast table reminded Jemma of the drugstore tables in

16

Chillaton where she and Papa drank chocolate shakes after the trips home from her art lessons in Amarillo.

"Mom liked the roses," she said, inhaling a vase full of them on the table.

"It was Neb's hobby, you know. I do hope he is watching from some cloud when I tend them because it is back-breaking labor for an old sort like me. Now, Jemma, I have been thinking about your accommodations, and here it is: I would like for you to move in with Chelsea and me. I have two guest rooms and neither has been used in years. You could keep that oven of a flat over the garage as your studio."

Jemma gawked at her. "Whoa. Thank you, Helene, but I can't afford two rooms. I'm barely paying for one."

"Don't be silly. We are too close for you to pay another penny for anything. This is completely my idea and it's quite shameful that I haven't suggested such an arrangement sooner. You may choose which room suits you best, and then we shall call your parents and ask their blessing. There you have it."

Jemma shut her mouth. She already knew which room she wanted. It was like a set from a movie. Her mom would croak when she heard about this.

She moved her things as soon as Helene got Alex and Jim's grateful approval. They were thrilled that Jemma wouldn't be living alone anymore. Rose toile wallpaper graced the walls and the ceiling was at least twelve feet high. The curtains were gold, patterned with hydrangeas. There was a skirted dressing table fit for Miss Scarlett, who might brush her hair there and then leave the room in a huff, overturning the stool. The bed was a four-poster with white linens and needlepoint pillow shams. Jemma could almost see herself in the cherry hardwood floor, she had her own bathroom with a claw-footed tub, and altogether, she was as close to heaven as a twenty-year-old artist could get.

Helene watched as Jemma pushed a large cedar box under the bed. "Whatever is that lovely thing?" she asked.

"It's my hope chest that my grandpapa made for me. It's a tradition from way back. My Gram had one and I'm supposed to keep things in it for, you know, if I ever get married."

"And so you shall," Helene said and went to the dresser to examine Spencer's senior picture. "Who is this handsome young man?

I didn't know you had a special someone."

"That is Spencer Morgan Chase."

"Ah, the reason for the hope chest."

"Spence and I grew up together. In our first-grade Christmas program nobody would hold hands with Lena Purl Sweeney because they said she had cooties. Spencer let go of my hand and took Lena Purl's. You have to love somebody like that. It was always our plan to marry someday, but we have been dating other people this year." Jemma shrugged at his picture. "He may not love me anymore."

Helene tapped the frame with *Class of '63* emblazoned in gold across the bottom. "If I were a young lady, I would be quite concerned about letting this one loose in the wide world of college women."

Jemma turned back to her unpacking. Everybody was full of advice. She may have learned a few things this year. First off, she missed him more than she had ever planned, and, along that same line, she needed to pray about important stuff rather than asking for help afterwards, like she was doing every night now.

Her new bedroom kept her awake or maybe it was just Spence. She turned on her bedside lamp and reached for her sketchbook. She drew his face, then thumped her pencil on the pad. *Would you* (crossed that out) *Could you* (crossed out) *I miss you so much and I'm sorry that...* She couldn't write it. She got his picture off the dresser and propped it up on her knees. She lay back against the pillow and just told him. It was a very long conversation. She would call him tomorrow night when she got home from cleaning the offices. Maybe her lonesome days would soon be over.

⧸⧹⧸⧹

The trash didn't even smell at Turner & Turner's. There were four offices for the lawyers, a conference room, a reception area where the secretaries worked, and two bathrooms. The mahogany furniture, floor to ceiling bookshelves, and the lack of windows conjured up the feeling of being trapped, like Papa's hogs must have felt at killing time. She shook off that icky thought and got to work. She polished the wood, especially the conference table, to a perfect shine. There were a few paintings on the walls, but nothing of merit. They were no more than furniture store prints.

Jemma remembered what her mother had taught her—top to bottom—dust, then vacuum. The vacuum cleaner was extra loud so she turned up her transistor radio full blast, pulled her hair back with a rubber band, and made a production of it, singing over the roar and dancing with her metallic partner. Spencer's favorite song was playing, "Mean Woman Blues." She was barefoot and in the middle of a torrid move when something told her that she had an audience. She turned around and squealed, as much in delight as in shock.

He was almost as tall as the doorframe he was leaning against. His black hair skimmed his collar and his eyes, jade green, were boring a hole through her. High cheekbones and square jaw spread into a grin, making him, without a doubt, the most delectable cowboy she had ever encountered.

"That's quite a show, darlin'," he yelled.

Jemma's tongue was as heavy as the vacuum that was still running. She fumbled around for the switch. "What did you say?"

"I said that's some show."

"You're on the photo wall, aren't you?"

"Yeah, I'm one of 'em. Hey, don't let me keep you from your work. I just thought I should let you know that you're not alone anymore."

"Thanks," she said, not knowing where to look. The photo hadn't prepared her for the real thing.

"No thanks needed. You made my day." He turned and went back into the conference room and sat at the table. His jeans were creased and the sleeves on his blue starched shirt were rolled up. Those jeans looked good, but the clincher was the black snakeskin boots. Lucky reptile to end up with this guy. He opened his briefcase and spread papers on the tabletop that she had just buffed to a fine sheen. He concentrated on his work, but Jemma couldn't take her eyes off him. He looked up and winked.

She finished the rooms, raked the shag carpet, washed the coffee maker, and cleaned the bathrooms again in no time at all, hoping he would come out of that conference room before she had to do it all over again.

He did. He leaned against the doorframe again and clicked his pen, staring at her. "I knew they hired someone, but I don't know your name."

"Jemmabeth, but you can call me Jemma. Most people do."

"Pretty name. I didn't see a car outside." Her daddy was six-three, and this guy was taller than that. He looked like a man who knew how to take charge and he was in good shape, too. There was no wedding ring on his finger. She had checked.

"I walked because my car is basically out of gas," she said, like a dumb bunny.

"You shouldn't walk around town at night, darlin'. Where do you live?"

"I live with Helene Neblitt. Do you know her?"

"Sure, the big stone house on the edge of town. When you're ready to go, I'm taking you."

"Actually, I'm ready now," she said, surprising herself.

He opened the passenger door to a baby blue Ford pickup and moved some packages out of the way. "Sorry. I just picked up my laundry." He put on a black cowboy hat. "So, you're a Roy Orbison fan, huh?"

"Yeah, Roy's the best." The hat was almost more than she could bear.

"Where did you learn to dance like that?"

"I like to dance. My mom won a jitterbug contest in college." That sounded stupid. Rats.

"What I saw back there was a far cry from the jitterbug. You were gettin' with it."

"I thought I was alone. You need to turn right here," Jemma said. "It's really not that far."

He pushed his hat to the back of his head. "Too far for a pretty thing like you to be walking at night. How long have you lived in Wicklow?"

"My family moved here two years ago, but I moved out last fall because I wanted to be more independent. My dad was the high school football coach. He has a great job now as an assistant coach at Arizona State College in Flagstaff. Did you play football?" She couldn't shut up, but she might as well have had cotton in her mouth. It was the hat.

"I played back in the fifties. I don't ever remember seeing you at any recent Wicklow games, and I would have noticed if you had been there, darlin', believe me." He drove past Helene's lane and had to back up. They sat in her driveway. As he put his arm on the back of the seat, his fingers skimmed her shoulder. She shifted and squared her back against the door handle.

"I bet you played basketball," he said. "Anybody with your moves and height had to be on the court."

"I had a good jumpshot." She lifted her hair to cool her neck. "I like your hat."

"Why, thank you, ma'am," he said, his voice like satin. He pulled it low over his eyes and smiled. "I wear it when I'm not trying to look like a lawyer."

"I thought good guys always wore white hats."

"That's just in the movies. You can't believe everything you see there, darlin'."

"I know, but I did want to be like Roy Rogers. He was my hero. My grandpapa had a hired hand that was a cowboy. He used to ride up to my grandparents' farm on his horse and pick me up with one arm. We'd go for a ride around their house. I had a crush on him when I was about five years old."

"You didn't want to be Dale Evans?"

"Absolutely not. One Christmas I asked for a Roy Rogers outfit and Santa brought me a Dale Evans one instead. I was so mad."

"So there are two Roys in your life, huh?" He moved his finger across her arm. "Any other men that I need to know about?"

Every hair on her arm stood up. "No more than a cello player or two." Spencer crossed her mind, but not long enough to stop her.

He walked her to the door and studied her face in the glow of the porch light.

"Thanks for the ride," she said, avoiding his eyes.

He tipped his hat. "Anytime, Roy." He started down the walk, his boots crunching the gravel between the stones.

She took a step after him. "Wait. What's your name?"

He walked back, putting his hat over his heart. "My apologies, darlin'. I'm Paul Turner, son of Stephens Turner. I guess I thought you already knew that." She was very aware of her own heartbeat since it was drowning out all the crickets in the yard.

His gaze was steady. "I've never seen eyes the color of honey before. You have to be the sweetest thing in Texas, no, in the universe." He moved his finger under her chin. "I hope you have some fine dreams tonight, Jemmabeth Forrester," he said, his perfect lips curving into a smile.

"You, too, Paul Turner," she whispered.

He took a few steps backward, then turned towards his pickup.

He gave her one final look over his shoulder before getting in.

"Whoa." Jemma stood staring long after his lights had disappeared. She'd better wait a while before she called Spencer. After all, she could be delivering flowers for Mother Bates, but she wasn't, so Paul Turner just might be The One.

℮⁐⁐

She cleaned the offices really slow, in hopes he would come, but was about to turn off the last light before his baby blue pulled into the parking lot. She held the door for him and held her breath as well. *English Leather.* Oh, man, she was a goner. He had on the works— jeans, white shirt, the hat, and those boots. His eyes were as green as Helene's emerald earrings, and his smile gave Jemma goose bumps.

"Hello darlin'. How are you tonight?" He set his briefcase on the conference table. "You work late."

"So do you." She couldn't help but notice that his shirt was almost too tight for his big neck.

He sat on the corner of the table with one boot still on the carpet and the other swinging like a hypnotist's watch. "What do you do with the rest of your day?"

"I'm in a summer mentorship at my art school," she said, glancing into his eyes. "How about you?"

"Law school at SMU." He gestured at the shelves of casebooks as though it were his fate.

"Hey, I went to SMU, too."

"Really, when was that?"

"Cheerleading school, summer of '61."

His laugh was raspy, what Gram called a whisky laugh. "Good one. I bet you were cute in your little cheerleading outfit."

Jemma leaned against the open door. She swayed it back and forth, her hands clutching the doorknob behind her.

"Are you on your way out?" he asked.

Actually, she had forgotten what she was doing. "I think so."

"You didn't walk again, did you?"

"No, I didn't walk. I'm using an old bike from Mrs. Neblitt's garage."

"Let's go," he said and put the bike in the back of his truck.

"I just keep owing you for all the favors you're doing me," Jemma said.

"I guess I'll just have to think of a way to collect. Are you hungry? How about a cheeseburger basket and a milkshake?"

"That sounds good. This is a really nice pickup," she said, knowing nothing about pickups.

He turned up the soul music. "Thanks, I just got it. It's a '66, with an eight-track tape built in."

"So, you're a real buckaroo?" Jemma asked in her best drawl.

"That's right, darlin'. Actually, I just help out the family with our ranching ventures. By the way, you're fixin' to have the best burger in the state. It's down the road a bit, but worth the gas."

She rolled down her window and let the breeze dry her damp face and neck before she undid her ponytail and let her hair fall around her shoulders. She knew good and well that he was watching. They got their food and sat by the creek that ran behind the burger joint.

The floodlight, which was attracting an assortment of insects, went off. After the last car pulled away from the parking lot, only crickets and bullfrogs filled the humid night air, as well as English Leather.

"Are you about to graduate from law school?" she asked. That sounded like an old lady question, but his hat was pushed back like Paul Newman's in *Hud*, driving her nuts.

"Yeah, this month, then I have to take the bar exam. What about you?"

"I just finished my second year in art school at Le Claire. The summer program brings a well-known artist to Dallas who mentors a few lucky students."

He sat way too close to her. "Are you as good at painting as you are at dancing?"

"I've never considered doing anything else. Have you always wanted to be a lawyer?" Her nostrils flared, just a bit, filling her senses and messing with her good sense.

"Pretty much. I decided for sure when I got out of the army. I was in ROTC at the University of Texas. Hey, check out the fireflies over there." He nodded towards the opposite side of the creek.

She jumped up like she'd never seen one before. "Wow! How do they do that?"

"The female puts out the brightest light, but I think only the male can fly."

"I wonder how they decide when to light up for romance?" Jemma asked, teetering on the edge of the creek bank.

He winked. "That's the universal question. The trick is knowing the answer."

A shiver rippled through her. Lashes like his belonged on a girl.

They rode home singing along with his eight-track.

Paul leaned the bike against Helene's garage. "Do you work two or three days a week at the office?"

"I work Tuesdays and Fridays."

"I'll see you on Friday then."

"Okay, but I'm going to look up fireflies and see if you know what you're talking about."

"Good." He ran his finger down the bridge of her nose, touching her lips. "You take care, darlin'."

Jemma swallowed hard. "I'll pay you back for the burgers."

"Don't you even think about it. I like the idea of having you in my debt," he said over his shoulder.

She shut the door and slid down it in giddy anticipation of Friday.

They went again to the Best Burger Stop, talking until the place closed. As the fireflies came out, he popped the question that she'd been thinking about all week.

"Are you in the mood for some romance?"

She gulped.

He ran up the steps to his pickup, leaving Jemma like a limp French fry on the bench. He came back with a tiny flashlight and a jar. "I used to do this at camp, but I haven't thought of it in years." He squatted on the grass by the table and handed her the jar. "Be ready." Then, just like the real thing, he turned the flashlight on and off in short bursts. Another firefly responded to the call and flew right to Paul, landing on his arm. "Gotcha," he said as Jemma put the jar over the bug and screwed the lid on tight.

"It's magical," she whispered.

"Works every time."

They sat on the table, watching the show in the jar. "I guess it's kind of sad, though," she said. "I feel like we've sentenced it to jail."

"Or worse," Paul said, sliding his arm around her waist and making her sweat.

She opened the lid and shook it out. The firefly took off and they followed its path until it was lost among the others.

"Oh, rats!" Jemma said. "What time is it?"

Paul looked at his watch. "Eleven thirty."

"I was supposed to call my little brother because he got home from church camp tonight."

"Close family?" He pulled her to him.

Her pulse rocketed. "My parents met at the University of Nebraska. Daddy was on a football scholarship, and my mom was a cheerleader, the daughter of a big shot newspaperman in St. Louis. Daddy joined the army after Pearl Harbor, and they got married as soon as he got out. My grandparents weren't exactly thrilled about her marrying a farmer's son."

"I take it they weren't football fans or they would have liked your dad. Did love last for them?"

"Of course it did. Daddy always says that he was a lucky man to find a Midwestern girl with all the charms of a Southern belle. He likes to tease."

"You're the cutest belle I've ever shared a milkshake with, darlin', and that's the truth."

"Aw, shucks," Jemma said in her Scarlett accent. "You stop that, or I just might swoon."

Paul laughed and moved his hand towards an unauthorized spot.

"I think it's bedtime for me," Jemma said, quickly deflecting his move.

"Well," he whispered. "We don't want you sleeping out here. Unless I am with you and then what would people say?"

He walked her to the door, and Jemma wanted him to kiss her so bad that her lips quivered. Paul took her hand instead, kissed it, and looked her in the eye.

"You know that I think about you all the time," he said. "I want to see you more than twice a week. How about if I come by here tomorrow night?" He was so close she could taste his breath in the midnight air.

"I can't wait to see you either. Come every night."

He grinned down at her. "I'll be having some sweet dreams about you tonight, darlin', guaranteed."

Jemma watched from the door until she couldn't see his lights on the road. She took a long bubble bath and went to bed, hoping that maybe tonight she wouldn't dream about Spencer Chase.

CHAPTER THREE

Against Her Heart

S he was, perhaps, smitten. That's all she could come up with. When she least expected it, a word or a touch would remind her of Spencer, but Paul's green eyes and snakeskin boots hustled those memories right out. How could her plans turn around so quickly? It was just over a week ago that she was dying to talk to sweet Spence. Now words came out of her mouth to which she hadn't given much thought until she heard them. Rats. She was tumbling into a wild hole with this cowboy, but he made the trip so easy on her. Spence could be engaged to some debutante by now. That was a troubling thought. She considered how it might feel to see Spencer with some other girl, but then she considered the fact that Cowboy Paul still hadn't kissed her. If he were a rotten kisser, well, what a waste of those perfect lips. There was nothing better than a great kiss, and she needed a sample by the end of the month. Then again, Spence could also be missing her kisses right now rather than being engaged. Double rats on her lifelong weakness for cowpokes, but, oh well, she was in this curious hole too deep to crawl out just yet.

"The French have a name for this time of day that is more romantic than our 'twilight'," Paul said. "They call it *L'heure bleu*, the blue hour."

Good grief, he speaks French. "I love the way you said that," she said, but then suddenly recalled Spencer was learning French the last time she saw him, too.

"Why thank you, ma'am," Paul said. "I had to take some kind of foreign language at college. Girls always seem to like French, so I took it. How's your mentorship going?"

Jemma tossed a kiss into the air, "Fantastico!"

"So you like Italian, too."

"I'm having so much fun in my class. We examine classic paintings with a magnifying glass to see what technique the artist used. After we figure it out, we try the same technique and paint a toss-away piece. Isn't that great? Eet is zee European way."

"You've never told me your favorite artists."

"I hate that question because there are so many, but I'll try. There's Vermeer, of course. Frank Benson, Mary Cassatt, and Andrew Wyeth are wonderful. The painting of the last Russian Tsar's wedding is dazzling; it's by Laurits Tuxen. Oh, and I just did a paper on William Bouguereau. I love that man."

"Maybe I'll have to learn about some guy you love."

She looked away and he put both of his nice arms around her. Jemma's mouth parched.

"You are something else," he whispered. His lips touched her ear as he spoke, then he turned her chin towards him and kissed her. It was perfect, just like she had imagined. He had made her wait on purpose. Only an unexpected twinge of guilt kept her from floating off with the swarm of fireflies. He rubbed the back of her neck. "I can't quite figure you out. You've got those bedroom eyes, but you keep giving me a Sunday school smile. How about we stop by my apartment on the way home, darlin'?"

She drew back. "No."

"A good girl, huh? I kind of figured that, but you can't blame me for asking."

"Yes, I can."

"I'm glad you said no. I really am. You just may be the darlin' that turns me into a one-woman man." His eyes were half closed as he smiled at her. For an instant, he resembled a cobra emerging from its charmer's basket in a cartoon that Jemma had seen at The Parnell with Spencer.

She blinked. "So, normally, you are not a one-woman man?"

"If I had somebody like you, I could learn that life. I just need a woman with your looks and your morals because I already know that I like your style."

"My style?"

"Yeah, innocence and something extra."

"I am innocent."

28

"Yeah, but you've got some stuff seething in the wings, darlin', right down to that husky voice of yours. I know it when I see it."

Jemma looked at him hard. She'd never had a conversation remotely like this one with anybody except her mother or sort of with Spencer. Paul knew how to twist things around and he was not yet a solid part of her heart. Spencer still was, though, and the promise they had made about not fooling around was very much intact.

"You're making me uncomfortable," she said and stood up.

He grabbed her hand. "Let me tell you that the feeling is mutual. So, let's talk about something else. I have to know everything about you."

Jemma hesitated, then flopped down on the wooden steps. He was smart to let her cool off, and he extended the time out by stroking her hair as though she were Helene's cat, Chelsea.

"I love flowers," Jemma said. "Someday I'm going to have fresh flowers all over my house. I'll grow my own roses, especially the old ones that smell so good. I'll have Asian lilies, peonies, lilies of the valley, lavender, sweet peas, but no carnations."

He eased his arm around her again. "What do you have against carnations?"

"They remind me of funerals," she said, moving his arm away.

He bumped her with his shoulder. "I like carnations. They smell like cinnamon. Something about you sure smells sweet."

"It's probably my shampoo."

"Hmm...what's your favorite perfume?" he asked.

"I haven't found one I really like. My Gram wears something called Moonlight Over Paris. That sounds intriguing to me. I like mysterious fragrances because I don't want to be like everybody else."

"Darlin', I don't think there could be anybody else like you."

"Thank you, cowboy." She looked at his watch. "We'd better start back."

It was a quiet ride to Helene's, but she did sit next to him, and unless he was shifting gears, his arm stayed around her shoulder.

"I've never known any girl named Jemmabeth," he said.

"I'm named after my daddy, Jim, and it's become a tradition in his family to add 'beth.' My great-grandparents named my Gram, their firstborn, Lizbeth. Then came Annabeth, Marybeth, Sarabeth, and Julia—the Jenkins girls."

"Julia doesn't fit the pattern," he said.

"We call her Do Dah. That's how my uncles said her name when they were little. Papa said that Gram's parents had worked so hard to have a boy that when Do Dah came along they were all out of 'beth'— get it? My grandparents raised Do Dah because her mother died giving birth. She was born about the same time as my Uncle Matthew. My grandpa, Papa, was from a Scottish family. He wore his father's kilt on holidays or just to aggravate Gram. I spent every summer with them on their farm while my parents finished college. There. Now it's your turn."

"You already know my dad and my mother died when I was in high school. I have two sisters that live in Dallas. Say, how'd you like to go dancing? There's a place in Kensington called the Handle Bar that has a great band. Let's go tomorrow night."

"What should I wear? Is it a dress-up place or what?"

"Not exactly." Paul smiled. "Wear jeans." He leaned across the seat and kissed her. She did have to watch out for those buckaroo hands of his.

❧❦

He picked her up with his snakeskins polished and ready. She wore her jeans and a long-sleeved, muslin shirt that her mom had given her. He didn't seem to mind that her red boots were a little on the shabby side.

"Every guy there'll be jealous of me tonight," he said, making her scalp tingle. He cranked up the eight-track player and they sang along until he turned off the road and into a parking lot already crowded with cars.

"Wait." Jemma said, her eyes like two fried eggs. "This is a bar."

"Yeah. Remember, I said it was the Handle Bar."

"I thought it was the handlebar, like on a bike or a moustache. I've never been to a bar."

"Oh, come on, darlin', I thought you told me you'd been dating every man in Dallas this past year."

"I don't drink," she said flatly, staring at the flashing neon signs.

"Really? Well, you don't have to drink. Just dance and it'll be fine. I know you're going to love this band, and old Paul will protect you from whatever dares to mess with you, I promise."

Inside, the Handle Bar was stale with smoke and beer. Jemma's twitchy smile waned as the bartender called Paul by name. They had just been seated at a table by the dance floor when the band broke out with "Treat Her Right." They moved onto the floor with several other couples. After the first few notes, Paul couldn't keep up with her. They danced every dance until he was tired and let other guys cut in, but she kept on until the band took a break. Paul ordered her a soda and winked at the waitress. Jemma needed to dance again to forget where she was.

"You're sure tearing up the floor, darlin'," he said, winking at her, too.

Another cowboy dragged up a chair and straddled it backwards. "What's up with you, Turner? I thought you were going to call me about our Vegas trip," he asked, nodding at Jemma and stubbing out a cigarette.

"Sorry, Kyle. Something's come up," Paul said.

The cowboy turned to Jemma. "Are you the something? You gonna break this bronco and put him out of his misery?" He took a swig of beer and planted the mug on the table.

Jemma said nothing, but watched the little bubbles slide down the insides of the glass. Her mother and daddy would be shocked to see her at this place and Gram would disown her.

"Jemmabeth, meet my friend, Kyle, who considers himself a dancer. How about you show him a thing or two?"

Jemma turned to the husky fellow with dark blond hair and bloodshot eyes. She paused but gave in to his crooked smile and outstretched hand. The band was playing "In the Midnight Hour." Kyle was big, but he was smooth and quick. Her daddy would have used him as a linebacker. He kept up with her, but nothing compared to Spencer. She was aware of Paul's eyes on her the whole time.

She went to the bathroom when the song was over. A platinum blonde was checking her makeup at the mirror, and she gave Jemma a long look before she spoke. "You're quite the little dancer, aren't you? Paul's fixin' to come unglued."

Jemma blushed. "Actually, I've never been to a place like this before."

"Drinking from the Devil's cup tonight then?"

"What do you mean?" Jemma asked as her hands dripped on the floor. "I don't drink."

"Paul Turner is what I mean."

"I like Paul," Jemma said, her stomach getting queasy.

The blonde arched an eyebrow. "We all like Paul, kiddo. I've been down a few roads with him myself. Every woman here would die to be his only darlin', and believe me, he's a real prize. Just watch yourself. That's all I can say because I don't think you know what you're up against." She blotted her lipstick then left.

"The Devil's cup?" Jemma whispered and looked in the mirror, blinking back tears and now feeling a solid swell of nausea. It would break Papa's heart if he could see her right now. She only hoped the world didn't come to an end in the next five minutes before she could get out of that place, but first, she had to throw up.

❧

It was a humorless trip home. She had drunk two Cokes, chewed a whole packet of gum to free her taste buds of barroom air, and had kept her head in the open window to rid her hair of cigarette smoke.

Paul took off his hat and put it on the seat between them. There was plenty of room, too. He ventured a comment. "I loved watching you dance tonight, Jemma."

She kept her eyes off him for once. "Isn't that what you do in places like Las Vegas?"

"I'm not following."

"If you're not going to dance with me, I'm not dancing."

"Looks like I've missed something here."

"Yeah, well, you could be missing me after tonight."

He reached for her hand, but it was quickly withdrawn. He drew a heavy breath.

"Look, darlin', I'd like to settle down. It would make my family very happy and probably be good for my health, but I'm going to need somebody to lay down the law and keep me on the straight and narrow. What do you say?"

"You want me to be your mother?"

"Heck no, I want you to be my woman."

Jemma chewed on her lip. "Just how bad are you?"

"That's not the point. The issue is that I want you more than anything, and I can see that's going to force me to be good."

She touched the brim of his hat. It couldn't hurt to bring in the

Lord. "I know the Bible says not to judge people."

"Well, there you go, darlin'. I'm your man." He moved his fingertips across her cheek.

"Lesson number one is never take me to a bar again." She looked him in the eye. "And I mean it."

"Understood." He crossed his heart. "Am I forgiven?"

"Maybe," she said, half smiling. "I don't know what to make of all this stuff I've heard about you tonight. How do I know if you're really serious?"

"I'm serious all right. Don't worry about my past. It just makes me a better kisser," he said and gave her a sample.

Jemma sat up, moving his hands away from her. "Kissing doesn't cure everything."

"Well, it might help what's ailing me right now, my darlin'. Have mercy and give me just one more."

⇛⇝

Jemma came in from school and Helene met her at the door. "You have some lovely flowers, dear. They are quite intoxicating."

Jemma walked down the hall to the dining room. Four large vases of lilies, roses, delphiniums, and lily of the valley lit up the room with color and sweet perfume. She opened the envelope and pulled the card out just enough to see his note.

> *Hope this fills your senses for now.*
> *See you tonight.*
>   *P.T.*

"I assume they are from your young man, Spencer."

"No, ma'am." Jemma blushed at his name. "They're from Paul."

"Ah, someone new for the hope chest. Let's move them to your room."

Jemma bit her lip. "Let's leave them here." Nobody had said anything about Paul sharing her hope chest, but the flowers were an impressive start.

She raced upstairs to change. The evening could not come soon enough.

She finished cleaning around dark and drew cowboys in her sketchbook until she heard his truck. Her temples tightened when he opened the door. He was a shiny red apple in that Stetson, like the cowboys who came into Chillaton for the Fourth of July dance.

He grinned at the sight of her, sitting cross-legged on the floor. "Hungry?" he asked.

"First, I have something for you." She held out a small package. "It's just a little thank you for one of the best surprises I've ever had."

He tore off the tissue covering and held up the painting. "You did this? It's not a Monet or something?"

Jemma giggled. "The flowers were stunning. This is just a little watercolor."

He looked right into her eyes. "No, darlin', you're the one who is stunning."

"I think you call all women 'darlin'."

He shrugged. "Could be, but when I say it to you, it's different. Remember that."

Sandy Kay called her from an army base in Germany, where her husband, Martin, was stationed. Jemma reported that it was the most thrilling summer of her life, and that her time with Paul was romantic, but never juvenile. She didn't mention that he made every attempt to fool around, and that she had to stay on her toes to keep the eighth-grade pledge to Spence. After all, a promise was a promise, regardless of the circumstances or participants. She didn't report that information to Sandy because within twenty-four hours, it would have been all over Chillaton and melting like butter on the sizzling tongues at Nedra's Beauty Parlor and Craft Nook.

"Aren't you getting a little carried away with this guy?" Jim asked her during their weekly phone call. "I sure hate to hear that. Maybe you should at least call Spencer, just to see how it feels."

"I don't know, Daddy. I really like Paul and I think you will, too." She didn't mention that he was almost ten years her elder, a fact she didn't dwell on herself.

"Don't rush into anything," Alex said. "You have plenty of time."

Robby was more succinct. "Cowboys are goofy, Jem. Spence is cool."

If she had never kissed Paul, things would have been easier because she did admire a great kisser. Spencer probably had himself a good kisser by now, too. Rats. That thought continued to thwart her otherwise perfect summer.

It wasn't as though Paul was everything to her. Art was her first love. At least that's what she'd told Spence the night they broke up. That memory carried her off for a few seconds, but then she snapped out of it and chose the fattest brush from one of her first-grade cowboy boots. She loaded it with white and splashed broad strokes across the canvas, giving her the base coat she wanted for the outdoor setting. She checked her notebook to study sketches of the stone walls of the garden and the Tiffany rose that would serve as background for Helene, then drew it in. She positioned Helene's head, neck, and torso on as well, then stepped back to see if she liked the composition. She added clusters of lupines and delphiniums to break up the line of the wall behind the roses. Helene would be pleased. She jotted notes in her book, selected her color palette and opened up her portable stereo, the last gift Spencer had given her. He flitted through her brain again for a second, which wasn't unusual, but rather unprofitable, in light of the last couple of weeks.

Jemma put on her favorite Fritz Kreisler song and dipped her brush in the glistening mixture of pigments. She guided the bristles across the knobby texture of the canvas. Her fingers pulsated with the initial sensation of bringing form to fiber. She dashed and tipped the color against the canvas, as it responded to her touch, interpretation, and design. The music was inside her. The bristles struck in bursts, like milk hitting the side of Papa's bucket in the barn, then softened as the paint absorbed into them, settling into strokes like the ebb and flow of the surf when she slept on the California beach with her family. Nothing compared to recreating life on canvas. She had known since that day in the second grade when the school principal hung her watercolor painting in his office, that her talent was a gift from God.

⤷⤶

"Talk to me about your hometown." Paul said as he straddled the bench like a horse. They didn't even have to place their orders anymore because the cook knew what to do when the baby blue pulled in.

"Well, Chillaton isn't nearly as big as Wicklow. It's about sixty miles from Amarillo, the biggest town between Dallas and Albuquerque. Main Street and The Boulevard are paved with bricks and we have trains that fly through town about four times a day. That's what Wicklow needs, a train."

Paul shook his head. "Once there are train tracks, it opens up all kinds of social issues."

"Surely you don't think that's the train's fault. Social issues are people problems. The tracks are just an excuse."

He sensed trouble again. "Tell me more about this Chillaton."

She was somewhat perturbed, but his smile was so inviting. "My Gram's house is one of two houses on the last street before crossing the tracks, about eight blocks away from The Boulevard. Lots of Papa's friends tried to talk him out of buying a house so close to the tracks. Gram took a liking to it, and nothing would do but for Papa to get it for her. It's a great location if you love trains like I do."

"There are always nosy people in small towns," Paul said.

"I guess you could call them nosy, but it's more like a huge family. If you're having trouble, you'll get prayed for in various prayer circles around town, and if somebody gets sick or dies, there will be a steady stream of casseroles at your door within an hour. The postmistress, for example, knows everybody. You can write a letter to somebody in Chillaton with just a first name on the envelope and Paralee will get it to the right person. We should try it. Let's send a letter to Lester, Gram's next-door neighbor, and see if he gets it."

"I don't know as I like you writing to some man."

She laughed. "Lester is about eighty years old. So, I can't write to any men, huh?"

He pointed a French fry at her. "You can if you want to, I just

36

wouldn't like it. I want you all for myself."

Jemma leaned over and looked him in the eye, nose to nose.

"What are you doing?"

"I have to look people in the eye when they say something important."

"You'd be a good horse trader because nobody could fool you."

"Say it again."

"I want you all for myself, darlin'."

She stayed in his face. "What exactly does that mean?"

"It means I'm hoping you won't be going out with any more piano players."

"Cello."

"Them too."

"Are we going steady, then?"

"It's been a long time since I heard that, but yeah. If you'll have me, it would make me happier than I've ever been in my life."

Jemma kissed him like he was her steady. He did take the prize for wandering hands. The cook's radio crooned in the background.

"Oh, listen. 'True Love's Ways,' my favorite Buddy Holly song," she said.

"C'mon, then." Paul put both arms around her waist and held her close, bending low to dance cowboy style. Jemma closed her eyes, her temple against his cheek. When the song was over they danced in place anyway. Paul kissed her neck, sending those chill bumps all over her.

"I can't believe you've never had a serious boyfriend," he mumbled.

"I, uh, had the same boyfriend all through school, since the first grade."

"And?"

"He still likes me, I guess."

"Likes?"

"There's a chance that he loves me."

"How do you feel about him?"

"Oh." She stumbled over the words. "I don't know. We're kind of like brother and sister."

"Puppy love."

"How about you?"

"I do like the ladies, darlin'. Remember, I warned you that I have a reputation."

"I keep hearing that."

"I hope you aren't in love with that kid."

She responded with only the slightest negative movement of her head.

"Good."

"It's getting late," she said.

He drove home singing along with the radio. It was just as well because she was thinking about the golden-haired boy who had loved her most of her life, and that she should have had a firm answer to Paul's questions. She didn't though, and to top it off, when she dreamed, it was still of Spence.

❧ ❧

Their favorite place soon became Helene's garden, and occasionally, her conservatory. Helene made herself scarce when Paul came over, but Jemma never asked about it. She was more curious, however, as to why she never got to meet Paul's family. He talked of his sisters' visits to the family home, but Jemma was never a part of the gatherings. She figured that maybe they had something against artists.

❧ ❧

"This is a great old place." Jemma said as she tilted her head back and scanned the gilded ceiling of The Grande Theater in Dallas while they waited for *Doctor Zhivago* to begin. "Hey, want to go to a concert? The violinist is a good friend of mine."

"I suppose I have to wear civilian clothes."

"Do you have some? I figured you wore cowboy boots even when you played football."

He grinned. "Naw, the cleats kept falling off."

Jemma could not imagine a more romantic movie to complete their night. Back in Wicklow, they held hands on the marble bench in Helene's garden.

"Close your eyes," he said, then draped her hair over her shoulder. She felt something cool and light around her throat, followed by Paul's kisses, warm and soft. "Okay, open." Even in the starlight, she could see the silver rose. "I know how much you love flowers so I thought this would be perfect for you."

"Paul, I don't know what to say." Jemma lifted the rose, then raised her eyes to his.

"Say that you won't love anybody else, ever, darlin'." He kissed her with such tenderness she knew he was becoming a one-woman man. "You and I were meant to be, and I hope this sweet feeling never ends."

"Me too," she whispered.

"I remember the first time I ever touched you. We were sitting in the pickup right over there, and I put my arm on the back of the seat. I wanted to kiss you, but we'd just met, so I touched your shoulder, just to connect. That was a whole new attitude for me."

"I wanted you to kiss me," she said.

He took a deep breath. "I have to really watch it with you, and I'm not used to that. I've always had it easy with women, but you are a tough one. You've got me feeling like I'm sixteen again."

"I love the necklace," she said. Rats. What a pitiful response.

"Could you miss church next Sunday? I have to take some horses to the hill country, and I really want you to come with me. We'd be gone all day."

"Just tell me when to be ready."

He twisted a lock of her hair around his finger. "How about four?"

"In the morning?"

"Yeah, it'll be all day, darlin'."

"I can't wait." She kissed him good night, then watched him drive away.

She switched on the light in her bedroom to see her new necklace in the mirror. Spencer's senior picture was looking right at her, staring at the rose. She picked him up and touched his lips. He had to have a girlfriend of his own after a whole year. She closed her eyes and held him against her heart for a moment, then tucked the photograph, face down, into her hope chest.

She said her prayers and asked God for some kind of big sign if Paul wasn't The One. She lay in bed, trying her best to concentrate on him and their special evening, but saw instead Spence's sweet face. She didn't even try to hold back the tears. They made a slow, steady descent into her pillow.

CHAPTER FOUR

A Big Sign

The red brocade dress with the mandarin collar that her Grandmother Lillygrace had sent when Jemma was Homecoming Queen was only a tiny bit snugger. She did her hair up in a cascade of curls and wore a touch of red lipstick, the necklace, and ankle strap heels. Paul whistled when he saw her. Helene and her elderly neighbor friend, Sophia, were already seated as Jemma waved from their front row seats.

Paul slid his arm around her. "Every man in here is looking at you, darlin'." She knew every woman in the concert hall was looking at him. Even in his civilian clothes, he was something to brag about.

She didn't hear anything else once Melanie began tuning up backstage. The house lights went down and Michael slipped in and sat at the piano. Melanie entered and nodded to him. The music began. Her long, red hair flew around her like a lighted torch.

Melanie's passion became Jemma's, and she, too, was exhausted when Melanie took her bow.

She was also unaware that Paula's eyes had never left her during the performance. He was under a spell of his own. She clung to his arm as Helene and Sophia approached.

"Delightful," Helene said. "I am so glad we came, Jemma."

"I knew you wouldn't be disappointed."

Helene turned to Paul. "What do you think, Mr. Turner?"

He kissed Jemma's hand. "She's something else."

Helene and Sophia exchanged glances and excused themselves to get some punch. Melanie played a wild gypsy song after intermission, then the final three pieces included Clayton Burgess, the cellist that Jemma had gone out with a few times. He of the folded lips did know how to play the cello.

Melanie caught her eye just before she raised the violin to her shoulder for an encore piece. Jemma held her breath for self-preservation. It was Papa's favorite song. The Scottish tune sang from his fiddle every holiday that she could remember. Papa's cousin had played it, too, at his funeral. Jemma was a wreck, but she loved Melanie for choosing it. She hustled Paul backstage to thank her and to show him off. Melanie gave a wide-eyed nod of approval when his back was turned. They moved to the foyer where Helene and Sophia waited, but Paul was ready to leave. They passed right by the two women and Jemma could only smile.

"These shoes are killing me," he said as they raced to his pickup. "Listen, I have to help my uncle and my dad tomorrow. We're working on a big case at the office all day because the trial starts Monday."

Jemma stopped. "Could you come by Helene's for lunch? She's teaching me to cook, continental style."

"What else can you do continental style?"

"You mean like, zee French kiss, monsieur?"

"Yeah. Cook me up one of those, darlin'."

"Maybe next year, if you've been a good boy," she said.

"I'll keep that in mind," he said and kissed her while they walked.

Jemma, though, was lost in thoughts of Spencer at that remark. It was too close to a private joke they shared from a line in *Hud*. She broke away and ran ahead of Paul, to clear her mind, like that would matter to her heart.

∾ʠʠ

There was so much green in the Texas hill country, making it a complete contrast to the Panhandle. Jemma took it all in for future paintings. They had delivered two horses to a ranch that sprawled alongside the Guadalupe River. She was singing harmony with Wilson Pickett when Paul pulled off the road. He led her through a pasture that sloped down to the river.

"Nice, huh?" He rested his chin on her head. "My dad and Uncle Lloyd own five hundred acres through here. Over those hills is a spot called Rustler's Roost where stolen cattle got zapped with bandit brands. I think there's even a boot-hill cemetery over there. Someday, I'm going to build a cabin in this meadow. What do you think about that?"

"Perfect," Jemma said, not referring to the land. She could marry him if he asked her at that very moment, and she would build the cabin for him, too.

"Maybe you could paint this for me sometime." He folded his arms around her, and she held his hands to keep them out of trouble.

"I'd love to do that."

"Good. In the spring, this pasture is full of bluebonnets. The only thing that could make it more perfect would be to see Jemmabeth Turner standing in the door."

That particular combination of names roused a tender longing first engaged in junior high when she wrote *Jemmabeth Chase* and *Mrs. Spencer Chase* on every page in her diary. She looked away. He pulled her down beside him on a rock and kissed her so hard that it was almost a relief when it was over.

"Darlin', you know I've fallen for you big-time, and I'm more than ready to pop the question. I've never been so sure of anything in my life. Problem is, I have a lot on my mind right now, and I need to see some stuff through before we go over the brink. This sounds crazy coming from me, but I can't do squat for thinking about you, Jem, and I need a clear head to take the bar exam."

"You're not saying that you don't want to see me anymore, are you?" she asked, big-eyed.

He returned the look like a spooked horse. "What? Good grief, no! You own my heart, and I have no intention of ever giving you up. I just need a couple of weeks to study." The sun was gone, leaving a shimmering mix of pinks and oranges behind. They were fast becoming a part of the night. He took a deep breath and looked straight into her eyes. "I might as well say it, Jemma. I love you. I've never said that to a woman and meant it, but I do now, and with every breath I take, I love you more. I only want to cool off long enough to pass the bar."

"I suppose I can wait two weeks," she said.

He held her until the stars came out. She closed her eyes so she wouldn't look for Orion. They left the river and headed for the truck, but she had no idea how she could stand to go two weeks, even two days, without him. It was very late when they got home.

He leaned against the gate at Helene's. "Got a question for you. What's your middle name? I can't believe I don't know that."

"Alexandra, after my mother. What's yours?"

"Jacob."

"Nice name. Paul Jacob Turner; it'll look good on a law degree."

"And on a marriage license," he said. "I like yours, too. It's beautiful, like you."

"Why are you asking about my name?"

"I need it here," he said, thumping his heart. "I want all of you, even your middle name." He reached for her, his hands massaging her spine until she thought she was going to melt.

"Paul," she said, catching her breath. "Do you believe in prayer?"

He frowned. "What brought that up?"

"We've never talked about religion. I've been told all my life that the Lord answers prayer, and I've started praying about us."

"Oh yeah?" he said, letting her go. He propped a boot on the railing and folded his arms. "I prayed for God to make my mother well, but He didn't. I'm not really into religion, darlin', although I'll have to start thanking God for your precious self."

"You don't get *into* religion, Paul. It's always there, as the heart of life." She needed something. "Do you read the Bible?"

"All I know is that I love you, and if religion is a part of the package, so be it. We can talk about this some other time. I just want you to remember one thing. You are mine forever, and I'll do whatever it takes to keep you. You are my one and only woman." He kissed her just like he had done at the river, and Jemma's lips hurt like they'd met hot metal.

He moved his finger under her chin. "Good night, Jemmabeth Alexandra Forrester. You remember what I said tonight and I'll see you in two weeks. It'll be smooth sailing after that. He laid his English Leather cheek against hers. "I do love you, darlin'," he whispered, "like no other man could."

He walked to his truck but stopped, like he was looking for something in the gravel. She thought he might come back and kiss her again, but he didn't. Instead, he saluted her from the brim of his hat. His lights disappeared down the road and Jemma went to her room, her head full of romance and her heart full of love, or something close.

⇟⇞

There was one more day to go, but she couldn't wait. She loaded the painting into her car and headed to the office. All the lights were on. Her plan was to take the piece inside the office and surprise him, but his baby blue was not the only car parked in the lot. She decided to set it in the pickup. The overhead security light was not exactly museum quality, but it would be sufficient for her surprise as it beamed through the windshield and onto the canvas Guadalupe riverbank, replete with bluebonnets. Jemma opened the back door to the building.

A pretty blonde sat in the conference room looking at a magazine. Her bare feet were propped on the table, displaying hot pink toenails. She glanced at Jemma and flipped a page.

"Well, who let you in?" she asked, and made a popping noise with her chewing gum. Her makeup was flawless and her Wind Song perfume packed the air.

Jemma smiled. "I'm sorry to bother you, but do you know where Paul Turner is?"

The blonde popped her gum again, but gave Jemma her full attention as their eyes met. "Well, of course I know where Paul Turner is, darlin'. I'm his wife."

CHAPTER FIVE

Tara

Helene assumed that Jemma was working in her studio, and was quite surprised to find her sitting on the stone bench in the garden. Chelsea jumped in Jemma's lap, expecting a good petting, but got nothing more than a blank stare. They sat in silence while the caged lovebirds in the conservatory chatted away.

Helene adjusted her hearing aid at this somber sight. Jemma's puffy eyes and tear-stained cheeks were cause enough for alarm. "Is it your family, dearest?" Helene asked. "Has there been an accident?"

Jemma blew her nose. "Not an accident, more like a major disaster. Helene, I have to go to Chillaton for a while."

"Oh my." Helene put her hand to her chest. "Then I shall make you a boxed lunch for the journey. It won't take but a moment."

"No, really, it's okay. I meant to leave sooner, but I just couldn't." A wounded look swept over Helene and Jemma relented. "On second thought, yes ma'am, a lunch would be nice."

They went inside and Helene puttered around in the kitchen, taking much too long to prepare a sack lunch. Finally, she turned to her. "Tell me, dear, is it that Turner man?"

Jemma bit her lip and nodded.

"Men can be such beasts. Even my dear Nebs would just shut down without warning." Helene sighed and nestled the lunch in Jemma's hands. "Please give my regards to your grandmother. Chelsea and I shall miss you terribly." Jemma nodded again, but Helene lifted her young friend's chin. "We are all but a breath away from joy or disappointment. Such is life. You know that my heart goes with you. Now, carry on, dear."

Jemma lost it and collapsed against Helene's double strand of pearls. They dug into her face as Helene guided her to the little kitchen table.

"I'm sorry," Jemma wailed into a tissue. "It's just so embarrassing."

"Nonsense. You sit right there and let me make you some tea. You know, dear, sometimes it helps to talk."

"I have to get going, Helene, but thank you." Jemma picked at a spot of dried paint on her jeans. "Paul is a big fat liar. Actually, that's an understatement. He's a devil because I met his *wife* last night." The words hung in the air.

Helene gasped. Jemma took the neatly folded bag from the table and did her best to smile as they walked to the Dodge. Belongings were stuffed every which way inside. "I love you," she said, and kissed Helene's cheek. "I just can't talk about it now. Sorry."

"You are dear to me," Helene said, her voice unsteady. Scooping up Chelsea, she retreated into the house. Jemma sat for a minute, then backed down the lane. Miss Scarlett went home to Tara, and she could go home to Chillaton.

The worst shame she had ever known until this was 'fessing up to the Sunday school superintendent when he asked if she'd been the one to scramble all the numbers on the hymn board in the sanctuary. That was a long time ago. Now a sickening thought ran ice cold through her brain. If Spencer heard that she was messing around with an old married cowboy he would lose all respect for her. That would be far worse than never seeing Mrs. Turner's husband again. If she'd anything left to throw up, she would have. That seemed to be her special way to deal with things these days.

As though she weren't distracted enough, it began to rain. She rolled her window down halfway to keep the windshield from fogging up, and to keep her awake. Papa could have eased her guilty pain. He always claimed that he could fix anything but the weather.

When walking from one chore to another, he would set his straw hat on the back of his head and examine the sky. She would ask, "Are those rain clouds, Papa?"

Usually, he responded with "I hope so, the coos need a wooshing."

Jemma would giggle at the old saying that he had learned from his Scottish Granny about the cows needing a washing. As she grew up, it became apparent that no weather was specifically intended for the Panhandle. Most of it had no particular place to go between the west and the Midwest, so it wandered in, sort of like Mr. Turner.

46

A beat-up blue pickup passed her. Rats on the Devil's cup. There must have been more warning signs along the way that she missed, like that woman at the Handle Bar "going down a few roads with him." What an idiot she'd been. Her mom would know how to help. No, she couldn't tell her parents. She would tell Gram. Maybe.

The pickup was just ahead of her, its taillights guiding her through a downpour. Papa and Gram used to have a pickup. It was red and black with yellow wheels. In the hottest part of summer they'd leave it in the tractor's turn rows, and spend the day chopping weeds and Johnson grass out of the cotton. If necessary, they hired Negro field hands to help. Whole families would work until sunset, then they crammed into the back of Papa's pickup and he drove them home to colored town.

Little Jemma had been in the fields, too, in her makeshift tent off the bed of the pickup. She played with Papa's old dog that was there to fend off rattlesnakes while she drew in her Big Chief tablet. The old fellow was grateful for the shade and usually dozed while Jemma drew portraits from photographs in the *National Geographic* magazines that Gram left for her. The people in the photos seemed to know things that Jemma wanted to know. Secrets sparkled in their eyes, so she whispered make-believe secrets to the people in her drawings so that their eyes would shine even brighter. It was a little girl's game, but now The Devil's secrets were another matter.

An hour away from Chillaton, the rain stopped and she turned on the radio. There was nothing but country music and scratchy radio evangelists. She turned it off and sang some of Roy's songs. The starry water tower finally came into view. It was always Christmas in Chillaton because the framework of two giant stars attached to opposite sides of the tower could be seen year round. The day after Thanksgiving, they would be plugged in to rev up Chillaton's holiday spirit. Chubs Ivey broke his hip changing the bulbs in 1959, so the town council had voted never to replace the bulbs again. In a few years it would be pretty much dead, like she was now. Folks might as well start bringing in the casseroles for her family.

Just outside the city limits, she turned down the "farm to market" county road, past the Chase castle, to the Citizens' Cemetery. The sun was beginning to set as she rolled to a stop at the Forrester family plot. She sat in the car a few minutes before moving to the wrought iron bench. There were fresh flowers in the sunken pot that she and Gram had put there at Easter. She stared at the headstone.

Cameron Andrew Forrester
Born to Andrew & Mary on February 10, 1887
Departed this earth on September 12, 1962
A Scotsman Glory Bound

It had been her daddy's idea to add the last line so that future generations could share Papa's pride. She ate the grapes and bread from Helene's boxed lunch, but the cheese had begun to sweat; she knew the feeling. There was nothing between her and the glitzy sunset, save a scrawny cloud and a windmill on the horizon. Movie directors sometimes came to Connelly County to catch a sunset and splice it into their films. Rats. If only the last twenty-four hours had been a movie. What happened to the big basketball captain who was cool and calm no matter what? For the last two years, she had jumped into the middle of things with no prayerful consultation whatsoever. That wasn't the way she was raised, but now the Lord might click His tongue at her prayers since this mess with Paul. She was no better than the women so disdained in the gossip at Nedra's Nook. Good grief, she had even danced in a bar, but at least she hadn't done it on the counter, half naked, like Missy Blake did at the Western Tavern in Amarillo.

The bullfrogs by the cemetery pond began their nightly chant. She couldn't put it off any longer. She laid her hand on the tombstone and asked the Lord that if Spencer ever heard about this, the news would come from her own lips. As she drove past the Chase castle, she looked to see if his Corvette was there, but it wasn't. Good. She needed to get herself back together, big-time, before she faced him.

⮜⮞

Lizbeth's phone had rung while she was still asleep and before she had her teeth in, scaring the wits out of her. Jemmabeth had spoken so softly that Lizbeth wasn't sure what she was saying. It seemed that she wanted to come and stay with her for a reason she didn't reveal or Lizbeth couldn't hear. It had to be this new boyfriend, the one she talked about all the time and wanted everybody to meet. Lizbeth had always hoped that Spencer would be the Lord's intended for her granddaughter. There was something in Spencer's eyes that made her know he was a golden boy, but she didn't mention her preference to Jemma even when the child had announced, over a year ago, that she was going to go out with other young men.

Lizbeth had dry-mopped and dusted the front bedroom, changed the sheets, and emptied out the chest of drawers. Jemma did not say how long she would be staying, and it was very peculiar for her to leave college like this. She loved that art school so much and she was surely their star pupil. Maybe Jemma would put some new paint on Cam's sad birdhouses. She had come at Easter and followed Lizbeth around for two days, pencil and sketchbook in hand, then mailed her a Polaroid of the final painting. It was of Lizbeth reading a letter from her baby sister, Julia. The painting was as good as anything Lizbeth had ever seen in a book. She kept the photo propped up on the television set.

Gram had not asked why her eyes were puffy, but she had made her eat some toast and drink a 7-Up, the standard cure-all. Papa's clock was striking three when Jemma crept to the pouting room off the dark kitchen and lifted the hook. The door creaked as she ducked under the doorframe and felt for the soldier box lid. The moonlight cast a thin beam onto the contents. She undid the necklace, felt her way to the bottom of the box, and let it drop. She stood over the trunk for a moment, then closed the lid and left. She snuck out the back door and walked to the tracks. A watchful dog barked on the other side. She sat on the rails, the icy steel penetrating her thin nightgown. She didn't care. Maybe a freight train would come along and squash her like the worm that she was.

CHAPTER SIX

Lost Lamb

Lizbeth got up early, thinking it would be a good time to polish the medals while Jemma slept. The child needed some rest. She looked just like she did when she had the Asian flu and ran a high fever, worrying everybody for a week.

She cleaned the pouting room and opened the soldier box. As she reached for the velvet containers, something odd caught her eye at the bottom of the trunk. She lifted out the necklace. The silver rose glinted in the early morning light. Lizbeth sank to the floor and leaned her head against the wall for a good while. She struggled to her feet and put the necklace back where she had found it, then poured herself some strong coffee. She had polished mementoes long enough. Lord willing, her granddaughter wouldn't pick up where she left off and start polishing something of her own.

❧❦❧

Jemma shot up in the bed, bumping her head on the quilt frame that Gram kept tethered to the ceiling. She hadn't a clue why she was there, but then it came back like an avalanche. She slumped down to her pillow. The curtains moved with a sudden breeze that bore the sweet perfume of honeysuckle from the front porch.

Gram tapped on the door, then sat beside her on the bed. "You know that you are welcome to stay, sugar, but you should call your folks. They'll be worried."

"Yes ma'am. I will." She paused. "It's just that I think I was in love, and I got my heart hurt pretty bad."

Gram stroked her hair. "Well, I'm here if you want to talk about it, but for now, let's get some food in you."

Jemma walked around Chillaton and wound up across from her family's old house, wishing for the days when she and Spencer were the king and queen of hearts and nothing hurt for very long. What if he pulled up right that minute and looked her in the eye? He would know. She jumped as a horn sounded in front of her. Shy Tomlinson waved as his pickup disappeared around the corner. Shy had filled the bed of his pickup with dirt thirty years ago and still grew things in it, including a blue spruce. Only in Chillaton, she thought, and trudged home.

She called her parents saying she needed some time off to work on her portfolio. Her daddy was adamant that she should either get back to school or come to Arizona. Her mom was more sympathetic, and they finally agreed that she could stay with Gram if she got a job and went back to school after Christmas.

⤥⤦

When he was a toddler, Robby ran from room to room in Lizbeth's house, opening and shutting the bevy of doors, much to the adults' aggravation. To get from the living room to the kitchen, it was necessary to pass through the *good* bedroom. Before Cameron died, it was their bedroom, but since his death, Lizbeth could not bear to sleep there. She slept, instead, in the cozy shed attached to the house that Cam had enclosed the same year he passed away. The bathroom, pouting room, pantry, and a screened-in porch all branched out from the kitchen. Beyond the porch was Lester Timm's driveway that led to his garage and Lizbeth's backyard where the hollyhock patch, pecan tree, storm cellar, and the car house all beckoned to an adventurous little guy like Robby.

Jemma was comforted by the scent of coffee brewing and Gram's perfume that seemed to find its way into every corner of the house. The extra bedroom opposite the living room was hers now. Tall windows were propped opened in the summer with broom handles that Cam had sawed in two. Crocheted pull rings dangled from the

51

shades, and in the center of the ceiling was a bowl shaped light fixture adorned with golden tassels. The wall switches were hefty pushbuttons. Lizbeth's tethered quilting frame was used once a month when she took her turn as hostess for the North Chillaton Quilting Club.

Quilting didn't interest Jemma at all. She craved instead, the ground-jarring rumble of the train. That opportunity now presented itself less than a hundred yards away. Dancing on those tracks had always given her a thrill. No secrets could lurk there and she knew just when to jump out of harm's way. However, instead of growing up safer and smarter, it appeared she was even dumber than she used to be. She had developed into a genuine nitwit.

⤬⤬⤬

She spread the *Chillaton Star* on the kitchenette, as Gram called it. The yellow Formica-topped table had come from Sears with its own matching vinyl and chrome chairs. There were two ads. Byron Blankenship was hoping to trade a homemade trailer for a rifle scope, and an anonymous person had lost a license plate near Farm to Market Road 2485. Jemma grinned. That bumpy dirt road led to The Hill, local parking spot for teenagers.

Lizbeth was busy making biscuits on the wooden countertop while Jemma moved around the room, touching things. The black and white checkered linoleum was laid over the uneven wood floor where Robby had scooted his metal cars. She stopped at the framed print of a lamb lost in a snowdrift with a sheepdog howling for his master to rescue it. She used to think of herself as the rescuing dog, but now she was the lost lamb, plain and simple.

"Gram, do you know of any jobs in town?"

"Lester knows what's going on, and he'll be over soon, once he smells these biscuits."

Jemma was well aware that the latest gossip was all that was ever going on. The citizens of Chillaton liked to stretch out an event until it was only a shadow of the truth. That common trait probably came from enduring the wicked Panhandle wind all their lives. It had whipped them into a gentle orneriness. Lizbeth's neighbor, Lester Timms, was the best storyteller in the county. Cam had called him Windy Timms. He was a "long drink of water," according to Lizbeth, meaning he was taller than she was. Lester was skinny enough to be carried away by a chicken hawk but his heart was golden.

Lizbeth concentrated on her Sunday school lesson after she put the biscuits in the oven. She indulged Lester unless he got on her nerves, then he had to watch it. Cam always got a big kick out of him, but since Cam's death, Lester had his heart set on Lizbeth. She had never learned how to drive, so he took her on all her errands. He beat a path to her door two or three times a day under the guise of bringing her mail from the post office. The mail was only put up once a day, so Lizbeth knew that he was holding some back and doling it out. Were it not for the sake of good manners and lack of company, Lizbeth would have put a box on the porch and asked him to put the mail in it, but she didn't and Lester was a patient man. Jemma knew, though, that he didn't have a chance with her Gram. Papa's robe and slippers were hanging in their closet and his shaving set still rested on the shelf under the bathroom mirror.

As predicted, Lester showed up at the screen door. "Mornin', ladies. Here's the mail crop, Miz Liz." He loved to say her name that way, drawing out the vowels in typical Texas style. He took off his hat and sat down, his silver hair reflecting the kitchen light. "Well, Jemmerbeth, it's sure good to see you. How are things down to Dallas? Run over any armadillers lately?"

"Jemma is here to stay with me until Christmas," Lizbeth said. "She's going to be painting."

"Is that a fact? Well, sir, you got yourself in a dangerous business then. I worked on a paintin' job one time and like to have died. We was paintin' a water tank over to Cleeber and I got up right near the top and run out of paint. I hollered down for a refill just as my rope come loose. I was scramblin' around that tank like a chicken on a windmill. Yes sir, dangerous business." Lester helped himself to some coffee.

Lizbeth ignored his story. He knew good and well that Jemma was an artist.

"I'm looking for a paying job, Lester," Jemma said. "Do you know of any?"

He rubbed his chin. "I seen a help wanted poster at the fillin' station, but that ain't no place for a young'un like you. The Judge has that poor little child with polio. Eleanor Perkins stays nights with her, and a right nice colored woman took care of her for years, but she passed away. Her girl took over for a while, but she broke her hip, so then the granddaughter come on, but I heard she up and quit."

"I'll talk with him," Jemma said.

"The Judge stays down to his office all day or he could be holding court," Lester said.

"Then I'll talk to Eleanor," Jemma said.

Lester tapped his foot on the linoleum. "Jemmerbeth, you watch your step around that old McFarland goat. He's the meanest judge in six counties."

She smiled. "I just want a job. I'll go tomorrow."

After supper, the phone rang and Lizbeth held it out to her. "It's that fellow," she whispered. Jemma hung up the phone and went to sit on the porch swing. He called about the same time every night, but it was no use. She would not talk to a married man.

CHAPTER SEVEN

Carolina

She sat on the tracks as the sky faded from flat cobalt to sparkling tangerine, then transformed into a blue-white spray, silhouetting the trees like a multitude of Creatures from the Black Lagoon. The wind that had kept her awake all night now mustered the tree row of elms into a frenzy of leaf and limb, summoning the arrival of the 6:23. Jemma moved off like a deaf old dog to let it pass. Sleepy-eyed passengers blinked at her wild hair and threadbare chenille robe that stirred in the force of the great Zephyr. The silver lady with the golden eye could do her a great favor now and melt away little pieces of shame in the sparks of her steel, but then it always had been a lopsided relationship. This magnificent thing enchanted her, frightened her, but never did her any favors. All Jemma could ever do was get out of the way.

As she walked to The Judge's house, Pud Palmer honked at her. He was on his way to man the Chillaton Volunteer Fire Station. Pud's job was to blow the tornado warning whistle every day at noon, just to make sure it was working right. Most adults still recalled that early morning in June of '37, when a twister came through town and killed eight good Democrats. After that, everybody with a lick of sense dug some kind of a storm cellar. They got in it, too, if the whistle blew and it wasn't high noon. Folks outside the range of the whistle had to rely on radio weather bulletins and their own two eyes—or just one eye in the case of Bernie Miller, the town barber and WWI veteran.

She made her way to The Boulevard. There, separated from the rest of Chillaton by ornate wrought iron fences, remained the trappings of wealthier days when ranchers built town homes to display their good fortunes. The Boulevard was wide and paved with bricks all the way through Main Street. In the middle of The Boulevard were patches of blacktop where great old trees once stood. In a rash decision, they were removed to make way for motorized traffic, but it had been a super place for bike riding when Jemma was a little girl.

Although once grand, Judge McFarland's house was now in sore need of care. A three-story beauty, it was accessed by a long walkway with cedar bushes lining both sides. The porch made a horseshoe around the front of the house. Jemma had seen The Judge's little blonde daughter sitting in a wheelchair on that porch many times as she walked to her dreaded piano lessons. She remembered her slightly from the first grade, too.

Eleanor Perkins had the absolute largest bosom in the county. Gram said that you could see her coming around the corner a full five seconds before she actually did. Now her double-chinned face appeared at The Judge's door. Her little pea eyes were totally lost as she flashed a toothless grin at Jemma. She whipped open the door with one hand and planted her dentures on her gums with the other.

"My stars, hon, I'd know you anywhere. You sure are a good looker, just like your mama. I know your grandma, too. She's a fine quilter, the best in the county. I remember when you was born. Now you just call me Eleanor. I knew that ever who we found to watch over our Carrie would be ever who the good Lord wanted. And there you were on the phone. Come on in and let me show you around. You can start tomorrow." She dusted off a side table with a tea towel slung over her shoulder, then clicked her teeth.

Uneasy at this sudden employment, Jemma hesitated. "I haven't talked to The Judge at all. It wouldn't be right to assume that he would hire me."

Eleanor poo-pooed that suggestion. "Don't you worry none about that, hon. The Judge and me go way back to kingdom come. If I want you for the job, he'll go right along with it, rather than listen to me talk."

That self-assessment made Jemma giggle. She drew her first taste of McFarland air, a heady mixture of cigars, disinfectant, and freshly baked sweet rolls, then followed chatty Eleanor around the house. The rooms were laid out just as she had imagined. There was a great staircase going up the middle of the house, and on the left was a parlor and to the right, a dining room. The foyer extended on both sides of the stairs and met behind them with one door to the kitchen and breakfast room, then double doors that opened into The Judge's study. On the stairs was an odd chair mounted to a platform. A track wound around the bottom of the banisters all the way up to the top of the stairwell.

Eleanor caught Jemma looking at it. "Here, hon, I might as well show you how The Crawler works. Have a seat." Jemma angled onto the foam-covered chair. "You don't have to buckle in, but you'll want to make sure our Carrie does. Of course, she'll be downstairs during the day, you know, but she needs the lung about sundown and sometimes during the day and all. Anyhoo, you'd best get used to this contraption." She pressed a button on the side of the chair and it began to crawl up the track like a snail. Robby would love it.

Huffing with each step, Eleanor gave a tour of the second floor of the house, too. Faceless ballerinas danced across the wallpaper in a corner bedroom. It was an odd little girl's room with a white canopied bed, dresser, numerous stuffed animals, and an ominous iron lung. The metallic monster resembled John Glenn's space capsule, and Jemma listened intently as Eleanor explained how to use it.

There were several closed doors, but the one she assumed was The Judge's bedroom stood open. A massive bed and antique wardrobe filled the space. There was very little art to be seen in the whole house. A portrait of the late Mrs. McFarland hung in the dining room, but it was only a cut above a truckstop print in Jemma's eyes.

The tour ended on a screened-in porch, where Carrie sat in a wheelchair. Her body, like a stem of baby's breath, was bent over a book. Her pale blue eyes met Jemma's with no hesitation.

Eleanor patted her arm. "Carrie, this is your new helper, Jemmabeth Forrester. Ain't she pretty? I've knowed her since she was a baby, and she's gonna take fine care of you, so get acquainted ever how you want to. I've got to check on something in the kitchen."

Carrie sized Jemma up with a quirky grin. "I've seen you in the *Star*," she said. "Homecoming Queen, cheerleader, all-state basketball, and Miss Chillaton High School. You and your ex-boyfriend were the darlings of everything." Her blond hair was cut very short, like a boy's. A long smock hung on her and made her look like a paper doll whose clothes could be changed on a whim.

Jemma caught the *ex*-boyfriend reference. "I'm not exactly sure that I have this job because I haven't talked with your father at all."

Carrie's eyes were intense, making Jemma look away first. Surely she didn't know about Mr. Turner. That hadn't made the paper yet.

"Sorry I was staring, but you used to take lessons from Miss

Mason next door," Carrie said.

Jemma laughed. "Yeah, for some reason, my parents thought I was going to be a great pianist, but after a few years of lessons, they gave up. I remember seeing you on your front porch."

"I hope you don't get bored around here. It's not exactly scintillating fare. You should bring books or something," Carrie said.

Jemma, impressed with Carrie's straightforward approach, nodded. "I might read, but I'll probably draw. I'm an art major. Or at least I was." It was the first time she had admitted that status to herself.

"Oh, yeah. You won some kind of national competition. Are you a college dropout now?"

"I suppose you could say that. I think I'll just call it a semester off. How do you spend your time? Apparently, you read the *Star* a lot."

Carrie shrugged. "I'm not exactly helpless like Eleanor makes me sound."

"So, you *were* rolling your eyes a minute ago."

"Well, obviously I can't dance, but I do play the piano. I took lessons from Miss Mason, too. She came twice a week, sort of like a house call. I think my father paid her big bucks to make the effort."

"What kind of music do you play?"

Carrie pointed to a leather ottoman. "Open that thing up and take a guess."

Jemma peeked inside. It was filled with classical sheet music. "I have a friend in Dallas who is a concert violinist," she said. "You two would get along great."

"Someday I want to break out in a rock 'n' roll frenzy. I can pick up songs by hearing them once. Do you have any records? Eleanor listens to country and western music, and Dad never plays music at all."

"I'm loaded with records and a portable stereo."

"Bingo." Carrie stuck out her hand. "It's good to meet you, Jemmabeth. I think our destinies are sealed."

Jemma clasped the slender fingers in hers. "Call me Jemma. What's that you're reading?"

"*The Feminine Mystique.* I have to hide it from my father."

"Really," Jemma said. "I didn't know anybody in Chillaton would read that one."

"I like to live on the edge of propriety."

Jemma laughed, liking her even more. "I'll see you tomorrow."

In the kitchen, she addressed Eleanor's broad back. "What time should I come in the morning?"

Eleanor wiped her hands. "Oh, my lands, hon, I should have told you that. Get here by eight, then you can leave ever when I come back. Now, we'll both be here of a morning, but I'll be doing housework. Plus, I can't miss my shows. I don't have a TV set at home, you know." Eleanor stirred a steaming pot as she spoke. She raised a spoon to her lips, then shook her head. "I shouldn't do that 'cause just a spoonful of beans sends me higher than a kite. I'm right up there with that astronaut fellow. Gas, you know. It's a good thing that you're a strong Panhandle girl, because you've gotta do things around here—ever what comes up." She went into The Judge's office and came right back with his typewritten instructions.

"Is Carrie her real name?" Jemma asked as she folded the paper and put it in her purse.

"Let me see," Eleanor said, her lips puckered in concentration. "We've called her that for so long. She was named after one of them states, ever which one her mama was from. The Judge calls her by it when he's of a mind to."

"Carolina?"

"Why just look at you, figuring that out so quick like. I think you're gonna be real good for Carrie. Law knows she needs something, poor thing."

"Thanks for the tour." Jemma skipped down the front steps.

Eleanor pushed open the screen door. "Hon, this ain't none of my business, but I sure did hate to hear that you cut things off with the Chase boy. He's had a hard time of it, what with his mama being a drunk and all. Maybe you'd better think on it. He's such a sweet one."

Jemma's head bobbed in agreement. *Welcome home.*

She walked home against the wind, holding on to her skirt so it wouldn't blow up. Dirt peppered her bare arms. Panhandle winds could blast a fleet of ships across the Atlantic in one afternoon. Papa always said that a smart man would spit every five minutes just to make room for more grit to sift into his mouth. Even the trees that lined the highway were bent from years of yielding to the wind. On the other hand, it kept windmills whirling and thus water flowing for farmers and ranchers. Only on hot summer nights, when it was actually welcome, did the wind die down to nothing. Kind of like love.

Lizbeth had the table already set for supper.

"I have the job, I guess," Jemma said as she filled her plate with tomatoes and fried okra. She added a small portion of meatloaf to keep Gram happy.

"It'll be all over town tomorrow," Lizbeth said. "Eleanor's quite the gossip. Did you meet The Judge?"

"No, ma'am. Did you know that his daughter is a pianist? I can't believe that she still has to sleep in that iron lung. Good grief, we have sent monkeys and people into orbit. Haven't we learned anything about polio?"

Lizbeth was thinking about something else. "When you were about five years old, we all went to hear the Governor give a speech. It was after the 4th of July barbeque and you were playing with your dolls on the courthouse lawn. The Judge's little girl came over and the both of you were having a good time until her mother came looking for her. I guess she'd wandered away. You probably don't remember that she was in your class in school. It was the next summer after your first-grade year that her mother died in that wreck, then the child got polio. Such a shame. Most folks believed she caught it when The Judge sent her down south to stay with her mother's people for a while."

Jemma moved the meatloaf around her plate. "It doesn't seem fair. Why her; why not me?"

"All I know is that we can't be second-guessing the good Lord. He is our Creator and we are His creation. We mustn't forget that."

⋞⋐⋞⋐

The Judge was still at the table, reading the Amarillo *Globe*, when Jemma arrived early for her first day of work. He filled the chair with his dark brown suit. Jemma could detect a partial comb-over, too.

Eleanor was fussing around in the kitchen, so Jemma walked right up to him. "Hello, sir, I'm Jemmabeth Forrester. I hope that you approved of Eleanor hiring me to help take care of Carrie. That's sort of funny—*care of Carrie.*"

The Judge folded his paper and looked at Jemma over the top of his glasses. "My daughter's health and comfort are not a matter for childish humor, so I assume you will take your responsibility seriously. I pay a dollar twenty-five an hour, and I expect you to remember that you are an employee, not a guest, in my home." He stroked his beard, his eyes boring through hers, like she'd already messed up. He scooted back his chair. "Eleanor, that was a fine breakfast, as usual. Good day, Miss Forrester."

"It's, ah, good to meet you, sir, and don't worry; I'll take great care of her." Jemma extended her hand, but he ignored the gesture.

"I'll be the judge of that," he said and left the room.

CHAPTER EIGHT

Latrina

Her wimpy plan was to leave the Dodge at home and walk everywhere in case Spencer happened to be driving around. She'd probably hide if she saw him, but it was worth a chance. Maybe she could pretend to faint or something. She'd just crossed the street that ran behind the tennis courts at the high school when she spotted a tall black girl shooting baskets on one end of the courts. She couldn't resist.

"Hey, want to play some one-on-one?" she yelled, pulling her hair up into a ponytail.

"Sure," the girl shouted back.

It felt good to play her old sport again. After about half an hour, though, it was a draw.

"Let's quit," Jemma said, panting. "I'm so out of shape, I may faint. You're good. What's your name?"

"Trina Johnson. That's some jumpshot you've got, girl. I'd be outta shape too, but I've been playing on a junior college team," she said with a dimpled grin.

"That makes me feel a little better. I'm Jemma Forrester." She wiped her forehead, and like any good artist, studied Trina's face. Her eyes were like slanted almonds and her lashes were extra long, like Paul's. "I always wanted dimples like yours," Jemma said. "In the first grade, I drew them on with my mom's eyebrow pencil, but they looked like moles. Do you live in Chillaton?"

Trina jerked her head towards the tracks. "Right over yonder, all my life."

"Really? We could've used you on our basketball team. That would've been fun. We came in second at state my senior year. When did you graduate?"

"In '63. I went to the colored school over in Red Mule."

"Whoa, that's an hour from here."

"Hour and forty-five minutes on the bus, one way, what with stopping to get kids," Trina said.

"You're kidding." Jemma chewed on her lip. "I'm really sorry you had to do that. Listen, I need to get home, but I live near the tracks myself, with my grandmother. You want to walk with me?"

"Thanks, but I need to shoot some free throws. I'll see you around." Trina resumed her dribbling.

"Maybe we can play again if I get in shape," Jemma shouted.

Trina flashed her dimples and waved. Jemma walked home, thinking of what she would have done for almost four hours, round trip, to get to school and back for twelve years. It was a ten-minute walk, even against a stiff wind, from her old house to her own high school.

After supper, Lizbeth took her quilt pieces out of the cigar box, and glanced at her granddaughter. "Are you doing math, sugar?"

Jemma read from her page of figures. "Around eight thousand—that's about how many hours those kids sat on a school bus for twelve years, just to get to Red Mule and back. Over a year, wasted. I can't believe that happened in this country."

Lizbeth put her sewing aside. "Well, honey, we let them do it. We probably felt real smug that we were even sending colored children to school."

"It never even crossed my mind," Jemma said. "I went about my big social life and never gave it a thought. Where did I think they were going to school? At the Dew Drop Inn?" She wadded up the paper and pitched it on the coffee table, then slumped on the couch. "I'm ashamed of myself. I could have written letters to Congress. I should have done something. Rats."

"I'm not sure folks would have paid you any mind," Lizbeth said. "It was a part of life that nobody talked about. Why didn't I say something? I knew where all those little children were going to school. We've been boxed up in our own little world, but maybe things will change now."

Jemma went outside. She sat on the rails surveying the ramshackle houses on the other side until the sun went down.

Lizbeth watched from the kitchen window, heavy with her own fresh sense of guilt.

"Boy howdy, it's so hot, I seen dirtdobbers carrying an ice cube into their nest," Lester announced. "Don't see that every day." He waited for a laugh, then proceeded. "I'm thinking about sleeping on my porch tonight in my new swimming shorts. Got the pinkin' shears and whacked off about two feet of my oldest overalls. Maybe I'll run through the sprinkler, too."

"I trust you'll be in your back yard for that," Lizbeth said.

He closed his eyes and inhaled. "I smell a piece of heaven done come down to earth."

Lizbeth tried not to smile. "The pie has to cool, Lester."

"No offense, Jemmer, but you been giving any thought to the Chase boy?" he asked.

"Lester. That's none of your affair," Lizbeth said, but she kept a close eye on Jemma's reaction.

"I'm too busy with my job and painting for boys," she said. Now she could add lying to her list of sins. She jangled her car keys. "I think I'll run to the grocery store before it closes. Do you need anything, Gram? Remember, I'm sharing the bills around here."

"I'll go with you," Lizbeth said, depositing her sewing on the end table. "I'm making a new recipe to take to the quilting club tomorrow."

"Well, now, looks like I'd better get on home myself," Lester said. "Gotta get things set up for my sleepin' arrangements tonight, but I could sure use a piece of that pie when you get back."

"Don't fall off your porch, Lester," Lizbeth said. "We'll see about pie later."

Jemma, fresh from the bank, stood in the middle of the kitchen, sizing up the walls. "I want to paint something different."

Lizbeth looked up from her reading. "Not another picture of me, I hope."

"No ma'am, I want to paint a room. I know that you like blue."

"Help my life, you are your Papa's child," Lizbeth said. "I don't think this old wallpaper will hold up under paint."

64

Jemma waved her hand. "Oh, I'm ripping that off. We're going to do this right. I've got it! We can do a *trompe l'oeil* and knock the socks off your quilting club." Jemma ran her hands across the wallpaper.

"A what?" Lizbeth had seen this behavior before when Cam would get a wild hair.

"It means to fool your eye. It's a mural, only very realistic. What would you like? A countryside, a garden, a river?"

"Sugar, you are making my head spin. I need to think about this."

Jemma put her hand over her mouth. "I'm sorry, Gram. Maybe you like your walls just the way they are, and here I'm trying to change them."

"No, no, it sounds like a fine idea. I'll sleep on it and we can talk in the morning. Maybe you could paint something that your Papa would have liked."

"He loved flowers and he loved his farm," Lizbeth said.

Jemma grabbed her sketchbook. "I'll do both or whatever you say. I can make the background from wall paint and I'll do the details with the acrylics Helene sent. Maybe just one corner could be a mural. I'll use lots of blue since that was his favorite color, too."

Lizbeth was not listening. She watched as the wind rippled through the pecan tree. Jemma stopped yakking and kissed her grandmother's cheek. "I know you miss the farm, so maybe this is not such a good idea."

"I miss him, honey, but the old home place was a part of him. Once he had that heart attack, the doctor said no more farming. Cam couldn't live on that place and not farm. You know all that. I'm just going on, showing my age." Lizbeth poured her coffee into the sink and wiped the table. She leaned against the counter. "Flowers. We need flowers in this room. I don't have to wait until morning to see that."

❧ ☙

Working with Carrie had to be the best job anybody could have and still get paid. Carrie was smart, quick-witted, well read, and could play the piano like nobody's business. She watched the TV soaps with Eleanor who got into the characters and plots like they were for real while her false teeth soaked in a jar by the breadbox. Jemma brought her portable stereo every day so Carrie could listen to rock and roll.

Carrie was in the "circus cannon," as she called it, for a scheduled breathing session, so Jemma brought the stereo into her bedroom. She moved the lamp table to reach the outlet and spied a necklace on the floor. The clasp was broken but a small locket was still attached to it.

Jemma held it up to the cannon. "Is this yours?"

Carrie shook her head.

"There's an *L* on it. Who would that be?"

"Latrina," Carrie whispered.

Jemma put the locket in her purse. On her way out that evening, she stopped in the kitchen. "Eleanor, how could I find Latrina, the girl who was here before me?"

"Law, hon, just go across the tracks and her mother's house is on the first street to your right. You'll know it by all the flowers out front. Why are you askin'?"

"I found her necklace so I thought I would take it to her," Jemma said and shut the door.

Eleanor turned back to her work. "Just don't go after dark, is what I say."

❧❧

Jemma had been "across the tracks" with Papa when he went looking for day workers. He drove around the neighborhood until someone came outside to the porch of a house. Then Papa would stop and talk with the grownups while she sat in the pickup and stared at the kids who appeared from nowhere to stare back at her. She was too young to pose any abstract social questions. Life was concrete—she was in the pickup and they were on their porch. The differences in skin color did puzzle her. Once in a while she would see some of the children and teenagers going up the balcony stairs at The Parnell on Saturday night. She even asked her daddy why she couldn't sit up there, too. Yet, even now, the cluster of shacks, outhouses, the Negro Bethel Church, and the Dew Drop Inn store remained a murky reality.

She scanned the street for dogs and spied a scrawny one emerging from under a porch. He barked a few times then retreated. The house with all the flowers was easy to spot. Anything that would hold soil was full of petunias. Old boots appeared to be a favorite, and some looked better than Jemma's own. She made her way up the hard dirt path leading to the house. A homemade sign was nailed to a porch post—*Does Ironing and Guarantee Her Work*. It shimmied in the wind. A sturdy rocker and two odd chairs rested on the plank porch, and inside, a radio was tuned to the same station Papa had liked. On the screen door were scattered puffs of cotton held there by bobby pins. Jemma knew about those human-crafted spiderwebs designed to scare off flies. She touched one.

A stocky young man appeared in front of her. "What do you want?"

Jemma stepped back. "I'm looking for Latrina. Does she live here?"

"Trina, some white girl's here," he yelled.

"What's the matter, Weese, don't you have any manners at all?" Trina pushed open the door and grinned.

Jemma shook her head. "Dumb me. I didn't make the connection. We played basketball last week."

"Yeah, I know," she said. "You wore me out."

Jemma motioned towards the kitchen. "Is that your brother?"

"Weese?" Trina laughed. "Naw, he's one of Mama's strays."

"I think I have something that belongs to you," Jemma said and handed her the locket.

Trina clinched the locket in her fist and moved to the path, glancing over her shoulder. "My boyfriend thought that Latrina sounded too much like a latrine and he said he dug way too many of them in the army to kiss one." She took a few steps into the street and lowered her volume. "I thought I might've dropped this somewhere in her room. Thanks."

"You're welcome." Jemma followed along. "How weird that we both worked with Carrie."

Trina exhaled. "I miss seeing her. She made me laugh."

"She says the same thing about you. Why did you quit?"

Trina looked towards the house where Weese had perched on the steps. "Carrie wasn't the problem."

"Ah, His Honor. He's such a grump, and he keeps Carrie shut up in the house like she has leprosy or something. Did you have a fight with him?" Jemma asked, watching Weese, too, though she didn't know why.

"Something like that," Trina said.

"Well, if you ever want to talk about it, I live just across the tracks. You can see the big pecan tree from here," Jemma said.

"I know," Trina said. "Mama told me."

"Come over and we'll get a Dr. Pepper at the little Ruby Store. I guess I'd better be getting back. I try to paint every day and I don't want to get behind. See ya." Jemma moved to the high grass by the tracks.

"Hey, wait," Trina yelled and caught up with her. "The Judge, well, you don't want to be around him by yourself if he's been hitting the bottle heavy."

Jemma nodded. "I thought as much, but thanks for the warning. Is that what happened with you?"

"Yeah. He kind of got friendly with his hands, if you know what I mean."

"I can guess," Jemma said.

"My mama doesn't know, so please don't tell anybody, okay?"

"I won't say a word."

"It's just that The Judge has been real good to Mama, and she would be upset if she knew that he was messin' with her baby."

"Did he hurt you?"

"That old tub of lard? He didn't do much of nothin' except blow his whiskey breath down my shirt. Claimed he liked my necklace and wanted to get a better look at it."

"Well, if he ever tries anything like that with me, he's going to get a surprise. I've seen my share of Saturday Night Wrestling on TV."

Trina laughed, then clamped her hand over her mouth as Weese moved off the porch. "I don't think The Judge will mess with a white girl. He probably doesn't even remember."

"So, that guy you mentioned, is he still your boyfriend? What's his name?"

"Nick Fields. He's in Dallas, studying to be a doctor, and I'm stuck here. Mama said your boyfriend was that Chase boy, but that you dropped him. Mama irons for the Chases when their housekeeper is out of town."

"News sure gets around in Chillaton," Jemma said.

"So you're looking for love, huh?"

"I don't know what I'm looking for," Jemma said, meaning it.

The screen door flew open and a large woman wearing a feed sack dress and a white, starched apron held it back with a cane. "Latrina, who you talkin' to out here?" she shouted.

"Mama, I thought you were gonna take a nap," Trina said. She turned to Jemma. "C'mon, now you've gotta say hello."

Jemma smiled and walked up to the porch, "Hi. I'm really glad to meet you. I'm Jemmabeth Forrester." They clasped hands and Jemma was struck with a feeling of sweet honesty at Willa's touch. There were no dimples, nor were her eyes slanted like Trina's, but they met hers straight on.

"I'm Willa Johnson. Ain't you a pretty one. We seen you grow up, child. Ever time your grandpap come over looking for hands, I'd peek out the door and see how much littler you were than my Latrina. Now it looks like you two are just about the same."

Jemma's smile wavered. "I'm sorry that I never met y'all until today. That makes me mad at myself."

"Well, we can't do nothin' about the past, can we?" Willa said. "All's we can do is keep on walkin' the road that Jesus give us, and try to do right by each other in the here and now."

"Mama, she doesn't want to hear a sermon. Thanks for coming over, Jemma," Trina said.

Willa stood in the doorway. "It's good to say hello and see you all growed up, face-to-face like this. You come back any time."

"Thanks. I will." Jemma walked to the tracks and looked back. She had missed out on something over the years, and it had left a vacant corner in her life that she had never noticed. Rats. She vowed right there on the tracks that things would change.

CHAPTER NINE

Assumptions

"Did I ever tell y'all how my second wife died?" Lester finished off his bowl of Golden Vanilla ice cream and set it on Lizbeth's front porch. "Well, sir, we had a storm come along 'bout dinnertime, and I'd just gone to shut up the hen house. The missus was still at the table when I left. The rain was movin' in fast, so I was tryin' to move even faster. All of a sudden my armhairs—excuse me, Miz Liz—come hence to pricklin', then BAM, this ball of fire knocked me plumb to the ground. When I come to, there lay the missus, flat out in the dirt no more than ten feet from me with one of the milkin' buckets atop her head. She was a goner. For the life of me, I still hadn't figgered out why she come outside with a metal bucket on her head like that. Beat all I ever seen. Ruint my bucket, too."

"How many times have you been married, Lester?" Jemma asked.

"Well, let's see. First there was Bertie, who died with the flu. So I married Mae Ella, the one I was just talkin' about. Then here come Zippy. Of course that wasn't her real name. It was somethin' like Zipporah. My last, Paulette, was part French. I ain't sure which part. Anyhow, she had a bad ticker and keeled over one mornin' with a dad-gummed heart attack. I hated to see her go. She was a ringtail tooter."

"You were married four times?" Jemma asked.

"I reckon that's right. Truth is, Zippy run off, and after a few years batchin', I went before The Judge and he figured she was a goner, too. So I married Paulette. She had a good bit of money from her first husband. Thanks to him, I can live on my railroad pension. Paulette was workin' at the drugstore when I met her. She was makin' malteds and whatnot, but she didn't need the money. Maybe that old Zippy will show up here one of these days, and I reckon we'd still be married."

Lizbeth cleared her throat and Lester changed the subject. "I don't know if y'all know it, but I heard down to the post office that Shorty Knox is lookin' in windows again. He must be near seventy by now, and he's been peepin' in windows for sixty of them years. Back in the Dust Bowl days, folks come hence to askin' Shorty when the next duster was comin'. He could predict them nasty things. I reckon he had extra sense about that kind of stuff 'cause he knew it was coming before the radio did. Anyway, you ladies best keep your doors locked up tight. 'Course Shorty don't do nothin' but look in. He's got himself a foldin' stool now. The sheriff took his old stool away the last time they hauled him in. I reckon that's hard on a fellow to be a peepin' Tom and himself no taller than a cookstove. He took a fancy to one of them high school teachers last year and come hence to starin' in her window at school until the principal had to call the sheriff. Shorty heard the police car comin' so he climbs up on top of the announcer's stand at the football stadium and won't come down for nothin'. Only come down when the sheriff promised him a new stool. That takes the cake, our own sheriff helpin' a criminal. I guess y'all know I'm just a holler away if y'all ever need a man to protect you."

Lester clicked his tongue in Lizbeth's direction. She, of course, didn't look up.

⊰⌀⊱

Eleanor stayed late to shell a bushel of black-eyed peas. She dumped the contents of a basket on the kitchen table and gave Jemma and Carrie each a lapful to work on. "Jericho McKinney is in the hospital up to Amarillo. Do you know her, hon?" she asked. "Lives over by the old skatin' rink." Eleanor's teeth were in the jar, so every S whistled, like Sylvester the Cat.

Jemma grimaced at the peas in her lap. "Yes, ma'am. I know her."

"Jericho was at the football game on Friday. They follow all them games even though they never had any kids at all. Ever where the team goes, they go. I don't know why she ever give that man of hers the time of day. Law knows he's chased ever who wore a skirt in this town and even got Vela Crane p.g. down to Cleebur. 'Course he can't hold a candle to Max Chase, but Mr. Chase never got nobody p.g. that I know of, exceptin' Mrs. Chase. Law knows how she puts up with him, 'course they had themselves that sweet child, Spencer. Now, that boy is a wonder."

Jemmabeth flushed at that revelation and wondered what Eleanor would say about her if she knew about Mr. and Mrs. Turner.

"Anyhoo, Jericho was at our own football stadium, and you know all they've got is them dinky little bathrooms. It beats all I ever seen how they can build a fancy ball field, then throw up them scrawny necessary rooms, thinkin' ever what's built is good enough to do your business in. They're probably nasty, too. Well, she was in one of them stall things, and it seems she had on a new kind of girdle that's got legs in it, not like the good kind that's shaped like a water hose. There's no tellin' how much them new ones cost. Ever how much that man of hers makes over to the light plant, it can't be enough to put up with him anyway. Now where was I?"

"Jericho had a new girdle," the girls said in unison.

"Law, yes, hon. Anyhoo, she hitched up her dress, got that thing halfway down, lost her balance, and slipped clear down to the filthy floor. I heard she hit hard, too, but she didn't just hurt herself. She got her feelings hurt. Went down between the commode and the cinderblock wall, and couldn't get up to save her life or reach her dress to cover certain things up. She was stuck like a wienie in a bun. She let out a holler for help, but it all happened towards the end of the game when the score was tied and everybody was carryin' on so loud that you couldn't hear nothin'."

Eleanor burped softly and went on with her story. "Sheriff's deputy, Faylon Price, was having to go himself right next door, and heard the racket that Jericho was makin' so he busted in the door. She had it latched, you know. He claims that he shut his eyes as soon as he saw her state, but I figure he had himself a good peek."

"Faylon saved her then," Carrie prompted.

"Law, no, hon. It took a plumber to do the job. They had to take the toilet out and her with a smelly locker room towel draped over her while they did it. Ever how you look at it, Jericho had a bad deal. She was mortified to the point that the poor thing won't even talk now. I bet she burns that girdle riggin' as soon as she gets home. I know I would, plus I'd throw her mister on the pile, too. They say she cracked a couple of ribs, but I think she's havin' a nervous breakdown, myself."

Eleanor collected the shelled peas and rinsed them in the sink. "I'm takin' a loaf of bread over to her mister and I sure hope he don't try nothin' with me." She sighed and stared out the window. The girls didn't dare look at one another.

Eleanor cut herself a generous slice of bread. "Now Jericho herself runs a nasty kitchen. I personally seen her cat walk around on the table just before they come hence to eatin'. That cat was lickin' the gravy only five minutes before I had a servin' of it. When folks ain't clean in their kitchen, they ain't clean in life. That's what my mama said. Of course that don't mean she deserved to have a nervous breakdown. Jericho's been packin' on the pounds lately, and that's why she was tryin' a new girdle. I reckon she squeezed into a large, on account of wishful thinkin'. I'm out for comfort myself." Eleanor hoisted her significant bosom right onto the tabletop. "Anyhoo, you given any more thought to the Chase boy, hon? He's a keeper."

"Uh, maybe," Jemma said. She didn't mention that she drove by the Chase castle every day to see if his car was there. She didn't have a clue what she would do if it showed up.

❧ ❧

"Did y'all have dances in high school?" Jemma asked Trina as they sat in the sunny hollyhock patch, painting their toenails with Rose Sensation polish and listening to Jemma's transistor radio. They were easy company and had shared most of their secrets.

"We had the best," Trina said. "The school over in Monroe would come too."

"Monroe?" Jemma asked. "Isn't that a hundred miles from here?"

"Yeah, from here, but not from Red Mule. They had some fine-looking boys."

Jemma rubbed baby oil on her arms and legs. "We had ours at the old WPA barracks across from the feed store. They knocked out some walls and it was just one long, rocking place. Once we got started on the Chillaton Stomp, the light bulbs would swing like crazy. Sometimes you could taste the dust from the thirties falling out of the ceiling and into the punch."

"What's the Chillaton Stomp?" Trina asked.

"The jitterbug and bop combined. You know how Chillaton is. It's always behind any new style of dancing, clothes, or you name it. I think they just heard about hula hoops last week." Jemma laughed.

Trina gave her a sidelong glance. "You really think I knew how things were across the tracks?"

Rats. Jemma took off her sunglasses. "Trina, I hate it that you were just right over there and I never knew you. I am ashamed of that. Honest."

A sudden breeze caught Lester's wash on his clothesline, flipping a dozen socks into motion.

"I always wondered why the good Lord didn't leave everybody as skeletons, then we could all be alike," Trina said. "Nobody would be a different color or too fat or real ugly."

They giggled at the idea.

"Good one, but then my art would be really boring," Jemma said. "Didn't you feel weird every time you saw how different things were across the tracks? It's so unfair and unequal. I think I would've been angry at the injustice."

Trina raised her brow. "Like Weese? Naw, Mama wouldn't put up with that kinda attitude. She's got her own way of living and behaving. It doesn't matter to her who you are or where you live. That's why folks are always sending their lost sheep to her. She makes 'em toe the line."

"So you toed it."

"I never really wanted to step off it. Mama has a good handle on the Scriptures and that's the way she raised me. How about you?"

"I've been going to church all my life, every Sunday," Jemma said.

"Going to church doesn't mean you really live by the Scriptures, though."

"I'm a good girl. I believe everything that's in the Bible and I say my prayers every night."

Trina shook her head. "I'm talking about the Lord taking care of every day. I mean just flat out giving it over to Him, on purpose. Even when things don't seem to go the way you're hoping, you still read the Scriptures, do what they say, and tell Him your worries. He'll do what's best for you. That's living by the Scriptures."

"Then why pray if God's going to take care of everything?"

"We're supposed to thank Him and praise Him. It doesn't hurt to ask for your way, too, but you have to be willing to live with His answer. I don't make a move without listening really good first."

Jemma gave that some thought. "How'd you get to be so smart?"

"Mama, Grandmama, and Brother Cleo," Trina said.

"I think I must not have been listening in church. I was probably thinking about Spencer." Jemma got lost in that memory for a minute.

"So, how come your team didn't win the state basketball tournament?" Trina asked.

"Rats. I hate this story. We were behind one point with five seconds left in the game. I got the ball and jumped one in with three seconds on the board. They threw the ball down court, picked up a foul, and won with two free throws. It was the pits. I should have waited and run out the clock before I shot. You would've thought of that."

"Maybe." Trina shrugged. "Sometimes two heads are better than one. I guess it wasn't meant to be."

The 3:37 Zephyr blew its horn, punctuating their thoughts.

❧ ❦

That night Jemma bought everybody burgers from Son's Drive In, and they ate them on Willa's porch. Weese left his in the sack.

"What we need around here are more fireflies. Did you see many fireflies in Dallas, Trina?" Jemma asked.

"Yeah. We called 'em lightning bugs. I guess they're the same thing."

Weese spat a wad of chewing tobacco. "Why you bringing food over here? Just give us the money instead."

"Weese!" Willa banged her cane on the porch. "Mind your manners, young man."

"There are all sorts of bugs that can light up," Jemma said, tentatively. "There's a beetle in Europe that can shine, but only the male can fly. The females spend their whole lives crawling everywhere they go."

"Sounds just like people to me," Trina said and shot Weese a look. "Men strutting around showing off, and the women down on their hands and knees, scrubbing."

Willa planted her cane and stood, ready to call it a night, but first she fired off a few choice comments. "Just like them little bugs makin' their own light, you can't wait on nobody to take care of you. If'n you crawl 'round on your belly all your life, don't be puttin' blame on nobody else. Ask the good Lord to show you the way, then pull yourself up and work it out. If you get to fly, well then, that's Him puttin' a blessin' on you and helpin' you along. Goodnight, girls, and you watch your mouth, Weese."

Weese stepped off the porch, spat another glob of tobacco near Jemma's foot, and ambled down the dirt road.

Lester was on his third cup of coffee. It was so hot that he poured it in the saucer and sipped it like soup. "I bet Jemmer don't know about the big floods we used to have around here. Some fields was taken as fishin' holes by city folk. Scratch Mason's outhouse floated clean out in the middle of his field with himself yellin' out for dear life from the roof. Beat all I ever saw. 'Course we ain't had that much rain in twenty year or more. Not since the Republicans got into the White House."

"I believe JFK was, and LBJ is, a Democrat," Lizbeth said, rolling out pie crust.

Lester tapped his foot and looked out the window. "That Kennedy feller was a Catholic, though."

"There are a lot of good Catholics in this world," Lizbeth said, "the same as with any other church."

Lester sniffed. "Used to have whoppin' sandstorms, too. When the sky turned black with dirt and it was the middle of the day, we called it a duster. A feller could see one comin' for a hundred miles off. 'Course Shorty knew it first. The wind come hence to howlin' for two or three hours, solid, and the sand would pile up and wedge itself between your teeth and your gullet. It was like a swarm of chiggers on your bare skin. If the missus left the wash on the line, it'd look like you drug it behind a plow horse. That sand would drift plumb up over barbed wire fences. Why, half our dirt's bein' plowed in Oklahoma right now. The other half got here from New Mexico yesterday. That's why farmers gotta work so dang hard to make a living. It ain't even Texas dirt."

"Lester, you're giving me a headache," Lizbeth said.

He lowered his voice. "Well, now, I'm just trying to educate this young lady here. 'Course nobody can ever forget what happened to old F.G. Powers durin' one of them big dusters."

Lizbeth sighed as she cut slits in the top crust. "Jemmabeth doesn't even know F.G. Powers."

That was all the invitation that Lester needed. "Well, sir, him and his missus were leavin' church when one of them dusters let loose and turned day right smack-dab into night. He come hence to yellin' for the wife and she was yellin' right back, to get their bearings. Old F.G. climbed up into his wagon, all the time still hollerin' over to the wife to make sure she was in the wagon. The Powers place was just down the road so their old mule lowered his head and pulled them up right by the front door. Now this is the gospel truth. F.G. helps his wife down and into the house. They get inside and, lo and behold, if F.G. don't give his wife a little celebration hug only to find out that he's got ahold of old lady Pinkerton instead of the missus. Old lady Pinkerton claimed she was as surprised as F.G., and that she couldn't tell for sure which wagon she was gettin' into. 'Course everybody knew that she was lookin' for herself a man and had been for near fifty year. Her face stopped many a decent clock."

Lizbeth reached for the aspirin on the rack above the kitchen sink. She shook it, too, for effect, but Jemma wasn't sure if Lester even noticed.

⊱⊰

"Hi, cutie pie," Jemma said and gave Lizbeth a kiss on her cheek. She hung her purse on the hall tree and set the table. "I'm so excited about using the car house as a studio. Lester is going to help me do a few things to it tomorrow."

Lizbeth cleared her throat. "A letter came for you today; it's on the table there. The return address is that law office in Wicklow. I thought it might be your last paycheck."

Jemma circled the kitchenette twice then sat at the opposite end from the envelope. She recognized the handwriting. Besides, only Paul would know he could get by without a post office box number. Lizbeth was mashing potatoes at the counter. She didn't turn around but spoke instead about the weather.

Jemma interrupted. "Gram, I'm not going to open it. Would you mind putting it in the soldier box?" For what purpose, she had no idea.

"All right." Lizbeth wiped her hands on her apron and unlatched the pouting room door. Jemma closed her eyes when she heard the

77

trunk lid close with a thump. Only Lizbeth's occasional humming leaked into her head during supper.

Afterwards, they sat in the porch swing. The extra bit of chain on the swing made a clinking with each movement, and a dust-settling sprinkle came up from nowhere to cool things off.

"Whatever is in that letter can just wait at the bottom of the soldier box with all those other sad things," Jemma said. "Someday I'll throw it away."

Lizbeth laid her hand on Jemma's arm. "It's getting chilly out here. I think I'll go in."

Jemma stayed on the swing with her legs pulled up under her chin until the sun went down, then she went inside. Lizbeth had lit the flame in the gas heater.

She laid her head on Lizbeth's shoulder and fixed her eyes on the flickering reds and oranges behind the patterned grill. "Gram, I'm ready to talk about Paul." She inhaled warily, but let it out in rapid fire. "I went to his office to surprise him with a special painting I'd done. There was a woman sitting in the office, and I asked her if she knew where Paul Turner was." She glanced at Lizbeth. "The woman told me that she was his *wife.*"

Lizbeth caught her breath. "His wife! Are you sure?"

"Yes ma'am. I knew it was true because I could see it in her eyes. They were cold."

"Oh, my." Lizbeth held her close. "How you must have felt, honey. I wish you could have told me sooner."

"I just couldn't because I think I loved him and he was married."

"You didn't know."

"So what could he have to say in a letter—that he was sorry I met his wife? The rat. I am so embarrassed."

Lizbeth took her hands. "The good Lord knows your heart and everything that happened."

"If Spencer finds out, I'll just die."

"God doesn't give us anything we can't handle. He has a plan for you, Jemmabeth, and it will come for you in His own good time. Your job is to be patient, trust Him, and pray for His guidance. Listen to Him and you'll see."

They watched the flame from the little stove as it warmed the room around them. Jemma sniffed into a tissue. "Gram, today is Spence's birthday, and I don't even know where he is."

She could hear them laughing in the dark as she arrived with a carton of Dr. Peppers. Willa waved at her. "Jemma, come and set yourself down. This here's Brother Cleo. He's been our preacher for about forty year. He knows more about Jesus than old Paul himself."

Brother Cleo took off his fedora. He was a big man, almost bald, and carried himself well. His voice bellowed like a fine-tuned bass. "I don't know about that, Miz Willa, but you are right about me preaching the Word of God, but for more like fifty years. That's a long time for folks to be listening to an old codger like me."

"I'm glad to meet you, Brother Cleo," Jemma said, shaking his hand. She didn't see Weese standing in the doorway behind the screen. He kicked it open and stood on the porch, lighting a cigarette.

Willa pointed her cane at him. "Don't be kickin' my door, young'un."

"Maybe that's not all I'm gonna kick," he mumbled, then took a swig from a bottle.

"When did you start smoking?" Trina asked, fanning the fumes away. "I thought you were chewing these days."

"And what are you drinkin'?" Willa frowned at him. "That don't look like no Dr. Pepper."

"I wonder what these mosquitoes do if they can't find a warm-blooded animal to feed on. Maybe they just die," Jemma said, hoping to change the subject.

"They just move back and forth across the tracks," Trina said.

"There's lots of warm-blooded animals over here to feed on, always has been, always will be." Weese flicked ashes on the porch. "Just one more thing owed us."

"I'll show you who owes who if you burn down my porch with them ashes." Willa shoved at the glow with her cane.

Brother Cleo took out his handkerchief and wiped his forehead. "My way of thinking is that folks of every color have to find their own way in this world with the guiding hand of the Almighty."

"You're so full of it, old man." Weese hissed and moved to the grass. "You still livin' on the Massa's place."

"Weese!" Willa jammed her cane onto the porch floor. "You mind who you talkin' to." She narrowed her eyes at him. "Don't you be usin' that kind of sass with Brother Cleo."

Jemma knew it was her presence that caused the outburst, not the venerable preacher. Even in the dim light she felt Weese's glare.

The words oozed from his mouth like sour milk. "Gov'ment comes along and says we can go to school in our own town, then do-gooder whites like you poke your nose across them tracks and say, 'We got coloreds livin' around here? Where are they? Come over here, you dirty little black children and let us give you our old clothes and junk. Now you be sure and give us a smiley thank you right out of your poor little hearts.' "

"That'll be enough, young man." Brother Cleo's voice echoed down the street.

Willa struggled up and cracked her cane against the porch post. "I'll not have you talkin' that way in my house, Weese. If you know what's good for you, you'll be tellin' Jemma just how sorry you are for them words."

Weese jutted his jaw. "She knows I'm right."

"It's okay, Willa. I know what Weese is talking about," Jemma said quietly. "I hope you don't think that about me, though."

"I don't care about you." He turned towards the tracks.

"Where you off to? Jemma brought us some Dr. Peppers. I know I got my mouth all set for one," Willa called after him. "You're gonna be sorry."

Weese disappeared into the dark, but not before he tossed his cigarette. Everybody watched it glow in the grass.

Trina broke the silence. "Good thing it looks like rain."

"I swear, sometimes that boy ain't got the sense that the good Lord give a one-eyed pee ant," Willa said. They all heard the sound of a bottle as it hit the packed earth and rolled to a stop. "That boy's done shucked my last cob."

"He's just baring his teeth, Miz Willa. Nothing's gonna come of it," Brother Cleo said.

Willa exhaled. "I done all I can do for that boy, so it's up to Jesus now. He's either gonna get himself throwed in jail or else he gonna get struck by the Holy Ghost and turn his sorry self around." The wind stirred around them and the first fat drops of rain pecked at the roof.

"Yes, ma'am," Brother Cleo said. "You've done more than his own mama would've. I'm gonna have to say good night, y'all. I don't want to get caught out in a storm, though I do like the smell of wet earth."

"I think I'd better go home too." Jemma smacked another mosquito. Lightning sliced the sky and thunder rattled the ironing sign.

Willa gave one last look down the road. "You're fixin' to get soppin' wet, child."

"I'll see y'all tomorrow," Jemma said and took off. The rain came on hard. She quickened her step through the tall grass and sunflowers. She and Trina had almost worn a path up to the tracks, down the other side through the tree row, and across the vacant lot behind Lizbeth's house.

A great flash of lightning revealed that she wasn't the only one on the trail. A crouching figure shared the path. It had to be Weese. Her scalp tingled and she broke into a run off the trail, then bounded up the tracks in a new spot, hoping to avoid him. Adrenaline coursing, she paused between the rails, then jumped at a noise behind her. The blinding headlight of the 9:04 pierced the darkness only yards away. Jemma screamed and stumbled off. She slid down the slick right of way, taking rail-bed rocks with her. The train horn blasted and the ground shook as the train shot past. Sparks hissed in the water and a gush of heat from the driving metal on the rails enveloped her. She lay in the mud and watched the cars flash by. A few passengers were lingering over their late evening meal in the dining car, unaware of her brush with death.

Her head pounded in rhythm with the clamor on the tracks and her stomach was in her throat. How stupid of her to come within a few feet of her own funeral. She slipped again, as she thought she heard something on the tracks. Her mind was a jumble, her clothes were soaked, and she had a big scrape on her arm. To makes things worse, she upchucked the burger and fries. Jemma was a muddy, stinking mess when she at last pulled open the screen door. She halfway hoped Lizbeth was still awake, and then again, she hoped not.

"Jemmabeth, I was a little worried," Lizbeth whispered. "That was a cloudburst."

"Sorry, Gram. I'm okay, but I think I'll take a bath."

Jemma stayed in the water until it was cold. If Lizbeth knew about her close call with the train, she wouldn't be snoring—"cooling potatoes," as she called it. Jemma would tell Trina tomorrow and together they would confront Weese. That would've been a nice headline in the *Chillaton Star:* "Former Miss Bigshot Run Over By Train." She didn't even jump off the tracks; she stumbled.

Spencer, her sweet Candy Man, was better off without her.

∾∾

It was half past seven when she woke up the next morning. She was gulping down breakfast when Lester came in with the mail.

"Mornin', Jemmerbeth," Lester nodded. "Where's Miz Liz?"

Jemma pointed to a note. "She took a casserole to Mrs. Schneider."

"Oh, the Germans," he said. "Old man Schneider's always laid up with somethin' or the other. I just wanted to let her know that Shorty's at it again. I heard down to the post office that he was peepin' in windows last night. You know he lives in a dugout just over yonder across the tracks. Sheriff spotted him out in that little storm we had, runnin' the rails right back here behind us, carryin' his metal step stool on his head. Pitiful feller. He could've got lightin' struck pullin' that kind of stunt, like my Mae Ella."

Jemma gave him her full attention. "I'm sorry, Lester. What did you say?"

"I said Shorty Knox was prowlin' around the tracks durin' that storm we had last night."

Jemma washed her hands and face in the kitchen sink, something she'd never done before, but had seen Papa do many times after a rough day in the field. "Thanks, Lester, I'll be sure and tell her about Shorty."

She exhaled in the morning air, rubbing the bandage on her arm. It was a brisk walk to work as she considered the trouble that she could have caused an already bitter young man.

CHAPTER TEN

Good Enough

"Well, well, if it's not Jemmartsybeth. So, big-city college was just way too much for you."

Jemma turned to face the wickedly beautiful Missy Blake.

"Moved in with your Granny, huh?" Missy pushed her pink sunglasses back on her head. Suntan lotion and Chanel #5 served up a pungent blend. Her signature high-cut shorts and very low-cut top showed the best of Missy—drum majorette legs and cleavage that belonged on a fat girl.

"Missy. I didn't know you were in town," Jemma managed.

"Oh, I'm here all right. What happened to you and that art school in Dallas?" Missy's indigo eyes scanned the sidewalk for other victims.

"I'm taking a break," Jemma said, noticing a big hickey on the otherwise perfect neck before her.

Missy waved at someone across the street. "Come on," she said to Jemma. "Let's go to the drugstore and get a Coke."

"I don't have time," Jemma said. She'd sooner be chased by a big snake.

"Yes, you do, because I want to talk about *Spence*." At that, Jemma allowed herself to be dragged away. Missy's nails gleamed in a sugary pink. "Do you like this color? It's called Cotton Candy. Oh, and I'm called Melissa now. I'm dumping 'Missy.' It's so juvenile. I assume that you and Spence have called it quits forever because he and I had several dates this summer. He was very interested, but it was me that didn't want to get serious. I'm way too busy at UT for a steady right now, but he was a temptation. Spence has gotten even cuter and everybody's talking about him."

Jemma flushed and focused on a display of antacids. Rats. She didn't know he would go out with CHS alumni, most particularly,

Missy Blake, and most especially several times. She drew a face on the side of her frosty glass. "I haven't seen him yet so we haven't talked," she said.

Missy cocked a perfect eyebrow. "Really. I thought he told me that he was coming home early this semester or something weird like that. I have a good feeling about us, so I know we'll be going out again." She was distracted mid-sentence by a well-toned deliveryman who was giving her equal attention. "Now that Spence is a free man at last, anything can happen and it usually does, with me," she added. "I have…what's the word…uh…"

"I don't know what you're trying to say," Jemma said.

"You know, that stuff that JFK had," Missy said.

"Back pain?" Jemma suggested. "Intelligence?"

"No. The stuff that made people want to be around him."

"Money?" Jemma said, enjoying the moment. Missy suffered from a limited vocabulary. It was her only flaw—that, and her personality. Jemma caved in. "Are you trying to think of *charisma*, Missy?"

"Yeah, cha*ri*sma," she said, as though she'd heard it at least once before.

Jemma sipped her soda. "So, what keeps you so busy at the University of Texas?" she asked, not caring at all.

"My sorority, of course. Is there such a thing as an art sorority? I mean, for parties and meeting guys and all that good stuff? I just love my sisters. I have really found myself. We have the same interests and goals. You wouldn't believe what serious f-u-n we have. You know, party time," she said, making circles in the air with her finger. "And the guys." Missy rolled her eyes. "If you are a Delta, you have more frat boys than you can handle. So, what did you do for fun in Dallas? Do you still play basketball and make your famous leaping shot or whatever you call it? I bet you don't have to write those boring term papers and junk like that at art school."

Missy folded her arms and sipped the last of her Coke. "It's so cool that you aren't going to start dating Spencer again because I'm thinking about my future." She put on fresh lipstick that matched the nail polish. "I can tell when a guy's, you know, interested in fooling around with me." She shook back her hair as the deliveryman passed by again. "Spence is hard to read, which is weird because he is just so hot. Did I say everybody is talking about him, only I've got dibs, if you know what I mean."

Jemma swallowed a big chunk of ice and tried to make eye contact with Missy to see if she was telling the truth about Spence fooling around.

"I heard that you were taking care of some crippled girl," Missy said, her nose wrinkled up like she smelled a hog farm. "Do you have to, you know, change a bedpan for her or does she wear diapers?" She leaned back in her chair and ran her fingers through her thick, flaxen hair. She looked like a TV commercial for shampoo and she knew it.

"The girl's name is Carrie," Jemma said. "She is smart, funny, and really pretty. Her hair is the same color as yours and that's her natural shade. She was in our class and in my Brownie group, before you moved here."

"How weird. I also heard that you're hanging around with a colored girl, but I couldn't believe it. I mean, that's just too tacky for words, even for you. Oh, and Miss Priss Sandy's wedding was kind of cute, in a hokey way. Marty's not good looking, but he's something else on a date. We went out once when she was mad at him. He only had one thing on his mind. Uh-oh, promise you won't tell Sandy that. It's just me—I bring out the passion in guys. All of them." Missy looked at her watch. "Didn't you say that you have to be somewhere?"

"Sandy and Martin are in Germany," Jemma said, "so I doubt she's worried about a date that he had with you when he might have to go to Vietnam, and yeah, Trina Johnson lives across the tracks. She's one of the nicest friends I've ever had. If you'll excuse me, I need to pick up Gram at the beauty shop." Jemma scooted her chair on the wood plank floor.

Missy's jaw dropped and she slipped some Dentyne into it. "How completely weird. Oh, well, to each his own. Your hair has gotten so long. I guess you're trying to go for my length, but it does sort of help tone down your height. You should try this thing I read about in a movie star magazine. Daddy gets them because of all the theaters we own, I guess. Anyway, you put mayo in your hair. I know that sounds crazy, but it makes your hair shine."

"Really?" Jemma paused. "Mayonnaise?"

"It sounds goofy, but it's so healthy for your hair roots or something. I'm trying to be more health conscience," she said. "Have you rolled your hair on o.j. cans yet? They are the coolest for long hair. It might help with those weird waves you have, too."

"Orange juice cans and mayo. I guess I'll have to try that."

"Yeah, just leave the mayo in. Don't rinse it out." Missy sized up Jemma's silk blouse and long skirt. "You're still trying to get by with the bohemian look. I guess I just love fashion way too much to go that route."

"Bohemian?"

"Yeah, you know, artsy, backwoodsy, like those cowboy boots you used to wear with everything. I guess there are guys who could overlook that, but not the fratties, trust me." Missy tapped her long nails on the tabletop. "Spence looks like James Dean's twin brother now. It's so freaky. I probably don't know him as well as I could because y'all were like Siamese twins or something in school. Did you know that he joined a fraternity? He told me all about it. We were so close. Listen, if you're ever in Austin during school, call the Delta house and ask for me. Maybe my sisters and I could give you a makeover or something. It would be a cool project, but you might bring some extra money to pay us back."

Missy propped a rhinestone-studded sandal on her chair, and frowned at a mosquito bite that dared to spoil her bronzed leg. She flashed her faultless smile at Jemma. "Thanks for letting go of Spencer. You did him a big favor and me, too, for that matter."

"Good-bye, Missy," Jemma said.

"*Melissa*. High school just seems so long ago." Missy took out her compact and checked the corners of her mouth and her eyeliner.

"Right," Jemma said, forgetting the question.

Missy swiveled away like she was still leading the band. "Say hi to Sandy. Anything you want me to tell Spencer the next time we're out?" She yelled it so everybody could hear.

"No." Jemma turned down the sidewalk to Nedra's, her nose and eyes burning.

Rats. If Spence took Missy to The Hill or to the river, she didn't know what to think about him. Maybe Fraternity Brother Spencer would do that. Maybe dumb Jemmabeth would do that with Mrs. Turner's husband. Everybody in their class did not call the only girl who could afford braces "Missy." Most just called her The Cleave, for obvious reasons.

Subsequent to The Cleave encounter, Jemma was wishy-washy about seeing Spencer. It was driving her bananas to think he might know about Paul. His whereabouts remained a mystery and she was too ashamed to ask anybody. She stopped driving by the castle, but each time the phone rang, she jumped. Like just now.

"Jem, can you hear me?"

"Sandy? There's lots of static. How's married life?" Jemma asked. "I had a disaster with Paul," she added, waiting for the sarcasm.

"Mr. Perfect Cowboy?"

"This is just between you and me, okay? I met his wife."

"Cheezo! The rat fink. I can't believe that he was married. What a cheating liar."

"I feel like dirt."

"How could you have known he was married?"

"I guess I could've asked him."

"Oh, sure, that comes up a lot on a date. He's not worth worrying about." Sandy always shot to the heart of things.

"He called for a while and now he writes me twice a week, but I'm not opening the letters."

"Burn them," Sandy said. "He's just digging himself a deeper hole. Good gravy! If Marty ever did that to me, I'd kill him. That poor wife."

"I think I loved him, Sandy."

"More than Spence?"

"I don't know if I really loved Spence. You know that."

"You never knew what you had with Spencer, Jem. You two were like that Jacob's ladder experiment in science where the voltage shoots across from one side to the other."

"I wasn't gah-gah like you were with Marty," Jemma said.

"Oh, yes, you were. Don't forget who you are talking to here."

"Yeah, but I was crazy all the time I was with Paul," Jemma said, "I mean crazy. He was so smooth. He was not your average buckaroo."

"Just a cheating married man. Jem, how many times did we run the bulls on the Fourth of July? I know you. Once you see a cowboy hat pulled down low over dreamy eyes with long lashes, and that 'howdy, ma'am' attitude, you're done for. Tell Spencer to get him a Stetson."

Jemma lay back on the good bed. "I'm not sure he's still interested in me. Besides, I don't want to mess up and hurt him."

Sandy snorted at that. "That's big of you since you already hurt him. I've heard he's been dating everything in sight since you broke up, just like you have. Aren't you the least bit jealous? Haven't you missed him?"

She closed her eyes. "Yes to both."

"He was always my second choice for a boyfriend," Sandy said. Remember our list? You and Spencer need each other; it's been too long. My phone time's about up. I'll call you next month. Get off the guilt train about the cowboy."

"Say hi to Marty. Oh yeah, Missy said your wedding was kind of cute," Jemma said.

Sandy laughed. "The Cleave said that? Well, that's exactly what I was shooting for—kind of cute."

"Spencer went out with her several times."

"Jemmabeth."

"Okay." Jemma hung up. Maybe she shouldn't have told Mrs. Blabbermouth about Mrs. Turner.

❧ ❧

It took her just a week to save up enough orange juice concentrate cans to cover her head. She bought o.j. for everybody on the condition that she got the cans back. She also bought a large jar of mayonnaise and got all set to have hair like a sorority sister and good enough for a certain fratty, should he ever show up. Jemma shampooed, then dipped her fingers into the oily mixture. "This had better be worth it," she said under her breath. The mayonnaise made the cans slippery and she winced at the smell. She had to use about four bobby pins per can to make them stay in place.

Lizbeth watched the proceedings with grave misgivings, as did Lester, who gaped at Jemma as though she were wrapping her hair in hundred-dollar bills. "I reckon you know what you're doin', Jemmerbeth, but I ain't never seen nobody put food in their hair, on purpose, excepting babies."

"It's okay," Jemma muttered with bobby pins in her mouth. She rolled the last greasy section onto a can. "I've heard of people using lemon juice to lighten their hair."

"Now that you mention it, Paulette, my little Frenchy, used to put beer on her hair. Of course, I never asked where she got the stuff," he said with a righteous look.

She sat outside to hasten the drying process. The wind whistled through the cans. She wore her sweater and sat in the hollyhock patch, knowing full well that Gram and Lester were taking turns watching her out the window and snickering. It would be worth it because she was going to have luxurious hair. After the first hour, she tested a strand, but it remained limp and greasy. She rolled it back on the can and propped her feet up in the extra chair. She closed her eyes, thinking about Spencer and his possible reaction to her new look.

"Girl, what planet did you come from?" Trina's voice woke her up and the cans clinked together like a bagful of garbage.

"Trina, you scared me to death," Jemma said.

"Well, now you know how I felt when I saw you." Trina giggled. "What are you doing?"

Jemma shoved a chair towards her. "I'm trying something new on my hair," she said and unwound another can to check it.

"You been eating sandwiches or potato salad?" Trina asked, waving her hand in front of her nose.

"No, why?" Jemma said, clipping the bobby pins back to the can.

"Something stinks."

"I think it's my hair. I put mayonnaise on it."

"Like for a baloney sandwich? Girl, you've lost your marbles. Have you ever seen that stuff after it's been setting around all day? It separates and looks like chicken mess. You wouldn't find me putting that stuff on my dog if I had one."

Jemma was perturbed. She unrolled the cans and let them drop on the ground. "What do you think?" she asked, running her fingers through the gooey mess. Trina erupted in laughter as Jemma ran inside to look in the mirror. Her hair was a clump of seaweed, glistening with mayonnaise and dumped by the tide in Chillaton. Tricked by The Cleave. Rats.

Lizbeth stood in the bathroom door, laughing and covering her nose. "Honey, I've been thinking about this," she said with great control. "I've seen Nedra give some kind of oil treatment, but she does it a little differently, seems like. I think she rinses the oil out before she does anything else."

"Oh." Jemma looked in the mirror again and started to giggle, despite her consternation. "Well, I guess this is what happens when bohemians try to join the ranks of sorority girls. Would you mind asking Trina to come in? I've got to wash my hair."

"I was hoping you would," Lizbeth said and handed her a towel. Jemma used up her bottle of shampoo, and her hair finally smelled like flowers again, like it did that night with Paul.

CHAPTER ELEVEN

The Candy Man

Nedra Porter could intercept a tasty tidbit of gossip from thirty yards upwind. The sign in her beauty shop window—*Hair's where it all begins*—spoke to the heart of Nedra's real business. She didn't pump her customers for information during a shampoo and set in order to run home and whip up a casserole or form a prayer circle. Nedra was pumping for the sheer thrill of knowing things first or secondhand or at least a good third.

Twila worked part-time at Nedra's Nook. She caught the tail end of gossip after Nedra herself had snooped it out. Twila Trout was in Jemma's class, but she married Sandy's older brother, Buddy Baker, two days after high school graduation. She was the one that Jemma and Sandy could count on to be on their side in a girlfriend spat. She was sweeter than she was smart, could cook better than their home economics teacher, and hadn't missed any meals. Her dark blonde hair was cut in a Nedra Helmet. That's what Jemma and Sandy called the hairstyle until Sandy got one, too.

"Guess who's in town?" Twila asked, broom in hand as Jemma came through the door.

Sweat beaded instantly on Jemma's upper lip. "The cast of Gilligan's Island?" she asked, her heart swirling around.

"You're so weird. It's Spencer and he's even better lookin' than he used to be. I mean really cute, Jem, and so nice," Twila said with a big sigh.

"I'm going to tell Buddy you said that."

"Hey, just because I'm married doesn't mean I'm blind. I don't see why you have to be so stubborn about Spence. He's cute, he's rich, he's so smart, and you were such a cute couple."

"If you say cute one more time, I'm leaving," Jemma said.

"He still loves you. Everybody knows it."

"He's dated all the girls in this town and several other towns, I'm sure, since we broke up. Just sell me some shampoo." Jemma opened up her purse.

"You told him to get lost. Everybody in Chillaton knows that, too." Twila shut the cash register drawer. "Buddy got a call from Sandy. I sure miss her. She makes me laugh, but I bet she gets lonesome so far away from home. They were a cute couple, too, but not as cute as you and Spencer."

"That's it," Jemma said with the snap of her purse. "Good-bye, Twila. Say hi to Buddy for me."

"Well, if it's not the long-lost darlin' of Chillaton." Jemma turned at the word *darlin'* to the waiting arms of Nedra Porter herself. Her frosted Helmet was backcombed and sprayed solid atop her long neck like a ripe dandelion, ready to blow. She dusted hair from her pink smock and smiled, revealing a tiny smidge of orange lipstick on her front tooth.

"You have come back for him, haven't you?" she asked. "I knew you would 'cause y'all are just made for each other. It's like a movie. Now you take that Missy Blake, for instance. Nice hair, big busted, but the angels must not have been holding their mouths just right when they made her. She ain't never easy to take, being so sweet on herself, plus she's too forward with the boys. Throws a basketball like a girl, too. Nothin' like you, hon. You coulda been on a college boys' team with that jumper of yours. I wouldn't worry too much about her and Spencer. Missy must bathe in #5 and a little of that goes a long way. Spencer's Corvette probably still reeks with it. Now are you gonna let me do up that nice head of hair before you see him? I could fix it just like mine. What do you say, hon?" Nedra stubbed out her cigarette.

Jemma flashed a smile and shook her head.

"Well, you give me a call if you change your mind. I could work you in."

Nedra moved back to the chair where Betty Kate Richards, towel-wrapped and poised for curlers, resumed reading her magazine, as did the rest of the hungry Nook patrons, most of whom had lifted their hair-dryer hoods so as not to miss a word. Jemma swore she would never wear Chanel.

He called that night.

"Hi, Jem." The sound of his sweet voice stirred a yearning in her, deeper than she ever expected. She wilted onto the dresser stool.

"Oh, Cassanova." What a stupid opener. After all the ideas she had practiced, too. She twisted the cord around her finger and chewed on her lip.

"Hey, it wasn't my idea to break up," he said.

"I can't believe you went out with Missy." Rats. It came out earlier than she planned.

He ignored it anyway. "Your year was up a long time ago, so let's go to the movies tonight."

"You've seen me before and the last time we agreed that would be the last." Dumb, dumb, dumb.

"You agreed all by yourself, Jemmabeth. Right now I miss you and I want to be in your presence."

"Smooth talker."

"Heartbreaker."

"Frat boy."

"Siren."

"Truce." She wanted to see him so bad that she ached.

"I'm coming over because I've missed Gram," he said, in his cute way. Twila was right about that.

"Fine. Maybe I'll be here."

She was, and she had picked out the least bohemian thing she owned—a tailored, violet pantsuit from her mother. Her heart hammered when she heard the Corvette in Lester's driveway. She stood just inside the foyer so that she could see him before he saw her. What if he knew about Paul? She hadn't been this nervous in a year.

He stood at the front door a few seconds, and then pulled the little knob that substituted for a doorbell. Jemma took a couple of deep breaths and opened the door. She tingled from her scalp to her knees at the sight of him. It was the same Spencer, but oh, he did look fine. His sandy blonde hair was parted and still cut short. He had that gentleman's nose, high cheekbones, a full mouth – she wanted to kiss it, and the tiny scar on his chin. His eyes were the color of old pewter, and she looked into them briefly. He was still taller than she was. Always the smart dresser, he was wearing tan slacks and a black shirt. James Dean never looked so good. Her tongue wouldn't work.

"Hi," she said and smiled, her lips sticking to her teeth. He stepped in and stood very close to her, but she didn't recognize his aftershave. It was probably something he got in Europe.

"Hello, baby," he said, just above a whisper. Neither knew what to do with their hands. He played with his car keys and change in his pockets. "You look beautiful," he said, his eyes twinkling.

Yes, yes, he still called her *baby*. "You don't look so bad yourself." She wrung her hands behind her back.

"I've missed you."

Jemma nodded. All she could think about was the way they used to kiss. Her heart was about to fall on the floor, but they just stood there like abandoned marionettes.

"Hey, I want to say hello to Gram," he said, at long last.

She led the way to the kitchen, where Lizbeth was politely lingering over her coffee.

"Spencer! Give me a hug, son," she said, patting his back. "It's a real treat to see you, but I think you've lost weight."

Spencer patted his stomach. "Maybe a little. It's the food back east. I need some of your cooking."

"Do you have time for cobbler? I just made it this afternoon."

"Thanks," he said, eyeing it, "but we are off to the movies. Do you want to go?"

"Let me get my purse." She laughed and hugged him again. "You two have fun."

They walked to the car in silence. She was ready to check it for Chanel, but it was the latest Corvette Sting Ray convertible and candy apple red.

"When did you get this one?" Jemma asked, remembering the way he walked.

Spencer touched her arm as he opened her door. "Today. It's my 'welcome home' gift and belated birthday present from my dad."

His touch didn't go unnoticed. "What's showing at the movies?" Jemma asked, too jittery to think of anything else to say.

"*Mary Poppins*," he said, backing out of the driveway. He put his hand on the back of her seat to check behind him. His eyes darted into hers for a second.

She held her breath until he moved his hand. "I've already seen it."

"Me too. So, what do you suggest?"

"What's at the Drive In?" she asked, like she really cared. She did care about who he took to see *Mary Poppins*.

Spencer peeled out at the first stop sign. He always did drive a little fast for Chillaton and had his own share of warnings from Sheriff Ezell. He pulled up to the marquee, creating a small duststorm behind him. *Darlin'—starring Julie Christie* was on the marquee. "The Chillaton spelling," he said and laughed. She didn't. "What do you think?" he asked, watching her.

"It's up to you." She had almost forgotten how he made his smile. It started with his eyes, not his mouth, and she liked that.

Spencer made a U-turn and headed towards the Salt Fork of the Red River.

"Whoa, what happened to the movies?" she asked.

He threw it into another gear. "I want to talk."

Jemma got a colossal knot in her throat. Rats. He must know.

He turned off the road onto a little dirt lane that she knew all too well, then pulled up to their river spot. The clock and their synchronized breathing made painful little explosions in her ears.

"Look at that sunset," she said, buying time.

"Be honest with me, Jem. We broke up so you could see if there was more out there than what we had. Did you find it?"

"I don't know. Why the third degree so soon?"

"Look at me, baby."

She kept her eyes on the gearshift. "Maybe."

He stopped breathing. She licked her dry lips.

"Why are you here?" he asked.

"You drove us here." She knew that kind of logical wordplay drove him nuts. "I also needed some time to work on my portfolio." It was not a total lie.

"Jemmabeth."

She closed her eyes. "Okay. I got caught in a bad situation and I decided to come home."

"What kind of bad situation?"

"A relationship." Maybe he didn't know. "I was in a relationship and it went bad." She watched the rise and fall of his chest, but didn't dare look him in the eye again. "Spence, I didn't want to tell you this, but you are making me."

"Did you love him?"

"I don't know." She laid her hand on his arm, setting off

fireworks in her stomach. He let it rest there a few seconds before touching her fingertips. When he did, every nerve she had overloaded.

"Spence," she began.

He held her hand, the one she painted with. "It's okay. Do you want to go home?"

"Only if you do."

He started the Corvette and adjusted his rearview mirror.

Her heart sank. "Wait," she said. "Stay a while."

He turned off the motor.

She traced the scar on his thumb where Sandy's cat had scratched him in the third grade. "Let's start over, Spence, okay? Just pretend we don't know each other's every thought, habit, and memory. Just have fun. What do you say?"

He shook his head slightly. "I don't think I can do that. I'm afraid that I've already lost you. I never thought you would find..."

"I missed you so much."

"Where did I go wrong? At what point did you decide it was time to look for somebody new?"

"You didn't ever go wrong, Spence. You couldn't. It's my fault because I always wondered what would happen if we got married and never really knew for sure that we were meant for each other. We had never even kissed anybody else."

"I didn't need to," he said, his eyes glistening.

"I know, but I did. I'm just made that way."

"There had to be some point, though, when you thought I wasn't enough."

She exhaled and looked out at the river. "All right, but remember, you asked for it. At Le Claire they have a May Day celebration."

"The pagans."

"I went with my friend, Melanie. She was trying to get a date with the guy that's her fiancé now, and I sort of went on a double date with her."

"There's no sort of."

"I just went along as a part of her plan."

"You liked it."

"I guess, but I didn't kiss the guy or anything, honest. It was just kind of exciting to be all new with somebody."

"Was he a cowboy?"

Her stomach flipped when he said the word. "No. He was a

cellist."

"Brought down by a cellist."

"I wish I hadn't done it, really I do." There she went, sounding like Miss Scarlett. "We could start over, though. Pretend I'm a new kid in town." She watched him out of the corner of her eye, then turned her head to look squarely at him. He loved that look. He could never turn it down, even when she asked if they could date other people.

He exhaled. "You're a mean woman, Jem. What choice do I have?" She grinned and he couldn't resist. "So, new kid in town, what do you want to do now?"

"This." She yanked him to her by his shirt, and kissed him like she hadn't kissed anybody all year. He came alive and she got her lightning bolts without even planning it. It was so easy to kiss him again and so very excellent. The Sting Ray was far too little for that kind of stuff.

Spencer got out and opened her door. They stared at each other, barely able to breathe, then he pinned her against the car. "Welcome to Chillaton, baby," he said and kissed the dickens out of her until their jaws ached.

They lay on the hood of his car and found Orion. She reached for his hand. "Whenever I looked at the stars last year, I pretended that you were watching them at the same time. Actually, it made life bearable without you."

"Was it really better than what we had?"

"It was different. I did worry that you had found somebody else."

"I want nobody else, Jem. I love you."

She suddenly wanted to say it back to him, but couldn't. "You are precious to me, Spencer," she whispered as tears rolled down her cheeks and onto his.

On the way home, they stopped off at Son's, the local drive-in hamburger joint.

"Why did you join a fraternity?" she asked after a loud slurp of her soda. "We always made fun of them."

He laughed. "How did you know about that? It's the American Institute of Architecture Students, not exactly a wild bunch."

"Oh." She had smelled like potato salad for nothing.

She dug in her purse and took out a small package. "Happy Birthday, Spence. You have always been my best friend."

"Not exactly what a guy wants to hear, baby." He unwrapped it, and lifted out a blue moon on a leather cord. "Hey, thanks."

"I made it for you in my ceramics class. Remember our last date, how we danced in the moonlight at the river? Now you will always have the moonlight with you. I wrote something on the back, too."

He turned it over and read aloud. *Near or far, I am where you are.*

"I really mean it," she said.

He draped it over his mirror. "I had to talk myself out of calling you every night. I nearly went crazy."

"I wish you would've called." She attempted a smile. "What are you doing home this time of the year?"

He grinned. "I needed to work on my portfolio. Actually, I'm doing an apprenticeship with an architect in Amarillo," he said, twirling the moon.

"All year?" Her heart jumped at the thought.

"I just finished orientation and I have to go back in May for culmination seminars." He gave her a sideways look. "Jem, I already knew that you had a boyfriend before you told me."

Rats. The question was how much did he know. "But you've been out of the country," she said.

He drew in his chin. "Come on…Sandy, Buddy B, Twila, Nedra, Mother, telephone."

"Oh yeah. The Chillaton chain of command," she said with a dry mouth. "What was it like for you the first time you kissed somebody else?"

"A big zero. I kept thinking that you were kissing somebody, somewhere."

"I know. It was the same for me." She didn't add *until I met Paul.*

"I missed your look." He kissed her hand, palm up, knowing she loved that. "I never realized how much I liked it until you dumped me. I hope you didn't give it to anybody else."

"I didn't do it on purpose if I did, and I didn't dump you. That's an awful way to put it." She knew that was precisely what she'd done.

"Anyway, that little look makes me want to kiss you every time you do it," he said. She did it again with a great giggle. He reached for her. "Pucker up, woman. You asked for it." Spencer leaned against the horn as it happened.

The carhop appeared mid-kiss. "Do you want something or not?" she asked, arms folded.

"Nope, I've got everything I need now," Spencer said, coming up for air.

"I don't like this," Trina said, tiptoeing her way down the cross-ties on the track.

Jemma stretched out her arms and balanced on the rails. "You'll get used to it."

"Why can't we just walk in the street like other people?"

"I like the tracks," Jemma said. "They give you direction and security."

"Security? Girl, you've got a screw loose. We could get smushed like bugs on here."

"Tracks are wings. They can carry you off into the blue." Jemma demonstrated her theory.

Trina peered down the rails. "Most people use a plane for that."

Jemma wasn't listening anymore. She was dancing and humming a French song she'd learned at Helene's. They shot some baskets, then went to play board games with Carrie. On the way home, they were making good time until Jemma took a seat on the rail. The wind picked up, lifting her hair from her shoulders.

Trina reluctantly sat next to her. "Now what?"

"I'm waiting for the 3:37." Jemma pushed wisps of hair out of her eyes.

"You're crazy if you think I'm gonna sit here and wait for a train to come, girl. What if you get your foot caught or you faint or something?"

"I won't," Jemma said, putting her ear to the rail.

"Okay; this is weird. I read a story once about robbers who listened to the metal so they could tell exactly when a train was on its way," Trina said. "Is that your plan?"

"Yes. Now you're an accomplice because you know my secret."

"See, you're cuckoo. C'mon, I've got work to do for Mama."

They walked to the elm tree row and parted. Trina started down the trail to her house. She looked back and smiled at Jemma, who stood with her face to the sun and her eyes closed, dancing again. Spencer was in her life.

Some nights Spencer sat in Papa's car house with her while she painted. He read or did paperwork for his apprenticeship. Whatever else he was supposed to be doing, he mostly just watched her paint and she loved it. They usually ended up shooting baskets under the lights at the tennis courts, then eating something fried at Son's. It was in the war that Son Shepherd claimed to have invented the *spork,* a cross between a fork and a spoon, for General MacArthur. It had become the logo for Son's Drive In—a giant spork, flashing in red neon.

"Jem, you know that I love you or else I wouldn't let you eat in my new car," Spencer said.

"Yeah, me and ten other girls," she said, making a face at him.

"Why do you always say things like that?"

She shrugged. "Because it's true. Everybody in this town can't wait to tell me about your love life."

"I needed to keep my mind off you, but that's all it ever was. I'm still your Candy Man, if you'll have me. I can wait as long as it takes for you to love me like you used to."

"I can never love you like I used to," she said like an ignoramus. "People change, love changes; there's always the test of time."

"My love has stood the test."

Spence was staring her down and she knew it. He was like a faithful old dog that wouldn't stay put if you drove thirty miles away to drop him off in the next county, but that was part of his charm.

"Do you mind if we go up to The Hill?" he asked. "Just to talk."

He started the Corvette and every head at Son's turned. It was The Car in town. Even Son, burger flipper in one hand and cigar in the other, stood in the doorway to watch them leave.

When they pulled up to their old parking space on The Hill, heads turned again, then went back to their business. A breeze moved the warm night air and Jemma fanned at a mosquito. Spence caught her hand in mid-flight and held it. "I want to make you a deal like the one you made me at the river."

"Always the car salesman," she said, but with a touch of nerves.

"Just listen and stop being so sarcastic. You're not Sandy."

She pretended to focus her attention on a white mare grazing in the pasture just over the barbed wire fence. Spencer turned her chin.

"Jem, I love every single thing about you, even your temper. When you get tired of fooling yourself that you can find someone who'll love you more, I'll still be waiting for you. I want you to know that I'm keeping the promise that we made in the eighth grade. All the dating and all the good times, that's all they are. If we get married, it will be even more special to me."

She drew back, wide-eyed. "I'm keeping it, too. Did you think I wouldn't? Good grief!"

He had the same look the night she broke up with him. "All I ask is that you give me a chance to win you back before next spring. That's my deal. What do you say?"

Jemma was thirteen again, playing Spin the Bottle at Fountie Clark's birthday party. Spence did have a way with words, so she blinked and did the only thing she could do. She leaned over the gearshift knob and kissed him with more affection than she originally intended.

"I keep it in mind," she whispered.

Spencer held her face in his hands, backing up his deal with warm kisses that Jemma had known and loved since the seventh grade.

CHAPTER TWELVE

Common Ground

Lizbeth carried the basket through the chest-high Johnson Grass and up to the railroad right-of-way. Train tracks made her nervous ever since she and Cam lost a milk cow on them years ago. The silly thing had wandered through a downed fence and ended up dead, a mile away on the tracks. She had yelled like a banshee the first time she saw Jemmabeth dancing on these tracks, but the child would have her way, claiming some foolishness about dancing to make the trains come. That prompted Lizbeth to memorize the schedule, just to be safe. Now she made sure of solid footing before taking a step. She surveyed the small houses and shacks facing the tracks. One, in particular, stood out from the rest. Petunias lined the dirt path to the unpainted house. She made her way to the sign that Jemma had told her about and knocked on the door.

"Yes ma'am?" A large woman smiled through the screen door. "You got some ironin'?"

"Hello. I'm Jemmabeth's grandmother, Lizbeth."

"Mercy, Miz Forrester. What a surprise. Come on in and make yourself to home." Willa pulled out a chair from the small kitchen table and unplugged her iron.

Lizbeth looked around. The room was dense with the smell of starch and damp fabric. "I thought you might like these," she said and set the basket of plums on the table. "They are from our old home place."

"Why, bless your heart," Willa said. "I know your home place. My man and me worked it a few times. Jemma took us out to your creek on a ride just the other day. These plums will make good eatin'."

"They're good for cobbler and jellies, too," Lizbeth said.

Willa wiped her forehead with her apron. "There's nothin' like a cobbler to make a place smell good."

Lizbeth nodded, noting the stack of ironing to be done. "You must keep busy with your business."

"Ain't much business to it. Sure don't take no brains to speak of," Willa said.

"Jemma told me that you are fond of petunias. My husband, Cameron, was, too."

"Yes, ma'am. The old style ones. My Mama worked for The Judge for a good long while, and tended his 'tunias, too. The Judge don't cotton much to things that's cheerful, so he had 'em dug up. She chewed him out real good and told him she'd take 'em home, and that's what we got now. Mama never was afraid to speak her mind. The 'tunias are doing real good this year. I seen your house and it looks like a picture book."

A fly buzzed across the table and both of them took a swat at it.

"Would you like a Dr. Pepper?" Willa asked. "Jemma brought me some. I gotta hide 'em from the neighbor kids." Willa reached behind a washtub, pulled out a bottle, and emptied it into two small jelly glasses. "Sorry it ain't cold and we ain't got one of them freezers to keep ice. How 'bout we go sit out on the porch, Miz Forrester. That might cool us off." Willa grabbed her cane. "There ain't no breeze in here today, but sometimes a stray one will come along outside."

"Please call me Lizbeth," she said, holding the door. "Would you look at that? I haven't seen rope bottom chairs since I was a girl."

"They're sturdy as a boot, too. They gotta be strong to hold up this old caboose." Willa laughed. "My man and his pap used to make 'em to sell in Amarillo."

"Is that so? I wish I'd known that. My father made them, too, when we lived in the hill country. Have you ever been to that part of Texas?"

"Law no, Miz Lizbeth, I ain't never been past Amarillo or Red Mule. I bet you miss them hills."

"I do, but of course Cam and I have lived in Connelly County so long that it seems like home. How about your family?"

Willa tapped the porch post with her cane. "I was born in this house in 1927. My pap and his brother built it, and it took them near three year to get it done. My mama and pap come from Georgia. Their folks was plantation workers, but my husband's family come down here from way back in Harlem."

"New York?" Lizbeth asked.

"Yes ma'am. My husband's pap was a Buffalo Soldier in France— they was all colored boys, you know, then he come home and hauled his family clean across to Texas. I'm thinkin' his money run out in Chillaton," Willa said. "No other reason to stop on this windy stretch."

"I've heard of those Buffalo Soldiers," Lizbeth said. "They did themselves proud. I surely do like your daughter. Is she your only child?"

"Yes ma'am. Latrina's daddy got hisself killed way over to It'ly. That's his picture there on the wall. He was a Buffalo Soldier, too, with the 92nd Infantry. His mama named him Samuel but we called him Sam."

"I'm so sorry," Lizbeth said, looking at the military issue photo much like her own boys' pictures.

"That's all right. I done cried a creek full of tears over losin' him, but he's gone to a better place. He was a righteous man, that one. Jemma told us that you've plumb near lost all your menfolk, too."

"Yes," Lizbeth said. "We had three boys, all good sons, and we raised my baby sister, too. My oldest boy is buried in Italy and his brother rests in Africa. Only Jemma's daddy is left. His name is James, Jimmy to me."

"That's gotta be a powerful pain, what with your husband gone now. He was always more than fair when our folks worked the fields for him."

"I'm not sure I'm up to it sometimes," Lizbeth said, smoothing her cotton dress over her knee.

"I know the feelin'," Willa said. "I get the blues real bad sometimes, but I believe the good Lord give womenfolk the backbone to carry heavy loads. That's what my mama always held with. She said men take to hidin' behind the bottle or the barn when they got troubles coming down around them."

"What do you suppose she meant about the barn?" Lizbeth asked.

Willa's brow creased. "I reckon she was talkin' about workin' themselves to the bone. How did your man handle hisself when you lost your boys?"

"The barn. He wasn't a drinking man. He farmed until he had a heart attack, then he kept busy with his flowers and birdhouses from dawn to dusk after we moved into town. He never stopped."

"Was he a serious man?"

"Goodness no. He was a talker and a joker, too, but very

spiritual."

"Yes, ma'am, I figgered that. How'd he pass?"

Lizbeth twisted her wedding band. "He came in the kitchen gray-faced and perspiring one morning while I was making biscuits. He made it to the refrigerator and got some nitroglycerin tablets to put under his tongue, then he passed out. He never came to, so I didn't get to say good-bye. I think the last thing he heard from my lips was a scream, and I do hate that."

"Well, where he is now, it don't matter about that, Miz Forrester. The Lord don't want us dwellin' on them things. My goodness, how did you hold up under such a lot of grief?"

"I tend to sweep my sorrows under the rug and go on," Lizbeth said quietly.

"To my way of thinkin', folks need to lay open their hearts until all that sadness and misery is spilled out so they can move on with livin'. It's gotta get out of you one way or another, so that it don't eat you up like the devil that it is. I've seen too much of that in my day. Coloreds and whites chewin' on this and that until that's all they think about. Just listen to me, I might as well get me a pulpit." Willa slapped her leg and laughed.

Lizbeth smiled. "There's a lot of sense in what you are saying. Jemma told me that you are a wise woman."

"That Jemma. I don't know when I've enjoyed anybody's company as much as your grandbaby. She's got a good heart and a gift straight from Heaven. Them paintings beat all I ever seen. Why, some of 'em are better than real life. My Trina and her sure are havin' themselves a time. I figger there's folks on both sides of the tracks wonderin' why them two parade around town like there's nothin' funny about it. Good thing is, they don't seem to care. What do you say about it, Miz Forrester?"

"I say it's high time. If I would have stepped across that silly track years ago and met your mama and bought a chair from your father-in-law, we'd all be the better for it."

"Well, yes, that's the truth, ain't it? I guess you and me are just little specks when it comes to the whole country. We can't undo what happened up to now," Willa said. She tapped her cane and they watched as a butterfly lit on the lavender petunias nearest the porch, its wings opening and closing over the blooms.

"Do you ever wish you could visit your husband's grave?" Lizbeth asked.

"Yes ma'am, I reckon I'd like that. I'd just like to reach out and touch it. It'd be a comfort to say a proper prayer over it, too."

"That would be nice. I don't think my Cam wanted to see our boys' graves. We didn't talk about it much, but I think that's why he wanted them buried where they died so it wouldn't ever be final, like it was a dream and they could walk in the door and we could hug them again. It's my opinion that funerals and cemeteries give us someplace to go and know it's real."

"I know it's real 'cause I got that old yeller letter in there from the gov'ment," Willa said.

"I have too many things like that in my soldier box." Lizbeth covered her eyes as a big dust devil blew down the road. "It's really just an old trunk that Cam and I had. It was his mother's, but when we lost the boys, I couldn't bear to see anything that belonged to them, so we put all of it in there. One day I got out their Purple Hearts to polish them, and from then on, I felt like I was doing something. Where do you keep yours?"

"What's that, Miz Forrester?"

"Your husband's Purple Heart."

Willa shrugged. "He didn't get no heart that I know of."

"That's odd. The Purple Heart is a military medal given for being wounded or worse," Lizbeth said.

"I don't know nothin' about no hearts. I just got that old ugly letter, and a chain with his name on a piece of metal." Willa's voice trailed off.

Lizbeth frowned. "That makes no sense."

"They's lots of things I don't understand in this world. I reckon my man had to die way across the ocean so Latrina could go to college."

"That doesn't make you miss him any less," Lizbeth said.

"No, ma'am, it don't. That man could make me laugh until I was fixin' to pop. He was a dancer too. I wasn't as big as a barn back in them days, and we did cut ourselves a rug on the dance floor." Willa's eyes crinkled up.

"Jemma moves around like silk when she's dancing," Lizbeth said. "Of course our church isn't real big on dancing, even now, but that child has a mind of her own."

"Well, I figure the good Lord wants us to dance or he wouldn't have give us Elvis." Willa tossed her head back and howled with laughter, and Lizbeth couldn't help but join her.

"I've had such a good time visiting with you, Willa. Let's do this more often. We have a lot in common, you know, despite our age difference. Now I hope that you'll come over and visit me sometime." Lizbeth rose and extended her hand.

Willa clasped it and smiled. "That's mighty nice of you to invite me. I appreciate the plums, too."

"I mean it. Please come over and I'll show you around Cam's garden. Maybe you can give me some advice because I'm no flower gardener."

"It takes me a good while to get around, but I'll come. I like puttin' a face to your name, Miz Forrester."

"Call me Lizbeth."

"Yes, ma'am, Miz Forrester," Willa said. "I'll sure try."

CHAPTER THIRTEEN

Silver

Jemma dried her hands on the dishtowel and grabbed the phone. She said hello a few times.

"Jemma? It's Helene here. How are you, dear? Just a moment, these horrid hearing aids are ringing in my ears. I'm missing you terribly, and telephone chats just won't do. I would like to visit your little village, but I want to consult with your Gram before proceeding any further."

"Great! We would love to see you."

"Now, I insist that you tell her every meal is to be dined out, and I shall stay in a hotel. There you have it."

"Okay, I'll be right back." Jemma found Lizbeth sitting under the pecan tree. At her news, Lizbeth stood, ready to receive Helene at that very moment. Jemma ran back to the phone. "Come as soon as you can because we can't wait."

"That's lovely. I shall get my ticket and be there next weekend, if all goes well."

"It will." Jemma beamed. "We'll have fun."

"I want to meet Lester, and I do hope he will have some stories for me."

"Lester is never without stories. If nothing else, just ask him about trains."

"Ah, a railway man. Lovely. Now, can you make arrangements for my hotel room?"

"We haven't had a hotel in Chillaton since the thirties, Helene."

"No? Then there must surely be one of those motor hotels," Helene said.

"A motel? We have one called 'That'll Do.'"

"What do you mean by that?" Helene asked.

"I mean that's the name of the motel. You might as well give up, because we want you to stay with us. Gram has a guest room waiting for you. If you stay at That'll Do, you'll be all alone."

"Such an odd name for a guest house. Are you certain it won't be an imposition?"

"I'm certain," Jemma said.

"I suppose that will do, then. Good-bye, dear. I'll call back with the schedule."

Jemma suppressed a giggle at Helene's unintended play on words. "Good-bye. See you soon."

The great silver engine creaked and moaned its way to a stop. The Zephyr, like mercury halted in a hasty rise on a thermometer, waited impatiently for Helene to disembark. The smell of hot metal and well-oiled mechanisms permeated the air. The conductor put out a little step, then offered his hand to Helene, who was dressed as though she were meeting The Queen. Her silver hair was done up in a French twist and her cerise linen suit was somehow unwrinkled. Her pearls and emerald earrings lent a decidedly regal tone to the station. Jemma wrapped her arms around her. The conductor set Helene's baggage on the platform and signaled to the brakeman. The Zephyr disappeared down the tracks.

Helene held Jemma back by her shoulders. "Let me look at you. Good. You are happy and it shows. That sets my mind at ease."

"I'm much better than the last time you saw me," Jemma said.

"Nothing could make me happier. Now, I must meet your Gram straightaway." Helene peeked around Jemma to spy Lizbeth.

Jemma introduced them, her two favorite silver-haired women. They hit it off, and she followed them around the rest of the day. Lizbeth and Helene went over each of her paintings, comparing observations. By nightfall, Helene had spent more time with Lizbeth than with Jemma. She insisted they go out for supper, and took it as great fun that the only place for a sit-down meal was the truck stop. Lester came over later for pie and coffee. He had his eye on Helene because he wasn't quite sure what to make of an Englishwoman in the house. He was quiet, but Helene had a good memory.

"I am quite fond of the railways," she announced. "In England, they were our main method of transport. I lived just outside London, but I once rode five hours to see my cousin in northwest Wales. It was lovely to chat with all sorts of travelers and see the countryside without the bother of a motorcar."

Lester shifted in his chair. "Well, sir, I reckon I know a thing or two about trains."

"Oh, and how's that, Lester?" Helene asked.

"I worked for fifty year down to the station. I done everything from sweepin' up to sellin' tickets. I know the Burlington Route like it was the back of my hand. I even rode me some rails when I was a young'un. I took boxcars out to California and back, then all the way to Chicago. I caught me another line that went to New York City itself. I must have been on one train or another for two weeks, give or take a day."

"How clever of you," Helene said, giving him her full attention. "Those must have been adventurous times."

Lester tapped his foot. "It was just life on the rails."

"Do give us an example," Helene said.

"Well sir, first thing that come upon me was just about Grants, New Mexico. I seen this right nice lookin' woman in a boxcar by herself, so when the train stopped, I figgered I might as well have me some company. I hopped in her car and I was doin' my best to be friendly and all, but then she come hence to moanin'. I figgered her for a gypsy fortuneteller or somethin', and I give considerable thought to gettin' out of there. There ain't much to slow up a freighter across New Mexico, though, if you know what I mean. Of course, I walked all over France and there weren't much happenin' there neither, except the Big War."

"So, this young lady was not amusing?" Helene asked.

"Well, sir, somethin' was going haywire because she worked herself up into a tizzy, then got kind of quiet-like. I thought maybe it was over. I give her a quick look, and I'll be Uncle Johnny if she wasn't sittin' the corner like a bullfrog. She let out a coyote howl, and the next thing I knew, she was holdin' a young'un and wipin' it down with her skirt. Beat all I ever saw. She just looked at me and grinned. I come hence to sweatin' and shakin' all over. That seemed to tickle her funny bone because she was laughin' and that baby was wailin'." Lester shook his head. "My ma had a similar story when she was in a family way. She'd been cleanin' out the chicken pen and it struck her to pay a visit

110

to the outhouse—no offense, ladies. We had us a two-holer just in case things got busy. Not many folks had a two-holer in them days."

Helene's eyes widened, and Lizbeth hid her smile behind her coffee cup.

"Ma took a seat, but come hence to feeling woozy. She decided to sit on the floor until she got her bearings. That's when I come into this world, smack-dab on the floor of the two-holer. Ma said she reckoned she'd about had enough young'uns when they started droppin' in the outhouse. I figger I'm a lucky man because if I'd come a few seconds earlier, I could've been at the bottom of the two-holer instead of eatin' this fine custard pie with you ladies. Now, back to my rail-ridin' days."

"Helene, let me refresh your coffee," Lizbeth said.

"How about some more pie?" Jemma asked.

Helene got the picture. "Lester, thank you for sharing these fascinating bits of history with us." She stifled a laugh.

"I've got plenty more, ma'am, whenever you're ready." Lester took a chance and winked at the Englishwoman.

⋙ ⋘

No matter if company was in town, Nedra wouldn't change a long-standing appointment. So, Jemma took Helene for a drive while Lizbeth was getting pumped for information as she got her hair done. Helene was interested in the farms, asking questions and taking photos. "Parts of this country remind me somewhat of the moors in England. Nevertheless, I am sure that working the land gives one a different perspective."

"I know that my Papa loved it," Jemma said, "He believed farming was a kinship among the earth, the forces of nature, and the wisdom and labor of the farmer."

"Nicely put." Helene looked out at the rows of struggling, dry land cotton.

"We also have some big cattle ranches around here," Jemma said as she turned away from the farmland and took the road to the sprawling Bar C Ranch, which belonged to Spencer's family.

"Jemma, have you heard from Paul?" Helene asked.

It took her a few seconds to answer. "He writes me every week, but I won't read letters from a married man."

"I am quite puzzled concerning that revelation," Helene said. "You were openly dating, dear. It was no shady tête-à-tête. Although he did strike me as a man who was familiar with the art of romance."

Jemma swallowed. "I'm glad to be here now. I love being with Gram and living in my hometown. I have discovered people that have been here all my life and I never knew them, and, of course, I have Spencer."

"I see." Helene looked out at the vast acres of sagebrush and mesquite trees. "Does Spencer expect to share the hope chest with you?" Helene continued to observe the scenery since her question went unanswered. The ranchland gave way to farmland and soon they were back on the streets of Chillaton.

Jemma parked the car in front of Nedra's Nook and toyed with the steering wheel. "Spencer loves me."

Helene adjusted her hearing aid and took Jemma's hand. "And how do you feel towards him?"

"I feel safe and happy, like it's going to be blue skies forever around him. That sounds silly, I guess."

"On the contrary, dear," Helene said. "It sounds like love."

Jemma opened the door. "I'll be right back. I think Gram wants to show you the old home place."

Helene touched her shoulder. "Do be mindful of the suffering heart, Jemma. You mustn't become a passage for pain in your indecision."

Jemma nodded. How could she cause him pain? He was still her Candy Man.

❧ ❧

For a while, Jemma sat in the car sketching the two women as they strolled through the field. She decided to walk up a small rise and make other sketches of the place while Lizbeth and Helene continued to meander around, talking. They made an interesting pair because Lizbeth loomed over the diminutive Helene.

"This is where you lived during the war?" Helene asked.

"Yes. When all of them were overseas, I'd sit at the south window and listen to the wind moaning through the cottonwoods. It was the same window where I watched for their school bus every day when they were little. See the windmill near the house? The boys played many summers in the shade of it." She smiled. "Once, they tied a rope from the platform at the top down to the fence below and rigged up a washtub with my baby sister in it. I can still hear her squealing as she slid down. Those three boys were full of the dickens."

Helene shaded her eyes. "I'm sure that you felt cheated when they died. I know I would have."

"My Cameron kept up a brave front for the both of us. He took a stand that our boys died in a noble cause. I supported that, and I wanted to believe it, but they were so far from home and very young. I just wanted to hold them one more time. I know that mothers all over the world felt that pain."

"This is not much consolation, Lizbeth, but my family suffered through the London Blitz. Many Europeans wondered what took America so long to get involved in the war, but my father said, 'Be patient. Liberty will call America to battle as it did her forefathers, then she will fight with extraordinary vigor because her people burn with freedom.' He was right, just look at your sons. No one in my generation will ever forget the sacrifice made by them and our own British boys in those horrid wars."

Lizbeth stopped. "Thank you for those words. They were fine young men with high hopes for the future, but I believe that in God's Great Plan, they were born to be warriors in the name of freedom."

"Well said, my friend." Helene took Lizbeth's arm in hers and they walked down a turn row.

"Now tell me about Mr. Neblitt," Lizbeth said.

It was Helene's turn to smile. "I called him Nebs. You know we English love our nicknames. I think he was much like your husband— very outgoing, full of energy, ideas, mischief, and quite the romantic. We traveled extensively because of his profession. He was a freelance geologist for a consortium of oil companies, and quite successful. Nebs died the same day that he suffered a massive stroke, poor darling. To my deep regret, we had no children. I know he would have been a good father, but part of it was our own fault. We kept postponing the decision to have children at all. Then, when we decided we could drag the little things around the world with us, I couldn't seem to get pregnant."

The women rested on an old cedar bench that Cameron had built and placed under an elm tree so he could eat his lunch and look out over the crops. It was in good shape to have endured so many Panhandle winters.

Lizbeth ran her hand along the wood. "Do you have family still in England?"

"Sadly, they are all gone. My grandfather was a Member of Parliament and my father was the British diplomat to France. I grew up in Paris, but after his retirement, we took up residence near London. You know, Jemma is rather taken with the French language. Like her, it is beautiful—so expressive and romantic."

"Did you know this Turner fellow?" Lizbeth asked.

"Evidently, I did not know him well enough. His family is quite upstanding in the community, and I simply cannot believe that he would have been having a lurid affair with Jemma. He was very much the charmer, that one, and oh, so splendid on the eyes. She seems content now with her friend, Spencer."

Lizbeth smiled. "You'll have to meet him. Spencer is the kind of young man that you want for your daughter. He's like a member of our family. Everyone thought that they would marry some day, and I know he loves that girl. I pray that she is not giving him false hope."

Helene looked towards the little knoll where Jemma sat, intent on her work, and seemingly unaware of their presence. "She is a rare child who will become well-known for her art, Lizbeth. We shall see her work in New York, Paris, and London galleries."

Lizbeth raised her brow. "My, my. Well, as I said, I do believe that the good Lord has a plan for all of us. It will be a true pleasure to see Jemmabeth succeed. She has brought such joy to her family and friends."

"I believe joy follows the child around," Helene said, still watching her.

"And joy sometimes follows pain," Lizbeth added.

⮞⮜

Helene's last day included a tour of The Boulevard and a visit to meet Carrie, who played several classical pieces, finishing with the two of them in an impromptu duet. Their next stop was Willa's, where they lingered for an hour on the porch while Helene laughed until she cried at the irrepressible wit and wisdom of Willa.

Lizbeth declared it would be an insult if Helene didn't allow her to prepare just one home-cooked meal; therefore, supper was a feast. She pulled out all the stops to show off some real Texas cooking. Jemma invited Spencer, and Helene was very much taken with him. They talked on and on about Europe and architecture. Spencer was buoyant. His family never talked with him about things close to his heart.

"What are your plans after you graduate?" Helene asked.

"I'd like to work in a large city, but live in a small town, like Chillaton. Sometimes I think it would be great to work in Europe, too," he said, glancing at Jemma.

She knew his plans backward and forward, and truly believed that his love for architecture began when they played with blocks in the first grade. Spencer could talk all the kids out of their blocks then build something that would prompt Mrs. Hardin to stop the class and have everybody look at it and clap. He was the smartest and most motivated person she had ever known. Somehow Jemma had ended up in his heart and she knew it was a sweet place to be.

"You're my hero, Spence," she said as they washed the dishes.

"C'mon, don't mess with me. Since when did you think that?"

"Since the first grade. Girls always say you are so cute, but I know your heart, my handsome, Candy Man hero. They know you're cute but only hope that you're sweet, too. That's the way girls think."

"So, you don't think like most girls?"

"Nope. You should know that." She put a dab of dishwater bubbles on his nose.

He wiped it off. "It's because you've had cowboy fever all your life. It's weakened your brain."

"Don't start," she said and flicked a handful of suds at him, giggling.

He hit her with the dishtowel and it was a standoff around the kitchenette.

"Let's finish this conversation in the hollyhock patch," she said and ran out the door into the night.

In the living room, Helene was ready for more Lester. "You know, Lester, there is something about you that reminds me of my husband. He had the same silver hair, but it's something about your eyes. Of course Nebs had a moustache, always did. How is it that you remain a single gentleman?" she asked.

Lester basked in the compliment. Maybe his foolhardy wink had paid off. "Well, I had me some fine womenfolk in my time. Now I just go around doin' good deeds here for Miz Liz. I figure it's worth it just to get a smile out of her, and that's all I'm askin' in my old age."

Lizbeth sniffed.

"Do you have children?" Helene asked.

Lester scratched his ear. "No, ma'am, never did. I reckon the good Lord figured on me bein' a husband several times over and havin' no time for young'uns. I had me some good dogs, though. Had me a mutt named Floyd that could gather eggs from the hen house."

Lizbeth, being well acquainted with farm chores, snickered at that notion.

Lester leaned forward in his seat. "I ain't jokin'. Most folks used to keep hens and a milk cow no matter what they did for a livin', even here in town. When I'd get up of a mornin', I'd set me a basket by the hen house door and by noon Floyd would have her filled up. Now you may think old Lester's full of beans, but I wagered a buddy of mine that Floyd could do it, so we spied on him. He wiggled the latch on the door until it come open, then in he went and sure enough, a few minutes later out he came holdin' a egg just as gentle as you please, between his teeth. He did it over and over until the basket was full."

"Did Floyd milk the cow, too?" Lizbeth asked.

"No, Miz Liz, not in his youth, but as he come hence to losin' his teeth, he give 'er a try a few times," Lester said, tapping his foot and grinning.

❧ ❧

Helene insisted she had things to do in Wicklow that couldn't wait, so she bought a ticket on the 6:23 Zephyr. Jemma hugged her tight. "Promise you'll come back to see us."

"How could I refuse such delightful company? Thank you, Lizbeth, for your lovely hospitality and companionship," Helene said. "Jemma, I dreamt that I saw your work in a London gallery."

Jemma laughed. "That would be a miracle. I love you, Helene, and you are always in my prayers."

The Zephyr roared into the station and screeched to a halt. Helene read the name on the silver engine and turned to Jemma. "Do you know the meaning of *Zephyr*, my dear?"

"No ma'am. I never thought about it," Jemma said.

"It means a west wind, something that just passes through, much like a summer romance."

Jemma nodded, staring at the metallic letters. Helene blew a kiss and boarded the train. Jemma bit her lip. Okay, so the definition might be appropriate, but this Zephyr didn't smell like English Leather and it didn't have eyes like…a big rat. Get over it, carry on.

CHAPTER FOURTEEN

Old Moves

"Have you ever had a boyfriend?" Jemma asked as she got Carrie ready for the cannon.

"I did," she said, "in the first grade. His name was Fountie Clark. I claimed him as mine when he swallowed the class goldfish the first day of school. Why are you asking me about boyfriends? You must have somebody in mind for me that had polio, too. Maybe he and I could line up our circus cannons and stare at each other."

"Stop it. If you get out into the world, you'll find love," Jemma said.

"Ah, but will it be true love, the kind you're still whining about?" Carrie asked. "I thought true love is what we watch on *As the World Turns* every day."

"What *you* watch," Jemma said.

Carrie spoke now in regulated gasps as the iron lung did its work. "So, you really think that some pitiful guy could fall in love with me?"

Jemma wagged her finger at Carrie. "Not a pitiful guy. He would be your Prince Charming. I don't see how it can happen in Chillaton as long as your father hides you in this house."

"I know."

"Maybe I'll talk to your father sometime," Jemma said.

Carrie smiled. "You're nuts."

Jemma smoothed Carrie's hair. "Nah, I just don't like it when people aren't fair."

The cannon took over the conversation for a while.

"Why do you keep fighting the fact that you've found your true love?" Carrie asked.

"I don't know. I need a big sign to come down from Heaven that says HE'S THE ONE."

"You're not fair to Spencer."

"You need to be quiet now." Jemma turned off the lights and moved to the window. A stray cat sat in the light from the streetlamp, then jumped up to capture a moth. It played with it for a few seconds, then moved on down the dark Boulevard, leaving the moth to flail hopelessly on the ground. Jemma chewed on her lip; she was not being unfair to Spence. Carrie just didn't understand.

❦

The static on the line always gave her away. "Sandy?" Jemma asked.

"Hey, Jem, how are things in good old Chillaton? Twila told me that you and Spence are going out again. That's the best news I've heard."

"We're having fun. How are y'all doing?" Jemma asked, flopping back on the good bed.

"All Marty talks about is Vietnam. Did Spence go for the cowboy hat idea? Is that what changed your mind?"

"I didn't fall for Paul's clothes."

"Really. Well, that's behind you anyway."

Jemma hesitated. "I guess."

"Hold it right there," Sandy said. "The guy was married."

"My head knows that, but my heart is still a little tender in that department."

Sandy's tone changed. "You'd better not hurt Spencer again."

"See? I'm in trouble if I don't go out with Spence and I'm in trouble if I do," Jemma said.

"What does he know about Paul?" Sandy asked, but received no answer. "I see. Just as much as your parents know. Buddy said that you have a new friend."

"Yeah, Trina Johnson. You'd like her."

"You relish the gray area, don't you? Always ready to dispense Jemma justice."

"That's not it at all. I hate the fact that Gram's house was so close to Trina and her family all this time, but I never knew or cared about them. She's funny, talented, wise, and a good person. They've had a hard life, Sandy."

"Do you think Chillaton is ready for that kind of thinking?"

"It had better get ready. Anyway, remember The Judge's house that you always wanted to skip at Halloween? I'm working for him now, as a sort of companion to his daughter. She's smarter than anybody in our class, except Spence, of course, and you should hear her play the piano. She's another one that I should have taken more interest in. I was too wrapped up in myself in high school."

"We all were, Jem. You don't have a corner on guilt. I assume you're still painting. Are you going back to Le Claire?"

"Next fall," Jemma said, "or Daddy will kill me."

"I wish we could come home for Christmas. Just pray they don't send Marty to Vietnam because we are hearing horror stories about that place. Gotta go. Say hi to Spence for me. Love you."

"Love you, too." Jemma hung up the phone and sat on the side of the bed, thinking about Mr. and Mrs. Turner. Good grief.

❧ ❧

The Parnell actually had a line at the ticket window. It was their first showing of *Torn Curtain*. Paul Newman had a following around Chillaton ever since *Hud* was filmed just down the road. Jemma and Sandy had stood around the *Hud* set so long that he walked right by them—after they got out of his way. His eyes were the same sky blue as Carrie's.

The theater was built just before the Depression, not grand by any means, but it had a certain flair that Jemma liked. The maroon floral carpet was now worn and the beveled snack bar mirror had a small crack down one side. The signs that read *coloreds* and *whites only* had been removed from the restrooms, water fountain, and the stairs leading to the balcony. The wallpaper was still vivid where the handmade notices had once hung. The only bad thing about the Parnell was that The Cleave's dad owned it.

After the movie, they sat on the hood of the Corvette and ate fries with their jackets on. The moon cast ribbons of light in the slow moving waters of the Salt Fork, and the stars were brilliant. One streamed across the sky.

"Make a wish," Spencer said.

Jemma crossed her fingers and held her breath.

"So, what was it?"

120

She held up a fry and lowered it into her mouth. "You can't ask that."

"Did it involve your Prince Charming?"

"Maybe you're my Prince Charming." She meant it to be funny, but looked at Spence, his blond hair ruffling in the breeze, then exhaled. "Okay. The guy's name was Paul. He was a law student in Dallas, and he was older than me." She bit her lip and turned away. She did not dare mention that he was a cowboy, of sorts.

"How much older?"

"About ten years."

"Ten?" His voice pierced the otherwise quiet night and bounced against the rocks. "You're in love with somebody over thirty?"

"I didn't say I am in love with him."

"What are you then?"

"I don't know, Spence. I don't want to talk about this anymore."

"You haven't anyway."

Jemma got off the car and walked to the riverbank. Spencer followed her, easing his arm around her waist. "I just want to know where I stand. Look at me, baby." Jemma stared at the ground instead. "I love you, Jemmabeth. If you are hurting, no matter the reason, it hurts me, too."

She put her arms around him, playing with the short hairs at the nape of his neck, and their muffled conversation mingled with the sounds of the Panhandle night. She had never felt so close to anyone.

❧ ❧

Dr. Huntley hadn't missed a day to check on Carrie. She only had a cold, but for her, that was major. Anxious to cheer her up, Jemma wanted to take her into the parlor just as the sun was making its way through the big windows. It was Jemma's favorite time of day and she wanted to share it.

"How was your nap? Do you feel any better?" she asked.

"Maybe," Carrie whispered.

"Do you feel like going downstairs?" Jemma asked.

"For five minutes." Carrie said.

Jemma strapped Carrie into the crawler, then lifted her into the downstairs wheelchair and rolled her into the parlor. "See how the shadows on the wall look like a leaf dance? The light plays with the wind and we get to watch. It's great."

"That was my dream," Carrie said, "to dance in the spotlight. I took lessons in Amarillo when I was only three years old. We saw the New York Ballet perform once and my mom said, 'Carrie, you'll be up there someday,' and I never forgot it. The room next to mine upstairs was my practice room. Dad even had a bar and mirrors installed, but of course the door is locked now. I've checked."

"Can you move your legs at all?" Jemma asked.

"A little, if I really concentrate."

"I suppose you've had all kinds of therapy."

"No," Carrie said. "Dad doesn't want me to be disappointed."

The rhythmic dance pattern faded before them. Jemma sketched as Carrie watched the final shadows. "I can still dance or I can even fly, Jem. It's all up to me and what I choose to put in my head."

Jemma kept drawing. "Do you ever wonder why this happened to you?"

Carrie shot her a look. "All the time. Miss Effie, Willa's mom, said it wouldn't change things to sit around and wonder why this or that, but she wasn't the one sitting in this chair. She'd say that the Lord's in charge and He knows what he's doing. He uses all of us for something."

Jemma quit drawing. "Has God used you?"

Carrie coughed. "I don't know. Miss Effie said we might go our whole lives and never figure that out. I read the Bible, but as you know, I don't get out much to apply what I learn. Miss Effie was my preacher, I guess, because I never go to church. Dad forbids it."

"Your dad has a lot of nerve. Maybe too much. Oh, yeah, I got you those books you wanted; hang on." Jemma was nearly to the doorway, but glanced over her shoulder. Carrie was still watching the wall, though the light had long left. In about ten minutes it would be time to get her into the cannon. Jemma sat on the floor and took out her sketch pad again. Her hand flew over several sheets of paper until Carrie wheeled up next to her.

"Where are the books?" Carrie asked, coughing. "You just can't get good help these days," she said with some effort, but sounding more like herself.

Jemma jumped up. "Sorry, I wanted to catch you in that light. I'll grab those books right now."

Carrie clutched Jemma's sleeve. "Just get me upstairs before I croak." Jemma took her up the stairs herself and put her in the cannon. Carrie closed her eyes. "You think you're Wonder Woman, don't you?"

"No, ma'am. I think you are," Jemma said, then called home. "Gram, I am going to stay with Carrie tonight. Please ask Spence to come over, if he can." She went back to the cannon, but Carrie was asleep, her breathing controlled by the lung.

Life wasn't fair. Maybe sometime she would have to sneak Carrie into church. The Judge had never told *her* that it was forbidden.

∞∞∞

They were the first ones in the church the very next Sunday. Carrie could not stop smiling through the service.

∞∞∞

Spencer and Jemma went to the Chillaton Homecoming celebration and danced every dance. The Buddy Baker band was, naturally, playing only Buddy Holly. The last dance was "True Love's Ways." Jemma put the Best Burger Stop out of her mind which was easy to do with Spencer holding her so close, but Buddy B had one more song.

"Ladies and gentlemen, I know you'll enjoy a little Roy Orbison to finish off the night, by special request," he said. As Buddy pulled out his harmonica, Spencer led her back onto the gym floor. Jemma knew what was up. He was not only a smooth talker, but Spencer was the smoothest dance partner she'd ever had. This song belonged to them in high school. Every time it was played, the floor cleared for Spencer and Jemma to strut their stuff. They had their own particular interpretation of the Chillaton Stomp, worked out in Jemma's living room when they were in junior high. Buddy belted out his version of "Candy Man," which wasn't too bad for a garage mechanic, amid wolf whistles and cheers. The old moves came back, and the eye contact they were giving each other was obvious to everybody in the gym. The crowd joined in, still giving them wide berth.

"You are in so much trouble, Spencer Chase, I mean big trouble," she shouted over the music. "How much did you pay him?"

"Just hush up and dance, so I can get my money's worth."

Jemma did love to dance with him. When the song was over, he held up her hand during the applause. Turning it palm up, he pressed it to his lips, looking her straight in the eye. She felt a lightning bolt shoot up her arm and straight into her stomach. Maybe he was The One.

CHAPTER FIFTEEN

Arizona

Something had bothered Jemma all night, then the call came at breakfast. "Hi, Sweet Pea." Her voice was all wrong.

"Mom, what's happened?" She paced around Gram's dresser as far as the cord would allow.

Alex sighed like she'd been up all night. "He's okay now, but your daddy fell off the roof and broke his leg. It's a bad break, so he'll be in the hospital a few days. He just had to get that silly Christmas star up before the Festival of Lights tour this weekend."

"Good grief! Can I talk to him?" Jemma asked.

"He's asleep, thanks to the pain medication," Alex said. 'We're lucky he didn't break his neck."

"I guess y'all won't be coming to Chillaton."

"I'm sorry, Jem You know we were looking forward to it. Robby is so disappointed. Now we're hoping you two could come here."

"I'm afraid the Dodge won't make it. Spence thinks it needs to go to the shop."

Alex sighed again. "Well, keep your chin up, honey. There'll be other Christmases. Let me talk to Gram. We love you."

Jemma gave the phone to Lizbeth, then slumped on the couch, tears welling up. She looked around the house. Spencer had bought a tree in Amarillo and they had spread soapflake snow on its branches. All but one of Papa's bubble lights were ready to shine in Robby's eyes.

She took the car to Chase's Cadillac & Chevrolet the next day. Buddy called her at The Judge's house with more bad news, which she relayed to Lizbeth. "It's going to cost at least seventy dollars to fix the Dodge," she said, "and the worst of it is that they have to order some part that will take a week to get here. Spencer already said he'd pay for it, but I'm scared it'll break down again."

"Help my life," Lizbeth said. "I guess we could ride the train, but that would cost more than the repair bill."

"What about the bus?" Jemma asked.

"I just got off the phone with them and there are no seats left. It's the holidays."

"Rats."

"We could go for New Years Day," Lizbeth said, half-heartedly.

"Maybe. I guess I'd better get off The Judge's phone. I'll see you later, Gram."

"You never know what the good Lord has in His plan for us, sugar," Lizbeth said.

During supper, the Lord's plan showed up at the back door. He was still in his suit.

"Come in this house, Spencer," Lizbeth said. "Have a bite to eat with us."

He was all smiles. "I have a proposal for you ladies. I would like to see Arizona this Christmas and I need some company."

Jemma squealed.

"I get off day after tomorrow and I'll be ready to hit the road if you are," he said.

The ladies each planted a big kiss on his cheek, like grateful bookends.

Lizbeth pulled out a chair. "Now, eat, son. That's the least we can do for you."

"What about your family?" Jemma asked, "Won't they be upset if you are gone for the holidays?"

"Mom is oblivious to the holidays, and Dad will be relieved he doesn't have to stay home on Christmas Eve, trust me," Spencer said.

"I do trust you," Jemma said, and kissed him on the lips while Lizbeth's back was turned. She grinned at him the rest of the evening. Everything about him was perfect, right down to his French aftershave.

❧❦

Flagstaff's mountains and pine trees surprised her. There was a dusting of snow on them at sunrise, so naturally, she went out in her pajamas and coat to sketch.

"You look cute in your jimmy-jams," Spencer said, sneaking out when she wasn't looking. "Mind if I watch you think?"

Jemma gave him a dirty look. "You aren't supposed to see me in my pajamas. Gram would have a fit."

"That coat is thick enough for a blizzard," he said, pulling her collar up around her ears. "I think you're safe in it."

"I wasn't expecting company. Missy told me that I had a bohemian look. What do you think?"

"Since when did you care what Missy says?"

"Since you went out with her more than I wanted to hear about."

"*Voila!* I've found the way to your heart. It's through The Cleave."

"Don't you dare try that route. Let's go in. I'm too cold to draw."

"Not until you give me a kiss, you bohemian."

"I haven't brushed my teeth yet."

"Me neither," he said, moving in closer.

She kissed him just as her mother opened the door.

"Good morning. Anybody out here want breakfast?" she asked.

"You bet," Spencer said and walked inside, holding Jemma's hand.

"Hmmm." Her mother raised her eyebrows a couple of times as Jemma passed by.

It was a lazy day. Lizbeth and Robby played dominoes and checkers while Jemma and Alex made pies. The men watched football in the den, with periodic wails and whoops.

"I know the time's going to fly and you will be on the road again," Alex said as they relaxed in the living room.

Jemma put her head in her mother's lap. "I miss you."

"I miss you too. By the way, that wasn't a sisterly kiss you gave Spence this morning," Alex said.

"True," Jemma said, "but don't draw any big conclusions from that. You know I have to love him in some way. It's just that I don't know if I love him above all others."

"You mean above Paul?" Alex mouthed his name.

"Mom, Paul made me wild inside, like my senses were starved or something. I think I loved him," she whispered, "but I never said it, even to myself."

"It was probably a physical attraction," Alex said. "That can be powerful at your age. You hadn't been attracted to anybody else in such a long time. Does Spencer know all about him?"

"I can't talk to Spence about that. I know he must feel about me the same way I felt about Paul."

"Felt?"

Jemma shrugged. "I haven't seen him in over four months. Maybe I need to see him again so I can sort things out."

"You haven't told me why you broke it off. Was there somebody else?" Alex asked.

Spencer appeared in the door. "I'm being sent out to get burgers."

Jemma jumped up, covered with guilt.

"That sounds great!" Alex said with gushy enthusiasm. "I'll set the table."

"So, what hot topic have you been chewing on?" Spencer asked as soon as Alex left the room.

"Girl talk," Jemma said, straightening the throw pillows. Spencer caught her as she turned and kissed her. Jemma's conscience made it a good one, too.

⤙🙢⤚

She knew that her daddy had questions. Talking to her mother was one thing, but she wasn't sure how she would hold up with him. He was a "look you in the eye" man. That's where she got it. Spencer offered to drive them around Flagstaff to see the Christmas lights, but Jemma stayed with Jim, to get it over with.

"I'm already tired of this cast," he said, laboring to sit on the couch. "Now, what's the deal with this Paul guy? Your mother and I thought you were going to call us any day and say you were bringing him to meet us and plan the wedding. The next thing we knew, you were calling from Chillaton to say you weren't going to school and you were going to live with Mama. Did this guy break your heart overnight?"

Jemma chose her words with great care. "There was another girl, a woman."

"I see. He was a jerk. Then what's going on with Spencer? You know that we love that boy. He may have money, but he's had no real love in his life, aside from us. I'm not saying that our feelings for him should make any difference to you, but he's a great kid and I don't want to see him hurt, especially by my own baby girl."

"I know." Jemma felt like she did when she was six years old and told the whole class that Eddie Parker had fleas, making Eddie cry and hide in the boys' bathroom.

"So, is Spence your boyfriend now?" Jim asked.

"I guess."

"Not much of an answer."

"I'm sorry, Daddy," she said. Then the tears came, but Jim was used to this. He handed her a box of tissues.

"Come over here," he said. She inched her way across the couch, not wanting to make his pain any worse. He put his arm around her. "Now, tell me why you left Wicklow like that."

Jemma could not bring herself to say the words that would send Mr. Turner straight into eternal fire as far as her daddy was concerned. "I just couldn't stay."

"How'd you give up your school? That was the biggest shock to me."

"I'm going back, Daddy, but not until next fall, if that's okay. I know y'all said for me to go back after Christmas. You should see all the paintings I've done, and I have made some really good friends in Chillaton. I think the Lord wanted me to go there." There she went again, using the Lord after the fact.

"Well, I know you've been good for Mama, too. I already heard about the change of plans for school, but back to Spencer. You're a good girl, honey, but I think you underestimate yourself when it comes to the effect you have on boys. You're just like your mother in that department, so you must use your power for good."

He shifted his leg with a moan. "When you played ball in high school, Digger Randall told me that he never worried about losing a close game. He just needed you to get the ball. All it took was just one good jumpshot from you and the game was in the bag. You were always in control. Second place at state wasn't your fault. Digger takes the blame for that one." He grinned at her with some amount of coaching pride. "The thing is, you are in control of more than just a game now. You have to watch out for Spencer's heart. Life is not a basketball game despite all the analogies we coaches like to draw from it. Remember that. Deal?"

Jemma exhaled. "Deal." She had escaped the third degree.

"Good. Now let's talk about something else. Tell me about these paintings you've been working on before these painkillers kick in, and I fall asleep."

She opened Spencer's gift and touched the gold Florentine heart; a diamond dazzled from its center. She laid her head against his chest.

Since he was a little boy, he had loved giving her things. "It's in the Etruscan style and diamonds are your birthstone," he said. "There's something on the back, too." He watched her face as she turned it over to see *Always* engraved there. "Don't forget that, baby."

He had endeared himself to her again. "Thank you so much, Spence. I love it, and I thank you for this trip." She kissed him before she had to choose any more words with such care. "Now open your present."

Spencer slipped off the wrapping paper and blinked at the painting inside.

"It's my first self-portrait as a grown-up," Jemma said, wrinkling her nose as she waited for his response. "Well, almost grown up. I've done some others, but nobody's ever seen them."

"You are an incredible artist," he said, shaking his head in disbelief at the painting. "I don't understand how you can do this."

"I do it because it is given to me. I don't know how."

"Could you marry me, Jem? This is not a formal proposal, but I need to know if it's even a possibility."

It was a solid hit to her heart. "Let's not do this tonight. I…don't understand my feelings for you right now." She was sorry as soon as she said it.

"Is there hope?"

Jemma could hear her daddy's words and she didn't know what to say. "Spence, I know that we could get married and live happily ever after, but I just don't want to marry anybody right now." There. That should buy her some time in this silly game she had created.

"Then promise that you will tell me when you are ready to marry—anybody. Promise?"

"Okay. I promise." She winced even as she said it.

They all played board games late. Lizbeth went to bed, but Robby was entranced with the model airplane kit that Spencer had given him.

"We'll take it out tomorrow, okay, Rob?" Spencer said.

"'Night, Jem. You, too, old man Chase." Robby yawned. "I like the plane."

Jim got up on his crutches. "Hey, I'm beat. Y'all excuse me, but my pain pills just took over again for the evening."

Alex drew Jemma and Spencer to her. "Merry, merry Christmas, you two."

Then they were left alone in the lights of the tree.

"Happy Christmas, baby," he said.

She put arms around him. "You too."

"Thanks for the portrait."

"I didn't just give it to you. I painted it for you. There's a difference." She touched his chin.

He tucked her hair behind her ear and kissed her neck. "Do you think they have a parking hill in Flagstaff?" he whispered.

"Probably, but why go out in the cold when we can just stay here?"

"You're right," he said, walking her backwards until her legs hit the couch. "Sit down, woman, and let's smooch until Santa comes."

Giggling, she did, and for a while, forgot her deal with her daddy.

⤫⤬⤫

Christmas morning, Robby flipped on the light and jumped on Jemma's bed with her stocking. "You got the fattest one." His red and white striped pajamas made him look like an electric candy cane in the bright light.

She sat up. "What time is it?"

"Almost six o'clock," Robby said, checking his new watch while he continued to jump.

"Good grief." Jemma flopped back on the pillow. "Can't we do this later? You're going to wake up Gram."

"She's already up, drinking coffee with Daddy." Robby crash-landed next to her. "You'll hurt Santa's feelings if you wait."

"The sun's not even up yet."

"C'mon, Jem. Please."

She tried to focus on the lumpy stocking in her lap as Robby crawled in bed with her. "Let's see," she said. "Here's an apple, and oh, look, an orange."

"I saw that apple on the dining table yesterday. See, it's got a dent in it right there."

She turned her sleepy eyes on him. "Hey, Santa put these in here. Who cares where he got them?" She pulled out a plaid tam with a pompon on top, matching scarf, red mittens, and a bottle of French perfume she'd never heard of before. "I bet you didn't see these on the dining room table yesterday,"

"No, but I saw Spence getting all of it out of his suitcase last night."

Jemma put on the tam. She used her best Scottish accent. "Did ya, now, my wee laddie? Well, goot. Did you see this a-coming, too?" She threw back the covers and tickled him until he couldn't breathe.

"Jem, stop! I gotta go to the bathroom," he said.

"You'd better run or I'm gonna get you again," she said, yawning.

Robby streaked out of the room and down the hall.

She turned off the light and got back in bed, hoping for sleep, but she got more little brother.

"So, how did God make the world?" he asked.

"Good grief, Robby. It's too early for this."

"My friend told me that He used electricity."

Jemma buried her face in the pillow. "Go back to sleep. You can stay in my bed if you want."

"Okay." He snuggled close to her. "You know what else? He said that God was just a teenager when the dinosaurs were alive."

Jemma cleared her throat. He lay still for a whole minute.

"Are you in love with Spence?" he asked. "I saw you kissing him last night."

"It's none of your snoopy business. Just let me sleep a little longer."

Robby covered his head with the sheet. "My girlfriend wants me to kiss her."

Jemma turned over and pulled the sheet back. "Who's this girlfriend?"

"Kimmy Sutton. She has short hair that goes all the way around her head like zurrrp." He made a halo around his head in the faint light. "She wears a different colored bow every day, and her hair is

132

yellow like Spence's. Mom says she's cute, plus she draws me pictures of monkeys. I'm going to get a real one someday."

Jemma laughed. "Girlfriend or monkey? What does Mom think about you kissing a girl?"

"Mom says kissing is for high school, but Kimmy says that I have to kiss her so she'll know I love her."

"Are you going to?"

"I don't know. I think I should because she's my best friend, and I want to make her happy. Jem, are you asleep?"

"Nope. I'm wide awake," she said, thinking of her own best friend since the first grade, asleep in the next room, and that Santa's helper had better get up to stuff Spence's stocking.

⚛⚛

After lunch, Spencer took Robby to the school playground to fly the model plane while Alex and Jemma went for a tour of the college.

Lizbeth and Jim had visited for an hour, enjoying the empty house.

"It was a real blessing to see you, Mama," Jim said. "I'm sorry that I was all banged up for your visit."

Lizbeth patted his arm. "I'm glad you are better, son. I've had a fine time."

"I think you and Jemmabeth are good for each other, don't you?" he asked.

"You and Alexandra have done a first-rate job raising that child. She's a joy, and I am not the only one who thinks she is going to be famous someday. You wait until you see the paintings that she has done in Chillaton, and to think that she did them in that dusty old garage."

"Do you know why she left Wicklow?" Jim asked, hoping luck was with him for an answer.

"She had some hard grief that she just couldn't hold up to, James."

He tried again. "I don't suppose you would share that information with me, would you?"

Lizbeth puckered her lips and Jim knew that look very well.

"Well, I guess I'll just have to put my trust in the Lord to take care

133

of her," he said.

Lizbeth smiled, at last. "That's always the best place to put it."

⧴⧵

Robby and Jemma finished up a jigsaw puzzle while Alex loaded the stereo. She and Jemma took turns jitterbugging and bopping with Spencer. The young people were dancing to "Mean Woman Blues" when Lizbeth entered the room. If her brow could go any higher, her eyes would have popped out on the floor. She could say with some certainty that Cam would not have liked seeing his little Jemmabeth move around like that to music. It wouldn't have even mattered that it was Spencer who was her partner. Alex and Jim didn't seem to think anything of it.

Lizbeth returned to the kitchen for more pie and coffee. She peeked out at the snow-covered mountains and wondered if Jemma had danced like that with this older man, Paul. No wonder he kept writing her letters. Jemma, with her looks and chaste ideals, would be irresistible to a man of the world. Things were so different when she was young. In her college physiology class, the professor pulled down a chart of the human body on the first day and the girl sitting behind her fainted. She thought of her own courtship with Cam. There were no dances at all. They went to socials where stern faced church deacons and their poker faced wives stood over them like crows watching the corn grow. She and Cameron played silly games and longed to be together, walking in the moonlight, bravely holding hands.

Cam had kissed her full on the lips once during their courting days. It made her so angry that she didn't speak to him for nearly two years. Had he not come to her school and played his fiddle under the window, she might have still been an old maid. He had to propose in front of her students so she wouldn't yell at him. Schoolmarms couldn't be married, so she gave up her career for him, and it was the best thing she ever did.

She washed her dishes and went to the linen closet to get a clean dishtowel. She opened the door to find Jemma and Spencer kissing. Red-faced, they stepped out.

"Hi," Jemma said, grinning.

"Sorry, Gram," Spencer said. "Watch out. There's some mistletoe in there."

Lizbeth couldn't help but smile back at them. Her own heart was full of youthful memories at the moment, now well over half a century old.

Jim leaned on his crutches and watched them load the car. Robby sat on Jemma's lap just like he had done when they left Wicklow nearly seven months ago when Alex reminded her to take her vitamins. Only this time, Jemma wasn't left on her own. She had Spencer. Now she needed to figure out what to do about it.

CHAPTER SIXTEEN

BB & Scarlett

Jemma shook snowflakes out of her hair at the post office counter.

Paralee Batson, the postmistress, gave her stamps and change. "We've sure had us some sorry basketball teams since you graduated, Jemmabeth. None of them girls will ever have a jumpshot like you. It took the cake. 'Course nobody is as tall as you either," she said. Her face was white with powder and set off with two rounded splotches of rouge. Joan Crawford had inspired the use of her eyebrow pencil, and tight brush curlers peeked out of a hairnet. A column of smoke rose from an ashtray on her desk.

Paralee leaned over the counter to check both ends of the lobby. "Hon," she whispered, "are you in some kind of legal trouble? I know it ain't none of my business and I shouldn't be talking about it, but I've known you since before you were born. Nobody gets a letter a week from a law office, so I've been worried about your state of affairs." Paralee's cat, H.D., raised his head from his perch by the scales in anticipation of Jemma's reply.

Jemma blushed. "I'm all right, Paralee. Thanks for worrying about me, though. I worked for that office and I guess they want me back." It could be the story.

Paralee thought for a second. "Well, I'll say. You must have made a good impression on somebody. I'm sure glad to see that you and Spencer are having another go at it. You two could make some cute young'uns, after you're married of course."

Jemma turned red again and reached to give H.D. a pat on the head. She couldn't think of a response to that. Chillaton—no secrets. Well, maybe one.

The snowy New Year came in at the Country Club dance. The Buddy Baker band was rocking and Spencer brought his mother. He had stewed over it for a week. Jemma came by herself so that he could spend most of the time with his mom. Mrs. Chase, fresh from Nedra's Nook and her own makeup drawer, was probably a smooth dancer in her younger days, before the drinking. She was still pretty, despite all that alcohol had done to her. Spencer kept his mom on the dance floor as much as possible. Jemma knew he was steering her away from the spiked punchbowl. He danced with Jemma only at midnight, then took her to say hello to his mother before they went home. She had dreaded it all night. Rebecca Chase had never liked her, not even when they were in grade school.

"Hello, Mrs. Chase. It's good to see you," Jemma fibbed, then clamped down on her lip.

Mrs. Chase glared at her. "So, did you find yourself a new boyfriend? My Spencer wasn't good enough for an overgrown, stuck-up hussy like you, I guess."

Spencer was humiliated. "C'mon, Mother, let's go. I'll see you later, Jem."

"You'd better not ever hurt him again, you little...!" She yelled something horrible as Spencer whisked her outside. The party turned silent for what seemed like forever.

Back home, Jemma's cheeks burned as she sat in Papa's chair waiting for Spence. Not only did Mrs. Chase dislike her, now she was calling her vile names in public and threatening her, too. Jemma closed her eyes. She truly didn't want to hurt him ever again. She heard his car and ran to open the door.

He was loosening his tie. "Sorry I'm late, baby. Mother got sick. She's asleep now, but I need to go back out and stay with her. I just wanted to apologize."

"I'll come too," Jemma said, getting her jacket. "Are you sure she's asleep?"

"Jem, about what she called you...," he began.

"Let's not talk about it now. I'm over it, really," she said, fibbing again.

"I don't know, maybe she's caught the flu or something. I shouldn't have taken her, and I'm so sorry about what she said."

"I deserved it." Jemma smoothed his hair. "She looked pretty, and y'all were great on the dance floor."

Every light was on at the Chase castle. Jemma hadn't been in the house for a couple of years. Everything about it said *money*, although nobody ever saw it except the three of them and their housekeeper.

They sat at the top of the big staircase, just outside his mother's room.

"This could be where Rhett carries Scarlett up the stairs," Jemma said, keeping her volume low.

Spencer almost smiled. "Don't ask me to carry you up it tonight."

"I think I must be like Scarlett because I am so bad."

"You are anything but bad. Mother didn't know what she was saying."

They sat thinking of things they couldn't talk about.

She took a deep breath. "Your house belongs in a magazine."

"Not in my opinion. An interior decorator redid it last year and got it in *Southern Comfort* magazine, but it's the palatial design that I hate."

"Everybody around here thinks it's magnificent."

"They don't have to live here." Spence took her hand. "Come on, I'll show you my room." He ushered her down the hall and into a large, very organized bedroom that included a drafting area.

"My goodness," Jemma said as she walked around looking at the numerous photographs of her. "You have way too many pictures of me."

"Nope. I can never have too many until I have the real thing. There's my favorite." He pointed to a black and white photo of a practically toothless Jemma in braids, her now famous cowboy boots, and a frilly little dress.

She picked up a framed drawing of a fox. "I can't believe you have these from grade school. They are so funny, but where did you get all this artwork, may I ask?"

"Your desk." He said, leaning against the door frame.

"You stole my drawings out of my desk in school?"

"Yup. They are in safekeeping until you are famous. Then we can publish them in a book."

"Spencer, you love me too much." She kissed him.

"Let's get out of here," he said and took her home.

⚜

Lizbeth heard the delivery truck pull in Lester's driveway. "Honey, let Kenneth in, please. I'm on the phone with Do Dah."

Jemma opened the door. "Hi, Kenneth. Just set the groceries on the table."

Kenneth Rippetoe's claim to fame was that one of his eyes was brown and the other blue. Their senior year in high school, Kenneth had outbid Spencer for her box at the student council's box supper. Kenneth, who was just a freshman then, paid fifty dollars to eat fried chicken and potato salad next to Jemma while she stared daggers at Spence. Spencer said he was giving him the thrill of a lifetime, but it must have cost Kenneth over two months' worth of delivering groceries. He wasn't all that bad looking. He was just one of those guys that didn't fit in, coupled with the fact that he had a silver front tooth, and Gene Autry style pants with the cuffs rolled up. He was undersized, but bigger than a cookstove.

"Jemmabeth, I've been hoping to catch you at home so I could tell you that you're looking more like BB every day." He moved his eyebrows in an impressive series of lifts. "Actually, you're prettier than she is."

"Thanks, Kenneth, but isn't Brigitte Bardot a blonde?"

"I wasn't talking about her hair. I was talking about her lips...I mean her mouth or something." He turned bright red at that revelation.

Jemma signed the delivery slip. "It's sweet of you to be thinking of me when you see BB."

He lingered at the kitchenette. "What I was wondering was, if you'd come to my Eagle Scout award ceremony."

"I didn't know you were going for your Eagle. Congratulations, Kenneth. When is it?"

"Seven o'clock, Thursday night at the Methodist Church. There'll be cake and punch, too."

"I'll be there," she said. "Thanks for asking me and here's a quarter from Gram."

"Thank her for me." He headed for the door. "Wait. Have you

139

noticed that my blue eye looks like Paul Newman's now?"

"Really." She bent down to check. "Not quite, but that's a nice line."

Kenneth grinned, his silver tooth glinting in the noonday light, "See ya Thursday." He tossed the quarter in the air and caught it.

❧ ❧

On Thursday Trina came over to Carrie's and the three of them were still playing Clue at a quarter to seven.

"I gotta go if I'm gonna shoot some hoops," Trina said. "You're too good at this game, Carrie."

"I'm just a lucky gal," Carrie said, patting the arms of her wheelchair.

Jemma made a face at her. "I think you cheat."

Carrie cupped her hands and shouted, "Eleanor, come and throw these people out of the house."

"She can't hear you; she's hanging out the wash," Trina said. "We'll leave quietly."

Trina dribbled along the sidewalk, taking care to miss the cracks and buckles. "Want to shoot some?"

"Sure," Jemma stole the ball and dribbled across the road. "Did you swipe this basketball? It says Metro College on it."

"My coach gave it to me when I left. He said for me to practice and try to walk-on for a team at a four year school."

"Did you?" Jemma said, popping in a long shot.

"Nah. That was about the time that Mama broke her hip, but I'm still working on my game. Brother Cleo fixed me a goal by the church, but this is better dribbling. Anyway, I don't know if I still want to play on a team."

"That's because you're in love," Jemma said.

"No more than you are."

Jemma took another long shot and missed.

Trina laughed. "Rattled you, didn't I?"

"I don't love anybody." That sounded tough.

"Sure you don't. You should see the way you look when you talk about Spencer or when somebody says his name," Trina said.

"Maybe you need glasses." Jemma missed a jumper.

"Maybe your jump shot's getting rusty," Trina said as she swished one through the net.

"You're on," Jemma said, popping one in herself. They battled it out until they were both tired and thirsty.

"What time is it?" Trina asked, wiping sweat on her shirt.

"It's seven thirty. Rats!" Jemma took off, tucking in her shirttail. "I'm late. I'll talk to you later," she yelled.

She stood outside the church and faced the wind to evaporate the sweat. She dusted off her jeans, undid her ponytail, ran her fingers through her damp hair, then pushed open the door.

In the choir loft, a whole troop of Boy Scouts was ready to sing. Explorer Scouts held flags at attention and Kenneth was in the middle of his speech. Jemma eased herself into a pew at the back of the church. He smiled when he saw her. The Boy Scouts sang "God Bless America," then the color guard walked down the middle aisle with the flags and it was over. Kenneth came right towards her.

"Thanks for coming," he said.

"Kenneth, I am so sorry that I was late. You gave a good speech."

"I made my mom cry."

"I'm sure she is very proud."

"Come and meet her."

Everybody was dressed up for the ceremony, but Jemma didn't even look bohemian, she looked like a field hand.

Mrs. Rippetoe hugged her son. Her thin arms held him for a long minute, then she turned her attention to his guest.

Kenneth grinned. "Mom, I want you to meet Jemmabeth Forrester."

Jemma shook her hand. "Congratulations on your son's accomplishments," she said, hoping his mother didn't notice that her hands smelled like a sweaty rubber ball. She recognized Mrs. Rippetoe's dress as one that had belonged to her own mother.

"You're Alex and Jim's daughter, aren't you? Your mother is one of the nicest people I've ever known. She cleaned my house for me when we lost Kenneth's father. She brought us food and called me several times to see how I was doing."

"My parents are very kind," Jemma said. "I hope that I can be like them someday."

Mrs. Rippetoe's voice was soft and tender. "I've heard nothing but good things about all the Forresters, and it sure means a lot to

Kenneth that you came tonight."

Jemma smiled. "It was my pleasure. I've never been to an Eagle Scout ceremony."

"Then I'm glad you got to see mine first," Kenneth said. "Now let's eat. Mom made cowboy sheet cake."

They ate the chocolate cake in the fellowship hall.

"Aren't you a senior this year?" Jemma asked, having her second piece.

"Yeah," he said.

"Going to college?"

"Junior college, at least I hope so. I applied for a bunch of scholarships, but my grades aren't real good."

Jemma scraped the last bit of icing off the plate. "I bet you'll get one. I'm sure your Eagle award will impress them. What do you plan to study?"

"I'd like to study business because I think I've got a good head for it. I want to manage a nursing home. My granny was in one that she hated, so I'd like to change that. I'd make it something special," he said, looking right at her with his blue and brown eyes. "I'll tell you my ideas sometime, if you want."

Jemma's heart melted. "You keep trying for those scholarships. Something good will happen." She set her plate and cup on the table. "Your mother is a great baker."

"Thanks," he said. "I'm glad she's out with other folks because she's been sad too long."

"Well, I'd better be getting home," Jemma said. "Gram will wonder where I am."

He stuck his hands in his pockets. "You probably don't remember this, but when you were in junior high and I was still in grade school, you said a poem over the loudspeaker one morning, right after the pledge."

She thought for a moment. "I do remember. It was a Dickinson poem. She's my favorite poet."

"One of the lines is about helping a fallen robin into his nest again," he said. "That's what I'm gonna do at my nursing home, and I'll put that poem on a plaque and hang it above the door. Life should be about helping others."

Jemma stared at him. "I can't believe you remember that day."

"I remember everything about you." He looked at the floor.

"Spencer is a lucky guy."

"You are a special person, Kenneth. You'll make a woman very happy someday."

He glanced at her.

Jemma started to leave, paused, then bent down and kissed him right on the lips. Kenneth drew back a second, then responded. She left him, stunned, at the church. She walked past the courthouse just as The Judge was getting into his car. She waved, but he ignored her. She smiled anyway at the thought of Kenneth, his dreams, and his eagle moment in the sun.

⚜

Lizbeth sat in her porch swing waiting for her family to arrive. The honeysuckle vine behind her was in its first flush before summer. She broke off a stem and savored its sweet fragrance. Too bad the blossoms didn't keep their fragrance longer off the vine. At her age, even a flower could set her thinking about the brevity of life.

Things seemed to revolve around arrivals, departures, and uncertainties. "Who Can Know What God's Great Plan Will Reveal?" That had been the title of her father's sermon when she and Cam had their first date on a warm spring day in 1905. It was about a year later that he messed up with the kissing business. She quickly realized that she had been too hard on him for that, but in those days it wouldn't have been proper for her to contact him and apologize. He proposed by asking in a great Scottish voice, "Will you stand with me, Lizbeth Jenkins, in front of God and man, and say that you will love me forever?" In spite of all schoolmarm etiquette, she had promised loud and clear, in front of her students, "I will stand with you, Cameron Forrester, forever and a day, and I will love you."

The Great Plan, though, had waxed hard, and she longed for the days when all her menfolk were with her, when joy was within reach. She didn't consider herself a bitter woman. It was just that she had nothing left to give, save small gestures of Christian kindness. Each day was the same now. She just went through the motions, playing out the past in her mind. Jemmabeth had brought a glimpse of the old joy back into her life.

She watched as a whirlwind caught a tumbleweed and sailed it skyward. They had named their sons from the New Testament—Matthew, Luke, and James. Cam had wanted to use Scottish names, Angus being a particular favorite. She had prevailed by choosing a Scripture for each son and Cam liked that idea. Lizbeth's faith in the truth of those Scriptures remained, but two of her three boys were gone, buried in far-off places she had only seen in an atlas.

She had adopted a verse of her own now, James 1:2-4: "My brethren, count it all joy when you fall into various trials, knowing that the testing of your faith produces patience." She was still standing, as promised, but in the shadow of a sorrow she did not want to confront. Maybe it was time she did. Jemmabeth was not the only one in the family who could do with some advice. Lizbeth recognized that she needed to count the joy, to take the advice of the Lord. The crunch of gravel in the driveway stirred her into a smile. They had arrived, signaling the onset of yet another sad parting.

Jemma ran out of the house to pick up Robby. "Goodness, you have grown," she said. There was a knot of conversation and laughter for several minutes.

"What's new out here?" Alex asked, looking around at the yard. "You've painted the birdhouses and planted more bulbs. I see the honeysuckle is in bloom."

Robby tugged at his sister's arm. "C'mon, Jem, show me the bird's nest." The group migrated to the nest tucked in a cluster of branches in the pecan tree.

"Jimmy, it's a cardinal's," Lizbeth said.

"I don't ever remember seeing one around here," he said, squinting up at it.

"I saw one last year, the day you moved to Arizona. First, I heard it outside the pouting room, then I saw it in the pecan tree. It's a cardinal all right."

"Let's see these paintings we've heard so much about," Jim said. Jemma and her daddy took the bar off the car house door. Alex gasped when she saw inside.

"Baby girl," was all Jim could say, over and over.

Alex clasped her hands to her heart and cried. Jim slipped his arms around his wife and daughter, but nobody said anything more.

Robby broke the silence. "Wow! This is just like that wax museum in California. Hey, there I am, almost," he said, pointing to the one unfinished piece.

"I can't believe I gave birth to you, Sweet Pea," Alex said.

Jim chuckled. "Papa's bragging would have been impossible to deal with."

Leaned against the walls were paintings so detailed that their subjects appeared to be waiting their turns to speak. There were so many – Willa in her rocking chair, fanning and laughing; Lester, hat in hand, concocting his next story with an eye on the train tracks; Trina bent over her old Singer sewing machine; Eleanor's hands in bread dough and her teeth in a jar; Lizbeth and Helene walking arm in arm in the sandy turn row; and Carrie engrossed in a piano piece while leafy shadows danced on the wall behind her. There were also landscapes of the home place and the Salt Fork of the Red River; a pastoral piece depicting two laborers, one black and one white as they hoed a field of cotton; a sunset behind a windbreak of perverse, leafless trees; a small bird on a wrought iron gate in a snowstorm, its black eyes piercing the swirls of white; the North Chillaton Quilting Club members hovering over their work; the half-completed one of Robby under his tree house; and a big one of Spencer on the hood of the Dodge, watching the stars.

Her family discussed each piece, lingering over their favorites. Robby was the first to leave, running to visit Lester. After an hour or so they went inside.

"Heavenly days," Alex said when she saw the kitchen. "I bet this is the only *trompe l'oeil* in Chillaton. Jemma, it's truly a garden."

"See, there's the home place. The sun is shining right on the windmill." Lizbeth pointed with pride to the house. "Now I can look at it any time I like."

Jim shook his head. "I have to say that you haven't wasted your time, baby girl. This is something."

"Robby can sleep on the cot in my room," Jemma said, holding their bags.

"Thanks." Jim said. "I need to get my circulation going again."

"How's your leg?" she asked.

"It gets a little stiff riding that far. How's Spencer? Are things okay with you two? I sure like that painting of him."

"Things are good, Daddy."

"Are there wedding bells yet?"

"Jim," Alex said, "aren't you being a little nosy?"

"Hey, I'm getting tired of waiting, and I'm sure Spence is."

Jemma played with her necklace, "Daddy you will be one of the first to know because I'm sure that whoever my future husband is, he'll do the right thing and ask you for my hand."

"That doesn't qualify," he said. "Give me a simple yes or no."

"I don't have an answer," Jemma said, with some impatience.

"Let's go look at the flowers," Alex said. "There'll be time for questions later."

⤦⤧

The guys went fishing at Pearl Lake about fifty miles away while Jemma took Alex to meet her new friends. She was so proud of her beautiful mother. She watched her talk with Willa and Trina like she had known them all of her life. As they walked back to Lizbeth's, Alex stopped on the tracks and took her daughter's hand.

"Jemma," she said, "I want you to know that I'm ashamed that I never reached out to the black community in all the years we lived in Chillaton. The most I ever did was send food and clothing to the Bethel church. That's inexcusable. It's my loss and my family's. I set a poor example for you."

"I know the feeling, Mom." Jemma squeezed her mother's hand. "We have a second chance now."

Carrie was dying to meet Alex. Jemma had never seen her so nervous. She fretted over her clothes, her hair, and which song to play for her on the piano. There was no cause for worry because Alex breezed in and took Carrie's breath away. Carrie was hungry for a mother and Jemma was eager to share her own. They laughed and played the piano while Jemma talked with Eleanor, who was doing double duty to give her time off with her family.

"Jem, would you please help me get Carrie on the sofa," Alex asked from the hallway.

Carrie couldn't take her eyes off Alex. They sat together on the sofa talking about things that Jemma couldn't hear. She didn't want to intrude, so she went for a long walk. When she returned, Carrie had fallen asleep on her mother's shoulder and Alex had been crying. Neither spoke of it. When Carrie woke up, Jemma left her mother to say good-bye in private.

"Thank you, honey," Alex said on the way to Lizbeth's. "I don't know when I have been so touched by such a starving, sweet spirit."

"I know," Jemma said.

Alex blew her nose. "She needs a mother."

"I'm glad she had you, even for a little while," Jemma said.

⟡

Spencer, who couldn't help himself, walked with Robby and gave him hints about where to find the candy eggs that he and Jemma had hidden for him. Alexandra sat with her daughter in the hollyhock patch. "I recall when your second grade class had the big Easter egg hunt in the park," Alex said as they watched Robby race around yelling each time he found another one.

Jemma sensed a lesson coming on. "I remember. There was a prize for finding the most eggs and for finding the fewest, too."

"You wanted to win so much that Spencer gave you some of his to fill your basket."

"Typical Spence, always looking out for me," Jemma said.

Alex kept on. "Somebody else had found more eggs than you. So, all the way back from the park, you kept dropping eggs out of the car window."

"I thought maybe I could get the prize for having the fewest," Jemma explained. "I know what you are going to say, that I was the loser all the way around because Eddie Parker won that prize for being late and not even getting to hunt."

"Now that you're a big girl, do you see any life lesson there?" Alex asked, taking her daughter's hand. "Maybe that's something to think about, Jem."

⟡

Alex took a box of clothing to the Rippetoes. Jemma meant to go with her, but took Robby to the park at the last minute.

They decided to end the week with a cookout at the river. Spencer and Jim bought the groceries and Jemma went to invite the Johnson ladies.

"You young'uns go on. I'll stay here and get some work done," Willa said.

"No, Mama. You're going with us. You never go anywhere," Trina said.

"It's true, Willa. You rarely go when I invite you to do something," Jemma said.

Willa chuckled. "I'm just a homebody."

"Then I won't go either," Trina said and plopped in a kitchen chair.

Jemma rolled her eyes. "Well, this is just great. I want both of you to come and if you don't, I'm going to have to tell everybody it's because you don't like eating with white folks. How do you like that?"

Willa and Trina exchanged glances, then Willa burst into laughter. It was one of her rolling, roaring ones. She slapped her leg and shook her finger at Jemma. "You are a sneaky one, Jemmabeth. You come here and give me a hug. I'll go."

Trina grinned. "Mama will make some cobbler."

෴෴

Jemma found her daddy in the good bedroom. He was in the rocking chair, eyes fixed on the big portrait of Papa.

"Want some company?" she asked.

"Sure," he said, blowing his nose. She sat in his lap. "That's a perfect likeness of him. It's almost too much."

"Thank you, Daddy. I wanted him to be watching us out of the corner of those blue eyes, with a twinkle in them, of course."

"You did well. That's the way he disciplined us kids in church. It just took one look. Of course we knew that he was thinking of some mischief of his own the whole time he was giving us the eye. I sure miss him."

"I think about him a lot, especially when I hear a fiddle."

"I don't know if I could bear to hear that old song he loved again," Jim said. "It got to me at the funeral, and I always wondered how Mama stood it. She never flinched. It was the same at Matt and Luke's memorial services."

"You never talk much about your brothers, Daddy."

"I keep it all here," he said, patting his heart. "If I didn't have your

148

mother back then, I don't know what I would've done. We were so close, and to have them both erased from my life in the same year, well, it was tough. It must eat Mama up sometimes."

"I think Gram is changing. I think she's letting go a little."

Jim shifted his leg. "Is she feeling okay?"

"She never mentions anything. Why?"

"Mama's always been healthy, but age is creeping up on her and I'm not around. You be my eyes, Jem, and remember, as much as you miss Papa, it's the Lord who always has his eye on you."

"I will," Jemma said. "How's your leg?"

He shook his foot. "Right now it has no feeling in it at all."

She jumped up. "Oh no! Do you need to go to the doctor?"

"I just needed you to get up. You must weigh a ton."

Jemma put her fists on her hips. "I do not. I run to work nearly every morning. You have to take that back."

He laughed. "Okay, okay, but you aren't exactly my baby girl any more, are you?" Jim stood and looked at the portrait again. "You find yourself a man like Papa, Jemmabeth, and you don't need to look very far."

She leaned against his shoulder. "I know, Daddy, really I do."

⤔⤕

So many people she loved were together in the same spot. She watched them as they joked and unloaded the cars. Spencer worked harder than anybody as he built the fire. He looked across at her, smiling, and she saw it all. He was so worthy of love, but she still needed to know if it was the marrying kind.

"You eat up these big productions, don't you?" he asked.

Jemma grinned. "I do. Hey, where's Mom?"

"She's on her way."

As they spoke, Alex drove up in the Rambler with Carrie.

Jemma ran to the car. "How did you swing this?"

"You could say that I used my womanly wiles on The Judge, but she can't stay long, so make the most of it." Spencer got Carrie out of the car and into a lawn chair, but first he took her to the river and dipped her feet in the water. She giggled and was the queen of the party until Jim and Alex had to take her home.

Robby, who built a whole city in the sandy banks, ate four hot dogs. Jemma and Lizbeth had no idea that an April girls' birthday celebration was in the works. Spencer had bought a fancy cake in Amarillo. It looked a lot like Sandy's wedding cake. Lester played his favorite song, "Red River Valley," on the harmonica, and they all sang along to whatever else Lester could play around the big campfire. Jemma watched Spencer work his charms on Willa as he talked her into singing a solo of "What a Friend We Have in Jesus." How could anybody resist him? Only a nitwit like herself could accomplish that.

"You'll get my present when it's your real birthday," he whispered to Jemma when it was time to go. She knew it would be something special.

⟨⟩⟨⟩

They left the next morning before the sun came up. Robby was still asleep when Jim put him in the back seat.

"You know everything that I am going to say to you, Sweet Pea," Alex said. "Be wise and listen to the Lord."

"Bye, Mom. I love you," Jemma said.

"Love you, baby girl," Jim said. "You'd better be registered for school next fall. No more extensions."

Lester's light came on just as the Rambler's taillights disappeared down the street.

"I'm going back to bed." Jemma yawned.

"I think I'll just stay up and do a little reading, sugar. You go on." Lizbeth reached for her Bible. Her father had given it to her when she learned to read. She turned to the first Psalm and read the words under her breath. "He is like a tree planted by streams of water which yields its fruit in season and whose leaf does not wither. Whatever he does prospers."

She laid the Bible across her heart and ran her fingers along its leather spine. Jimmy was the last of her men. They had all been trees planted by the water, but he was the only one whose leaf did not wither and die.

She closed her eyes. *May he prosper Lord, and may his wife and children reap the fruits of Your Spirit. Amen, Sweet Jesus.*

150

CHAPTER SEVENTEEN

A Whirlwind

It was May Day and Jemma had wasted a page in her sketchbook, doodling. Exactly two years had passed since she had agreed to go along with Melanie on a double date. That was her first sip from the Devil's cup. She felt weird about doing it even then. Now look where it had gotten her.

Lizbeth bent over the mail and tore open an envelope. "Uh-oh."

Jemma looked up. "What?"

"Julia is coming next week."

"Great! There's nothing like a dose of Do Dah."

Lizbeth laughed. "Julia is so much like my mother—boss of the world. She's nothing like Father. He was a man of few words until he got in the pulpit. Preachers in his day were fire and brimstone men, but he believed in following the Lord's example of teaching in parables. He taught us that life is like a jealous crop which we must always be tending. Some of us have a short row to hoe and some have a long one. Regardless of the length, there will always be an abundance of work to be done. Mercy me, sugar, I've gone and preached a sermon to you."

Jemma put her arm around her. "What did your father think about discrimination?"

"Oh, there was plenty of that when he was alive. It's a mystery how even good people justify prejudice. He used to say, 'We are all sinners, even if our sins are ones of omission, but it's never too late to change.'"

"I think we get used to things being a certain way and get lazy," Jemma said.

"I suppose." Lizbeth put on her apron. "I know Cam said that the Devil loves a lazy man."

"Or woman. Does Do Dah get along with Lester?"

"Lester?" Lizbeth laughed again. "That man is hard to find when she comes."

"Then Lester doesn't know what he's missing," Jemma said.

Lizbeth smiled. "Maybe so."

⚜

Julia came in like a whirlwind. "Let me look at you, Jemmabeth. You've got Jim's height and Alex's good looks. Those are his eyes, too, but you look out of them like your mama. Now, what are you doing here in Chillaton with Lizbeth when you should be in Dallas, painting? A man, I presume." Julia was not known for her tact, but for her generosity of opinion, affection, and money. She was shorter than Lizbeth, but had the same gentle eyes and high cheekbones. Her hair was dyed a little too red, and Lizbeth was right, she was building herself a front porch that she camouflaged with classy clothes. Lizbeth might have one too, if she had a cook and a maid.

"I am painting," Jemma said. "I'll show you my studio in Papa's car house." Jemma grabbed her great aunt's arm and caught a wink from Lizbeth.

"I never could get Cam to call it a garage," Julia said. "He did things just to aggravate me sometimes, the stinker."

Jemma lifted the homemade bar and let it swing aside, and Julia entered the odd studio. "Mercy," she said. "You need to get a padlock on that door. Somebody could rob you blind the way it is now. Oh, my!" Her head swiveled as she stepped around the garage, and her high heels made little dots on the canvas tarp that Lester had spread for a floor. "Jemmabeth, this is sensational! Why, I've got friends at home who would pay a fortune for one of these. You can't leave them out here in this outhouse of a studio. You have to take them inside. They should be in a vault somewhere. I'm serious. Where do you get money for these huge canvases?"

"I have a friend in Wicklow who buys the materials for me, and I make the canvases myself," Jemma said, moving her easel out of the way.

Julia looked at her. "That Dallas boyfriend bought the materials?"

"No. Helene was my landlady."

She lingered at a new portrait of Carrie. "This one is so sweet."

152

"It's a gift for a friend," Jemma said.

Julia whistled. "Amazing. They show such personality and I like that. It gives me a connection. That has to make you feel good, as the artist."

"Yes ma'am, it does. I hate to break into that connection, even a little. That's why I don't like to put my name on the painting itself. I'd rather sign the back of the canvas."

Julia sniffed. "You have man troubles, sugar. I can spot it a mile away. We can talk about it because I know a thing or two about men. I'm not an old fogey, you know."

"Nobody would ever think that about you, Do Dah," Jemma said, not knowing how this was going to turn out.

"Oh, heavens, call me Julia. Only in Lizbeth's house does anybody still utter that silly name."

"It's cute," Jemma said. "Mom calls me Sweet Pea."

Julia waved that notion away with one bejeweled hand. "Speaking of cute, what happened to Spencer? I hope you didn't run that boy off. He's a winner if there ever was one. Maybe you're looking for greener grass on the other side. It usually turns out to be crabgrass, by the way."

Julia was hard to keep up with, especially when she was sniffing out an injustice.

"Spence and I were taking a little break, but we're seeing each other now," Jemma said.

"Well, all righty, then. Now tell me the truth about my sister's health."

"Daddy asked me the same thing. Should I be worried about Gram?"

"I'm not talking about her physical health," Julia said. "I mean does she still mess around with the old trunk in that pouting room."

"The soldier box? I'm not sure," Jemma said.

Julia hopped up on the painting stool and kicked off her heels. "It's not healthy the way she holds her feelings back about those boys. It broke all our hearts, but Lizbeth never shed a tear, that I'm aware of, and I was living with them. When Cam died, Dr. Huntley told me that she went in the pouting room and threw a fit, excuse me, sugar, from you-know-where. She screamed and hollered and beat on the walls and kicked that puny little door until it came loose from its hinge at the top. It never has hung right since."

"Gram did that?" Jemma stared at her. "Surely she cried then."

"Nope. He said she came out of there wild-eyed, but composed. Lizbeth needs to let go and grieve like the rest of us." Julia pointed her finger at Jemma. "She's going to have a stroke one of these days."

Jemma's scalp tingled. "Oh, surely not, but then I've never seen her cry about anything."

"Well, I'm no psychiatrist, but it can't be healthy not to shed a tear over three losses."

"Why didn't they bury Matthew and Luke in Chillaton?" Jemma asked.

"The government said they would bring them home, but Cam wouldn't have it. He said Rest in Peace means just that, so they were buried in the closest cemetery to where they gave their lives. I think it would've been good for both of them to have those boys out there in Citizens' Cemetery, but what's done is done. Now Matthew is way over in Italy and Luke is in Africa. Who would have ever thought that?"

"Africa?" Jemma had never heard anybody mention that before or maybe she just hadn't been paying attention.

"Tunisia," Julia said, staring at the tarp. "Luke died in an air raid on the Ploesti oil fields. He was a gunner in a fighter plane. You know, at first, they told us that Matt was Missing In Action. About a month later, they sent another telegram saying…" Julia's voice broke. "That Matty was dead."

Jemma put her arm around her great aunt.

"If Lizbeth would go," Julia continued, "I would take her to those graves. You know that we love traveling to Europe, but I've never been to their graves either. They might as well have been my brothers."

"Have you ever asked her?"

"I have not. She won't even fly down to Houston to see our sisters. She rides the bus. That's why I flew them all here for her birthday last spring. She uses that old joke about the Lord saying: 'And lo(w), I am with you, always.' I know what she would say about flying across the ocean. She won't leave him." Do Dah stood in the door, watching the stars. "I hear you're making some new friends across the tracks."

Jemma pulled the chain on the light bulb and swung the big wooden bar into place. "Yes ma'am, and I wish I'd done it a long time ago. I can't believe that I never even considered it."

154

They walked arm-in-arm to the front porch. "In the bigger world, there's not quite as much prejudice towards people of color," Julia said. "Places like Chillaton, where it's no more than a wide spot in the road, old thinking runs deep, but that will all change in your generation, I hope. Who are these new friends?"

"Willa and Trina Johnson, they live straight across the tracks from here. Trina and I graduated the same year, we both played basketball, we like the same music, and *To Kill a Mockingbird* is our favorite book. Do Dah, I used to walk those tracks all the time and never once acknowledged their existence. It's like I had a gift that I never opened."

"I know, honey. Don't forget that I grew up here, too. Blacks were just a part of the landscape back then. None of us would've considered crossing those tracks for social purposes. It's the shameful truth. I also heard you've been working for Judge McFarland. You know I dated him for a while in high school. I don't suppose Lizbeth told you that."

Jemma's jaw hung open. "No! What was he like?"

"Let me see, I would give Johnny about a five out of ten. He was like a king with no kingdom as far as social graces went. With me, he was more like a benevolent dictator, always keeping emotional score until I just quit. He was smart and nice to look at in his youth. It's too bad about his wife and little girl. What's she like?"

"His name is Johnny? I can't believe you actually dated him. He is such a fuddy-duddy." Jemma giggled. "Carrie has to be her mother's daughter in every way. She's so funny and talented. We were in Brownie Scouts together and we both took piano lessons from Miss Mason."

Julia stopped. "Brownies? It could be that I have a picture of you girls. Maybe of a fundraiser or something for the Negro church, I don't know for sure, but I remember there were some black children in it, too. I'll check when I get home and send it."

"All three of us were there?" Jemma asked. "Now that would be a real coincidence."

"We'll see. I just know I have a picture. I'm amazed at your art and I don't get that way often. You should paint your old aunty a picture. Whatever happened to the one you did of Lizbeth reading the letter from me about her birthday party?"

"I'm not sure where it is. Maybe in Dallas, at my school," Jemma said. "Ask Gram, please. She might surprise you."

"To go to Europe? When the time's right and if you'll come to see us in Houston. Now tell me what happened in Wicklow, and I'm not buying anything but the truth."

There was no use tiptoeing around it. Jemma released the bomb. "I think I fell in love with a married man."

Julia made a slight noise in her throat. "Sounds like you didn't meet him at church. Are you sure the passion bug didn't blind you? I bet he used all the tricks he had, and you just got a little carried away with things. Let's stay out here for a while." Julia took a seat in the wicker chair, and Jemma sat in the porch swing, pushing off from the cool concrete with her bare toes.

"Tell me about last summer," Julia said.

They talked until Gram's light went out in her bedroom, then Julia paced around the porch, sifting through the story. She stopped at the swing. "Scoot over, honey. Now I don't like all these letters. It's just common sense that if you send a few letters and they don't get answered, you try something else. This smacks of a Bronte novel. What did your parents say?"

"I haven't told them the whole story because I'm afraid Daddy would pound him," Jemma said.

"And you haven't seen this guy or written to him or anything?"

Jemma halted the swing. "He has a wife. You know me better than that."

"I didn't mean in a romantic way. I meant just to chew him out or something. Let that Jenkins' temper fly."

"No, ma'am," Jemma said. "I haven't done anything. It just wouldn't be right."

"Sugar, I'm glad you told me. Love can be a mean old thing, and I speak from experience. I had my share of love stories before I met Art, but it's worth it all when you find the right man. This Paul business should show you that it's all the more reason to stick with the Chase boy. He's gold."

Jemma nodded blankly. Everybody was so sure.

"I know what you're thinking," Julia said, "that nobody understands. Well, I gave your Papa fits with my love life. Cam was a patient man. Anybody who's a farmer knows patience. Of course he also learned a lot of that raising me. Those were exciting times, but he might have called them something else. I had boyfriends who made me break a sweat with their romancing, and a few whose idea of romance was to agree with me in an argument. When you pack on a few pounds and makeup won't cover your wrinkles, you can get down on yourself, but if your man tells you that you're beautiful, talented, smart, and he can't wait to see you in the morning, you know you made the right choice. Arthur still dances all the slow ones with me, sugar."

⚬⚬⚬

Julia slept in the next morning. She claimed it was part of her vacation routine.

"Good morning, ladies, what's the plan for today?" she asked, wearing her Chinese robe and slippers into the kitchen.

"I want you to meet Carrie," Jemma said.

"Good. I'd like to see how old Johnny Mac turned out."

Much to their disappointment, The Judge was not at home. Julia made Carrie laugh, though, with tales of her brief courtship with her father. Next they drove across the tracks so Julia could meet Willa and Trina. After listening to Julia and Willa trade jokes and stories for a couple of hours, the younger women went to Lizbeth's for supper. Julia came home during dessert, still laughing.

On her last day, they hit Amarillo hard for some shopping. Jemma figured her favorite great aunt must have spent over three hundred dollars. Lizbeth protested at each purchase, but her sister paid no attention to her and did as she chose. "That's why I drove, Lizbeth," she said. "When I fly I can't splurge on you the way I want because there's no place to put the booty."

"I have the Dodge," Jemma reminded her.

Julia flicked her hand in the air. "That old thing needs to be put out of its misery. It's going to conk out on you one of these days."

"Maybe I'll start driving it when Jemmabeth gets a new one," Lizbeth said.

Julia threw back her head and guffawed, attracting everybody's attention in Woolworth's coffee shop, her favorite. "That'll be the day."

Lizbeth sipped her coffee, then excused herself to the restroom.

"I think maybe I'm in the doghouse now," Julia whispered. "She didn't like me laughing at the idea of her driving."

"Don't you think she could learn?" Jemma asked.

"Honey, there is nobody in this old world that I admire more than Lizbeth. She is my mother, for all intents and purposes, and she is one strong woman. Did you know that during the Depression she had to have most of her teeth pulled? They were rotten, but we didn't have enough money to get dentures made. She went almost a year without any teeth and never complained, poor thing. It nearly killed Cam. Finally, he started selling off the furniture to get a dentist in Amarillo to fix her up. Now, if that's not strength and humility, I don't know what is. She just doesn't take teasing well, and I learned how to tease from the master, your Papa Cameron."

"Are you still entering contests, Do Dah?" Jemma asked, changing the subject as Lizbeth returned.

"Goodness, yes." Julia left a ten-dollar bill on the counter for the two cups of coffee and a soda.

"I don't know why you go to all that trouble when you already have everything you need," Lizbeth said.

"Once in a while, I win, and that keeps me going. When I pass away, I want everybody to just think of it as me winning the Big Contest in the Sky," Julia said.

"Julia!" Lizbeth set her cup down hard.

"Let's get on home." Julia winked. "Lizbeth is all tuckered out."

The next morning, Julia snuck out before they got up. She put an envelope on the kitchen table with a hundred-dollar bill in it for her sister and a note for Jemma.

Sweetie Pie,
I believe that once you pray about something and you sleep on it, then you go with what your heart tells you. How else is the Lord going to talk to you? I don't think that I've made so many bad choices in my own life. If I did, it seems more likely to me that the circumstances, when I happened upon them, were lacking in stability. If I'd had more information, I could've done even better. The same is true for you. I'm certain sure that you've been on your knees about your love life. Now you need to make a choice, Jemmabeth, and embrace it with all you've got. Choose Spencer. Thank you for introducing me to Willa and Carrie. I loved being with you and seeing your art. You make us all proud.
    Hugs and kisses,
    Julia a.k.a.—unfortunately—Do Dah
    P.S. I want a painting!

CHAPTER EIGHTEEN

Lucky Ducks

Their table at Cattlemen's, the Amarillo penthouse restaurant in the Golden Spread Building, was graced with a bouquet of twenty-one roses and a silver box tied with a black satin ribbon beside Jemma's plate.

She untied the bow and lifted out a porcelain music box. The top was adorned with a replica of Van Gogh's *Starry Night*. "I wanted to remind you of our stargazing," he said. She opened the lid and it played part of a song that she had heard on the radio, "I Will Wait for You." Inside the box was a pair of earrings—tiny flowers of pink gemstones and pearls.

"They're supposed to be sweet peas," Spencer said, "your birth flower."

Jemma was afraid to look at him. When she did, the tears had made it to her chin. "How do you think of these things?"

"I bought the box in Paris for your birthday last April, but you said to leave you alone for a year. So I had it inscribed when I got back to New York." He read her the inscription under the lid: *I think of thee*. "That's all I could do."

Her tears got fatter. "How did I get so blessed to have you love me?"

"If things were different, I would ask you to marry me tonight. That was always my plan, to propose on your twenty-first birthday," he said.

Jemma closed her eyes.

"I won't, but you have to remember, you're going to tell me when you are ready, no matter the circumstances."

"Spence, you deserve better than me." She leaned across the table and kissed him. It was the first of many before the night was over.

"Jemmabeth, are you brave enough to teach me to drive?" Lizbeth asked, her lips puckered in dread.

"Sure," Jemma said. "I'll teach you where I learned."

Lizbeth's glasses slipped. "The cemetery? Oh, my. Well, I suppose no one could see me there. This driving business is to be our little secret. Don't tell a soul."

Jemma couldn't wait to tell Spencer. He could keep a secret.

Lizbeth had her first lesson that afternoon while Lester was at the barbershop. She wore her paisley headscarf and held her Sunday purse in her lap on the way. They had agreed that she would not practice anywhere near Papa's grave. That meant they would have the lessons in the oldest part of the cemetery. "Do you think this is awful, driving around these graves with no intention of paying our respects?" she asked.

"No, ma'am. I think it will liven up the residents' day," Jemma said.

Nobody was at the cemetery except Scotty Logan, who was mowing in the newer section. Jemma pointed out all the stuff on the dashboard, and made a circle around a section heavily wooded with cedar bushes to show her how things worked. She made a second loop around the reflecting pond and the Chase mausoleum. Then it was Lizbeth's turn, but first, Jemma took her picture with the Brownie camera. It was not unlike a photo for a reward poster. The engine grated and screeched as Lizbeth held the key to start it after it was already running. She let go with a gasp.

"You're doing fine," Jemma said. "Just put your foot on the brake, no, the other pedal, that's it. Now press the button with the D on it." Lizbeth did, and at Jemma's direction, she lifted her foot off the brake. The Dodge began to roll. She gripped the steering wheel and Jemma braced herself. "Now put your foot on the brake again and press it real easy so you can turn up by that big cedar bush."

"Which way?" Lizbeth asked, her voice like Tweety Bird's.

"Either way," Jemma said, trying not to laugh.

She turned without slowing up at all and ran over the curb. Both their heads bounced up and hit the ceiling of the car. Lizbeth's eyes were like ping-pong balls behind her glasses. "Oh, help my life. This

160

was a bad idea."

"Try giving it a little gas with the pedal on the right." Lizbeth found it and the car shot forward past several plots safely enclosed with rusty iron fences.

After an hour, she was making turns. When it was time to go, she chose to drive by the Chase mausoleum and all the way back to the arched entrance, past the pond. Scotty was putting the mower away in the caretaker's shed. He looked twice as the car crept by.

"Fiddlesticks," Lizbeth said. "Scotty and your Papa were good friends. I hope he doesn't say anything."

"Gram, everybody will be amazed that you are learning to drive," Jemma said as she took over the wheel.

They were at the cemetery every day, provided Jemma could get home before dark. Sometimes they stopped at the pond so Lizbeth could feed breadcrumbs to a duck family that had taken up residence there. The pond was full this year, not like some years when there was no rain and it was more like a sandy bog, full of cattails. The Chase family had bought all the plots running down the incline from their mausoleum decades ago and created the pond as part of the memorial to the patriarch of the Chase family, Morgan Chase. Their mausoleum was probably the only replica of the Pantheon in the Panhandle. It was a good spot to wait out the rain, which they did one evening. Jemma read the inscriptions.

The Honorable Morgan Ashton Chase
Banker, Philanthropist
Member of the Senate of the Great State of Texas
Born—New York, New York—March 9, 1868
Died—Chillaton, Texas—August 19, 1954

Margaret Phelps Chase
Beloved Wife & Mother
Born—Teaneck, New Jersey, June 3, 1870
Died—Chillaton, Texas, May 1, 1949

"Did you know them?" Jemma asked.

"I knew them, but we were never in their home," Lizbeth said. "They were money folk. He came out to the Panhandle to get into the cattle business, best I recall. His family owned some banks back East. I heard Mrs. Chase came from old money and that she also survived the *Titanic*. She was never happy here, poor thing, even though he built her that castle."

"Spencer doesn't like his grandparents' house. He thinks it's out of character with the land or something like that," Jemma said.

"Well, it didn't help anyway. I believe she died of boredom."

Jemma nudged her. "Gram."

"That's what folks said."

"This stone must have cost a fortune," Jemma said, gliding her hands across the cool marble.

"They had it to spend," Lizbeth said.

"I wonder why they moved so far away from New York? I'll have to ask Spence more about his grandpa. It looks like he was a bigshot. Too bad his dad is such a jerk."

"Jemmabeth Alexandra."

"It's true, Gram. He's had fifty different girlfriends, and he knows nothing about Spence. All he does is give him cars."

"Don't judge someone's heart, sugar."

Jemma decided to take a chance as they headed back to the car. "Have you ever wanted to visit Uncle Matthew's and Uncle Luke's graves?"

"I've given it some thought," Lizbeth said. "I used to feel I couldn't do it even when I had Cam, but it's nonsense to talk about that anyway. They rest on other continents." Lizbeth drove to the Farm to Market road and reached for the door handle.

"Do you want to try driving home?" Jemma asked.

Lizbeth pushed her glasses up. "Do you think I'm ready?"

"I do indeed," Jemma said.

The car rolled onto the pavement. "So much sadness out here," Lizbeth said as she turned towards town.

Jemma smiled as an old tractor passed them. "There's one tombstone that's not too sad. It's the one that says, *Here lies Bodie Farlow's right foot. The rest of him is in Erath County.*"

Lizbeth had to agree.

The phone was ringing as they walked in the house.

"Jemmabeth? It's Kenneth Rippetoe."

Jemma could feel him blush through the phone. "Hi, Kenneth. What's up?"

"I wanted you to be the first to know that I got a scholarship to

Amarillo Junior College," he said.

"Way to go! I'm so happy for you," Jemma said.

"Thanks. My mom said that maybe sometime you and Spencer could come out to our place and have supper with us. She'd make that cake you liked."

"We'll do it, Kenneth. Thanks for sharing your good news."

He dropped his voice. "Thanks for the you-know-what, Jemma. It was the highlight of my day—" he hesitated—"of my life." Then he hung up.

⤙⤚

Jemma wiped off the TV trays and put them away after Hoss slapped Little Joe's back and guffawed, just like Do Dah, bringing up the happy ending music. *Bonanza* was Papa's favorite show. Lester, who usually joined them for it, had gone to see a John Wayne movie by himself this particular night. Lizbeth paced to the kitchen and back, arms folded, head down.

Jemma followed her. "Are you having a spell, Gram?"

"No, but I need to get my driving license. I don't want to break the law any more than I have already."

"You'll have to study for the written test, pass a vision test, and you'll need to parallel-park with an officer," Jemma said.

She quit pacing. "Surely I could pass a test. I was first in the state teaching exam, and my glasses are like new. Now, I don't know about the parallel parking."

"The Dodge is too long," Jemma said. "I have trouble with it myself. Maybe we could borrow somebody's car. How about Lester's?"

Lizbeth shook her head. "I don't want him to know yet."

"Maybe Spencer could get us one. He knows you can drive."

Lizbeth waved her finger at Jemma. "You weren't supposed to tell."

"I only told Spence. Besides, he'd love to help."

Lizbeth took up the pacing again. "I'm being too much trouble with all this driving business."

"You are not. I'll go by the courthouse tomorrow and get a driver's manual for you."

Lizbeth took off her glasses and rubbed the bridge of her nose. "I haven't studied much of anything but a Sunday school lesson and the Scriptures in nearly fifty years. The good Lord has His work cut out for him."

⸘ ⸙

She sat at the kitchenette, staring at the manual. The State of Texas had spent a lot of time making up driving rules. With the Lord's blessing, she might get the feeling again, that she could work hard and change things, like the Lizbeth before all the sadness had done. That person had hunkered down somewhere inside her ever since she had become acquainted with grief. She had wept at the death of her mother when Julia was born and for her father's long journey home to Heaven, but that wellspring of sorrow had gone dry and she could not see clear to bring it back. Grief had hollowed out holes in her that she longed to patch up, and overcoming her fears was a part of her plan. As silly as it might seem to her family, driving a car had always been a great fear for her. She wanted to win at least one battle.

Cam would have fainted to see her take this test. She smiled at the thought of those blue eyes crinkled in laughter over her parallel parking skills. Nobody had been able to help her do it right. Poor Jemma, bless her heart, had surely tried, too.

Lizbeth stretched and drew a weary breath. She wandered into the bedroom that she and Cam had shared. His portrait dominated the room. She wished Jemma were not so talented because Cam looked as though he were about to speak. It was bad enough to think of sleeping in the bed where he took his last breath, but to wake up and see him watching her, well, that would be too much. She smoothed the old chenille bedspread and adjusted the cross-stitched pillows that Annabeth had sent last Christmas. The room was never bright enough to suit Cam. "We should be able to cut off the lights in broad daylight," he had said at least once a day. Maybe Jemma was right. She should let her paint the room the color of butter, put a pretty quilt on the bed, and take down the heavy drapes. Nobody was going to look in her house anyway, except maybe Shorty Knox.

Lizbeth crossed the room to their closet and took down the wedding ring quilt top that was almost finished. It would be a quilt for newlyweds, whenever that happened, and if she were reading Jemma's heart correctly, she knew who would be sharing the quilt with her on cold winter nights. That's why Lizbeth had embroidered their initials in the heart at the center of the rings. It would stay in the closet, though, until Jemmabeth got her head straight and Jimmy gave his approval. It was the old-fashioned way, but she liked it.

"I've got a car for Gram," Spencer said as they walked to the car house. "A '64, two-speed, Powerglide, automatic Corvair."

"Does that mean she doesn't have to shift gears?"

"There are no buttons to push except on the radio, and it's much smaller than the Dodge." Spencer opened the door and turned on the lights. "She'll need to practice driving it." He sat in the rickety armchair Lester had loaned them and watched as Jemma made preparations to paint. "I told my dad that we needed the car for a couple of weeks."

"Thanks, Spence. It's nice of your dad to help us out." Jemma mixed her colors and applied them to her palette.

"He doesn't care. I doubt he was even listening. He'll sell it when she's done and make a good profit. I do have to pick it up in Lubbock, though." Spencer stretched out his long legs, and folded his arms behind his head. "I'm hoping that you'll go with me in Buddy's truck and we can tow it home."

"Sure. I'll work it out with Eleanor." She turned her attention to the painting in front of her, and he watched with everlasting admiration.

After two weeks' practice, Lizbeth had a cheering section when she emerged from the courthouse with the testing officer. She had even allowed Lester to come since he had discovered her hapless efforts to parallel-park in their alley. Now the official parking poles were set up next to the curb by the shady lawn. The officer stood outside the Corvair, writing on his clipboard. He opened the door and slid in the passenger side. Lizbeth inched the car away and was out of their sight for a long fifteen minutes.

She came creeping back on the other side of the courthouse. The officer got out of the car and Lizbeth pulled up next to the two upright yellow poles. Jemma couldn't look. Lester held his breath, then moaned. Lizbeth had parked between the poles, but at least eight feet away from the curb. Even the officer was laughing as he continued to write on his clipboard, then they disappeared into the courthouse.

Anxiety ran high as Lizbeth emerged, but she was practically skipping. "I did it, help my life, I did it! Can you see this, Cameron Forrester?" She held the paper overhead, laughing. "There's only one thing," she said after the clapping died down. "I failed the parallel-parking. The officer said he would overlook it, but for me to stick with driving in Connelly County. It seems there isn't a parallel-parking space in it."

The next day, Willa and Trina agreed to go for a celebration ride in the Dodge. Lizbeth treated everybody to soft-serve ice cream at Son's, then headed to the cemetery, her old training ground.

"I've never been here," Trina said. "White folks sure do spend a lot of money on fences out here. They must expect an escape."

Willa laughed. "I come here once with Mama to Miz McFarland's service. You know, The Judge's wife. There was a whole slew of cars out here then."

"Let's show them the ducks," Jemma said. "Just pull in there by the mausoleum, and we can walk down."

Lizbeth eased up next to the marble structure and stopped, angling in, as was her only parking style.

Jemma leaned in the back window. "Don't you want to come, Willa?"

"Y'all run on," Willa said, "I'll keep the car company. It would take me a whole hour to get down there."

"We won't be long," Lizbeth called over her shoulder.

The trio walked to the pond, the girls on either side of Lizbeth, to keep her safe on the incline. Jemma had a packet of sunflower seeds in her purse and she and Trina tossed them to the waiting ducks.

Willa watched as best she could from the back seat. She shifted around to get a good view, and the springs groaned at her every move. With considerable effort, she leaned up over the front seat to flip the sun visor out of her way, then plopped back with a resonant grunt. There was a slight movement in the car itself, a creaking sound, followed by the soft crunch of gravel beneath its tires.

Trina was the first to see it. "Look out, Mama's coming down the hill!"

"Oh, no!" Jemma took off right behind Trina.

Lizbeth froze in her tracks. "Have mercy."

The whole thing was over in seconds.

The Dodge came to rest where the water stood midway on the cattails just as the ducks lifted off at this extreme invasion of privacy. Its headlights were underwater, like a duck taking a drink.

Willa was sprawled across the seat when the girls got to the car. Her Sunday hat was willy-nilly at the side of her head and her purse was upside down on the floorboard.

Trina shook her. "Mama! Are you hurt?"

Willa's eyes popped open. "Now that's a whole lot faster than I figgered I could make it."

Jemma found Scotty Logan, the caretaker, still mowing on his tractor. He hooked a cable to the Dodge and pulled it out of the pond. Lizbeth was mortified. She half-expected Sheriff Ezell to show up and take her new license away. It didn't help that Scotty grinned the whole time he was helping them.

"I thought I'd seen you driving around here, Mrs. Forrester," he said, smoothing back his white hair.

"Well, I'm never doing it again, Scotty."

"I reckon you pushed the neutral button instead of the park button. It's a natural mistake in them Dodges. It could've happened to anybody."

"But it didn't. It happened to this old woman. I'm just lucky that my friend didn't drown."

Scotty and Willa exchanged nods as she fanned herself with her hat.

"The way I see it, Miz Liz, them's lucky ducks that they didn't end up on your cookstove," Willa said, then hooted with laughter.

"How much do I owe you?" Lizbeth asked stiffly after everyone had a good giggle.

Scotty wiped his hands on his overalls. "It was no trouble. Just my good deed for the day."

"I meant how much do I owe you to keep this quiet?" Lizbeth whispered.

Scotty chuckled. "Ma'am, I could write a book about some of the things that go on in this graveyard, and it's sure not the residents that I'm talking about. They're well-behaved. It's the visitors who get restless after they come through them arches yonder. Don't give it another thought, Mrs. Forrester. I was very fond of your Cameron. On his honor, I won't breathe a word."

"Thank you." Lizbeth extended her hand. "I'll make you some plum jelly, Scotty."

"Sounds like a deal," he said and drove off. Soggy cattails clung to the big tractor tires.

Willa loved being the center of attention. She was still roaring about it when they pulled up to her house with Jemma at the wheel.

"Miz Lizbeth, don't fret about this no more. I ain't had that much fun since a mouse run up Brother Cleo's britches when we was cleanin' out the fraidy hole. I mean it, now."

Lizbeth forced a smile. "I'm just glad you didn't get hurt, Willa. You'll never want to ride with me again. Not that I'll be doing any driving anyway."

"Hush puppies. The good Lord holds my life in His hands. He don't want me to be foolish, but He don't want me to sit around on my caboose all the time neither. I'll ride with you. Just honk and I'll come limpin' out." She was still giggling when she got to her porch.

Trina just shook her head. "See y'all later."

That evening, Lizbeth pieced quilt squares in the living room while Spencer and Jemma played chess in the kitchen. Jemma braided her hair and twisted rubber bands around the ends as Spencer contemplated his next move.

"Do you think she'll get over this?" he asked.

"She's just embarrassed," Jemma said, countering his move.

"I don't like those pushbutton controls," Spencer said. "They are confusing. Anybody could hit the wrong one by accident."

"I see now why they had a pouting room," Jemma whispered. "It's weird to see your own grandmother in a big snit like this."

"I'm giving her the Corvair. I'd get you any car you want, too, if you'd let me," Spencer said.

Jemma kissed him. "Nope. It was Papa's."

"Let's go watch the stars," he said, pulling on her braids.

At the river, they put a quilt on the hood of the still warm Corvette. They kissed, as was their stargazing ritual, then laid back, arms folded under their heads.

"Tell me about Paris," Jemma said, finding Orion.

"I want to show you Paris, baby."

She touched his chin, the way she'd touched his picture for that whole year.

"Spence, if you captured a firefly in a jar would you keep it there, just to watch, or would you let it go?" She had no idea why she'd posed such a thing to him.

He turned his eyes on the heavens. "I think that there's a secret about fireflies, Jem. It's the firefly's heart that gives off light, and if we hold such hearts captive, even for a few seconds, they must always be set free to rise above the earth and become the stars."

Whoa, whoa. The wind fluttered his hair at that very moment, and she was in awe of him. How many more incredible things like that did he have inside his head, or even better, in his heart.

***

Lizbeth stood over the flowerbed where Jemma was perfecting her weeding skills. "Honey, I'm worried about Lester. He hasn't come over in two days."

Jemma took off her gloves and wiped her forehead. "I thought maybe he was in the doghouse with you or something. Have you been over to his place?"

"No, but would you mind going with me to do that now?"

"I'll go, Gram. You stay here." She got no response when she knocked on either of his doors. She checked his garage and shed, too. "Do you know if he has a spare key?" she yelled.

"I think there may be one in the clothespin bag on his clothesline."

There was. Jemma opened his back door and stepped inside.

"Lester?" She rummaged through the old mail on the table. The dishes were clean in the drainer and his bed was made up. There was nothing unusual in the house. She put the key back and found Lizbeth wringing her hands in the driveway.

"I should have checked on him sooner, but I was busy on a quilt. Shame on me," Lizbeth said.

"He didn't say anything to you about leaving?"

"Oh, sugar, he talks so much he could have told me that he was running off to become a missionary and I wouldn't have noticed."

"You want me to ask at the barbershop?" Jemma asked.

"No, I don't want to scare folks. It's just not like him, poor old thing."

"Let's give him one more day."

Lizbeth nodded, but doubt lingered in her eyes. During the supper blessing, she said a special prayer for Lester, and Jemma heard her get up several times during the night and open the back door to see if Lester's car was in the driveway.

Two mornings later, as Cotton John rattled on about the price of pork bellies on his radio show, the back screen door opened.

"Morning, y'all." Lester stood in the door sporting a Panama hat, a Hawaiian shirt, and flip-up sunglasses. Lizbeth and Jemma looked at each other. He came in and set a paper bag on the kitchen table.

"Howdy do from the sunny state of Californ-i-a." He hung his hat on the chair next to him.

Lizbeth switched off the radio and folded her hands on the table. "Where in this world have you been? We've been worried sick about you."

"Beg pardon, Miz Liz?"

"Don't call me that."

"Missus Forrester, ma'am, I sat right here last week and announced my intentions to head out to California to learn the chinchiller business."

"The what?" Lizbeth asked.

Lester's voice was shaky, like a one-room student sent to the corner. "The chinchiller business. I'm gonna raise the little critters to sell. I told you the whole plan right here in this kitchen."

"Chinchillas?" Jemma asked.

"That's the ticket," he said. "Chinchillers. I expect everybody downtown knew where I was off to."

Lizbeth was in no mood for excuses. "Take off those ridiculous things."

Lester fumbled with his flip-ups. "Well, sir, I don't know nothin' else to say. If I caused y'all to worry, I'm sure sorry."

"You gave us a fright," Lizbeth added.

"Then, I'm askin' forgiveness, from the both of y'all." Lester's nose was scalded.

Jemma smiled at him. "It's okay, Lester. We're just glad you're

170

back."

Lizbeth was not so quick to let it go. "You're fixing to start peeling, too. A man your age shouldn't be out in the sun getting blistered like that."

Lester was a turtle, hopelessly abandoned on his back.

"Tell us about the chinchilla business," Jemma said. "I thought California had too many Republicans in it to suit you."

"It's gonna be my ship comin' in," he said, skipping the political comment. "I'm startin' off with a few newlyweds, then they'll be doin' the expandin' of my business for me."

"Where are you going to keep them?"

"In my shed. I got me some cages ordered and a heater so they won't get too cold in the winter."

"What exactly are chinchillas?" Lizbeth asked.

"Well, I have to say the little critters favor their cousins, right smart."

"I have no idea who such cousins would be," Lizbeth said.

He got quiet. "Mouse family."

"Help my life." Lizbeth cradled her head in her hands. "You mean to tell me that you've gone all the way to the Pacific Ocean to buy mice to multiply, practically in my backyard?"

His face drooped. "There's good money in chinchiller ranchin', Miz Liz."

"Mr. Timms, don't you ever bring one of those rodents in my house, no, not even anywhere on my property, and I don't want to hear a single word about them either. I detest vermin," Lizbeth said. "You might as well be raising snakes, in my book."

Jemma poured Lester a cup of coffee. "Are you going to be a rancher, Lester?"

He took an audible sip. "That's my plan."

Lizbeth arched an eyebrow and pointed at him. "Those folks saw you coming a mile away."

Lester gulped more coffee and Jemma bit her lip. The words lingered in the room until Lizbeth's shoulders began to tremble with laughter. "Since you're going to be a mouse cowboy, I suppose you'll have to brand them, too." She took off her glasses and wiped her eyes. "You can borrow some of my knitting yarn for the roundups, or maybe you could just set out some cheese and they'd come running." She took a deep breath, but started laughing again. She looked at

Lester, then headed for the bathroom, blowing her nose behind the closed door.

Lester's ears had turned the color of the Corvette. He picked up his hat and left without another word.

Lizbeth opened the bathroom door.

"Lester went home," Jemma said.

"Fiddlesticks," Lizbeth muttered and rushed out after him.

Jemma looked in the bag that Lester had left behind on the table. Inside was a giant conch shell and several peaches. In a few minutes, Lizbeth came back with Lester in tow.

"Jemmabeth, could you start some fresh coffee? I want to hear more about Lester's business, don't you? Oh, and get out the bread and dewberry jam, please. Here, Lester, have a seat. Let me take your hat."

Jemma hid her smile. Gram was probably right. Dewberry jam could be good with crow.

CHAPTER NINETEEN

Restoration

S pencer left for a weekend conference in Dallas, and Jemma got up her nerve. "Gram, I want to ask you a favor. If you don't want to do it, it's okay."

Lizbeth poured the rest of her coffee in the sink. "I'll be happy to help."

"When I was a little girl, you told me that someday you would show me the things in the soldier box. Do you think we could do that now?"

Lizbeth's fingers pressed into the yellow vinyl on a kitchenette chair. "I suppose so."

Jemma unhooked the latch and pushed the creaky door. She moved the TV trays out of the way. "Who named this the pouting room?" she asked, making an extra effort to sound cheerful under the circumstances she had created.

Lizbeth took a big breath just before she ducked under the doorway. "Oh, that was your Papa. When we first married he said I needed a place to pout when we quarreled. When the boys and Julia came along, that's where we would send them to settle down if they got into mischief. On the home place, the pouting room was more like a real room where Papa did his paperwork for the farm. This little nook has served the purpose though." Lizbeth blinked at the soldier box. Her visits had always been private.

"Should we move the trunk into the kitchen?" Jemma asked.

"No, no, I like it here. We can sit on the floor, if you'll help me up later." Lizbeth opened the trunk and set Paul's letters aside, as though they were not there. She took out two velvet boxes. "I used to polish these medals, but that seems a little strange to me now."

Jemma opened the containers and traced around the hearts with George Washington in the middle. Lizbeth lifted out more velvet boxes: Distinguished Flying Cross, Air Medal with Oak Leaf Cluster, Bronze Star, and Good Conduct Medals, among others. She carefully placed three mustard colored telegrams in her granddaughter's lap. Jemma unfolded one, curious at first, then a chill crept over her as she realized how it must have felt to open them for the first time. *The Secretary of War desires me to express his deep regret that your son...* Not wanting to read the other two, she touched Lizbeth's arm. "We don't have to do this, Gram. It was rude of me to ask."

"It's all right. I need to show you." Lizbeth withdrew several notebooks tied together with ribbon. "These were Matthew's Bible study notes. He planned to enter the ministry when he got home. Bless his heart." Lizbeth untied the ribbon and opened the top notebook. The penciled entries were organized by chapters of the New Testament. Pages were meticulously numbered and cross-referenced with notations in the margins. There was also a large, leather-bound Bible. Lizbeth held it for a moment. "This was my father's. We gave it to Matthew on his sixteenth birthday. He was always a serious young man, very caring. His girlfriend's name was Eileen Sittler. I heard she's married now and lives in California with her family, but she used to write to us." She exhaled. "Here are some of Luke's drawings. What do you think about them, sugar?"

It was like taking her uncle's hand. It was easy to see that he was good. The sketches were very detailed with no apparent erasures or second attempts on the subjects. They were all portraits of young women with each personality revealed in elegant detail. Most were suppressing a grin, some peering over their shoulders, a la Betty Grable, but all their eyes were fastened on the artist. "These are excellent," she said.

"Luke had a way with the young ladies. He was so outgoing and full of nonsense, like his pa." She opened a heavy photograph album filled with laughing babies growing into teenagers. Jemma looked over Lizbeth's shoulder as she turned the pages on their lives: chubby infants in lacy gowns; tow-headed, grinning boys and a tom boy girl dressed up for church; and lanky, barefooted kids on the train tracks. Other photos showed the foursome hiding their teeth with watermelon seeds, building snowmen, riding mules, climbing the home place windmill, forming a human pyramid, and wearing soldier uniforms with their arms around their pa. The last was of all the boys standing at attention, saluting Julia.

174

"Was Matthew more like you?" Jemma asked.

"Oh, yes, and Luke like Cam."

Jemma thumbed through a few photos that had come loose from their mountings. "What about Daddy?"

Lizbeth rested against the wall. "He is some of both, but they were all good sons. Your daddy, being the baby, took a lot of foolishness from his big brothers, but he was a good sport. He and Julia carried a heavy burden when we lost them. The government sent Jimmy home after we learned that Matthew was not just missing, but gone. Sometimes I forget how those two must grieve. Julia is open about everything, but Jimmy hides it. At least he has Alex and you children. He was my baby, but now he and Julia are my Gibraltar."

Jemma leaned into the trunk and felt around for something else to talk about. She took out two stacks of old letters tied with ribbon. One look at the return addresses and she laid them aside. She would not intrude on precious correspondence between parents and departed sons. There were several cigar boxes held together with rubber bands and filled with ribbons from track meets, little wooden toys, a miniature metal horse and two high school rings. She found several pages of poetry written by Luke and a program from a play.

"Whose rock is this?" Jemma asked, giving Lizbeth a white, pitted stone.

Lizbeth turned the rock over in her hand then placed it back in the trunk. "That was a birthday present from Luke to Matthew on his birthday. Luke must have been about three years old then and Matt about five."

There were several shirts at the bottom, wrapped in tissue. Jemma looked through them. "No wonder you treasure all this, Gram, it's like pieces of your heart."

Lizbeth touched the paper, then retreated. She cleared her throat. "I couldn't throw those shirts away, but I couldn't bring myself to seeing other youngsters wearing them, either."

"Let's stop for now," Jemma said. "We'll finish some other time." She replaced everything, closed the lid, then helped Lizbeth to her feet. They left the trunk as they had found it, like the Chase mausoleum. Lizbeth had done it and survived. They had both seen the necklace at the bottom, but neither had mentioned it.

It was Friday and Jemma was in a fizz, almost late to work. "Gram, I've been thinking about those shirts," she said, downing a glass of juice. "You've made quilts before out of old dresses and shirt scraps. Wouldn't it be nice to make one for your bedroom and use Matthew and Luke's shirts?"

Lizbeth folded her newspaper on the table. "I suppose. I know they aren't doing anybody any good in that musty old soldier box." She managed a smile. "Thank you for thinking about it."

Jemma waved and was out the door. Lizbeth blinked after her.

Lizbeth didn't feel like eating a noon meal. Instead, she made a pot of coffee and drank most of it, staring at the pouting room door. She set her cup in the sink and got the shirts. There were seven in all plus a skinny rag doll she had made for Julia from one of her old petticoats. Matthew's shirts were dark blue and brown, made of sensible and sturdy cotton. Luke's were cotton as well, a plain khaki, a bright blue, and the other a green plaid. There was one small item that all the boys had worn, a cream colored baby's undershirt. At the bottom of the stack was Jimmy's favorite shirt from high school—a faded red corduroy. She tried to brush aside visions of the three of them bounding over the fence to catch the rattletrap school bus, their hair still wet from the windmill pump, with Julia tagging behind. Those grinning, freckled faces with hands stretched high to catch the wind, would reappear as they raced home from school at day's end. Lizbeth swallowed hard, thinking she shouldn't have drunk so much coffee. She rested, hoping the queasiness would subside.

She took the shirts to the good bed and spread them out, cutting each into squares and saving the buttons in the nightstand drawer. Her hands made quick work of it, but her mind was overflowing with the past and it seemed to disconnect from the working parts of her, as though she had snipped the final thread that had secured her composure over the years. She tossed out the little bits of fuzz left over from her assault until only the baby shirt remained. Its fabric was cotton soft, worn almost to the fiber by use and washings. There were no buttons to remove, just small satin ribbons once tied across fat tummies. A stain on one sleeve was barely noticeable, but she knew it was there. Lizbeth stroked the tiny arms and positioned the heavy blade of the scissors under the widest part of the shirt, but her hand would not move the metal, it trembled instead with such violence that she let the scissors drop on the bedspread. She sank down to the throw rug beside the bed in the fear that she might faint, then leaned forward to let the moment pass.

She moved to the oak chair that was her mother's and caressed the fabric as she rocked. She lifted the shirt to her face with the desperate notion that some fragrance of her babies might still linger. The chair creaked in gentle rhythm with her body as the tempo increased, then came to a sudden halt, like a bird shot in mid-flight. The misery rose through her chest and throat until a pitiful moan shuddered out of her. Then, in waves of unrelenting sobs, she wept. Her cheeks became slick with tears until her glasses fell in her lap and she buried her face in the soft folds of the shirt.

The clock chimed another hour. Lizbeth steadied herself and went to the portrait on the wall to touch it for the first time. The brushstrokes of oil were hard against her fingers, the same as his dear face just before they laid him to rest. The faintest hint of violets and roses, like those she wore in her hair on their wedding day crept through her senses. She looked into the blue eyes on the canvas and whispered, "I'm still standing, Cameron Forrester. I am still standing."

She folded the baby shirt between two sheets of tissue paper and tucked it back in the soldier box. She shut the pouting room door and washed her face in the kitchen sink.

☙❧

Spencer called Jemma right after breakfast. "Hey, let's go to Amarillo for dinner, a movie, bowling, whatever you want."

"Putt-putt golf."

"I'll see you at five."

The evenings were getting warmer. They ate Mexican food and played eighteen holes at the Amarillo Fun Park. Spencer was in top putting form and won a banana split bet.

"You hate to lose, don't you?" he said, blowing his straw wrapper into her float. "Have you thought any more about us getting married? I need to know so I can propose and not get turned down."

Jemma was caught off guard again, even though she had thought of little else for weeks.

"We aren't just best friends, Jem." He leaned across the table. "Not the way we kiss."

"Remember, I'm not ready to marry anybody." It was probably the ice cream that zapped her brain as she spoke.

"I'm not going to sit by while you daydream about your summer romance. I know that you love me; you're just too stubborn to admit it. I'll refresh your memory. My conference at Syracuse is in three weeks, then I'm off to Italy," Spencer said.

"But you'll come home for Christmas."

"Maybe. It depends on you. I can stay in Florence and finish my degree or come back to Syracuse and graduate there. How far away do you want me? I can be in Europe or New York."

"I thought this was a study abroad program."

"If the program is as great as they say it is, I might stay. The university also has an impressive school of art, Jem. After all, it is Florence."

"You'll find some Italian bombshell and forget about me anyway." She could have talked all day and not said that.

He narrowed his gray eyes at her. "I want to spend the rest of my life with you, baby."

She pushed the float aside and bit her lip. "I don't know what else to say, Spence. I'm just not ready yet." There it was, a second zap to her brain.

Jemma lay awake that night considering the next year without Spencer. It didn't take a genius to make a commitment to the sweetest man in the world. What could she possibly get from Mr. Turner that she didn't already have with Spence? It had to be the hat and the snakeskins. She was so pathetic. She went to the living room and sat in Papa's chair for a while, sketching familiar faces on Lizbeth's lined stationery until she fell asleep. She awoke in the morning with a quilt spread over her.

Lizbeth was drinking coffee at the kitchenette. "Good morning, honey. I hope you slept well."

"Thanks for the quilt." Jemma yawned and got ready for work. It was going to be a late one. Eleanor's gall bladder was acting up.

❧❦

The Judge let her go home just before midnight when he got back from his poker game. She tiptoed inside and hung her coat on the hall tree. Lizbeth was still up and reading in bed. "It's way past your bedtime," Jemma scolded.

Lizbeth closed her Bible and swung her feet to the side of the bed. "I want to show you something," she said and headed to the good bedroom. She flipped on the light switch then stood back to watch Jemma's reaction.

"Oh, my goodness, it's beautiful!" Jemma caressed the shirts from the soldier box, now blended together with stitches in the Lone Star pattern. She smiled. "It has a blue corner. That's Papa watching, isn't it?" She turned to Lizbeth, then gasped. "Oh, Gram, I've never seen you cry. I know it was so hard for you to create, but it truly is a masterpiece."

"No, it's just a bunch of cotton, but it was my life, our life." Lizbeth rubbed her forehead. "I need to get some sleep. Goodnight, sugar." She paused in the doorway. "Jemmabeth, would you keep me company if I sleep in here tonight?"

"I'd be honored."

Lizbeth folded back the covers and reclined between the sheets. Jemma lay down beside her, still in her jeans.

"Sweet dreams," Lizbeth said. "Say your prayers."

Cam's portrait was faintly illuminated by the moonlight filtering into the room. Jemma's eyes rested on his and it came to her. "Gram, I've been thinking Papa's portrait is too big for this room. Would it be all right if I add it to my portfolio?"

Lizbeth sighed. "I do admire that painting, but I feel like he is standing in here, actually out of his resting place. Oh, my, don't tell anybody I said that."

Jemma reached for her hand. "I'm sorry that I did that to you."

"Hush now. You can't help being good at what you do. The way he's looking, well, you caught the little blue corner, too."

"Daddy says it was always on them, making them behave."

"It was, but with a twinkle. He was a special man."

"I'll take it to the car house in the morning."

"Thank you, honey." The gratitude offered was for much more than Jemma could ever realize.

CHAPTER TWENTY

Unto His Nest Again

Her transistor radio was blasting, but she sensed someone watching her. She let a brush drop on the tarp and, as she bent to pick it up, glanced at the window. Shorty Knox was barely visible at the window's edge, but for some reason, he didn't frighten her at all. He stayed about ten minutes. She did hear him leave and she watched out the window as he darted down the alley, step stool in hand. He came again the next three nights. After a week, he was on his stool for at least a half hour, watching various paintings evolve, not her. Jemma angled her easel to give him a better view, and she hadn't said a word to anybody—especially Spencer. He would have a cow.

Shorty came the same time every night. On the last Friday of the second week, she left the car house lights on but stood in the shadows of the pecan tree. Shorty arrived as usual, setting up his stool under the window. She had never realized how tiny he was. Lester was right about Shorty being the height of Gram's cookstove.

"Would you like to come in, Shorty?" Jemma asked. He tumbled off his stool then backed up on all fours.

"Didn't do nothin'!" he shouted.

"No, no, you didn't do anything at all. I would like to paint your picture, like I did this little boy. He's my brother. Please let me."

Shorty was halfway into the alley before he stopped.

"You callin' the sheriff on me?"

"No, I'm not. Let me draw your picture and then, if you like, you can watch from the window while I paint. It'll just take a few minutes, but I need the light to do it."

Jemma opened the door to the car house and stood back. "It's okay, just sit on my stool over there. It won't be long. See, no phones in here."

Shorty came in like a sick pup, but he smelled much worse. Jemma took shallow breaths and got her sketchpad. Shorty spent the time surveying the other portraits around the room, but her stool was too tall for him. His feet dangled, sporting two different kinds of boots with no laces. He was gotch-eyed, which had to make his peeping Tom business difficult, and he used his mouth like an antennae to detect sounds. His head was topped off with a tattered fedora perched on flapjack-sized ears.

"All done," she said. Shorty hopped off the stool without a word and evaporated. She added detail to her sketches and left the door open for some fresh air. Anything for art.

She began his portrait the next Monday. A cold snap hit the Panhandle and it brought much-needed rain with it. He didn't come that night, so she did the background work. He was there the next night, standing on the stool for almost an hour. Jemma would have worked longer, but she took pity on him as he shivered in the chilly air. The next night she left one of her winter jackets under the window. He came as usual and the coat was gone when she went to bed. The piece was coming along, but she had no idea what Shorty thought about it. He never made a sound, but lasted each night as long as she did. He left abruptly once when Spencer showed up and knocked on the door. Jemma went outside immediately to talk to him since she wasn't quite ready to explain her latest work to anybody.

"Hi, baby," Spencer said. "It smells like something's cooking in there. Are you staying warm?"

"It's just that old campstove," she said. "I got cold so I fired it up. It stinks, but I'm fine. What brings you out during my work time, you naughty boy? I thought we agreed that I can't paint with you in the room any more."

"I miss you," he said. "I drove over for a kiss."

She gave him one worthy of his trip across town.

"Could I come every night for one of those?"

"You may, and here's one for the road. Now, scram."

"Is Gram awake? I thought I might just visit with her a while."

"I don't know," she said, eyeing him. "See if her light is on."

"Love you, Jem." He stood there for a few seconds, then walked away.

Jemma went back to her work, but changed her mind. She cleaned her brushes and went into the house. All was dark, Gram was asleep, and Spencer's car was gone.

She grabbed her keys and found him at Son's. "Tell me what's going on," she said.

"You're supposed to be working."

"I'm almost finished with the piece anyway."

"That's good news." He avoided her eyes.

"Let's go back to Gram's and talk, Spence."

"I'll be there in a minute," he said, gesturing with his burger.

They drank cherry lime Dr. Peppers, a specialty of Son's, and Jemma gave him a shoulder rub. "Is it your family?" she asked.

"Yeah. The usual. They set an all-time high for being nasty tonight and I just couldn't take it anymore. It's not like when we were in high school. Then, I was so busy doing sports and stuff that I could be away from the house until they went to sleep. Living with them now is the pits. Mother yells and screams and tonight she was throwing stuff around. She actually started swatting at Dad with a lamp. It's a wonder somebody doesn't get hurt. I'd call Sheriff Ezell if he hit her back, but he's not made that way. Mother's the fighter. I guess it's sort of unfair that I don't call the sheriff on her, but when I have the nerve, I'm getting her into a treatment center. She needs help bad."

"I'm so sorry, Spence."

He leaned back against the couch and looked at her like a little boy. "Hope I didn't ruin your night, baby."

"You could never do that."

"I miss your Papa," he said. "I always wanted to be like him—a friend to everybody. He was the last of his kind, wasn't he?"

"Yeah. My Daddy is pretty special, too."

"Sure, but he has some coaching persona, too. Papa was just himself. He made me forget about my problems. I like the portrait of him that you did for Gram. Would you paint me one sometime?"

"I will. I'm working on a few things right now, but I will this summer, I promise."

He yawned. "Thanks, Jem. Sorry to be so down."

"I'm sorry that I paint at night."

"I guess it's time I moved out on my own," he mumbled, eyes closed.

That thought gave her a chill. It shouldn't have, but it did.

He soon fell asleep. She kissed his forehead and covered him with a quilt.

He was gone when she woke up the next morning, and the quilt was neatly folded on Papa's chair.

⟫⟪

The nights warmed up again and Shorty and Jemma continued their vigil until the painting was done. On that night, she turned to the window and smiled at him. "May I keep this, Shorty? I want to take it to my school, but I have some drawings for you. They are in that folder by the window. Thank you for letting me paint your picture."

He blinked at her then bobbed his head. She hung the painting on the wall next to the one of Robbie. A couple of times a week he came by to look at it. Jemmabeth acted as though she didn't see him so he would feel welcome.

⟫⟪

Carrie had just given her a sound beating in Scrabble.

"Hey, want to go to Son's for a Dr. Pepper?" Jemma asked. "I have the car today."

Carrie giggled. "Oh, my gosh."

At Son's, two teenage boys in the car next to the Dodge flirted with them as they sipped their drinks.

"Can you believe that they are looking over here?" Carrie asked.

"They have to be on their lunch break from high school," Jemma said.

"They must be looking at you, Prom Queen," Carrie said.

"Nope. It's you and your blonde hair. It's getting long, by the way."

"They'd change their minds if they could see all of me," Carrie said, watching them and twisting a lock of her hair around her finger.

Jemma started the Dodge. "That will have to remain a mystery because it's time to get you home."

"I hope they don't follow us." Carrie waved at them and grinned. "Then they would see me get out."

"Nah. They have to get back to school."

"That was so cool. Let's go back tomorrow," Carrie said, looking over her shoulder.

"It's a date." Jemma waved at Twila, who was walking home from work.

Carrie gave Jemma a sidelong glance. "Tell me what it's like to kiss a guy."

"Well, it can be the highlight of the day," Jemma said, thinking of Kenneth's remark. Rats. She and Spence hadn't been to visit the Rippetoes yet. Maybe she'd call them over the weekend.

"You told me that you dated half of Dallas last year. I bet you kissed them all," Carrie said.

"Hey, I didn't say that I kissed all of those guys. Some of them were real creeps."

"So, who's the best kisser, Paul or Spencer?"

She didn't really like hearing their names linked up like that. "The cowboy was smooth, but he's been around a while. Spence gets this look in his eye just before and, well..."

"Is that all you do, kiss?" Carrie asked.

"Of course," Jemma said. "We made a promise. No monkey business until after the wedding bells."

Carrie raised her brow. "What about Paul?"

"What about him?"

"You said the agreement was with Spencer."

"I couldn't promise that to Spence and give in to somebody else. I guess it never occurred to us that we would be dating other people. You're getting too nosy. Let's get you in the cannon." Jemma lifted Carrie out of the car and into her wheelchair.

"Do you think I'll ever kiss anybody?"

"If you can ever get out of this house for more than an hour." Jemma sat by the window and watched Carrie doze off in the cannon with an overwhelming urge to give her the joy that she deserved. This was worthy of a prayer. She asked the Lord to show her what to do. He was probably surprised to hear her asking for help before a wild idea rather than afterwards.

❧ ❧

Lizbeth stood on the front porch and looked skyward. "I don't like the feel of this. The sky is green and there's no wind."

"At least it's not raining yet," Jemma said. "I'm going over to Trina's, but I'll be back in an hour, okay?"

"You keep your eye on these clouds, honey."

An eerie calm hovered in the air as she walked across the tracks, but the 'tunias seemed bright and perky. Willa was standing on the porch as Jemma walked up. "I ain't no weatherman, but something's brewin'."

"You sound just like Gram. Is Trina busy?" Jemma asked.

"She's makin' a dress for Miz Lewis's girl and she's a big 'un, like me," Willa said, laughing.

Trina didn't look up from an ocean of pink taffeta when Jemma came in.

"I keep forgetting to ask you, where is Weese these days?" Jemma asked, watching Trina guide the fabric under the needle.

"Somebody told Mama that he got into trouble in Amarillo. The police thought he stole some money, but they couldn't prove it. That boy's meaner than dirt and about half as smart. He came slinking around the house the other day and told Mama that he was joining the army."

"They'll send him to Vietnam."

"Maybe that'll straighten him out," Trina said over the whir of the old Singer. "Too bad we couldn't put him in the cannon. That'd teach him a lesson if he spent a few nights in there."

Jemma studied a postcard of the Eiffel Tower that was tacked to the wall. "I wonder how long it's been since Carrie has been to a clinic. Did you know that she's never had any kind of physical therapy? She might be able to move her legs for all we know."

"Mama told me that The Judge doesn't trust doctors."

"Really?" Jemma turned to her. "Maybe I'll say something to him."

"Oh, boy, here we go," Trina said, shaking her head and refilling the bobbin.

"What does that mean?" Jemma asked.

"It means, The Judge better eat his Wheaties."

The wind came up and Jemma shut the windows, but it still rattled the roof. They joined Willa on the porch. Gusts whipped the branches of the elm trees and rippled the Johnson Grass in wanton, choppy waves. The sky was a canopy of moss colored pearls.

"You girls get my 'tunia boots." Willa held the door while the girls

186

brought in all they could carry.

Rain blasted the tin roof like the heavens just opened up.

Jemma held up her hands. "Listen." Through the pounding on the roof, they heard it.

"Oh, law!" Willa shouted. "That ain't no noon whistle. Get to the fraidy hole!" She threw a dishtowel over her head, grabbed her cane, and headed out the door. The girls followed, steadying her as she grunted down the steps.

"I'm going home," Jemma yelled.

"No, you're not," Trina yelled back, "you're helping me get Mama into the fraidy hole."

The whistle never stopped. Jemma glanced in the direction of the tracks. The elms thrashed and the rain turned to hail, pelting their arms. They leaned into the wind and half dragged an exhausted Willa to a metal door protruding out of the ground behind the church. Willa beat on it with her cane until the door cranked opened. It took several young men to shut it again as the women made their way down the steps. Brother Cleo helped bolt it with a heavy piece of lumber.

They quickly adjusted to the somber mood in the musky darkness. Lit by two coal oil lanterns hanging from the crossbeams, the room was crammed with people. Jemma stood out from the crowd, her face even whiter in the lantern glow. Brother Cleo gave her a hug.

"Sorry I'm so wet," she said.

"We're all sopping," he said and went to talk to Willa.

The noise overhead was deafening. "Over here," Trina yelled from a corner. They sat on stools fashioned from metal tractor seats. Trina shivered. "Aren't you freezing?"

"I just hope Gram is okay," Jemma said. "Surely she went to the cellar. I should have stayed with her."

"Lester will take care of her," Trina shouted, tucking her ponytail back into its rubber band. Jemma shook her wet hair. "Hey, cut that out, girl," Trina said as she brushed the extra dose of water off her arms.

"Sorry," Jemma yelled. A clap of thunder reverberated down the metal door. A little boy about Robby's age edged his way over to Trina and crawled in her lap. Jemma smiled at him as he nuzzled up to Trina with his fingers in his ears. The air was fraught with dust, damp clothing, sweat, and apples. In the shadows of the lamplight, she could see bushel baskets of old clothes, broken toys, canned goods, and overripe fruit.

"That's where we keep stuff for folks having a hard time," Trina screamed in Jemma's ear. It seemed to Jemma that everyone in the cellar could qualify. Something major walloped the door, causing shrieks from the children. Within seconds of their screams, another monstrous blow vibrated the room. Dust sifted from the rafters, and Jemma jumped up, her heart racing. The same violent tremors undulated above them that she had encountered with the Zephyr. The beams shook with such force that a lantern popped off its hook and crashed to the floor. Jemma grabbed Trina's arm and the little boy ran to his mother.

Brother Cleo's voice pierced the pandemonium. "Brothers and Sisters, let us gather in prayer."

The girls joined the circle and held hands with the others.

"Lord God Almighty, Creator of Heaven and earth and all who dwell upon it, we ask that you hold us in the palm of Your great hand, and, like the story in the Scriptures, we ask You to calm this tempest and deliver us to do Your glorious work until the day of reckoning. Amen."

A mother hummed "This Little Light of Mine" to her crying child and soon they all joined in singing. They were to the part about "won't let Satan blow it out" when a hush fell over the room.

Brother Cleo took the lantern off its hook. "Women and children move back yonder to the far corner. Men, come this way." The group did as they were told. Brother Cleo moved up the steps to examine the door. Jemma could hear the men straining until something heavy clattered down the stairs.

"Everybody all right?" Brother Cleo asked. There were reassuring responses, so the grunting and shuffling resumed, coupled with an intermittent pounding. Something was being used as a battering ram against the door. The sounds of metal being bent against its will were somewhat reassuring. Finally, a tiny shaft of light shot across the room, and collective sighs of relief rose up from the captives. "Now folks, we're going to see what can be done with the door. Stay where you are until we make sure it's safe out there."

Jemma said a prayer of her own. She would never forgive herself if anything had happened to Gram. At least Spencer should be home by now if he didn't get caught in this mess. The men spent another half hour working to remove something from the entrance, then the group filed silently up the steps and out through the twisted remains of the door.

The scene above ground was sickening. The little church was no more than rubble. A giant cottonwood tree was split into pieces with a big chunk of it sprawling across the fraidy hole and what was left of its door. Brother Cleo reached under a splintered piece of wood and pulled out part of a hymnal. Others did the same, gathering up what they could salvage, which wasn't much. Willa and an older woman held one another, crying.

Jemma picked her way through the shambles towards home. The tornado had taken a crooked, wicked path. Willa's house had a gaping hole in the roof. Jemma raced through the trail, dodging odd mixtures of muddy clothing, paper, chunks of metal, slivers of wood, and tree limbs. Several elms were down behind Lizbeth's house, their roots sticking up like Medusa's hair. Lizbeth's pecan tree was still there, as was her house. Jemma's shoe came off in the sludgy mess that had collected in the alley, so she was standing on one foot when her heart stopped. The roof of the car house was gone as well as one wall. She raced to look inside, then collapsed on her knees, breathless. All the paintings she had done over the last year were gone.

Lizbeth and Lester rushed towards her. They huddled together, stone still. Jemma's grasp was so tight on them that they couldn't have moved anyway. Lizbeth wiped her eyes. "I'm so grateful you are safe, but I can't tell you how sorry I am about the paintings. We should have moved them inside like Julia told us. It's all my fault, sugar."

Lester stared at the hapless remains. "That car house had a good roof. I helped Cam put 'er on in '61. Devil's work, that's what it is. Just a dang shame. There was a million dollars' worth of art in there, at least."

"Honey, you know strange things happen when a twister comes. Maybe we'll find them around the neighborhood," Lizbeth said, stroking Jemma's damp hair.

"I'll look for them tomorrow," Lester said, out of hopelessness. "I'm just as sorry as I can be, Jemmer girl."

Jemma sat on a splintered limb. Devil's work? Was she forever aligned with him? If she started now, maybe she could paint some of them again by August.

Where was God's plan in this? It was too painful for her to sort through and find some spiritual lesson. Maybe she was being punished for stepping foot in The Handle Bar. She picked up bits and pieces of the little birdhouses that were strewn around the yard, then wandered around to the front porch. The swing was impaled in the honeysuckle vine, but still in one piece.

They had water and that was it. Whatever Lizbeth had in the fridge they took to Willa's. Once there, Lester shifted his weight and sighed repeatedly. He had never paid a social visit to a home across the tracks. "Sorry about your church and all. I lost my chinchillers."

"Well, that's too bad," Willa said. "Losing critters is worse than me losing part of my old roof. I reckon the good Lord will take care of us."

"Jemmerbeth lost ever one of her paintings," Lester said.

"Oh, no, sugar pie, come give me a hug." Willa stretched out her arms.

"Girl, you didn't lose them all, did you?" Trina asked.

Jemma raised her chin. "Willa, what can we do about your roof? You can't sleep with it open like that."

"You're welcome to stay at my house," Lizbeth said, "and Lester has an extra bedroom if your neighbors need a place."

Lester looked at her like she had just announced she was a Republican.

"We'll be fine, Miz Lizbeth, but thank you kindly," Willa said. "I'm just glad it ain't rainin'."

"Lester, the tarp that was in Papa's car house is in the backyard. Couldn't we nail it up on the roof to keep the rain out?" Jemma asked.

"I think I could get up there." Trina sized up the hole.

"That'll work," Lester said. "I'll get my ladder."

"Mama, we'll be right back, okay?" Trina said.

Willa joined Lizbeth who was already making sandwiches.

The Sheriff was there when they returned.

"He's been here before, talking to Weese," Trina said as they dragged the tarp to the back of the house. They set up Lester's ladder and Jemma climbed up halfway with a corner of the thick canvas. Trina followed her with more of it, until they pulled it up the whole way. It was heavier than they thought. "My grandpap built this old house," Trina said, struggling with the weight.

"He did a good job," Jemma said. They stretched it across the hole as best they could, then drove nails through the tarp and into the tin. It looked awful, but it covered the hole and they didn't break their necks like Lester said they would.

"I could use a bath," Jemma said, wiping her face on her arm.

Trina brushed mud off her arms and legs. "Me too."

"What did the Sheriff say?" Jemma asked as they tied the ladder to the top of Lester's car.

"The road is closed to Amarillo, but he said the tracks are cleared off, so they can get supplies in," Lizbeth said.

"That means Spence is stuck up there. I hope he's okay," Jemma said.

Willa poked at a stray petunia blossom with her cane. "There's gonna be some gov'ment fellas here tomorrow to see if we need help."

"Well, that's not too hard to figure out." Trina slumped on the steps.

Lester cleared his throat. "The Sheriff said that some folks were killed over to the river."

Jemma looked up. "Who was it, Lester?"

"Well, sir, the only ones they knew for sure were Wilma Rippetoe and her boy."

Lizbeth covered her mouth. "I always liked that young man and his mama, too. They had a hard life. Such a shame, oh, I do hate to hear that."

Jemma leaned against the side of the house. "Kenneth was an Eagle Scout." She slipped down to the ground, her shoulders shaking.

⊰⟩⟨⊱

It was after midnight as she sat on the cold steel, waiting for the 9:04. As it passed, blowing its horn, she screamed with all her soul, the kind of scream she thought an eagle might have made, long and loud. The Lord had taken them unto His nest, but they did not die in vain. Jemma would see to that if she never accomplished anything else. She took a somber bath by candlelight, and went to bed. The Devil may have brought the tornado, but not getting around to having supper with Wilma and Kenneth Rippetoe was nobody's fault but her own.

CHAPTER TWENTY-ONE

Rescues & Risks

Jemma woke up at the sound of Spencer's voice, just as Lizbeth knocked on her door. "Honey, get up quick and put something on. We have company."

She threw on her old robe and padded out of her room, numb and depressed. Everybody scurried around rather suspiciously.

She ran to hug Spencer, but stepped back. "Are you okay?" He smiled and turned her shoulders. "Oh my gosh!" she said, then held on to the sides of the doorframe and bawled. "Thank you. Thank you, Lord. Where were they?"

"Lined up on the front porch," Spencer said, dusting off his hands.

"Oh, my goodness, they're all here." Jemma jumped from painting to painting, touching each one. She squealed when she came to her brushes, still in the little cowboy boots. "How is this possible? Lester, where did you find them?"

"Well, sir, truth is, I hadn't even started looking for them, no offense, Jemmerbeth. I don't know how the Sam Hill they got there. I worked on that porch swing last night and there weren't no paintings out there then."

"This calls for a celebration," Lizbeth said. "I'll make blueberry pancakes." She and Lester went inside, exchanging theories about the paintings.

"Any ideas about this?" Spencer asked, taking Jemma's hand. "There has to be a logical explanation."

"I don't have a clue. Look at my brushes and the boots. They're in perfect shape. It's all too weird."

They took the paintings to the living room and examined them.

"That must have made you sick, baby, to think that all your art was gone." Spencer frowned at the portrait of Shorty. "When did you do this one?"

"A few weeks ago," she said into a yawn.

"You didn't do this from seeing him around town."

Jemma tried to sound casual. "He posed for me."

"Are you crazy? Where did this all take place?"

"In the car house. He was watching me paint so I asked him to come inside and let me sketch him. He did."

"Jemmabeth Forrester, you need a spanking. That guy is not right in the head, and you were alone with him in the car house at night? Tell me that you will never do anything like that again."

"Okay, okay; I'm sorry, but he was like a lamb."

Spencer studied the portrait. "Doesn't he live close to Willa?"

"Yeah. He lives in that old dirt cellar at the end of her street." Jemma touched the painting of Papa.

"Look at this, Jem. There's sand on these canvases, but only on the bottom. You don't suppose that Shorty could have taken them to his place before the tornado hit, do you?"

Jemma's eyes widened. "I guess it's possible because I haven't painted the last two nights, and Lester said that Shorty could predict the weather when he was young. Oh, Spence, bless his heart. He even saved my boots."

"Let's not tell anybody, baby. Shorty did you a great favor. I'll think of some way to make it up to him, but he doesn't need a bunch of hoopla, okay?"

"He's like Boo Radley, in *To Kill a Mockingbird*, helping me," she said.

They talked about Kenneth and then sat looking at the paintings and the blotches of Panhandle dirt, most likely from a cellar across the tracks that had become an earthen stronghold against the Devil's work. She would never forget Shorty's kindness nor Kenneth's sweet invitation she let slip away like it didn't matter.

⋙⋘

Lizbeth was in the final stages of making her famous pecan divinity. She poured the hot corn syrup and sugar mixture into the egg whites while Jemma beat it in a heavy iron pot. Spencer had just left, and Lester watched from the kitchenette as he drove away.

"I sure do like that young'un, but I never could hold with his old man, Max-a-million Chase. His folks come from back East somewhere, big money people. Right there's the problem. That shifty feller's got money to burn. I bought a Ford truck off him about ten year ago. He was asking seventy-five smackers for it because it was supposed to be in such fine shape and he even showed me what low mileage it had. I was flabbergasted, so I bought it. Well, it wasn't worth a plug nickel. I went straight back to get shed of the thing. He come right out and told me a bald-faced lie, too. Said he got it off Buford Watson in Cleebur, who bought it new and only drove it to church. Seeing as how I went to school with Buford and knew he hadn't darkened a church door since he was in diapers, I paid my respects to him and the missus, then got the truth. Buford got that Ford off an old boy named Leroy Jessup during a trade for two blue ribbon sows way up to Sweetwater in '51. Leroy's son drove it to work in Abilene every day until the packing plant closed in '60. Plus, Buford and the missus took it on a whole slew of trips to Arkansas themselves. Why, it was on its last set of legs when he towed it into Chase's place behind his tractor. *Only drove it to church*, my foot. Bald-faced lie, just like I figgered."

"Was that the end of it?" Jemma asked.

"Nope. I drove right up to his car lot and waited 'til he come out for a cigarette break. I got so close I could tell his brand of smokes. He come hence to drinkin' a sody pop and took a few gulps with the bottle turned up right in front of my nose. I said to him, 'I'm drawin' back on your sorry hide, Max-a-million Chase. The truth ain't in you because Buford Watson done told me the truth. So you'd best draw back right now and may the best man win.' I was ready for him, too." Lester jumped up and assumed his boxing stance. He punched the air a couple of times then sat down. "Yes, sir. He's one sketchy cuss." He tapped his foot and Lizbeth and Jemma exchanged glances.

"Lester Timms," Lizbeth said, throwing up her hands. "You beat all I ever saw. What happened next? You get your audience all riled up, then quit at the most exciting part."

"Yeah, did you sock him?" Jemma asked.

Lester scratched his ear. "I drew back on him and I reckon that's all it took, 'cause my punch landed in thin air. He tucked tail and run off into that fancy office of his. Couple of days later, a check come in the mail for seventy-five big ones, and I kept the truck, too."

"Then you won the fight." Jemma couldn't wait to tell Spencer the story.

"You could say so," Lester nodded. "Fact is, I also took a spill on the concrete when I tried to land my punch. I kindly broke my nose," he said, sniffing. "That wasn't the only time I broke it, neither. First time, I must've been about eight or nine, me and some other young'uns was seein' who could throw a brick the highest. I probably won that match too, but the dang thing landed right across my nose while I was doin' my calculatin'. All the same, I throwed it up a good ways. Yes sir, this old arm's been right decent to me."

∽��

Jemma had been thinking about the painting of Robby. She set it on the bed, leaning the canvas against the wall.

Lizbeth stood back and admired it. "It gives me a chill, sugar. He is the image of your Uncle Luke. I just don't see how you can make those little dabs of paint put our Robby by that tree. It's like I'm looking out the window and there he is. I've seen him sit like that so many times, with his knees all drawn up. He looks like he just heard a little bird or something in the branches, doesn't he?"

"Gram, I am going to send it to the Lillygraces. Do you think that's a good idea?"

"Why, yes, honey, I do. Goodness, it is a big painting, isn't it? They'll have the perfect place for it in their grand house."

"I feel a little guilty because down deep I want them to regret the way they've ignored him."

"Well, they'll never know why you sent it. It'll be your heart that has to reconcile your motives. You need to forgive them, Jemmabeth. Some money folk have a hard time showing love."

"They could at least send him a birthday card once a year." She moved the painting off the bed and went to Papa's chair to write the letter.

∽��

A package came from Julia, and Lizbeth held up a polka-dotted driving scarf. A black and white photo fell to the floor. Jemma picked it up and got goose bumps. It was the picture Julia had told her about. She recognized the Negro Bethel Church and the big cottonwood tree. Standing to the left was Jemma's Brownie troop. In the front row was a little blonde cherub looking straight into the camera. There was no mistake; it was Carrie. It was impossible for Jemma to miss her own smiling face in the back row, but more than anyone else, it was an undeniable image of Trina Johnson with her slanted eyes and dimples. She stood in a cluster of little black girls, each holding a can of food. Brother Cleo was shaking hands with the troop leader, and Sandy Kay was holding a poster that read:

Troop 814—FOOD FOR THE POOR DRIVE—1951

She couldn't believe it, but there it was.

"Jemma, telephone. It's your Grandmother Lillygrace," Lizbeth said.

"What? It's not even Christmas." Jemma took the phone as Lizbeth swatted the seat of her pants. "Hello."

"Jemmabeth, dear. Your grandfather and I just received your letter, and we are sending a check to cover the cost of shipping for the painting. It sounds like you have been busy with your art. We are anxious to see the portrait of little Robert."

"Thank you, Grandmother. I didn't mean that y'all needed to pay for the shipping. I just wanted permission to send it."

"I'm sure it is nice, dear. Little Robert is a pleasant child. He writes to us now and then. So, it's all settled about the shipping?"

"Yes, ma'am. Thank you. I'll get it ready to go."

"We'll be glad to have it."

"Robby is a great little guy. I wish you could get to know him." Jemma threw that in just to be ornery.

"Yes, well, families live so far apart these days. Give my regards to Lizbeth. Oh, yes, and Trenton was here this weekend. He sends his love."

Jemma hung up and sat on the bed. Trent didn't love her. He didn't even know her. During the war, her mother's only sibling, Ted, was in the Air Force. His wife gave birth to Trent while he was overseas, but she took off when the baby was only a few weeks old. She gave him up to the Lillygraces to raise. "She just wasn't the type to be a proper mother," her Grandmother Lillygrace had explained, "too

196

nervous." Jemma overheard her mother say once that the Lillygraces had paid the baby's mom a sizeable amount for her to divorce Ted. The baby, Trent, then became the object of all their attention and affection when Ted made the Air Force his career. It was as though they had no other grandchildren. They were not at all pleased when Robby came along after such an embarrassing space of time. Jemma knew Trent about as well as she knew her grandparents. He had just received a degree from Stanford in structural engineering and, reportedly, had a great job in New York City. How could she say that Trent "sent his love"? Maybe that's how rich people make themselves think they care about each other.

❧❧❧

Lester was rosy with news. "Sheriff Ezell was down to the post office this mornin', and word has it that Shorty Knox done come up with a color TV for himself."

"How on earth could Shorty afford a color television? I don't even have one," Lizbeth said.

"It was bought and paid for by an anonymous person or persons. That's straight from the Sheriff."

Jemma grinned and finished up her oatmeal.

Lester went on. "I'd sure like to see Shorty in his dugout with a color TV. It's got a big antenner stuck in a slab of concrete right by the door, too. Even got its own generator. That just don't seem natural. Must've cost somebody a pretty penny."

"Maybe if Shorty has a television to watch, he won't be looking in windows," Jemma suggested.

Lizbeth nodded. "You could have a point."

"Well, be that as it may, that's not my best news." Lester beamed and waited for a query. He tapped his foot on the linoleum.

"Do we have to guess it?" Lizbeth said.

"Nope. Here it comes. Some feller down to the barbershop was going on about his young'un winnin' first prize for his school science project. Seems he showed how a varmint could follow a trail in a box or some such thing. Well, sir, he come hence to tellin' how the young'un found the varmint under the porch and it wasn't scared of them at all. They was pettin' it and the young'un was sleepin' with it."

"Are you thinking it is one of your chinchillas, Lester?" Jemma asked.

"It's Bruno. I figured it out right quick like when he said that the little critter likes to get under the pillow when he sleeps. Yes siree, that's my Bruno," Lester got a melancholy look in his eyes. "Them folks just live two blocks over."

"You don't mean to tell me that you slept with those things?" Lizbeth asked.

"Well, not ever single night, Miz Liz, but a feller has to have some company ever once in a while," Lester said, sipping his coffee.

Jemma waved good-bye to Lizbeth who looked as though she had just encountered a rat in her house.

⨎⨍

Lizbeth rarely got to answer the phone anymore, but she got a kick out of seeing Jemma run to get it before the first ring finished.

"Jemmabeth? Robert Lillygrace here, ah, your Grandfather. I trust all is well with you and your Grandma Elizabeth. I'll get right to the point. We received the painting today. I'm not sure what we were expecting, but often, with a subject matter such as you have chosen, the results are saccharine and rather clichéd. We were delighted and quite frankly, astounded with what you have done. It has a unique and fresh perspective and I look for that quality. Your mother has spoken of your art many times, but, well, we had no idea of the depth of your talent. We just got off the phone with your parents to share our accolades with them."

Jemma smiled to herself. "Thank you. I'm glad you like it."

"We were discussing your educational plans with your parents. As you know, I consider myself to have an eye for artistic talent. You may recall our collection from your visits."

"Yes sir, I do." Each visit, she had memorized a different painting and tried to replicate it with crayons on the trip home.

"What I am trying to say, dear, is that your Grandmother Catherine and I would like to make you a proposition. As you know, we have been generous patrons of the arts and find it quite satisfying to discover such giftedness within our own family. Our obvious reaction is to embrace your efforts. We are, after all, your

198

grandparents." He cleared his throat. "We want to fund the remainder of your education."

Totally stunned, she groped for words. "Even if I want to finish at Le Claire?"

"We can look at all options. I have acquaintances at numerous schools of art."

"Mom and Daddy know about all this?"

"Indeed. They consider it an opportunity to develop your talent without financial worries for any of you."

"Wow! This is such a surprise. I'll have to think about it, not that I don't appreciate it, but I like to sleep on things. Thank you and thank Grandmother for me."

"She's right here."

"Jemmabeth, dear." She sounded all smiles.

"Grandmother, I don't know what to say."

"The pleasure is ours. The painting is enchanting, and it is very touching that you sent it to us. We had no idea that our granddaughter was capable of such work. We cannot think of anyone else in the family with even the slightest flair for creating art," she said.

Jemma was quick with the answer. "My Uncle Luke, on my daddy's side, was an artist."

"How interesting. Well, then, we shall be talking with you very soon."

"Jemmabeth, it's Grandfather here again. The likeness of little Robert is brilliant. Is portraiture your forte?"

"Everybody calls him Robby, and yes, I am fascinated by it."

"Catherine and I have considered sitting for an updated portrait ourselves. Would you accept such a commission? You could come here and stay with us for a couple of weeks before the autumn term begins. That way we can become better acquainted and it would give us a chance to finalize your plans for the future."

"Yes sir, I guess I could do that. Everything is happening so fast."

"I will call you first thing Monday morning. Another thought. Would you like to have little Robert, Robby, come and visit at the same time? And perhaps Trenton, if he can get a weekend off?"

Jemma was about to pop, but she kept her cool. "That would be nice. Thank you."

"I'll call your Mother and work it out," he said. "Until Monday then."

She bounced on the good bed before leaping into the kitchen.

"Child, what's happened?" Lizbeth set down a steaming pan of potatoes, and Jemma danced her around the rippled floor while Cotton John compared fertilizer brands on the radio.

"You're not going to believe this," Jemma said. "The Lillygraces have offered to foot the bill for the rest of my college. All because of that painting I sent just to bug them about Robby."

"Well, praise the good Lord."

"Papa would say to sleep on it, right?"

"It was his policy."

"That's what I told Grandfather. They also want me to come to St. Louis and do their portrait."

"St Louis, my, my."

"Oh, and they are inviting Robby to come, too, and Trent. That should be interesting." She frowned. "I wonder what kind of control they'll try to have over me if they're funding my education. Good thing I asked to sleep on it."

Lizbeth said a prayer over their food while Lester played his harmonica on his back porch.

"God is blessing me, Gram," Jemma said, "and I wasn't even looking for it."

Lizbeth filled her plate. "We must always be looking for blessings, so we will be prepared to accept them. Cam was my greatest blessing, but I chose to make him wait and accepted him in my own good time. Looking back though, I could have been with him longer. I should have grabbed that blessing as soon as it came to me. Now I'm sorry for it."

Jemma reached for Lizbeth's hand. She touched the slender gold band, still worn on her wedding finger. "You think I'm being stubborn about Spence, don't you?"

"It's not that simple, Jemmabeth. You've muddied the waters with this man from Wicklow. I think you need to look this Mr. Turner in the eye so that you can get on with your life. I don't think you are being fair to Spencer." The clock chimed, interrupting a lecture that had been building for months. "It's a Forrester trait to look folks in the eye when it's serious business, but I think the time has come for you to look yourself in the eye, too, sugar. You need to do some serious business in your heart."

Jemma dragged her fork through her mashed potatoes. "I can't tell

Spence that I love him as long as I have a single thought about someone else. If I ever see Paul again, I might be bowled over by my feelings for him. He electrified me even though I shouldn't have been dating him. My brain is all tangled up and I just can't love anybody like this."

Lizbeth considered this rationale. "That doesn't say much for Spencer. As bad as I hate to admit it, you two weren't exactly acting like Sunday school children at Christmas. Granted, I'm an old lady, but that dance you were doing was electrifying enough. Love doesn't have to muddy the waters, honey, it can clear them up just as well. I had to choose between being a teacher and marrying your Papa because only single women were hired by school boards back then, but being with him would have made me a better teacher, I just know it. Blessings multiply when you act on them. I learned that and tried to raise my boys with that in mind."

Jemma sighed. "I'm not ready to marry. I need to sort out my feelings first, to be fair to everybody." She laid her hand on Lizbeth's arm. "You're a blessing to me, Gram."

"I came with the territory. You'll have lots more coming down your road."

"I think I will accept my grandparents' offer. I can live with Helene again. I know she would want me to," Jemma said.

Lizbeth didn't respond at first. She took off her glasses and pretended to have something in her eye. "I know that she will love having you with her because I surely have..." Her voice failed her.

Cotton John never missed a beat as he updated the price of pork and beef. Then again, old Cotton wasn't fighting back tears.

CHAPTER TWENTY-TWO

Chances

"Let's do something crazy," Carrie said, wheeling herself in circles around the parlor. "Dad doesn't go off like this very often and for you to be here instead of Eleanor is great. I hope he doesn't find out or he'll have a conniption fit."

"Let's redecorate your bedroom in polka dots or a Beatles theme."

"Oh, sure. Dad would really freak out then."

"Then what would you say if Trina and Spence come over and we play Password and listen to records?" Jemma asked.

"I would say yes, yes!"

Jemma wore a blue sundress that her mother had sent. They played board games for a couple of hours, then she couldn't stand it any longer. She took all the records off and loaded a new stack, heavy with Roy's songs. Spencer danced the Stomp with Trina. Jemma loved to watch him, but she loved to dance with him even more. When "Candy Man" came on, they didn't even have to think about it. Every subtle movement was built on the one before it. Carrie and Trina watched, googly-eyed. When it was over, Spencer kissed Jemma on the lips and whispered in her ear, "Baby, if you ever wear that dress again, I'm not going to make it through a dance with you."

Carrie and Trina giggled and busied themselves making a sign. They held up their creation: *HE'S THE ONE!*

Jemma made a face at them.

"Girl, if you don't marry that man, you are one dumb woman," Trina whispered. "You told us that you needed a sign, well, now you've had one."

Spencer scooped Carrie up in his arms for her last dance. The Everly Brothers sang their "Dream" song for them.

"All she needs is a glass slipper, plus she's going to be hard to deal with after dancing with Spence Charming," Jemma whispered to Trina.

The hallway clock chimed right on cue for Cinderella's bedtime. "Time for the cannon," Jemma announced.

"I'll do it," Trina said. "You stay here."

Spencer set Carrie in the crawler and kissed her forehead.

"If I could, I would steal him away from you, but you've been too good to me, Miss Forrester," Carrie said. She pointed at the discarded sign and glided up the stairs.

They were alone in the den and Roy was singing "Crying."

"May I?" Spencer asked, taking her hand.

"Of course. Are you wearing new cologne?"

"It's my magic potion. It puts ladies in a trance and they do whatever I say."

"Ladies—plural, hmm...then what is your wish, oh great one?"

Spencer lifted her chin. "Marry me."

"I keep it in mind." Jemma said and kissed him until the music stopped. She walked him to his car and they sat on the hood. "I'm going back to Le Claire, Spence," she said, straight out. "My grandparents said they would pay my expenses anywhere, but that's where I want to finish. I love it there."

He looked away. "Whatever you want, Jem, but I wish you would come to Florence with me. It could be something special. You might be surprised."

"Le Claire is so good for me. I've learned to be fearless and to trust my instincts. Last summer I was in a mentorship with a French painter. We studied famous artists' techniques and I learned so much. My last semester I wrote a paper on William Bouguereau. His work impressed me, but I identified even more with his passion. I actually memorized a little reflection he wrote on his work. Anyway, I think I have my style down now."

"So, what was the quote?" Spencer asked.

She closed her eyes and recited:

"Each day I go to my studio full of joy. In the evening, when obliged to stop because of darkness, I can scarcely wait for the morning to come. My work is not only a pleasure, it has become a necessity. No matter how many other things I have in my life, if I cannot give myself to my dear painting, I am miserable."

"Now I know what to do when you are miserable. Put you in

203

front of a blank canvas with some good lighting," Spencer said.

"That, or this," she said and kissed him in the moonlight.

⸙⸙

Late Sunday night the phone rang as Jemma wasfinetuning a sketch of Carrie.

"Jem, it's Buddy B. Listen, I need your help. We are going to have to cancel our big chance to get a two-night gig at Amarillo Junior College. Some of their homecoming organizers are coming to the Chillaton prom next week to sort of audition us. Now it may not happen."

"Why not?"

"It's Leon. He wrecked his dumb motorcycle. He's banged up, but he'll live long enough for me to kill him."

"Sorry, Buddy. Can't you do it without him?" she asked.

"Are you kidding me? Leon is lead guitar, sweetness. I do well to play rhythm and throw in some harmonica. I'm what we in the business call a vocalist."

"What about Wade or Dwayne?"

"Obviously, you've never heard those yahoos without Leon. Listen, I was wondering about that guy in your class who moved here your senior year. Leroy somebody. He was good."

"Leroy Sapp? He joined the army right after graduation. I don't know anything else about him. Surely you can find a guitarist."

"In five days? Nah, I'll just call and tell 'em what happened."

Jemma got an inspiration. "Buddy, what would you say to another instrument playing the lead?"

"What are you suggesting? We only do Buddy H.'s stuff."

"Buddy H. used strings on some songs and all kinds of weird percussion stuff. Do you want to get that college thing bad enough to take a chance?"

He sighed. "Okay, let's hear it."

"I have a friend who can rock out on the piano."

"I don't know about a piano. How good is he?"

"She's great."

"Is she good looking?"

"She's very pretty."

204

"Does she have some moves?"

"She's in a wheelchair."

After profuse begging by Jemma, Buddy agreed to come by on his lunch break and listen to Carrie play. She had to spend even more time talking Carrie into it. When he arrived, however, she could see the mischief return to Carrie's eyes. Jemma had done her hair in a flip, and she looked like an angel.

"Buddy, this is Carrie McFarland. Carrie, meet Buddy Baker. We call him Buddy B so as not to confuse him with Buddy Holly, Buddy H."

Buddy smiled cautiously, then took a seat on the big leather sofa. He ran his hand through his hair, freshly dyed black to maintain his professional persona, and waited. Carrie rolled up to the piano, laid her fingers on the keys, then busted out a medley of Buddy Holly songs. Buddy B's mouth hung open. He jumped up, whistling and clapping. "Hey, I think this might work," he said. "Can we practice here or what?"

Carrie flinched.

"No," Jemma said. "You'll have to practice at the gym. Do you think you could arrange it? If not, I could talk to the principal. He won't mind."

"I'll call him. Maybe we can rehearse tomorrow and Thursday night. Where'd you learn to play like that?" he asked.

"Miss Mason, next door," Carrie said.

"Aw, I know that old hen and she didn't play rock and roll. My sister took lessons from her and so did she." Buddy jerked his thumb at Jemma.

Carrie giggled. "Well, I sort of learned that on my own."

Buddy lifted one blond eyebrow, sorely in need of a dye job. "And the style?"

"Hey, I do what I can to keep my charge enlightened," Jemma said.

"Good for you, sweetness," Buddy said. "I'll see you ladies tomorrow night, but I don't think it was chance that brought us together. It was fate." As soon as he left, Jemma ran to Carrie and grabbed her around the neck, screeching for joy.

Carrie's eyes danced. "Do you think I can last through a rehearsal?"

"Or a performance?" Jemma asked. "I sure hope so. We're in too deep to back out now." She smiled at the fresh zing in Carrie. So, the Lord was going to use Buddy B—interesting.

⤜⤛

Jemma arranged to wheel Carrie out at five for a walk. They went down a block and turned towards the high school then circled back to the side entrance to the gym. Buddy had laid some wide boards for the wheelchair to make it up the steps. Once inside, Jemma and Buddy lifted her chair to the stage. The band had been forewarned by Buddy to keep a civil tongue and cut her some slack. She blew them away on the first song. The rehearsal actually went faster than Jemma had thought, and she had Carrie back and ready to get in the cannon by seven. The Judge was asleep in front of the television with his bottle nearby.

"At least he'll be gone Saturday night," Carrie whispered, drinking a soda.

"I told Eleanor that I was going to sleep over. We are just going to have to rely on the Lord and the power of poker. How late does he stay out?"

"It varies. Sometimes he stays until two o'clock, sometimes midnight, and sometimes he doesn't go."

"Don't tell me that. The dance starts at seven. I'm going to have to get Trina and Spencer to help us with this."

"Actually, I'm not too tired," Carrie said.

"That's just the Dr. Pepper talking," Jemma said as she fired up the cannon.

⤜⤛

The Judge left the house with two brown bags at 6:45, just as Trina and Jemma rolled Carrie out the front door. Then, when his car disappeared around the corner, they pushed the wheelchair across the street to the side door of the crowded gym. Spencer picked her up and whisked her through the boy's dressing rooms, out the storage room, and up the stairs to the stage. Trina met them with the wheelchair and Jemma got her set just right at the piano. As planned, Buddy went in front of the closed curtain to do his introduction. Carrie grinned at Jemma then took a deep breath. The curtain and the applause went up and Buddy B blasted out *Wellllll*…and Carrie came in right on cue.

The gym floor was alive with teenagers dressed in clothes that had set their parents' checkbooks back a month, but it was prom. Carrie was on fire. Her crew stayed backstage the whole time. At the break, they brought her some prom food, then Jemma and Trina carried her to the restroom.

"Are you worn out?" Jemma asked.

"This is the life," Carrie said.

"You are some kind of piano player, girl," Trina said. The trio made their way back up to the stage. By ten o'clock Jemma was keeping a close eye on Carrie. At the back of the gym, near the exit, another eye was on Carrie, too, an eye glistening with pride and old fears. During the final slow dance, The Judge slipped out the exit and made his way across the street to his empty house.

Carrie got the biggest applause of the evening. Jemma and Trina were in tears and even the guys in the band said nice things to her.

Buddy gave her a big peck, right on the lips. "Sweetness, you just got us a two-night performance at the Amarillo Junior College Homecoming Weekend next fall."

Carrie was jubilant. Spencer carried her home and up the stairs. "Do you think your father is here?" he whispered.

"I don't care. Let him see me coming home with a man."

Trina got the cannon going while Jemma said good night to Spencer.

"You always come through for me, don't you?" she said. "Thanks for fixing the car house for me, too. You're the best."

"I try," he said. "Sweet dreams, baby." A sudden breeze lifted her hair between them and he tucked it behind her ears.

"Good night," she said and gave him a superb kiss, then watched as he drove away. For a split second, the baby blue wiggled through her brain as the Corvette's lights disappeared around the corner. Rats.

Eleanor woke them up Sunday morning. "You girls gonna sleep all day? You better scoot home, Jemmabeth. Your Gram may not like you being late to Sunday school. I don't know ever who your teacher is, but I've been in your Gram's class before, bet you didn't know that. Anyhoo, she's got a head full of Bible learnin'."

Jemma scrambled out of bed. She and Trina flew down the stairs to the Dodge. Eleanor was right. She was late, but it had been worth it.

⚜

They were sitting in The Parnell, waiting for the movie to start, when Spence broke the news. "My dad told me that The Judge was at the prom the other night. He said The Judge was drinking and bragging at their poker game about how well Carrie played at the dance."

Her heart skipped a beat. She didn't know if it was bad, or halfway good, news. "Yikes. I'll have to tell Carrie."

"It was just a matter of time until he would have found out anyway. This is Chillaton," Spencer said.

"Maybe it's best that he saw her. Now he knows what she is capable of doing," Jemma said.

"We'll see. At least Carrie had a ball."

⚜

Lizbeth walked over the little path to Willa's house with a proposal in mind. She got right to it. "Willa, would you like to have a memory quilt in honor of your husband? I made myself one not long ago."

Willa wiped her brow. "Well, I'm no quilter, that's for sure."

"Now that's where I come in," Lizbeth said. "I guess quilting is my calling in life."

"Well, that's a different story." Willa leaned in to hear more.

"If you have saved any scraps from his shirts, I could get started."

Willa considered the assignment. "Law, seems like I saved some of Sam's things, but we'll have to look around."

"Have Trina bring them over this week, and I'll get going on it."

"Thank you kindly," Willa said, her face already lit up with memories.

Trina was at the door with an armload of fabric the next morning.

"Come on in and let's see what you found," Lizbeth said.

"It's sure nice of you to do this for Mama. She's real excited."

They dumped the fabric on the good bed. There was a pair of threadbare overalls, several bandana scarves, and a set of feed-sack curtains.

"Mama said this was all she had. The overalls and bandanas were what my daddy wore when he was working the fields. She didn't have any of his shirts, but the curtains were the ones hanging in their bedroom before I was born."

"These will all do just fine, Trina. You should help me choose the pattern. I know that you are handy with needle and thread."

"Yes ma'am. I like to design dresses."

"Well, there must be scholarships for that kind of thing."

"I'm not sure many colored girls go into that business."

"Now you listen to an old woman, Trina. I went to college. It was hard enough back then, but nowadays, there are money folk who will help you along no matter whether you call yourself a Caucasian or a Negro. Now let's look at some of these patterns."

"Actually," Trina reached in her pocket and pulled out several sheets of paper, "I have an idea." She laid the cutouts on the bed. "Here's a drawing of it when it's finished."

Lizbeth examined the samples and nodded her approval. "It's a fine idea. Let's get to work."

"I have some things to do for Mama, then I gotta get over to The Boulevard to clean a house. I could come afterwards."

"We'll start tonight, then."

"Thank you, Miz Forrester."

"Trina, please call me Gram."

Her dimples went deep. "Thank you, Gram."

❧❧

They worked well together. Lizbeth showed Trina something once and she had it. Lizbeth stayed up way past her bedtime each night, knowing that Trina had already put in a full day of work. She taught her all the tricks of master quilting. Trina's were tiny, even stitches, the kind so valued in quilting circles. On their last night of sewing, Jemma went to bed before the two of them were finished. She had to sleep in the little side bedroom since the quilt frame was lowered over part of her bed.

"Gram," Trina asked, "did you ever think you'd be sitting up at midnight making a quilt with a Negro girl?"

"Sugar, the good Lord surprises us all with His plans. I'm just proud that we got to know each other well enough to make this quilt for Willa. If you keep it up, you are going to be a whole lot better at this than I am. You'll be able to pass your skills on to your grandchildren." Lizbeth lowered her voice. "I don't think my little artist in there is going to be passing along any quilting skills."

"I heard that," Jemma yelled.

The quilt was finished just before Papa's clock struck two. Lizbeth hadn't stayed up that late since Jim was a baby.

❦❧

The next morning, they walked ceremoniously over the tracks together to give Willa the quilt. Jemma followed along with Lizbeth's camera.

Willa greeted them with an anxious grin. "Well, what are y'all waiting for? Show me what you got."

"Close your eyes, Mama," Trina spread the quilt over the kitchen table. "Okay, open."

Jemma had never seen Willa speechless, but this was close. She ran her big hands over the fabric and stitches and then backed up to look at it again. Trina's design was just the thing.

"That must be the most beautiful batch of 'tunias ever made by human hands. Sweet Sunday morning, how did you do it? Miz Lizbeth, I gotta hug you because this is a blessed quilt and I know it mostly come from your hand. I'll never be able to thank you proper."

"Call me Lizbeth and that'll be thanks enough," she said.

Trina and Willa held up the quilt and Jemma took a whole roll of pictures.

"It's a beautiful tribute to your husband," Jemma said.

"Our baby girl here is the beautiful one," Willa said, hugging Trina to her side again. "Don't really need nothin' else, but this quilt sure will keep me warm when the wind is howlin'. I can snuggle up in it like a big ol' baby. Latrina, your daddy would be awful proud. You done good."

CHAPTER TWENTY-THREE

A Matter of Opinion

The artist carried the big canvas into the parlor, then stepped back from the painting. "Drum roll, please," she said.

Carrie thumped her knuckles on her wheelchair. "Let me have it."

Jemma untied the blindfold.

Carrie blinked. "That's not me."

"Well, thanks a lot. I guess that puts the artist in her place."

"But you've painted my face on another girl's body. She's a dancer."

"No, no," Jemma said. "I painted the spirit I see in you." Then she noticed the tears and dropped beside the wheelchair. "Oh, rats. Carrie, I didn't mean to make you cry. I was hoping to make you happy. You told me that you could do anything in your head. So, you dance."

Carrie wheeled herself right next to the portrait. "I do love it."

Jemma followed her. "You're not going to do anything crazy are you?"

"You mean like slit my wrists with a letter opener and fall across the painting?"

"Yeah, something like that."

Carrie touched the ballet slippers. She closed her eyes and hummed a song she had been playing on the piano lately. She moved her body, within the confines of the wheelchair, not unlike Melanie's dance with the violin. Jemma looked away so as not to intrude.

"Dad won't like it because he's a complete realist," Carrie said.

"It's your painting, not his," Jemma said.

"I didn't say he would throw it out the window. You painted it for me and I couldn't love it more. Thank you."

"You shouldn't thank me, Carrie. I owe you."

"You aren't going to tell me how my weakness has become your strength or something."

"That's not what I was going to say."

"What, then?"

"I believe my art is a mirror of physical and emotional realities. I only take liberties with light and shadows and I try to paint from my heart, but this time I painted from yours, and, for opening up a new perspective in my work, I thank you."

Carrie looked away. "It's Dr. Pepper time. Forward, Jeeves."

Jemma rolled Carrie across the parquet floor, but she grabbed the doorframe as they passed and twisted in the chair for one more look.

"You're welcome," she said under her breath and then smiled up at Jemma. "It gives substance to my fantasies."

❧☙

Monday morning, Jemma arrived for work as usual. The house was much too quiet. Eleanor didn't yell out to her and Cotton John was not squawking from the radio, but more importantly, Carrie was not at the kitchen table.

Jemma dropped her purse on the floor and bounded up the stairs.

"Miss Forrester!" The Judge's voice catapulted behind her. She jerked around and came down hard on her bottom. He made no effort to help her up or inquire as to her health.

"Sir, where is Carrie?"

"Come to my study." He turned and disappeared around the dark paneled wall. Jemma followed him, rubbing the seat of her jeans. His back was to her as he stared out the bay window behind his desk, and he didn't seem in any hurry to talk. An annoying clock above the fireplace ticked off the minutes and leftover cigar smoke fouled the air.

"Has something happened to Carrie?" she asked.

"I knew your grandfather," he said. "We were on the bank board together. He was a good man, and it was very sad about his boys. Your grandmother has had more than her share of grief."

Jemma glanced around the room. The painting of Carrie was propped against the wall of bookshelves.

"I see that you have the painting. Where is she?"

"Sit down, Jemmabeth."

212

She remained behind an armchair. "If she's sick, why didn't somebody call me?"

"Carolina is out of town." He pulled out his big desk chair and lowered himself into it.

Jemma narrowed her eyes at him. "How far out of town?"

"She's in Houston." He leaned back and put his hands together like a church with a steeple. "Miss Forrester," he said, dragging the steeple through his beard, "I appreciate the spirit you have awakened in my daughter. I know you meant well and that you two have become very close. I have no malice when I say this, but it's time that you move on."

"Are you firing me?"

"Call it what you will. However, Carolina is a very sensitive, special person and she is quite vulnerable in most respects. You have ignited a kind of hope in her that has no future."

"Are you talking about the prom? You sent her away because she played the piano at a dance? She had a fantastic time. I only want Carrie to enjoy living and not spend every waking minute in this house wheeling around wondering what her life could have been like. I love Carrie."

"Those who love her guard her against false hope." He raised his brow, then leaned forward, his pudgy fingers pressing on the glass top of his desk. "Dispensing false hope is not an uncommon trait in your family."

Jemma came out from behind the chair. "I did not give her false hope. She isn't a memento from your past to put away in some old china cabinet. She's a talented, vibrant person. Carrie has something to offer the world." She paced around the room, gesturing like Professor Rossi. "How can she do anything cooped up in here? You won't even let her have physical therapy. She could walk for all we know."

The Judge rose up like Godzilla emerging from the sea. "Sneaking her out of the house to a huge gathering like that was unauthorized and endangered her life."

"She did fine. I would've asked you, but Carrie wouldn't let me. She didn't want you to say no."

He jabbed his finger towards the portrait. "No friend would paint her like that."

Jemma's cheeks burned. "It's how I see Carrie, her spirit. She told me that she could do whatever she wants in her head, so I translated

213

that power to canvas. Ask her. She understands."

"I find it a mockery of her."

"The painting is a confirmation of her, who she is inside that body."

The Judge looked past her and towards the painting. "Then it is an unfair portrayal and it breaks my heart." His breath was short.

Jemma had a sudden, yet fleeting, compassion for him. She did lower her volume. "I disagree and I am the artist. I believe it is spiritual justice, but maybe you aren't familiar with that kind, sir."

He turned his icy stare on her. She knew how it must have felt to stand before him in court, awaiting sentencing. He aimed his finger and erupted. "You have no right to superimpose your vision of Carolina onto canvas in the face of her reality and expect it to be interpreted as any type of justice whatsoever. It remains a haunting reminder of her handicap."

"It shouldn't be a reminder of her physical condition, but of her spirit."

They stood, unrelenting. The Judge's breath emerged in snorts as Jemma held hers.

He jerked out his chair and slammed his bulk into it. "I have kept quiet long enough about a number things that have happened in my home since you came. I tolerated them, thinking it might bring joy to my Carolina. However, you have begun to make decisions outside my control. Now you have toyed with my daughter's mind. Whether you approve or not, we are a family and you are merely in my employ. I realize the merit of your argument, but the fact remains that we need a rest from you, Miss Forrester."

She wiped her cheeks. "Why is she in Houston and who is with her?"

"Carolina is with experts in this type of polio. They, not you, know what is best for her. I am flying down today."

"How long will she be there?"

"Indefinitely." He fumbled through a stack of papers. "She is there for long-term treatment. You are not the only one concerned with her happiness. I admit that she has missed opportunities due to her confinement and that she might be more mobile than first thought."

"Why did you send her over the weekend?" Her voice broke. "We didn't even get to say good-bye."

214

"I've had these arrangements in the works for some time now, ever since your little church excursions. She left you a letter. It's with your final wages." He held out an envelope. "I know that you care for her, Jemmabeth, but you have exceeded your boundaries. I am not a cruel man, despite what you think. A young woman with your obvious talent will not remain in Chillaton very long, and those left behind suffer most in these cases."

"This is not one of your cases."

He extended his hand to her. "My regards to your family." Jemma could not accept it, and his fingers curled into his palm. "Very well," he said, withdrawing. "Take the painting as you leave."

"That belongs to Carrie. Ask her what she wants to do with it." She took a step towards him. "Sir, somebody has to take up the slack from you leaving Carrie stuck in that wheelchair to the point where she is up on a stage playing rock-and-roll. Who do you think will do that when I am gone? Eleanor?" Jemma paused for a moment, knowing that he didn't have an answer. "Carrie is my friend and you can't fire me from that." She turned to leave, but stopped in the hallway for one more look at the painting. The Judge lit up a fresh cigar and resumed his position at the bay window.

Jemma turned on her heel. "She wanted to go to church. Will you keep her from God as well?" she shouted down the hall, the words echoing into the rooms. She grabbed her purse at the foot of the stairs and saw Eleanor in the kitchen. It would be hot news by noon, but Jemma didn't care. She slammed the door on her way out. Her head ached with a creeping sense of permanent loss. She walked to the tennis courts, sat on the bench and opened the note.

Dear Jem—I'm off to Houston in case you didn't know it. Dad says that I am going to have a bunch of tests with some specialists. Maybe they can actually help me. It's all happening so fast that I can't believe it. I'm flying down there, and I can't help but think of your Gram's motto about flying. Ha, ha I don't know when I'll be back—maybe next week. Tell Trina and Spence 'bye for me and I'll see y'all soon. I guess you can get some extra painting done. I love my portrait, but Dad hasn't mentioned it yet.

Love you, Carrie

She refolded the paper and stared at a scrawny weed growing in the middle of the concrete. Carrie was smart and the Lord would take care of her, but was His plan? It was probably all her own fault. Typical Scarlett. Someone across the way was running scales on a piano. She should've taken his hand. That would have shown some class, even though he didn't shake hers when she first met him. Jemma walked home the long way, through the park and back up Main Street. She went past Gram's and down to the Ruby Store. Lester straightened up and waved from his rocking chair as she approached the porch.

"What's going on, Jemmerbeth? Are you 'tard,' but not feathered?" He slapped his leg at the joke.

Jemma handed him a cold Dr. Pepper. "Lester, tell me some stories. I've had a bad morning."

"I think I'll look for work in L.A. this summer. My uncle has a beach house near there," unemployed Jemma said as she watched Willa and Trina work.

Willa set the iron down with a thud. "Jemmabeth Forrester, I expect you got flowers in your heart and fertilizer in your head. Runnin' off to Los Angeleez ain't gonna solve nothin'. You're pulling Spencer around by his tongue that's hangin' out after you. Now, don't deny it and don't give me that look. I've seen many a lovesick child and he fills the bill. Marry that sweet man right now or get a job." She hung another crisp shirt on the line. "You'll find there's plenty of work once you start lookin'. Latrina has to turn folks down all the time in her housecleanin' business. You can help with that, if nothin' else. Now, c'mon over here and give me a hug." The damp warmth from the steam iron was still fresh on Willa's neck. "There ain't no shame in being mixed up about things, sugar," she said, looking Jemma in the eye. "The shame's in leaving it to fester."

CHAPTER TWENTY-FOUR

A Very Blue Corner

It was Lizbeth's idea for them to picnic at Plum Creek on the old home place. Jemma had been there a hundred times with her family. Papa always invited Spencer, too. Her favorite place as a little girl was a shady spot under the cottonwoods where the creek ran clear. Sometimes, when rain swelled the waters, a little island formed that Robby had claimed as his own. The creek would definitely be a good place for their last date.

As he drove under clear blue skies, Spencer talked about a Parisian chapel, the Sainte-Chapelle. "I want to take you there. You will feel God's presence in every square inch, I promise," he said. His smile was so easy and always part of his speech. She traced around his ear with her finger. He lifted his shoulder to defend himself. "Hey, you don't want me to have a wreck, do you?" She proceeded to nibble on his earlobe.

"That does it." He slammed on the brakes causing an explosion of dust behind the Corvette. He grabbed her and planted a red hot one on her.

"Whoa!" she said, catching her breath.

"Let that be a lesson to you," he said and resumed his lecture about the chapel.

They set the cooler under the cottonwood that bore their initials, threw off their shoes, and waded into the ankle-deep creek. The water was cool, even in the heat of the afternoon sun. Jemma wore her favorite silk skirt and a cotton peasant blouse Alex had sent. It was, without a doubt, bohemian. The silk was wrinkled and clingy against her skin, and she bunched it up to keep the hem out of the water as she scanned the creek for minnows.

"Jemma," Spencer called.

She looked up, pushing locks of hair out of her face with one hand as he snapped her photo.

"Stay right there," he said, taking several shots.

"Nice camera," she said, kicking water at him.

"Nice legs," he said. He sloshed over to her and took a closeup. "You look like a million bucks. Let's eat."

Jemma had packed a lunch of fried chicken, potato salad, and peach cobbler. Lizbeth had made it all. Spencer brought a big thermos filled with cold, sweet tea. Sitting on one of Lizbeth's picnic quilts, they ate until their faces and fingers were greasy with fried chicken. They washed up in the creek, and Spencer followed her every move, making memories for Florence.

"Sorry about Carrie," he said, "but I know you did the right thing by showing The Judge that she can do more than he wants to allow."

"Yeah, well, I thought that it was all a part of God's plan."

"It could be, Jem. Remember, the verse that says His ways are mysterious."

"I hope so. Right now it's a mystery how I'm going to get a job."

"If we got married, you would never have to do anything but paint."

"Spence."

"Let's have our own secret wedding right now."

She dug her toes into the sandy creek bottom. "What do you have in mind?"

"The honeymoon," he said with a smile like his third-grade school picture.

She leaned over, peering into the clear water. "Look, minnows."

The little fish scattered before he could see them. He led her back to the big tree and they relaxed against it. Her hair spread out over his shirt like ribbons of mahogany silk.

Spencer sighed. "I think that getting married might make us spontaneously combust."

"Gram says that marriage can clear the water rather than muddy it."

"Hey, I'm talking about fire here, not water."

"I know, but Gram waited to marry Papa and she regrets it now. If I were going to marry someone, which I'm not, I would want to wait until I was thirty."

"You're kidding, of course."

"No. I think thirty would be a good age."

"Jem, do you know how ugly you're going to be at thirty?"

"That's okay. It's what you have in here that counts," she said, pointing to her chest.

"Oh, really." He gave her a sneaky look. "Well, I'm not too familiar with that particular spot on you."

"Very funny. I was talking about my heart." She smiled like she loved only him, and, at that moment, it felt like she did. "Did I tell you that Gram is going to Europe with Do Dah?"

"Nope," Spence said, not particularly wanting to change the subject.

"Do Dah talked her into it, and I helped a little. They are going to visit my uncles' graves. I think it will help her heal after all these years."

"That would be something, to run into them in Italy."

"Maybe they could visit you. Do you know where you'll be staying?"

"Not yet, but I'll call Do Dah before they come."

The cottonwood leaves quaked in the breeze and she closed her eyes. Spencer went to the Corvette and came back with a guitar.

"What's this?" she asked.

"I spent all last year learning. I had to do something with my time, and I've finally got these two down, so here goes."

He sang "Candy Man." She moved her shoulders to the music and watched his long fingers move across the frets. Spencer was the only football player with enough guts to sing in their school choir. She danced barefoot under the tree as though she were alone on the tracks, but then it had always been Jemma's nature to dance anytime the music moved her. It was just one more thing that he loved about her.

"What else did you do last year?" she asked, settling beside him.

"Rode a motorcycle all over Europe."

"No! Tell me you didn't do that. You know how I feel about motorcycles. Remember what happened to the Kelseys?"

"Baby, they could have died in a car wreck. You wouldn't have me stop driving a car, would you?"

"Mom and I weren't the first ones to come up on a car wreck. At least in a car you have some protection."

"I have another song."

"Changing the subject, huh? Is there anything that you can't do? You really are a Renaissance man."

"Apparently, I can't make you love me." He played some chords.

"You can't dance to this one. You have to listen," he said, and sang Roy's "Running Scared" with more emotion than she was prepared to hear. She got the message. There was nothing to do but hold him when the song was over.

"Do you like pipe music?" she asked.

"Uh…you mean bagpipes?"

"Nope, the Uilleann pipes. Remember, Papa's cousin, Angus, drove all the way from North Carolina to play the Uilleann pipes at his funeral? I miss Papa's fiddle music. I wish you could have heard my friend, Melanie, play that song he loved at her recital."

"I wasn't invited."

She exhaled. "Do you remember the first time you ever touched me?" Not really a fair question and she knew it.

"The first time I ever touched you was at our first morning recess in the first grade. We played 'Red Rover' and I busted through you and Randy Jordan. I didn't like him holding your hand."

"I meant when you first touched me in a loving way."

"That's easy. It was noon recess the same day. I grabbed your hand as soon as you got to the playground to play Red Rover again. Afterwards, when nobody was looking, I kissed my palm where you'd touched it."

No other guy could have come up with that. He was truly a rare, beautiful man.

The bullfrogs warmed up for their evening chorus and a mourning dove cooed in the plum thicket. In the distance, cattle called for feed. Spencer and Jemmabeth sat on the banks of Plum Creek, under the generous branches of a cottonwood tree and a peach colored sky, soaking in one another but avoiding the obvious.

"You'll go with me to the airport tomorrow, right?" Spencer asked when they got home.

She nodded.

"Jem, you know this is going to be hard for me. I'm leaving you again with no idea about our future."

"I don't want to think about that right now," she said. It came out wrong, and she was too chicken to fix it. Rats. He was pouring his heart out to Miss Scarlett.

She had dreaded this day ever since she kissed him on that warm night at the river, a winter ago. Jemma wore the blue sundress he liked, the heart necklace, and the earrings. She tied a blue velvet ribbon in her hair, humming *Un Coin Tout Bleu,* "A Very Blue Corner," one of Helene's favorite songs. The morning was sunny even though Cotton John had predicted cooler weather. Spencer was cool already. He hadn't looked at her since she got in the car.

"Well, here we go again," he said just as they passed the city limits sign. His jaw was tight, like it was when his mother was yelling obscenities at the Country Club.

"I know," Jemma said, "and I'm sorry."

"Tell me what you want to do because you can't tell me how to feel."

"Spence, I don't know what to say. I have loved every minute with you these past months." She reached for his hand. He let her hold it, but he didn't kiss it. She had come to expect that.

"So, you still want to date around." He took his hand out of hers and gripped the steering wheel. "Looking for Mr. Skyrocket?"

Her mouth went dry. He wasn't like this even when she broke up with him. "I just have to see how things are when we're apart one last time. I'm not horsing around with you, Spence. If we are meant to be together, then I promise I'll make a commitment. You don't want me if I have any doubts, do you?"

"Doubts? It's us, Jem. It was us at Flagstaff and Plum Creek and dancing in the moonlight at the river. We aren't the prom king and queen anymore. This is grown-up love and you know it." He turned back to the road. "I'm curious how you'll figure all this out to your satisfaction. Let's see…maybe you'll record how many times you think about me and track that data on a calendar. Or I suppose it could be more like a rating system to measure the intensity of the thoughts. Well, I'm sorry, but I can't stand to think about you kissing anybody but me. Does it bother you at all that I will be with other women?" He gave her a look, his eyes piercing into hers. "Go with your heart, baby. Let our relationship be like your art—fearless and instinctive—but that can't happen because it's him, isn't it? The almighty Paul."

Jemma chewed on her lip and watched a cluster of sparrows on the high line wires beside the highway.

"I know that he's a cowboy."

It shot through her.

"You're still running the bulls, aren't you? Hemingway would be so proud. Only this is one bull at a time."

"Who told you he was a cowboy? I never said that."

"What difference does it make? You've found your fantasy, and nothing else matters. He's a wild, barhopping womanizer. That's fine. He lied to you. That's okay. He even forgot that he was married—not a problem. Good grief, Jem, married!"

Jemma's face tingled. Rats. Rats. Rats. The ceramic moon swayed wildly.

"So, that's it. You are waiting on Paul. Maybe he has kids and you can be a little mama sooner than you thought. You've just been killing time with me until he's a free man. Well, I can guarantee that I'll be dating every knockout that I find because I don't have anybody waiting on me. Enjoy your cowboy with a clear conscience, my friend. I won't be around to watch you like a hawk, so do as you please. I'm staying in Italy."

He stopped the car and put the top down so that the only thing they could hear was the wind. She couldn't look at him. This was not her Spence, the one who cried when she broke up with him, and this was certainly not the sentimental drive to the airport she had expected. Teardrops spotted her pretty blue dress.

"I can't say good-bye like this," Jemma said as they waited at his gate.

He turned to her, his face solemn, his gray eyes cool and glassy. "I'm sorry, Jem, but for the first time in our lives, I feel like I don't know you. How could you even consider loving somebody like him? It's not just your cowboy fixation; it's that you could mess with me all these months. You should have more respect for me or for yourself. You must take me for a fool."

"That's not fair. You are dear to me, and I didn't mean to hurt you." Her voice cracked. "I thought you understood last fall. I don't know how I feel about us, but I never, ever meant to cause you more pain. I want you to be happy. I want us to be happy. Can't you wait a little longer for me to make up my mind?"

"I have waited almost two years for you to make up your mind." He blew out his breath and hugged her to him. "For once, I wish I didn't love you," he said, his voice husky. "This is it, though. I've humiliated myself for the last time." He looked right into her golden eyes. "I can't play your game anymore."

She put her fingers on his lips, then struggled to say the words. "Spence, you and I are pieces of each other. The best that I am, I owe to you, and we can never be separated. We will never be far from one another's heart or mind, ever. Remember the quote on the moon. I must love you because I want to so bad. All the time I dated him, it was you I dreamed about. Just give me until Christmas to sort out my feelings so I can look you in the eye and say that I'll love you, and only you, forever and always. Just that long. I'll give you my answer then. I promise." She choked up. "Remember, we started over. I should get a little more time."

"No, baby, you should know by now." He wiped his eyes. "I won't be back," he whispered. "I just can't do it. For you to choose between him and me is like cutting out my heart."

"Spence, listen. I promise I wasn't waiting for him."

His flight was announced and she gripped his arm. He stroked the length of her hair, untying the velvet ribbon to fold in his hand, then cupped her chin and kissed her. It was a fireball kiss that stopped her heart. "Good-bye, Jemmabeth," he said. Then he was gone.

"Call me, okay?" she yelled, then covered her mouth. "Please call me, Spence," she whispered into her hand.

Jemma watched the plane lift off from the runway. She ran to the parking lot and squinted at the silver speck heading northeast. Her foolish lips still tingled. She was Frankenstein's bride getting the jolt that awakened her from the dead.

She drove home with the purr of the motor and beat of her anxious heart to keep her company. Even the ceramic moon was gone. She parked the car at the dealership, gave the keys to Mr. Chase's secretary, and walked home. Jemma knew that she had painted herself into this very blue corner.

CHAPTER TWENTY-FIVE

Quicksilver

T he summer blew in, literally, keeping her busy with work and painting. She teamed up with Trina and put her cleaning skills to work again. They landed the Farmer's Union Bank custodial job at night for a steady income, and she helped Trina with private homes during the day. She dropped off bags of food at Shorty's dugout every week, and could hear his television blaring.

Spencer never called. Her head was clear on that because he had said as much. She deserved it, too, but her heart hoped otherwise. Her heart hoped many things—most of all, that she had not lost him forever. She even prayed about it, remembering a sermon about the mercy of God. Maybe He didn't just reserve mercy for kings and nations, surely there was a drop left for complete nitwits like her.

She hadn't seen Eleanor Perkins since the day The Judge fired her. That is, not until she was paying for a half gallon of Golden Vanilla ice cream for Lizbeth at the grocery store.

Eleanor abandoned her cart and walked right up to her, bosom heaving. "Well, here you are hon, out and about. Ever who says to me these days, 'Iddinit a shame about the Chase boy running off to It'ly, and leaving poor Jemmabeth, I say, hold your horses right there. We ain't talking about Max Chase here because Spencer Chase is a perfect angel.' Anyhoo, the shame's on you for having yourself a high time with that sweet young man, then turnin' him down flat when he proposed marriage."

Jemma raised her head. "Who said Spence proposed to me?"

Edith Frame, sitting comfortably at the cash register, drew in her pointy chin. "Law, sugar pie, some things go without sayin'. Did you think he was just gonna date you forever?"

Eleanor went on. "Hon, you give up a good, good man ever how you look at it."

Edith clucked her tongue and opened the register, but Jemma was gone before Edith could count out the change.

⸎⸎

Next to the Cotton Festival, The Fourth of July was Chillaton's crowning glory. The same citizens organized both events and took their jobs dead serious. Depending on the event, they were in charge of the Cotton Queen pageant, town barbeque, parade, rodeo, and the cowpoke dance at the old skating rink. The Cotton Festival acknowledged a bountiful harvest and the Fourth celebrated America's independence from the British and dependence on beef.

All Jemma had ever cared about was getting a gander at the cowboys. The Fourth was a hat and boot jungle for one whole weekend, but then the cowboys disappeared to their ranching duties and reappeared en masse the next Fourth. They were a breed unto themselves, and she wasn't the only one that felt that way. They were of interest to every breathing female who would admit it. That's what she hadn't been able to resist and one thing, among others, that Spencer had tolerated about her. In high school, Jemma and Sandy put on their cowgirl outfits to mosey down to the rink without their boyfriends and check out the buckaroos waiting for the dance. "Running the bulls" is what she and Sandy had named their pilgrimage.

It was their expert opinion that if any decent-looking male put on a pressed pair of jeans, a starched shirt, boots, and a cowboy hat, he could pass as the good Lord's gift to women for five minutes—ten, if he wore English Leather or a Stetson. The real ones came across as so wantonly feral. It was the way they stood around in those jeans, like they could wrestle any large animal with one hand tied behind their backs and never mess up that crease. Or maybe it was the hat. A cowboy just sure knew how to make a girl feel special. She got roped for real once, and several times she had given in to a dance or two if they scored high enough on her buckaroo rating scale. She felt a need to do it one more time. Maybe it would cheer her up.

She pulled on her jeans, beat-up red boots, a long-sleeved white shirt, and Papa's old straw hat. She lifted her chin and walked straight past the prime candidates who leaned against the outside of the building. She walked through the appreciative, verbal crowd and into the rink. She turned down some good invitations to dance all night, but it was nothing. She waited under the rodeo announcer's stand to meet a reluctant Trina, as planned. If only there had been just one blonde with gray eyes and a tiny scar on his chin. If only.

The day took a turn for the worse. A sports car idled at the curb and the Voice of Doom called. "Hey, over here!" The Cleave waved to her from the car. Jemma hesitated, but walked over and leaned in the window. Great idea.

"That's some outfit, cowgirl." A stranger pushed his sunglasses up on his head and grinned at her from behind the steering wheel. He winked and took a drink from a bottle. "Wanna have some fun?"

"Chad, this is Jemmartsybeth Forrester," Missy said, eyeing Jemma's boots. "She's sort of the town's token hippie."

"Hi, Chad," Jemma said, eking out a smile.

He puckered his lips and kissed at her. "Missy may not last all the way to Amarillo. Why don't you hop in?" He jerked his head towards the tiny back seat.

The Cleave turned to Chad. "Jemma doesn't have fun. She's a Sunday school girl, and remember, it's *Melissa*, not Missy." Her *s*'s were slurred and her breath was foggy with beer.

Jemma drew back. "Y'all are in no condition to drive anywhere. You should just stay in Chillaton."

Missy flipped her mane over her shoulder. "I heard you and Spence are splits—for good this time. I guess He finally figured out that you're not Miss Perfect after all. Now it's my turn."

"Good-bye, *Missy*," Jemma said. "Good luck, Chad."

Missy gurgled a noise resembling a bored horse. "Oh, shut up. You're the one who needs some luck. Everybody knows you had a cowboy in Dallas and managed to lose him, too." Missy's laughter blended into the squeal of the tires as Chad threw the car into gear and sped away. A Greek fraternity decal glowered from the back window. Jemma clamped down on her lip and waited for Trina.

⇜⇝

The phone rang and she raced to it as though Lizbeth might try to get it first.

"Carrie! Where are you?"

"I'm still in Houston in a physical rehab program. I miss you so much."

"I miss you too. I would write, but I doubt your dad would give me your address and Eleanor claims she doesn't know it."

"I'll get it for you. Just a second." Jemma heard a male voice in the background, then a stranger came on the line.

"Hello there," he said. "Got a pencil?"

"Sure, I'm ready," Jemma wrote the address and Carrie came back on.

"So, is that your boyfriend?" Jemma asked, teasing.

"Yeah."

"Whoa. I was just kidding."

"I'm not," she said with a giggle.

"So, what's the deal? Is he cute or what?"

"Are you cute or what?" Carrie asked the boyfriend. "He says he is in the *or what* category."

"See, it didn't take you long to find somebody."

"It just happened, Jem. He is the head of physical therapy here and we just fell crazy in love. He doesn't even care about my other boyfriend."

"The cannon?"

"Yeah. His name is Philip Bryce and I'm so happy."

"What does your father say about this?"

Carrie lowered her voice as though he might be listening. "Dad doesn't know. Isn't that funny? Phil plays the drums. We could have a weird band if you wanted to be our singer."

"Did you know that your daddy snuck you out of town just to get you away from me?"

"I kind of figured that out. I'm sorry you lost your job."

"We had words, but what's important is that you are in good hands now."

"How's Spence?" Carrie asked.

Jemma fidgeted with her necklace. "He's in Italy."

"Oops. I forgot about that. When's the wedding?"

"We parted hard."

"Oh, c'mon, y'all are in love."

"It's my fault because I can't get rid of Paul."

"You gave up Spencer for that guy?"

"I just want to know for sure. I told Spence that I would make up my mind by Christmas."

"What did he say to that?"

"He said he wouldn't come home for Christmas, but I'm afraid he meant something else."

"Like what?"

"Like he is tired of messing with me."

"You can't blame him, Jem. If you were on *As The World Turns*, the writers would give you amnesia about now, and you'd be sent off to an island."

"I guess we've just known each other too long and too well. It's like we've been married all our lives."

"I wish I'd known Phil all my life. He's my hope for happiness. Remember when we talked about that?"

"I do and I'm glad for y'all. I promise I'll write, but don't tell your father. He hates me."

"He doesn't hate you. You scared him."

"Carrie, you keep the painting. I did it for you, not him."

"Don't worry; we've already talked about it."

"I'm going to send you another one and I hope you'll like it even better. It's from my heart to yours."

"I can't wait. Love you. Tell Trina about Phil."

"I will. Love you, too."

"Don't mess around and lose Spence, because y'all were magic. You were so right about kissing being the highlight of your day. I'll talk to you later, Jem. I'm the happiest girl in the world."

"Good for you, Carrie." Jemma hung up the phone and cried.

❧ ❧

It was propped up on the kitchenette between the salt and pepper shakers.

JEMMABETH ALEXANDRA FORRESTER
C/O HER GRAMBETH
CHILLATON, TEXAS

"It's time you dealt with this," Lizbeth said, her tone firm.

Jemma knew she was right. An odd sensation, layered in swirls of emerald and black, snaked up from her stomach. The answer to all her doubts could lie in front of her. The almighty Paul. He had messed with her life and, therefore, with Spencer's. She grabbed the envelope before she could change her mind and took it to the living room. She turned on the lamp by Papa's chair and ripped it open.

Sweet Jemmabeth,

How you must feel towards me, I can never know for sure because the hurt I have caused is your private pain. Why I didn't have the guts to tell you about my situation is beyond me. It would have saved us from all this grief.

Shelby is the woman that you saw the night you came by, and she was, technically, my wife. She and I met in college. We were both bad kids and we got married our senior year. Things went from wild to worse. We were stepping out on each other even before our first anniversary. We said it was over, but my dad wanted us to make it work. I had been in ROTC so I began my service right after graduation and stayed in a few extra years. You already know all about that. Shelby was with me for part of my service, then she stayed with her folks. At least that's what she said.

When I came home, it was like old times for a while, but it just didn't work. We were both ready for something else. When I met you, I was living alone and nobody knew where she was living, but we were legally separated. She called up one day and wanted a divorce. When you saw her, we were meeting to file. That was the first time I had seen her in over a year. The divorce was granted on Valentine's Day, and I am no longer a married man.

I should have told you this last summer. You were so perfect and I was not proud of the whole Shelby mess. I know you are a spiritual person and in your eyes I was out of line to be dating you or anybody else before I was divorced. My only excuse is that I must be weak when it comes to you, Jemma. Even your name gives me a chill.

I joined my dad and uncle in their law firm, but nothing else matters if I don't have you in my life again. Let me ask your forgiveness in person so that I can look you straight in the eyes. I know how you feel about that.

My feelings have only grown stronger for you, my darlin', and I will never rest until you're mine. I mean that.

I love you,
Paul

Jemma stuck it back in the envelope. Old pangs of guilt and shame seeped through her. She moved to the porch swing and pushed off, longing to be rocked by something or someone.

The next morning before Lizbeth woke up, Jemma crept into the pouting room and opened the soldier box. Lizbeth had bundled up the letters and put big rubber bands around them. She sat on the floor wielding Papa's shiny letter opener until she decided they were not letters at all. They consisted of a couple of lines jotted on the back of his business cards:

Jemma, please call or write to me.
I have to talk to you.
*   Love, PT*

How embarrassing. These bits of nothing had shared the soldier box with dear letters from her daddy's brothers. She pitched the cards in a cigar box and squeezed it into the corner of a shelf. She stood for a few seconds, looking into the open chest, then felt around the bottom of it until her hand touched the chain. She took out the rose. It was as beautiful as the night he gave it to her. It glittered in the first light of the day that filtered through the little window. She draped the necklace around the shade of her bedside lamp. In spite of everything, she still needed to see him, to be sure. Time had healed her pain, but now there was this solid longing for Spence. He was not tucked away in a corner of her heart—he filled it up or so it seemed.

∾∿

Each time the phone rang, her heart skipped two beats, thinking it could be either of them. She was truly hopeless. This call was full of static.

"Sandy, hi!" Jemma said. "I've got news about Paul."

"So what? He's got problems," Sandy said.

"I don't think so. He was legally separated when we dated and he still loves me."

Sandy exhaled. "Jem, he's weird, I'm telling you, and he's got history. Nobody needs history; it's no fairytale when you get married, trust me."

"You don't know him."

"Obviously, you didn't either."

"I need to see him."

"You just used Spence, didn't you?"

"I did not."

"What would you call it? As soon as the lonesome stranger comes riding back into town you drop Spence like he was nothing. 'Ooh, he still loves me.' What a bunch of bull. You are just plain mean, Jemma. You were born to hurt him."

"I was not. You were the one who begged me to start dating him again. Everybody wanted me to get with Spencer. He and I talked about our feelings for each other."

"I'll bet you did. You probably spent time on The Hill, too, and at your not-so-secret spot on the river. You probably danced your little heart out with him every chance you got. Don't be trying to blame me for anything. You're the girl who's been on this big campaign against injustice. All you need to do is look in the mirror. Excuse me, but I have to go now."

Jemma hung up and fell back on the bed. This was a solid hit with the double whammy from Saturday Night Wrestling. Sandy always had a good handle on things. That's something the two of them had in common since the first grade, and Sandy was right, despite the sarcasm. Rats. Maybe she had just unleashed her hormones with Spencer, or maybe she loved him.

She tore half a page from her sketchpad and wrote the note. It was short and to the point: *Paul, We need to talk. Jemma* She figured that was equivalent to the back of a business card. She took it to the post office herself.

Paralee stamped the letter with a lifted Joan Crawford brow. "I heard that Spencer is off in It'ly. I kinda thought you'd be whippin' out a letter a day to him by now." H.D., her cat, stretched and looked Jemma right in the eye before jumping off the counter.

"Yes, ma'am, I should do that," Jemma whimpered and left. She sat in the car and blinked back tears, but the letter was mailed and Paul would come.

❧ ❧

The hollyhocks were in full bloom. They didn't have the sugary aroma of honeysuckle, but they were heavy with pink blossoms. She leaned back and closed her eyes. A warm breeze moved through her hair.

"Jemma?" His voice surged through her like quicksilver and fond memories regained their throne.

"Paul!" She gasped at the sight of him and shot straight up, her heart pounding as she looked into his startling green eyes—just like when she froze in the lights of the 9:04 Zephyr.

"I am so sorry, darlin'. I was stupid and wrong." He kissed her hand, sending her into a familiar spin.

She didn't even think about it. "I forgive you." Good grief.

He kissed her a long one. It was nice, but she was cool enough to know that some of the feeling came just from pressing her lips against any man's after three months of abstinence.

Paul moved the chairs together and took her hands. "Did you get my letters?" he asked, almost innocently.

"Only the last one was a real letter."

"My father finally convinced me that you were worth risking the truth over. I hope that what I said explained things. I've missed you so much," he said, looking her over like she forgot to dress. "So, you're wearing perfume now, huh?"

"Someone gave it to me."

They sat for a while, breathing in rhythm with the swaying and bobbing of the hollyhocks.

"Why did you wait so long to tell me?"

"I don't know. The longer you were away from me, the more I felt like you weren't going to listen."

"No, I mean from the start."

"Like I said, I was ashamed of it."

"I don't see how you could keep such a thing from me," she said.

"Why wouldn't you talk to me on the phone?"

"I thought you were married, and actually, you were."

"I guess there's a lot to forgive," he said.

She nodded, fiddling with the heart necklace. "So what do we do now?"

"It's up to you."

She'd heard that enough to last a lifetime.

"Did you date after I left?" Curiosity, nothing more.

"I didn't for a while, darlin', but, well, I got lonesome."

The thought of him with other girls didn't have any impact on her at all.

He traced around her wrists and hands, like a blind man. "This morning, when I told my dad that I was coming here, he said that he hopes that you're the one to be the mother of his grandchildren."

He seemed older, heavier than she remembered.

"What are you thinking?" he asked.

"Do you still wear your hat?" Great choice.

He grinned. "What kind of cowboy do you think I am? Of course I wear my hat."

How weird. He had grown wrinkly lines around his eyes over the winter.

"What's your horse's name again?" she asked. What an idiot.

"His name's Cinco. Jemma, do you love me? You've never said the words, and I need to know." He was serious, but she couldn't say it. She had made such a big deal about him for all this time, and here he was, wanting answers she couldn't give. Just like Spence. "Do you love me?" he asked again, this time with a kiss.

She pulled away. "I don't know. You and I had something, but I don't know what it was. I'm not thinking straight. This all seems like a dream."

"I understand, darlin'. It's been a long time. I just thought that maybe down deep, things hadn't changed."

"People change, Paul. Love changes. I just don't know how I feel right now." Yikes, there were those words too. She kissed him because she didn't know what else to do. He knew exactly what to do because Paul was, after all, a ladies' man.

⧸⧸⧸

Lizbeth was gracious, and Lester came over for supper and told stories. Jemma, though, was edgy. It was not right, somehow, for Paul to sit in the chair where Spencer had left that quilt so carefully folded. At Lizbeth's suggestion, Lester invited Paul to stay overnight at his house.

"Gram, I'm going to take Paul to meet the Johnsons," Jemma said.

"You young folks run along. Say hello to Willa for me." She gave Paul a polite smile. "We're glad you came," she said, meaning more than he knew.

The lights were still on at Willa's house. Paul waited in the baby blue while she knocked. She wasn't sure how this would go over.

Willa opened the door. "Mercy me, child. Why are you gallivanting around at this hour?"

"What's going on?" Trina asked, yawning.

Jemma led them off the porch and along the 'tunia path. Paul got out of the truck and stood beside it.

"Paul Turner, meet Willa and Trina Johnson."

He took off his hat and bowed.

Trina stammered and stared at him with a silly grin. "Glad to meet you," she said, then looked to Jemma for help.

Willa pursed her lips. "You in town for long?"

"I'm here for one reason," Paul said, pulling Jemma to him.

Willa and Trina knew too much. "I just wanted you to meet him," Jemma said. She really wanted them to see what she'd been up against.

Willa read her mind. "It's good to put a face to a name." She turned towards the porch. Her cane whacked the path with each step.

"Bye, Paul," Trina waved. "Nice to meet you." She lowered her brow at Jemma.

"Y'all watch out for the 9:04." Willa said over her shoulder. "Be a downright shame to mess up that pretty pickup."

⁊6r

Lester pulled in his driveway with the morning paper and found Jemma sitting in the porch swing, wrapped in her old robe.

"Jemmerbeth, you're up early. Did you already milk the cow?" he asked, chuckling.

Jemma gave him a weak smile. "I'm just thinking."

"That lawyer is still asleep. He seems a bit peculiar around the edges. Sort of drifts off while a feller's talkin'."

"I miss Spencer," she said.

Lester settled into the wicker chair. "I know what it's like to be without your sweetheart and I've got lots of them to fret over. I loved 'em all, too, even the cranky ones." A rooster crowed across the tracks. "Yes, sir, the only thing worse than being in love is being plumb out of it."

"I think I'm going crazy, Lester. I have no control over my heart. It's separate from me, running wild."

234

"Well, sir, you know, back in the thirties, we had a runaway train come thunderin' through here. The engineer had hisself a heart attack and there wasn't nobody else with him at the time. That runaway was full throttle through four counties. Folks was gettin' off their deathbeds to see it fly by. The Sheriff and the Texas Rangers was trying to beat it down the road to clear the tracks. It had a mind of its own, too. Them kind of runaways have to hit somethin' to put 'em out of their misery. This particular one run smack dab into Eugene Richey's cotton trailers. He was pullin' a double load behind his tractor, right close to Cleebur. It rained cotton for a whole hour after the collision. Eugene got throwed thirty foot in the air, and his wires was crossed after that, poor old feller. He should've jumped off when he seen it comin', but he wouldn't leave his cotton, I reckon."

"I don't have any excuses," she said.

"How's that, Jemmer?"

"Helene warned me that Paul was just a passing fancy. I thought I was so smart, but it looks like I am no better than Eugene, when it comes to jumping out of the way of a real Zephyr."

Lester couldn't add anything to what she'd said. He tapped his foot and looked out over the yard.

Jemma gave him a kiss on the cheek. "I'd better get dressed. Thanks for the conversation, Lester."

⊰ᚪᚪ⊱

Paul and Jemma drove out to the river, but not to The Spot.

"Does this creek have a name?" he asked.

"The Salt Fork of the Red River," Jemma said, scanning the horizon.

"Sounds western, but it's not much of a river though."

She scowled at him. "It's ours."

Paul put his arm around her. "Seems like you're ticked off, darlin'. Surely you don't want me to confess every detail about my past. We could be here for a week." He laughed—that same old whiskey laugh—then crossed his heart. "No other secrets worth repeating, Jem. The only truth that matters is that I was hooked on you that first night at the office. Any man alive would've been, but you were such a good girl that I knew that I was going to have to straighten up. Then I realized that I really loved you and had to have you to love me back. That was the first time I'd had thoughts about a woman from my heart, and I knew that I should tell you everything. When I opened my truck door and saw the painting, I cried like a two-year-old...anyway, my dad and I talked for hours that night. He was hacked off at me for messing up again. He said that I deserved a good kick in the pants for hurting you."

"He was right."

"I saw your car at Helene's, but I couldn't bring myself to face you. I don't know why I fell apart like that. I let you leave town, thinking the worst of me. I will always regret that, darlin'. Always."

She watched the water as it curved around and made a little pool below them. It could be a spot for minnows to scatter if she and Spence went wading there. He was probably asleep now, across the Atlantic. She hoped he was having sweet dreams.

Paul lifted her hand to his lips. "I think you have become even more beautiful, if that's possible."

"A good heart is more important than good looks," Jemma said. As though that was why she fell for him.

"You do have a good heart, and I'm sorry I caused you pain."

"Nobody goes through life without pain," Jemma said. "The pain that Gram has endured makes mine insignificant. My friend Carrie has gone through physical and emotional pain, but she still has an amazing spirit. Trina and Willa, well, they know pain on a daily basis."

"Black people are resilient," he said, playing with her hair.

She drew back. "Excuse me? Black *people*? We've wronged each individual. It makes us feel better to think of people in groups, then we put the groups in boxes, like mementoes. It makes us comfortable. We close the lids and open them up occasionally for our own purposes. We need to face the people inside the boxes."

"Hey," he said, fending off the verbal barrage with his hands, "I wasn't inferring anything. I just meant, as a race, they have shown a remarkable ability to survive. It was a compliment."

"As a race? Like there is something in their blood?"

"Now hold on here a minute, darlin'. I'm not a racist. I was only making an observation."

"Integrity. That's what Willa and Trina have. When you ride the bus four hours every day when you're just six years old, there's nothing in your blood that says 'be strong.' It was Trina who got on that bus every day because she loved to learn. Willa does ironing for people across the tracks who won't do their own because they're too lazy. If she could've been on that bus like Trina, maybe she could have realized her dreams, too. You and I did that to her, our parents did that to her, and our grandparents, too, because we put people in boxes to keep our consciences comfortable. You were not making a compliment and you know it."

"Is this the temper you told me about?" he asked. "Are you about to throw something at me?"

"No. I throw stuff when I'm just a little mad. I was throwing things from my heart just now."

"Come here." He pulled her towards him. "Let's talk about the scenery," he said, nuzzling her ear. "There sure is a lot of flat land around here, except for some draws and a few hills."

She shrugged. "I guess it grows on you, like the desert."

He pushed his hat back on his head. "Dry land cotton, I suppose."

"Some farmers have irrigation wells, and there are ranches, too."

"Ranching's good, but farming seems like a hard way to make a living in this country."

"My Papa and Gram did it."

He moved his fingers under her chin. "It's interesting that someone like you came from a one-horse town like this."

"What's that supposed to mean?"

"Your art. It's way too sophisticated to have been nurtured by Lester, for example."

"Grammar has nothing to do with character or good sense," she said, daring him to say more.

Paul chuckled. "Well, you have to admit that he's quite the bumpkin."

Jemma looked him in the eye, ready to pounce. "Don't ever say that about my friends. What you see in them is exactly what's inside me."

Paul exhaled and readjusted his hat. The wind kicked up from the west. "Is it that I was married?"

"You have to be kidding me." Her hands sprang up in the air. "The problem was that you were *married and dating me*! Good grief. All this talk about love was going on while you had a wife and didn't have the decency to let me in on your little secret."

"I was afraid I'd lose you."

"You did anyway."

"I get the feeling now that you wished I hadn't come."

"No. I needed to see you to get my heart straight."

He touched her cheek. "I'm so sorry I hurt you, but I can't change the past, Jem. I don't believe in living like a monk, either, and I know your opinion of that. It's just the way I am, but I promise you, on my mother's memory, that I've never loved anybody but you and I never will."

The sun moved behind coral edged clouds, changing the color of the river. She touched the heart necklace. "You're right. Some things never change," she said, "and they shouldn't."

"Just give me another chance. I won't push you or stand in the way of your art. If you need to finish your education, that's okay with me. We both have things we need to do. I've got a career to get off the ground, and besides, we can get to know each other again. Have fun like we used to." He touched her lips. "What do you say, my golden-eyed darlin'?"

"I think I still love Spencer, my high school boyfriend." Jemma's heart sank when she said his name, as though she had summoned his ghost and he was with them now, watching.

Paul laid his hat on the rock, then his lips curled into a grin. "Well, I'm in this for the long haul, so I suppose I can handle a little competition from some kid." His arms were tight around her and he wouldn't let go. "I love you, Jemma," he whispered. "You'll always be mine." He kissed her like a man determined to start a fire with wet wood.

There they were, only a football field away from Jemma and Spencer's parking spot. A cinnamon colored hawk sailed just above them, its shrill cry startling her. She broke away from Paul's kiss and sat up, watching as the hawk circled, then flew into the sunset. She could still hear it on the wind as Paul wiped her tears, thinking they were a good sign.

ᛋ᚛ ᚜ᛂ

It was time for his return to Wicklow. "If there were any way to swing another night, I would," he said. "I realize that we have some more

238

talking to do. Problem is, I have a court hearing tomorrow morning, and nobody else in the office knows the case."

"I leave next week to spend the rest of the month with my Lillygrace grandparents in St. Louis," she said.

He stood by the door, touching her hair. "I do know about commitments, but I'll miss you and I'll call. One more thing I need to ask. Do you know anybody who would hire a detective to follow me around, then quiz my family and friends about my character and personal life?"

"A detective?" Jemma asked, suddenly interested. "I don't know. Unless it could have been my great aunt." She couldn't help but smile. "I bet you've been Do Dahed." At least that's who she hoped it was. He held her, cowboy-style, as they kissed good-bye. She should have told him right then that there was no hope for them, but being the Queen of Bad Choices, she didn't.

CHAPTER TWENTY-SIX

Fallow Ground

English Leather was still on her skin as she painted, even after playing basketball for an hour with Trina. Paul dazzled her last summer when she was ready to love again, but it was Spence she needed then and now. The initial surge of emotion she felt when she first saw him in the hollyhock patch was not worth the grief she had caused Spence and herself. It was neither earth-shattering desire, nor was it love. She had just been running the bulls, but this time she had tripped and let herself get caught up on a big horn.

She took a break from painting and walked the rails. Cotton John had predicted scattered showers. Only at the vanishing point of the rails was there a hint of blue. She smiled at Shorty's TV blaring across the tracks. Funny, how wood and steel could come to dictate social status. How easy things would be if all lines were so clean and clear cut as the tracks, creating tidy boundaries, boxes, for sorting souls. She knew now that lines must be blurred for people to achieve their dreams. Those were the gray areas. There was no gray area for love, though. She either loved Paul or Spence, and she knew the answer.

❦

"Let's drive out to cemetery and then to the home place," Lizbeth said after church. Jemma picked flowers from the garden and put them on Papa's grave. The stiff wind flipped the petals like broken pinwheels. Lizbeth kissed her hand and laid it on the tombstone. She said a prayer, then waited in the car.

"Papa," Jemma whispered, "I'll make it up to Spencer. I promise. I do love him." Saying it out loud, at last, made her feel better. It might be nice if she told him, too.

Lizbeth drove to the little rise on the far northeast corner of the home place. In the distance, the windmill next to their farmhouse was a prism, spinning and sparkling in the blazing sun. Lizbeth tied her scarf under her chin and got out of the car. Jemma followed her to the edge of the barren field, left unplanted for a growing season by the tenant.

Lizbeth surveyed the horizon as the wind flapped her thin, cotton dress about her legs. "Your Papa liked to let the land rest now and then, too. He said it worked hard giving us a living and needed time to regain its strength. He always talked about this place like it was a person. 'Let it go fallow for a while and it'll come back twice as strong,' he'd say and he was right. We had some fine crops over the years."

She gathered a handful of dirt and sifted it through her fingers. It sprayed back against her dress. "That's how he tested the fallow ground. Claimed he could feel if it was ready to taste life again." She put her arm around Jemma. "I sometimes think that I am like this old place." They stood together, wavering in the wild gusts that hissed through the fencerow grass. "You drive back, sugar," Lizbeth said, dabbing at her eyes with her hanky. "He was full of joy. I do so miss that man."

On the way home, Jemma admitted to herself that all she needed was a hoop skirt. She couldn't go back to Tara any more. She was already there. She couldn't sift the dirt through her fingers and know when the fallow ground was ready to taste life again. She had Spencer, gave him up, wanted him back, got him, and gave him up again. She was not even worth being called fallow ground.

❧ ❦

She heard the phone ringing as they drove up. She raced to it on the outside chance it was Spence.

"Hi, Jem."

"Sandy. Okay, I was wrong, and you were right. I'm so sorry."

"Yeah, well, it may not matter now. I hate to be the one to tell you this, but Spencer has a serious girlfriend."

Jemma crumpled to the floor, stomach churning. "No, no, no." Her fingers went to her lips where his good-bye kiss still smoldered.

"She's in that study abroad thing with him in Italy, and I guess they are quite the couple. Mrs. Chase said that he is bringing her home for Christmas. She was showing pictures to everybody at Nedra's."

"He hasn't been gone that long."

"Hey, it only took you a summer to fall in deep love, remember?"

"It was a mistake."

"Looks like the mistake of a lifetime. She's from New York. Twila saw the pictures and said that she is completely gorgeous. Remember when we used to do the Zephyr Dance on the tracks? You were always the last one to stop dancing, and you wouldn't jump off until the train blew its whistle. You just waited too long this time. It was bound to happen sometime. Well, hang in there, Jem. I have to go."

Scarlett barely made it to the bathroom to throw up. Afterwards, she sat on the bathmat and unleashed a deluge of sobs.

Lizbeth heard it all from the living room, but decided to let nature take its course. She had already heard the gossip at Nedra's. Unfortunately, it was the talk of the town.

Jemma stayed in the bathroom until dark, then when Lizbeth tactfully went to bed early, Jemma crawled onto her own bed and stared at the ceiling. The teardrops filled her ears, then trickled through her hair and soaked into the pillow. She was swallowed up with misery, the surly kind that gnawed with each breath to remind her that it was all her own doing.

Rain plinked into a watering can left on the front porch as the curtains billowed out with the damp breeze. She took the broom handles out of the windows, letting them slide shut, then she wandered outside.

It was a quiet shower that would rinse leaves and give the birds brief puddle water. She rubbed her arms at the sudden cool air. The knot that had lodged itself in her throat began sifting down to her heart, to a gloomy corner that harbored comfortless and pointless loss. She stepped into the rain and lifted her desperation to the Lord in prayer, but it was the night that pointed its soggy finger at her. She was without him—her hero, her best friend, and her own true love.

❧ ❧

Most of her paintings were gone, shipped to Le Claire in carefully packaged crates, designed and crafted by Lester, who knew a thing or two about shipping on trains. She was going on with the work at hand. Spencer had warned her that he was going to do it. Rats. Not just gorgeous, but completely gorgeous. Jemma blew her nose. "I won't come home for Christmas," she said to the walls. "I'll go to Arizona." She got the paintings and walked across the tracks.

"Hey girl, what's with the puffy eyes?" Trina asked as she opened the door.

"Spence has a girlfriend in Italy." Jemma said. She knew she was in for a sermon.

Trina shook her head. "I hate to say it, but everybody saw it coming, even though that cowboy was really something to look at. Man, you sure can pick 'em."

Willa made the face that mothers get just before they give a lecture. "Give me a hug, sugar. Now, you'd better get yourself some backbone. Just because Spencer's got himself a honey, don't mean that he's outta love with you, even though you were fiddlin' around with that pretty boy."

"Mama, don't start preaching," Trina said.

Jemma propped the painting up on the kitchen counter. "It's okay. There's nothing you could tell me that I haven't already beaten myself over the head with anyway. Here's my surprise."

Trina's eyes widened. "Oh, Jem," was all she could say.

"I painted three of them and I already sent one to Carrie. The one of Papa is for Spence, so would you take it to his housekeeper's for me? She'll make sure he gets it." Jemma might as well have been talking to the ironing board even though Trina nodded politely.

Willa wiped her eyes. "Jemmabeth Forrester, you are the sweetest child I ever knew outside of my Latrina. I need another hug."

The painting enchanted the Johnson women. The three little girls were dancing on the tracks with the wind in their hair. The smallest was a pretty blonde with eyes the color of cornflowers, the tallest was a beautiful little black girl with slanted eyes and dimples, and in the middle was an auburn-haired beauty with pouty lips, freckles, and golden eyes. All were laughing—heads back, arms akimbo, like there was no tomorrow.

"I gotta go," Jemma said. "I'll see you in the morning for the 6:23."

As she trudged home, something pink caught her eye. She pulled it out from an old pipe, sheltered by the cellar door. It was the remains of a candy Easter egg, wrapped in cellophane, a survivor of Robby's egg hunt and the tornado. Spencer had hidden that one. She put it in her pocket. Now she understood playing both ends against the middle and losing again. Like that did her a lot of good at this point. She called her family to get chewed out and get it over with.

Alex answered the phone. "Sweet Pea, you knew this was coming if you didn't make a commitment to him. He needs to be loved."

Her daddy was less tactful. "I don't know what to say, Jem. I'm happy that he has someone now, but it breaks my heart that it's not you. You'll just have to deal with it, baby girl. You're the one that let it happen."

Only Robby had anything encouraging for her. "I bet Spence is just teasing you. He likes to tease me. I'll see you tomorrow at the airport."

She stared at the stack of records under the dresser. Roy was calling to her. She might as well make herself as miserable as possible. She put on his album, but couldn't make it past the first song. Eleanor and Edith and were right. She'd had her time with a sweet man and tossed him aside, like those practice pieces in her mentorship. Even in Chillaton, there were no comforting casseroles for this particular brand of pain. She would have to buck up alone.

Paul had called every night. He talked for a half hour each time, droning on about his work. Jemma's ear was sore from it and from hearing *darlin'* every other breath. He had never even asked to see her work when he came. She should have thrown out those letters with the table scraps. She took the rose necklace off the lampshade and dropped it again, without ceremony, into the depths of the soldier box. She wrapped the letters in the Amarillo *Globe* newspaper, and dumped them in the trash barrel., along with a whole pack of lighted matches from the truck stop. The flames danced as tidbits of the ashes floated away. The 9:04 Zephyr flashed by on the tracks, quite appropriately. Jemma stood beside the barrel until nothing was left but a whiff of smoke.

❧ ❧

On the morning she left, they sat in the porch swing, holding hands.

"I don't want to leave you, Gram," Jemma said.

"I know. I won't be able go in your room for a while," Lizbeth said.

"You know I'll come to see you every chance I get."

"You're a joy to me, Jemmabeth, no matter where you are."

Jemma squeezed her hand. "I hope that I can be a strong woman like you someday."

"It was a hard row that brought me here, sugar. I pray that God's Plan will be an easier one for you. Nobody sets out to be weak or strong. Life just falls in your lap and you have to do something with it."

"Remember when Papa would say that we can ask the Lord about one thing or the other when we get to heaven? I could just imagine this long line of people waiting to sit in God's lap and ask their list of questions, just like the Santa line at a department store."

Lizbeth laughed. "Surely that's not the way it will be."

"I want you to live forever. Say that you will."

"I will, honey, but not on this old earth, thank the good Lord. You take care to guard your heart, Jemma. Sometimes the paths we consider are not the ones the Lord intends for us to follow."

"I've lost Spence. I hurt him again and now he has somebody else."

"That's your pain, and you'll have to bear it. You need to quiet your heart now, so you can hear the voice of The Holy Spirit leading you. Here, this is for you," Lizbeth said, taking a package from her sweater pocket. Jemma opened it to find a small white Bible. It was encased in a leather cover with a zipper and a tiny cross as the fob. Her name was written in gold letters on the cover, as was a Bible verse—*Proverbs 3:5-6.*

"It's beautiful, Gram. Now it's your turn." She took a bundle from under the swing and put it on Lizbeth's lap. "Go ahead, open it."

Lizbeth pulled back the paper and hooted with laughter. It was her own grimacing face, teeth bared, behind the wheel of the Dodge. The ends of her scarf were bent back in the wind and her knuckles were white on the steering wheel. They were still laughing when Lester walked up the porch steps.

"I figured I'd find y'all bawlin' like babies, but here you sound like a couple of settin' hens," he said. Lizbeth pointed at the painting propped up on the wicker chair. Lester lined up his bifocals and leaned over for a good look. "Jemmerbeth, you are something else. You look

245

downright scary, Miz Liz, no offense."

That set them off again.

Jemma loaded her bags in the car. "Just a second," she said. She ran to the tracks and gathered pebbles from the rail bed, then stopped at the honeysuckle vine and picked off a solitary blossom and pressed it between the pages of her new Bible.

Lester drove especially slow to the station, giving her plenty of time to think. "Gram, would you keep my mail for me? I might get some registration stuff from school. Just open it and call me if it's important."

"I'll do that. Tell Robby that the cardinals are doing fine, and give your grandparents a chance to show their love for you in their own way."

She wasn't too sure about that idea. "I can't wait to hear all about your plans for the trip with Do Dah."

"Oh, mercy. Don't bring that up."

"Gram, if you learned to drive a car, you can handle sitting in a plane."

"Lord willing," Lizbeth said.

Trina and Willa were there to see her off. No more tears, Gram had said, but she was the one waving backwards so Jemma couldn't see her cry. The Zephyr was on time. The conductor looked at his watch and brought in the step. She pressed her face to the window to get one last look. The sun was not quite up, but the Chase castle stood silhouetted against the horizon. It suddenly occurred to her that she used to call him "babe" when they were in high school. Since Paul, she had denied Spencer even that morsel of affection. *Selfish hussy.* That's what Mrs. Chase could've called her.

In six hours she would be in Dallas, then on a flight to St. Louis and the elegant Lillygrace mansion. Things would not be quite the same at all, what with someone to cook and clean, and a gardener who lived in a caretaker's house the same size as Gram's.

The Zephyr rocked along as the sun cast a red-orange glow on the fields. Jemma leaned her head against the cool window and watched the "man on stilts," as Robby had named the passing rows, striding to keep pace with the speed of the train. Each row helped the stilt man along like a cartoon flip chart.

She squinted into the sunrise as farmhands waved at the train. Weese would never know that life. Maybe he would send Willa a

246

photograph of himself in his uniform, just before he shipped off to Vietnam. If Spencer married his new girlfriend, she would lose him and become a wretched old maid, but if she lost him to a war, that would kill her.

She took out her sketchbook and wrote him a note.

Dear Spence, I promised that I would tell you when I am ready to marry. Oh, I am. Let's go back to Plum Creek and invite the whole county.

She wadded it up. She couldn't write those words to him when he had a girlfriend. She drew his face as he looked on the trip to Amarillo. She scribbled off a poem about her runaway heart, then put the book away. She was not born to hurt him, like Sandy said. She was born to love him.

∽∼

Lizbeth stood on the porch and watched the swing move in the wind. Jemma had been gone for the better part of a week. The soldier box now held the overflow of her granddaughter's hope chest. Her prayer was that Jemmabeth's trials would not increase, and that her menfolk would not come into life to be warriors, dying in far-off places, nor would they leave in her screaming presence.

She walked out back to the hollyhock patch. There were two Cardinals living in the pecan tree. Jemma had painted them for her and hung the piece where Cam's portrait had been. Lizbeth liked seeing them first thing when she woke up. They made pleasant company. If those stray little birds could adapt to a harsh existence in the Panhandle, surely she could find joy in her own solitary life. The 6:23 Zephyr passed, blowing its whistle. At least she didn't have to worry about Jemma dancing on those tracks anymore. She reached in her pocket for a tissue.

"Miz Liz, would you mind a little company?" Lester stood outside the patch, hat in hand.

"Help yourself."

"I've been thinkin' about Jemmerbeth. If I could've had me a child, I would want her to be like Jemmer. She made me feel good, always comin' and goin'. I kinda think she's the one that's like that

Zephyr, but not silver, 'cause she has them gold eyes like yours, no offense, Miz Liz. I looked forward to being around her every day. We don't have too many things like that in our old age, do we?"

"No, we don't, Lester. We'll just have to get along without her. I knew she would leave someday. She's headed for bigger things."

"A feller wishes though, that she could've stayed here and painted them pictures. I reckon she'll get famous and they'll be hangin' in museums."

"Helene thinks so and she should know." A squirrel scampered across the grass, catching their attention. It hesitated, then, with a swish of its tail, ran up the pecan tree.

Lester cleared his throat. "I've got a real lonesome feelin' today, so I was wonderin' if you would like to go for a little drive."

"That's a fine idea. Let's drive until we run out of gas, Lester. What do you say to that?"

"Now, Miz Liz, when I was in my courtin' days, runnin' out of gas was just an excuse to spark."

Lizbeth pushed up her glasses. "Mr. Timms, my sparking days were only with one man. You and I are friends, just like Willa and I are friends, understood?"

"Yes, ma'am. Your plain speakin' always reminds me of Paulette, my last wife. I think you must be part French, too."

She smiled and picked some flowers to put on her only sparking man's grave.

Lester brought in the morning mail and sipped his coffee, going on about mail-order brides. Not finding much of an audience for his story, he left for the barbershop.

Lizbeth turned down the radio and went through her mail. There was a letter for Jemma from her school in Dallas. She slid Cam's letter opener under the flap.

August 18, 1966
Dear Miss Forrester,

We have just received official notice that you have been awarded the Girard Fellowship at Le Academie Royale D'Art in Paris. The award was based upon your portfolio, staff and mentor recommendations, and, of course, your competition piece, Joie, Dans Lumière. This prestigious prize carries a full stipend for all expenses incurred during the Fellowship. Additionally, your work will be featured at the Academie's public gallery throughout your attendance.

We are honored, indeed, to have sponsored you in this international competition. You are the first American student to receive the Fellowship and it is only the second time a woman has won in over seventy years. We are fortunate that the competition date only recently expired and the award came within the time limits of your attendance and intent to re-enroll at the college. Your portfolio must be updated and we shall be in contact with your liaison at the Academy. There are many details that must be addressed.

Again, the faculty joins me in extending our warmest congratulations and most sincere appreciation for the attention this award will undoubtedly bring to our own program. We look forward to seeing you soon. Please do contact my office immediately.

Yours truly,
Dr. Edmond Crowder, Dean
Le Claire College of the Arts
Dallas, Texas

The sun glinted through the honeysuckle vine and its lacy shadows flickered across the letter in her lap. The Great Plan had begun for Jemmabeth. An odd tear slipped down Lizbeth's cheek and pooled in the fold of the paper. She blotted it with her finger, then touched it to her lips. Its taste conjured a long abandoned sensation. With a cleansing breath, she dialed the long distance operator, then waited while she connected her with St. Louis. Jemma herself answered.

"Lillygrace residence, Jemmabeth speaking," she said.

Her formality made Lizbeth smile. "Jemma, it's Gram. You have some mail."

"Something bad?"

"No, sugar, something of joy."

CHAPTER TWENTY-SEVEN

Being Still

*C*riticism is easy, Art is difficult—Philippe Nericault 1680-1754. Jemmabeth read it and exhaled. Her heart hadn't found a steady beat since Lizbeth's call. She was beside herself with the thought of studying in Paris. Her Grandfather Lillygrace had given her a French dictionary and phrase book to read on the flight to Dallas, but she had barely looked at it. Instead, she had memorized the foldout map of Europe that showed France and Italy, and she had marked Florence with a red heart.

"Jemmabeth!" Professor Rossi was waiting for her at the top of the steps. He held out his arms. "Bravo! Bravo! The school is buzzing with the news of the Fellowship. I am so proud of you. Now the world will learn what we have known all along—beautiful woman, beautiful art."

Jemma laughed. "I missed you, Professor, and I have missed Le Claire. I wanted the smell of paint in my nose and the sound of pianos and violins in my ears."

"No, no, Jemma, you have not lived until you see Paris and it becomes a part of you. That will be your new love, believe me. Now, when you are there, you must go to Italy, no questions asked. It will ignite your heart. I shall give you the name of my friend who teaches in Florence and you will stay with his family. They will love you."

Jemma's throat tightened at the name of the city. "Thank you so much. I'm a little overwhelmed right now, and I have to meet with the Dean."

"Yes, yes, don't let me keep you, but my wife and I will have you over for dinner to discuss these plans. Where are you staying?"

"Mostly with my friend, Melanie Glazer. I won't be here very long, but I do have to get my portfolio ready. Will you help me?"

"I am your servant, Jemma."

Le Claire was so eager to get the school's name in the international media that every effort was made to assure she made it to Paris. She was shuffled around from office to office while the staff took care of her. She had to get a passport quickly. Calls were made. There was so much paperwork to sign that someone joked that a lawyer would be helpful. An attorney appeared. It was a fun, mind-joggling experience. At day's end, Jemma and Melanie sat in the student center, eating and going over the excitement.

"You have caused all this, you know," Melanie said.

"What? The paperwork and phone calls and names I can't pronounce?" Jemma said with her feet propped on an empty chair.

"No, I mean the anxiety about your boyfriend."

Jemma sat up. "I know," she said, "I wasted a year on a wild cowpoke lawyer."

"Was he worth it?"

"Not really, but at the time it was like a rodeo poster—chills, thrills, and spills."

"What's your plan? I assume you have one," Melanie asked.

"My plans are worthless. I only know that I'm scared," Jemma said.

"Isn't it possible that this girlfriend is just a rebound thing?"

"Spence is not one to take romance lightly."

"You have to talk to him. If he knows your feelings, then it's his choice."

"It all comes down to Spencer getting to make the choice," Jemma said. "That's poetic justice, and I'm so big on justice, you know."

"It'll work out." Melanie said, "Look at my life. I just finished a world tour with a major orchestra, Michael and I are headed for Julliard, and we will be getting married after that. Two years ago I was only hoping to teach violin lessons and find a boyfriend who wasn't too pathetic. Besides, what happened to the old Jemmabeth who wasn't afraid of anything? Are you scared to let go of this problem? You do realize that the God who created the universe can figure out your little life."

"I know," Jemma said. "I just hope I'm not in the doghouse with Him, too."

⧉⧉

Paul knew she wanted to tell him adios. He was, after all, a lawyer and knew when he had a losing case. They had discussed it at great length on the phone before she left St. Louis. He had said he would meet her at The Big D coffee shop at Dallas Love Field. Jemma had given him the date and time of her flight. She called him from Helene's when she spent the weekend there, but he didn't answer. She even got to Love Field two hours early so they could talk, but he never showed up. After an hour passed, she called his office. The secretary said that something had come up and he wouldn't be back until the next week. Jemma asked, on a hunch, if his friend Kyle had gone with him, and the response was affirmative. They'd gone to Las Vegas. She hung up and stared at the jets taxing into the terminal, thinking about those words at the Handle Bar—*Drinking from the Devil's cup tonight?* She should've said her good-byes then.

⧉⧉

She had no idea that she would be hanging in the sky for thirteen hours, all flights totaled. Across the Atlantic, she watched the sun rise above a carpet of clouds, like puffs of pink whipped cream piled below the jet. As the sunlight spilled across the heavens, she noticed a sprinkling of ice crystals on her window. They cast tiny star shadows on the window frame. She could have still been finding Orion with him. As they dropped altitude the crystal stars evaporated, the clouds cleared, and Paris came into view. If she never got to set foot in it, just seeing it with her own eyes was enough to make her cry.

She had practiced French phrases until they sounded reasonable to her, but once she tried them out on the airport staff, she realized there was going to be a problem. To her relief, most of them spoke English. Her liaison met her at the baggage claim area, as planned.

"*Bonjour*, Miss Forrester, I trust you had a good flight. Permit me to introduce myself. I am Peter Neville, and I am ready to assist you in your acquaintance with the Academie."

Jemma liked his style. He reminded her of her cousin Trent—short, slender, very well dressed, and equally well mannered.

She shook his hand. "*Bonjour.* I'm Jemmabeth, but please call me Jemma. You'll have to forgive me, because I'm in a dream world right now and can use all the help I can get."

"You have a nice Texas accent, Jemma." He pronounced her name just like Helene did, *Zhemma.*

"How do you know about my accent?" she asked.

"My wife and I go to many movies, particularly cowboy movies. You sound somewhat like the woman in the movie, *Hud,*" Peter said.

She clapped her hands. "I can't believe you said that. It was filmed not far from my hometown. Paul Newman actually spoke to me. Oh, there's my luggage," she said, pointing to her new matched set, courtesy of the Lillygraces. "Have my paintings come yet?"

He lifted her suitcases onto a cart. "*Oui,* they have arrived. What did Mr. Newman say to you?"

"He said, 'Excuse me.' I was sort of in his way as he left the set. I know that's not much, but it is when you are in high school and you have a crush on him."

"What do you mean 'crush'?" Peter asked.

"Oh, you know, an infatuation. Surely you French know about that." She did, for sure.

"Ah, now you are speaking in the language of love. I am certain that you have had many young men with these crushes for you, Jemma," he said with a French grin.

Jemma flushed. "How far is it to the Academie?"

"We will be there within the hour. Here is where you should wait for me. I will bring the car and collect the luggage and you," he said, then blended into the crowd.

In Peter's car, she could neither sit still nor could she stop talking. She didn't even care that he drove fast, much like Spencer. He was gracious and smiled at her enthusiasm.

"I can't believe that I am here," Jemma babbled. "Paris is too beautiful to be a city. They should call it a museum; then every corner could be a painting. Can you believe the vanishing points? Where do all these people work? What is the name of that building? Where are we, approximately? Is that the Seine? Paris! I can't believe it!"

They went to her apartment on the third floor of an old building within walking distance of the Academie. The ceilings were high, as were the windows. The room, plain white, was furnished with the essentials: bed, dresser with a mirror, bench, desk and chair, an umbrella stand, chest of drawers and a wardrobe—no closet. Next to the door was a coat hook. There were shades on the windows, but no cabbage rose prints like at Helene's. She would have to do some fixing up to make it her own. Below was a courtyard with scattered trees, roses, benches, and a bicycle rack. Jemma's room was at the rear corner of the building with two sets of double windows. One pair looked down on the courtyard while the other looked out over the jumble of buildings in that part of the city. Across the rooftops, she could see a hill with a gleaming white structure at the pinnacle.

"Sacre-Coeur?" she asked with her nose against the glass.

Peter joined her at the window. "You have studied well. May I help you with your baggage?"

"No thank you. I will manage just fine. Could you help me with just one call later? It's collect to my grandparents."

"That is no problem. It will be a joy to hear you talk."

Peter was her constant companion throughout the day. He took her to the Academie and showed her the basics. The double doors at the entrance dwarfed them, but the classrooms were similar to those at Le Claire.

"All art schools must smell the same," she said, taking a deep breath. "It's the best perfume."

They toured the Gallery, too. She couldn't wait to get her materials and get started. He showed her the neighborhood markets and cafés, but she was amazed by the amount of dog poop on the sidewalks. Papa would have gotten a big laugh out of that. It was no different than dodging chicken mess, but she didn't mention that to Peter. He was very good at avoiding it. They stopped for lunch at a café near her apartment.

"Do you have someone in your life at the moment?" Peter asked, taking her off guard.

She blushed. "He's in Florence, but he doesn't know that I'm here."

"I see that you are in love," Peter said. "You are quarreling?"

"How did you know?" She recalled hearing a story about French fortunetellers. "Are you a gypsy?"

"I am a Frenchman," he said, laughing.

"Spencer and I grew up together and we've always been in love. Now he's seeing another woman."

"He could not be in love with her as long as you are alive."

Jemma smiled. "No wonder the French have such reputations. You have a way with words, don't you?"

"As I said, it is the language of love. We created it. Now tell me this story." Jemma gave him the basics about Paul. He listened, watching her face almost to the point of distraction. He raised a finger. "This is the plot of another American movie, correct?"

"No, unfortunately, it's my story."

"Everyone makes mistakes in life, Jemma. If one never does anything, one never does anything wrong."

"I hadn't thought of it like that."

"I am certain that you are weary. I'll take you back to your apartment so you may call your family, then rest. I shall see you in the morning. Sleep late, Jemma. You may suffer some of the jet lag," he said, arriving at the telephone near her room.

She made her call with his assistance. "Thank you so much, Peter. You've been wonderful."

∾∾

It was the first time she had been alone in a year. She looked around her room and unpacked a few things, but the sleepless flight was getting to her or maybe it was the rain that had begun to trickle down the window panes. She managed to move the furniture around, and she hung the driftwood Robby had carved for her on the hook by the door. On the dresser, she spread her great-grandmother's lace handkerchief and put Spencer's picture on it, and beside it, the music box.

She set out a picture of her on the tractor with Papa and the pebbles from the train tracks. Yawning, she opened her new Bible and read aloud, "Trust in the Lord with all thine heart; and lean not unto thine own understanding. In all thy ways acknowledge Him, and He shall direct thy paths." Trust—that was the key word, probably. She underlined it and fell asleep on the bare mattress before she could finish her prayers.

In the lonesome early morning hours, she woke up with a

pounding headache and serious rumblings in her stomach. The trip had caught up with her. She went to the window and looked out over the rooftops. The moon was a big snowball in the sky, like those she had made for Carrie to throw at her last winter. In its light, the mishmash of Parisian structures rose like ancient, pastel Monopoly houses up to the gleaming Sacre-Coeur. Jemma smiled. *Moonlight Over Paris.* Gram would be reading the mail by now, and trying not to laugh at Lester's stories.

At least Spencer was somewhere on the same continent with her now. He said that he wanted to show her Paris, but that was before he found out the truth about Paul. A wave of nausea overwhelmed her, and she ran out her door, down the hallway to the toilet, and lost her first French meal. She was back to her old ways of dealing with life.

She returned to the window and chewed her last stick of American gum. Arizona was a zillion miles away. Robby was most likely teasing some little girl, her daddy was almost certainly yelling at his football team, and her mother was probably worrying about her. For sure, the Lillygraces were having something served to them.

St. Louis had been such an odd experience. How her warm, generous mother and her uncle came from that stilted couple, she hadn't a clue unless it was due to their nanny. Something was done right because Trent turned out well, too. He resembled her Uncle Ted with his dark blue eyes and gentle smile. Trent was not arrogant, as she had once thought, but reserved, with a very dry wit. It was Jemma's full intention to open some kind of cousin door to him, and Robby was the key to that plan. Nobody could resist her little brother because he was such a tease, and Trent played along with him on everything. They found their family link in their funny bones.

She went back to the mattress. Tomorrow she would buy some sheets and a duvet, but she could live without those. Her greatest dread was finding out what it would be like to live without Spence.

Her morning sleep was interrupted by an argument. She sat on the side of her bed, collecting her thoughts. Meanwhile, the shouting intensified outside her window. She looked down on a young couple standing in the open alcove of a ground floor apartment. The man was shirtless and barefooted. He ran his hands through his already rumpled hair and leaned into the face of a woman in a satin nightgown. She stood her ground with her hands on her hips. Her hair was pulled back and tied with a ribbon. Jemma couldn't understand a word of their conversation, but she didn't need to. A little boy with a mass of curly hair pedaled up between them on a tricycle. He asked something, appealing to them both for a response. The man clenched his fists and turned away. The woman lifted the child from his seat and carried him into the house. She returned, speaking in low tones to the man, then slipped her arms around his chest and laid her head on his back. He turned to embrace her and took the ribbon from her hair. Jemma slid to the floor and cried.

⊷⊷

"How's my girl?" Julia's accent sounded so comforting on the phone. "Did you survive the trip? Everybody is still busting with pride over this fellowship thing. Now Lizbeth can't wait to get over there, just to see you. Sit down, sugar, I've got something to tell you because Spencer just called."

Jemma's stomach went bananas. "Oh, no. What did he say?"

"He was calling with information about Florence so we can meet him there. He said he got Papa's portrait, and he liked it, I could tell. I told him about you winning the fellowship and all, but he didn't say squat. There was nothing but those pregnant pauses."

Jemma bit her lip. "Somebody told him that I was dating a married cowboy."

"Well, be that as it may, I just couldn't stand it. I told him that even though it was none of my business, I had hired somebody to check out that man in Dallas and that he was from a good family, but wild as an acre of snakes and divorced to boot. I told him that you broke things off with him before you went to Paris. That's right, isn't it?"

"Yes, ma'am."

"Well, it's all been said now. You know I'm not going to let my little girl suffer any more than she has to."

"Did he sound happy?" Jemma asked.

Julia hesitated. "Oh, polite and sweet, as always."

"That's not the way he sounded the last time I saw him. Do Dah, I'm just like Scarlett. I want too much, I choose all wrong—if I make up my mind at all, I don't learn from my mistakes, and now my man has left me."

"Well, if that's so, sugar, don't forget what Scarlett said at the end," Julia said.

"You mean to go home to Tara? I already tried that."

"No. Scarlett said she would think of some way to get him back. Don't mess with your aunty, Jemmabeth. I know that movie backwards and forwards."

"I guess I forgot about that," Jemma said, "but then again, you can't believe everything you see in the movies." Like someone who wore a black hat once told her.

"No, you can't, but you can't believe everything people say when they are angry, either, honey."

"Did he sound like he was in love?" Jemma asked.

"Oh, my, you are pitiful, aren't you? You know your Papa always said that when you are between a rock and a hard place, just remember that your rock is Jesus."

"Yes, ma'am. I know."

"Don't go turning into some French free thinker on us now," Julia said. "Listen, I mailed you some folding money to spend however you want."

"Thanks, Do Dah. I love you. Call Gram for me and tell her I miss her."

"Jemmabeth, you are not Scarlett. Bye, now."

Jemma hung up the phone and went to her room. She stood at the window for a minute, then went to the dresser and got her scissors. She gathered a lock of her hair and clipped it. She tied a bit of ribbon around it and laid it in the music box. She said her prayers and asked the Lord for His will to be done. She promised to take it like a big girl, whatever it was.

⚬⚬⚬

Her schedule included a meeting with the Academie Director, Monsieur Lanier, to discuss the Girard Fellowship and her obligations. He was a thin, balding man with a trim moustache. His English was impeccable and his praise for Jemma's work was extensive. Her portfolio pieces had arrived intact. Lester's handmade containers were preserved in a tidy stack in a cavernous storage room. She had not seen the painting of Gram in over a year. She smiled, remembering that particular letter from Julia, and enjoyed the remarkable likeness created by her own hand.

Another faculty member joined Jemma and the director. He was Louis, the head portraiture instructor, and Jemma's advisor for her tenure as a Fellow at the Academie. The three of them spent hours going over the pieces, sustaining technical discussions and heated points of view. Jemma loved every second of it. She was both exuberant and articulate about her art, and their fresh perspectives had stimulated her creative juices. It was apparent to her that she had entered a higher level of exploration in her work. They briefed her on the timeline for the Girard Fellows Exhibition in October. It was traditionally the opening exhibit at the Academie gallery, and Jemma asked if she could add one more piece to her portfolio.

Her assigned workspace was in the west section of the Academie studios. She liked it because the afternoon sun was best there. She shared the area with a young Frenchman. He did not speak English, which suited her just fine. She had carried the brushes Helene had bought in her purse. The rest were packed in an old suitcase filled with her art supplies. She unpacked brushes, oils, acrylics, and watercolors. She checked them all to make certain that each had survived the journey in good condition and put the brushes, always wood down, into her first-grade cowboy boots. The Frenchman raised his brow at the boots, but smiled.

The Academie required all students to spend time in the shop making stretched canvases each week, but then they were allowed to use the canvases as needed. She had selected a large one for this piece and paced around it several times, brushes in hand. Then, like Melanie tuning her violin, she brandished strokes across the canvas with a dry brush. She had not painted in weeks and this one was to be perfect. She loaded the brush and began. It rushed back to her just as the old steps had come when she and Spencer had danced to "Candy Man" at Homecoming. She worked on it at a breakneck speed, not stopping to eat the first day. She had to force herself away from it, but when she wasn't at the canvas, she was thinking about it, and when she wasn't thinking about it, she was thinking of him.

Jemma was in the middle of an especially nice dream when a pounding at the door woke her up. A girl down the hall pointed to the telephone. She wrapped her old robe around her and picked up the phone.

"Jemma? It's Sandy."

"Sandy, can you believe I'm in Paris?"

"I can," Sandy said. "I knew you were going to hit it big someday, but I had no idea it would be in Paris. I'm so proud to know you."

"They eat, breathe, and sleep art. I love it."

"Nobody has heard from Spencer in a long time, Jem."

"I was afraid of that," Jemma said.

"I do know where he got his information about Paul. I know you said not to tell anyone, but I let it slip to Buddy, and he thought Spencer knew all about Paul. He said that the morning Spence left, they were sitting around talking at the dealership. Buddy made some comment about how he would like to horsewhip your wild cowboy and I guess that's all it took. Spencer grilled him about everything."

Jemma closed her eyes. "Oh, no. Bless his heart. He must think the very worst of me."

"He probably just thinks you would rather be with an old married guy than with him," Sandy said.

"Thanks, Sandy. You're making me feel worse, if that's possible."

"Sorry. Let's meet somewhere for the day, okay? I really want to get away."

"Ask me next month. I have this big art show now and I'm so nervous. I need my mommy."

"Yeah, right. You've never needed anybody when it comes to your art," Sandy said.

"Maybe so, but this is Paris. I'll talk to you next month." She paused. "Today is Spence's birthday, but I just can't call him, not with the girlfriend."

"Hey, you did it to yourself. Bye, Jem. Oh, yeah. Buddy swears nobody else knows."

She went to her room and sat in front of the big window. Sacre-Coeur rose above everything else. She wondered if Spence had ever been there. She got dressed and walked up the long, narrow streets to the church. The view of Paris was incredible, but Jemma went inside and got on her knees. She thanked God for letting Spencer love her all those years and for sending him someone to love him back. Those last words came hard. She sat back on the pew and peered up at the stunning mosaic of Christ. How silly of her to think that the Lord of the universe would not know what was best for her. It was time that she grew up in her faith, and she meant to do it too, with all her heart.

∾∿

Louis, her advisor, dropped by on a daily basis. His suggestions were brief and well received by Jemma, who was never one to bristle at technical criticism. As the piece neared completion, Jean-Claude spoke briefly with Louis, who acted as interpreter.

"Jean-Claude inquires if the man in your painting is your love?" Louis asked. Jemma glanced at Jean-Claude, who grinned and raised his brow, as seemed his habit.

She nodded. "*Oui.*"

Louis translated again. "He says that that the work flows from your brush with such emotion he knew that you must be in love with your subject."

"Tell him it has been so for a very long time, but only recently did I come to realize it," Jemma said.

"Ah, the best kind," Louis said, "true love."

CHAPTER TWENTY-EIGHT

I Think of Thee

The Girard Fellows Exhibition was scheduled for the middle of October. Jemma finished the piece on the last day of September. She stepped away from it for a final appraisal: Spencer reclined against the old cottonwood, strumming his guitar. His head was turned towards what Jemma knew was Plum Creek, and a faint smile played about his lips, tugging at her heart even from the canvas. The sun danced on the cottonwood leaves and in his golden hair. She did love him so.

Jean-Claude stood beside her, kissed his fingers, then tossed them towards the painting, just as Professor Rossi had done.

"*Merci beaucoup,*" Jemma said.

"Title?" he asked.

Jemma drew her breath. "*I Think of Thee,*" she said. Jean-Claude did not comprehend the words, but he did understand the look in her eyes.

❦

Peter met her for lunch. "You have exhausted even me with your attention to your new piece, Jemma. I assume it is of your Spencer. Is there some secret about the painting?"

"No secrets, just regrets, like I told you before."

"Regrets can be mended. We are all very anxious to open the show with your work. Louis and I agree that you must take a brief holiday and see our beautiful city. My wife and I would like for you to go with us to a concert tonight."

"I love concerts!" she said.

"It will be in the Sainte-Chapelle, our secret jewel of Paris, most

262

memorable, I assure you."

She smiled slightly. "Thank you, Peter, but I'm not ready to go there just yet."

"The painting, I presume?"

"Yes. I have to go to Florence." The words made her shiver.

⊰⊱

On Saturday, Peter took her to the train station. She had never seen so many trains in one place. She half expected Monet to materialize and set up his easel in the early morning light. The shrill whistles were more like Robby's toy train compared to the Zephyr, but she didn't care. Each clack of the wheels took her one more step closer to him. She would fall at his feet, if necessary, and apologize.

The last hour of the long trip, she couldn't breathe right. Her greatest fear was that she would see them together—Spencer and Miss Completely. She didn't want to cause him any embarrassment or worry, but she had to tell him that she was ready. As the train moved into the Florence station, she could hear her own pulse above the noise of the crowds and the trains. Peter had written phrases for her to use. She managed to catch a cab to the university.

After asking, in Texas Italian, for the location of the School of Architecture, she finally found it on her own. She walked past classrooms, thinking how she would react if he appeared in the hallway. She located the office and got out Peter's notes. She read something to a secretary, hoping she had asked where Spencer might be.

"Ah," the woman said in clear English, "Mr. Chase is not here. He is with the field group in Greece. He will return next Friday. You are his sister, perhaps?"

"No, ma'am, I'm not his sister," Jemma said with prickles rising on her scalp. "Could I leave him a message, please?"

"Yes, yes." The woman gave her a pen.

Jemma tore a page from her sketchbook. She didn't have to think about it, but her hand was shaking.

Dearest Spence,
I know this is bad timing, but please forgive me. There was never a choice to

be made. I love you and only you. You said to tell you, no matter the circumstances, when I am ready. Oh, I am, babe, I promise. I need to look you in the eye, if that's something you would like. If not, then may the Lord bless you both.

> *Always,*
> *Jem*

She took something from her pocket and folded it in the letter. It could be the last part of her that he would ever hold. The woman offered an envelope. Jemma sealed the note inside, then kissed it, right in front of everybody.

"I will see that Mr. Chase gets it," the woman said and put it in her desk drawer.

Jemma lingered at the door, but finally stepped away. She could relax now. He was in another country with the one who could speak four languages, or was it five? She knew the secretary had assumed that she was his sister because he already had a girlfriend. She bit her lip and repeated her new prayer of accepting the Lord's will. It was not easy. Jemma decided she would learn French. The first thing she would master would be the word for *fool*.

Professor Rossi had given her the phone number of his friend in Florence, Mario Grasso. He and his wife, Carlena, spoke English as well as Jemma, and they insisted that she spend the day with them. The couple took her in and treated her like family. She had fun in spite of herself. They gave her a guided afternoon tour of their city. It was full of all the things Spence loved—masterpiece sculptures and elegant buildings with extraordinary details, Gothic churches with brilliant stained glass, graceful bridges, and an amazing number of museums. Jemma was spellbound by the art collections in Florence. All that beauty and she hadn't been with him to share it.

Jemma wolfed down Carlena Grasso's sumptuous food until she was miserable. They went for one more stroll, this time along the Piazza della Signoria. When they returned to the house, she used her colored pencils and sketched Mario and Carlena sitting on a bench at the Piazza as a gift. She propped it up by a vase of flowers on the kitchen table along with a note of thanks. She caught the midnight train back to Paris and slept most of the trip. A sense of relief that she had made the effort was better than having no sense at all.

Peter picked her up at the station and took her to their usual café for a late lunch.

"Success?" he asked.

"No, he was in Greece," she said. "I left him a note."

"Ah, a love letter. *Très bon*. Now you must begin preparations for the show. The opening will be a very formal affair. Have you brought with you anything suitable to wear?"

Jemma considered her wardrobe. The closest thing she had was the red dress from high school she wore to Melanie's recital. "I don't have a thing."

"My wife, Ami, thought you might like to go shopping."

A sweet thought came to her and she nodded. "*Oui, oui, monsieur.*" She checked her mail, hoping it would be there, and it was—a plump letter from Julia. She took half of the money and put it in her purse to exchange at the bank. The other half she folded up in a pair of socks and put them back in the drawer. Her daddy would be proud of her. She knew also that Do Dah would approve of her spending the money somewhere along the Champs Elysees in Paris.

⧴⧵

All former Girard Fellows were invited to show two pieces of work and Jemma could show up to a dozen, but she had to title and write an artist's comment for each piece. It took her two days to do that with the help of a translator. The most difficult was his portrait. She asked for permission to let that title stand as sufficient statement for the work. It was small comfort. The big comfort would have been if he had called her from Florence.

⧴⧵

The day before the opening, Jemma was in her jeans and Le Claire sweatshirt helping the gallery manager make display choices.

"Miss Forrester, you have guests," an assistant called to her.

Jemma turned to the foyer, her heart racing. Surely Spencer wouldn't bring Miss Completely to her show. She blinked and caught her breath.

"Mom!" she squealed and ran like crazy. They hugged and cried and jumped around, much to the staff's amusement. Her Lillygrace grandparents stood by, smiling and inspecting the gallery.

"Sweet Pea, you look so thin. Have you been taking your vitamins?" her mother asked, holding her at arm's length.

Jemma laughed. "I can't believe this. I'm so happy to see you."

"Your daddy sends this hug and this kiss to you," she said, complying with his wishes, "and Robby says to tell you that he is now saving up for a pet lizard. You have your grandparents to thank for this surprise. It was their idea."

Jemma hugged them both at the same time. Their stiff arms relaxed in hers, but there was no jumping.

"Thank you forever!" she shouted.

Her grandfather almost laughed. "Our pleasure, Jemmabeth. We are very proud of you."

"Yes, congratulations, dear," her grandmother said. "We wouldn't have missed this, and we couldn't let Alexandra either." Her grandparents quickly became distracted by her art because they had seen little more than their own and Robby's portrait until now. They engaged in an animated side conversation with the manager, in French, and her grandfather proceeded to take over the placement decisions on Jemma's behalf. For once, she didn't mind.

Jemma turned to her mother and clamped her arms around her. "Come, look at my work." They went from piece to piece, reading her artist's comments. Alex was moved by the painting of the three girls. She looked at it for several minutes, sniffing into a tissue at the statement. When they came to Papa's portrait, they both cried at her reflection on the piece, *Corner of Blue*. Jemma kept an eye on her grandparents to see their reaction to her very personal reflection about him. They read it without reaction and moved to the next painting.

Alex patted her arm. "I'm glad you brought it over. I think it was too painful for Gram to have in her house."

"I feel like Papa is here and I like him watching over me. Here's my last piece, Mom," Jemma said, standing next to it.

"Oh, honey, *I Think of Thee*. The title alone breaks my heart. Have you heard from him?"

"No, ma'am," she said, touching the painting. "I went to see him in Florence, to apologize, but he was on a field trip to Greece, so I left him a note. I thought that was better than nothing. He hasn't answered, Mom, and I know he's back by now."

"After all that has happened, it must be in the Lord's hands, Sweet Pea."

"I know. The Great Plan. Well, I'm ready to accept it, whatever it is." Maybe saying it would help her believe it.

"So, I assume this is the Chase boy?" her grandfather asked, looking closely at the painting.

"Yes, sir," Jemma said.

Her grandmother read the French translation. "*Je Pense au Vous.* I see a longing in his eyes. Well, it has been some time since we had a wedding in the family. There is nothing that your mother and I would like more than to plan a wedding," she said and slipped her arm around Jemma's waist. "Oh, yes, and Trenton will be here tomorrow. He will serve as the family photographer. He's quite good, you know."

"That's great," Jemma said. "He can be my date."

∽ᎧᏟ∾

Trent arrived early the next morning. Jemma and her mom were already up, making decisions about shoes. Nobody knew more about footwear than Alexandra Forrester.

"I read an article about this show in the *New York Times*," Trent said. "There's even a paragraph about you, cousin. Oh, yeah, Dad sends his congratulations and says it's nice to have a celebrity in the family."

She shrugged. "I'm just me. God gave me whatever skills I have."

"It involves more than skill," Alex said. "You see details overlooked by most, letting us revisit life's joys, Jem. You see with your heart."

Jemma lowered her eyes. They should all know that her heart was blind.

"This is for you." Trent tickled her chin with a white rose wrapped in tissue.

"Perfect," she said. "I'll wear it tonight."

∽ᎧᏟ∾

Parisians knew how to throw a party. Great towering baskets of flowers, glimmering candelabras, elaborate tables of hors d'oeuvres, and a string quartet playing chamber music had transformed the gallery. Reporters, cared for with ease by Peter, took as many photographs of Jemma as they did of her work. The Lillygrace men wore tuxes and her grandmother was decked out in a black Chanel gown. Alex stayed close to her daughter's side. She wore an emerald gown purchased the day before, courtesy of her parents. She looked better than Jackie Kennedy.

Jemma's new dress was periwinkle blue satin. She and Ami had searched until they found an evening gown similar to the sundress she wore when Spencer said that if she ever wore it again, he wouldn't make it through "Candy Man." She wore her hair loose with the white rose pinned in it.

The attendance was elbow to elbow and the ever-patient Peter had to translate the many questions about her paintings.

"I wonder what these folks would think if they saw Papa's car house and knew that's where most of these were painted," Alex said. "I bet none of them have even seen a dirt floor."

Jemma smiled, thinking of their sojourn in Shorty Knox's dugout as well. Shorty was probably watching his color television as they spoke.

Alex went suddenly pale and clenched her daughter's arm. "Jemmabeth, look."

Jemma gasped. "Spence!" she yelled like a true cheerleader, then picked up her skirt and flew to him.

He turned from his portrait at the sound of her voice. "Hi, baby," was all he got out. She kissed him an embarrassing length of time while lightbulbs flashed around them. Spencer locked his arms around her and lifted her off the floor, returning the kiss tenfold.

She drew back and looked him in the eye. "Do you love that girl?"

He laughed, laying his head against hers. "What do you think?"

"Please say you forgive me, Spence. I've loved you since the first grade. I loved you then, I love you now, and all the time in between. I'm yours forever, if you'll have me."

"I keep it in mind, always." He inhaled the scent of her hair, then gathered her in his arms. She said something soft and low in his ear, making him grin. "Dance with me until the sun comes up," he said, "then I'm showing you Paris, you crazy woman."

The string quartet never missed a beat. The patrons, quite amused, resumed their festive endeavors, but Spencer and Jemmabeth danced through the crowd and her delighted family. It just so happened that some of their sweetest words came in whispers, quite near the portrait with the twinkling corner of blue.

Coming Soon...

In My Bones

Book Two, The Jemma Series

Sharon McAnear

Even though headstrong young artist Jemmabeth Forrester thought she'd patched up her love life in *Corner of Blue,* Book One of the Jemma series, there's more trouble headin' down her road. It's 1966 and Jemma gets soap opera amnesia, the Vietnam conflict wants her best friend, and a mail order bride invades the neighborhood. Jemma's grandmother, Lizbeth Forrester, has never been able to visit the graves of her soldier sons. They're buried in places she's only seen in the atlas. Will she get to see their final resting places while she's still on earth? And what is Jemma's great Aunt Do Dah up to?

Just when Jemma's longtime sweetheart, Spencer Chase, is ready to offer her The Ring, cowboy lawyer, Paul, plots his own proposals. Then jealous Missy Barnes, also known as The Cleave from her infamous baton-twirling days, stands nearby to do what she can to twist that ring right off Jemma. And there's the secret pact that Jemma and Spencer are determined to keep, despite frustrating situations and anxieties over the war....

CHAPTER ONE

Blessings

Paul Turner wedged the quart of milk between the other containers of liquid refreshment in his fridge. He tossed off his Stetson and ran his hand through his thick black hair. He wasn't all that hungry anyway. His dad's parting words as they had left the office still hung in his ears. "You're one sorry disappointment, son," he'd said, without humor. Not exactly something a grown man wants to hear, but it was better than some of the things his dad had called him in college. He knew the old man wasn't talking about his work in their legal practice because Paul was carrying that off with style. He was referring to Paul's private life and his dad was right—it was slime.

He had considered buying a few more groceries so he didn't have to eat all his evening meals out or maybe taking his little sisters up on their constant offers to cook for him. Neither of those options was appealing. If he went to one of their places in Dallas for supper it would haunt him for a month. They were both married with kids, and that was the root of the disappointment he'd brought to his dad.

Paul settled for cold cereal. He pitched his boots at the front door, then parked himself in front of the television to eat. He hadn't been to the Best Burger Stop in Texas since she left Wicklow. It was their place and he wouldn't go back without her. He didn't need his dad to tell him what he'd lost when he had messed up with Jemmabeth Forrester. She had been his one treasure in life and he had botched that relationship at every turn. She most likely was with that puppy love of hers right now in France. Maybe the kid would get drafted and shipped off to Vietnam.

Something solid shifted through the couch cushions. Paul felt around and pulled out a gold bangle bracelet. It probably belonged to the loudmouth redhead from the night before or one of the crazy blondes from the past Saturday. He sailed it across the room and into the trashcan. "Bingo," he said aloud and returned to his cereal. If his mother had lived, he might've turned out different. She was spiritual and smelled like flowers, too, like his darlin' Jemma, but God had other plans.

The painting Jemma had made for him hung behind his desk at the office. Most days that was his sole motivation to go in to work. He liked to imagine that they were together again, back in the hill country, watching that very spot from the river, and that Jemma was safe in his arms.

Paul set his bowl in the sink and ran water in it. He needed more of her paintings so he could have some at the office and others at home. Her art gave him hope and a chance to look into her pretty head. He stared blankly at a sparrow scratching at the fresh leaves on his lawn, then wiped his eyes. She was bound to come back to her school in Dallas sometime, and then he would have a chance to prove his love to her in ways that really mattered. Until that day, he would fill his evenings with whatever came along, because nobody could ever fill his heart like Jemma did.

He could wait forever for her because she was his solitary blessing from God. She was inside him, in his bones, and there was really nothing anybody could ever do about it.

About the Author

SHARON MCANEAR grew up in the Texas Panhandle, where cotton reigned as king and small-town drama was his queen.

"*Corner of Blue* is more than a love story," Sharon says. "It rekindles a sweeter time when family and friends were everywhere, and you were frequently glad of it. When needed, the good citizens of Connelly County stood ready to help out with chores, form a prayer circle, or stretch the truth about your situation. Take your pick."

Sharon and her family live in Colorado.

For further information about Sharon McAnear:
http://smcanear.googlepages.com/gentlefiction
www.capstonefiction.com